Mayne Reid

Gaspar, the Gaucho

A Tale of the Gran Chaco

Mayne Reid

Gaspar, the Gaucho
A Tale of the Gran Chaco

ISBN/EAN: 9783337079031

Printed in Europe, USA, Canada, Australia, Japan

Cover: Foto ©Andreas Hilbeck / pixelio.de

More available books at **www.hansebooks.com**

"DO YOU WISH TO BE FREE?"

p. 306.

Front. Gaspar the Gaucho.

GASPAR, THE GAUCHO

A TALE OF THE GRAN CHACO

BY

CAPTAIN MAYNE REID

LONDON: GEORGE ROUTLEDGE AND SONS, Limd.
Broadway House, Carter Lane, E.C.
NEW YORK: E. P. DUTTON AND CO.

CONTENTS.

CHAP.		PAGE
XXVII.—BETWEEN TORRENT AND TIGER		154
XXVIII.—SAVED BY A SPITTING-DEVIL		159
XXIX.—A ROCK-BOUND SLEEPING ROOM		164
XXX.—THE "SACRED TOWN"		168
XXXI.—PASTE AFTER POWDER		173
XXXII.—STOPPED BY A "RIACHO"		178
XXXIII.—A FISH DINNER AT SECOND-HAND		183
XXXIV.—ATTACKED BY GYMNOTI		189
XXXV.—UNDER THE CAROB TREES		195
XXXVI.—A CHAT ABOUT ELECTRIC EELS		201
XXXVII.—NOTHING FOR BREAKFAST		207
XXXVIII.—A COUNTERFEIT CRANE		212
XXXIX.—THE AVESTRUZ		217
XL.—ON THE SALITRAL		225
XLI.—TRAVELLING TANDEM		230
XLII.—PICKING UP PEARLS		235
XLIII.—IN THE SACRED TOWN		242
XLIV.—AN INDIAN BELLE		247
XLV.—AN ELEVATED GRAVEYARD		253
XLVI.—A DEAD MAN IDENTIFIED		261
XLVII.—GASPAR DESPONDENT		265
XLVIII.—BREAKING BAD NEWS		269
XLIX.—GASPAR MEANS MASQUERADING		275
L.—A MIDNIGHT PROMENADER		279
LI.—A DISPENSER OF SPELLS		284
LII.—A FRIEND UNEXPECTED		291
LIII.—A DELUDED JAILER		298
LIV.—AN UNLOOKED-FOR DELIVERER		305
LV.—AN UNLUCKY TUMBLE		311
LVI.—AN INFURIATED FEMALE		318
LVII.—THE CAPTIVE RECAPTURED		323
LVIII.—VA CON DIOS		328
LIX.—FRIENDS OR FOES?		332
LX.—SPEEDY RETRIBUTION		339
LXI.—CONCLUSION		344

GASPAR, THE GAUCHO.

A TALE OF THE GRAN CHACO.

CHAPTER I.

THE GRAN CHACO.

SPREAD before you a map of South America. Fix your eye on the point of confluence between two of its great rivers —the Salado, which runs south-easterly from the Andes mountains, and the Parana coming from the north; carry your glance up the former to the town of Salta, in the ancient province of Tucuman; do likewise with the latter to the point where it espouses the Paraguay; then up this to the Brazilian frontier fort of Coimbra; finally draw a line from the fort to the aforementioned town—a line slightly curved with its convexity towards the Cordillera of the Andes—and you will thus have traced a boundary embracing one of the least known, yet most interesting, tracts of territory in either continent of America, or, for that matter, in the world. Within the limits detailed lies a region romantic in its past as mysterious in its present; at this hour almost as much a *terra incognita* as when the boats of Mendoza vainly endeavoured to reach it from the Atlantic side, and the gold-seekers of Pizarro's following alike unsuccessfully attempted its exploration from the Pacific.

Young reader, you will be longing to know the name of this remarkable region; know it, then, as the "GRAN CHACO."

No doubt you may have heard of it before, and, if a diligent student of geography, made some acquaintance with its character. But your knowledge of it must needs be limited, even though it were as extensive as that possessed by the people who dwell upon its borders; for to them the Gran Chaco is a thing of fear, and their intercourse with it one which has brought them, and still brings, only suffering and sorrow.

It has been generally supposed that the Spaniards of Columbus's time subdued the entire territory of America, and held sway over its red-skinned aborigines. This is a historical misconception. Although lured by a love of gold, conjoined with a spirit of religious propagandism, the so-called *Conquistadores* overran a large portion of both divisions of the continent, there were yet extensive tracts of each never entered, much less colonized, by them—territories many times larger than England, in which they never dared set foot. Of such were Navajoa in the north, the country of the gallant Goajiros in the centre, the lands of Patagonia and Arauco in the south, and notably the territory lying between the Cordilleras of the Peruvian Andes and the rivers Parana and Paraguay, designated " EL GRAN CHACO." This vast expanse of champaign, large enough for an empire, remains to the present time not only uncolonized, but absolutely unexplored. For the half-dozen expeditions that have attempted its exploration, timidly entering and as hastily abandoning it, scarce merit consideration.

And equally unsuccessful have been all efforts at religious propagandism within its borders. The labours of the *padres,* both Jesuit and Franciscan, have alike signally failed; the savages of the Chaco refusing obedience to the cross as submission to the sword.

Three large rivers—the Salado, Vermejo, and Pilcomayo—course through the territory of the Chaco; the first forming its southern boundary, the others intersecting it. They all take their rise in the Andes Mountains, and after running for over a thousand miles in a south-easterly direction and nearly parallel courses, mingle their waters with those of the Parana and Paraguay. Very little is known of these three great streams, though of late years the Salado has received some exploration. There is a better acquaintance with its upper portion, where it passes through the settled districts of Santiago and Tucuman. Below, even to the point where it enters the Parana, only a strong military expedition may with safety approach its banks, by reason of their being also traversed by predatory bands of the savages.

Geographical knowledge of the Vermejo is still less, and of the Pilcomayo least of all; this confined to the territory of their upper waters, long since colonized by the Argentine States and the Republic of Bolivia, and now having many towns in it. But below, as with the Salado, where these rivers enter the region of the Chaco, they become as if they were lost to the geographer; even the mouth of the Pilcomayo not being known for certain, though one branch of it debouches into the Paraguay, opposite the town of Assuncion, the capital of Paraguay itself! It enters the river of this name by a forked or *deltoid* channel, its waters making their way through a marshy tract of country in numerous slow-flowing *riachos*, whose banks, thickly overgrown with a lush sedgy vegetation, are almost concealed from the eye of the explorer.

Although the known mouth of the Pilcomayo is almost within' gun-shot of Assuncion—the oldest Spanish settlement in this part of South America—no Paraguayan ever thinks of attempting its ascent, and the people of the town are as ignorant of the land lying along that river's shores as on the day when the old naturalist, Azara, paddles his *periagua* some forty miles against its obstructing current. No scheme of colonization has ever been designed or thought of by them ; for it is only near its source, as we have seen, that settlements exist.   In the Chaco no white man's town ever stood upon its banks, nor church spire flung shadow athwart its unfurrowed waves.

It may be asked why this neglect of a territory, which would seem so tempting to the colonist?   For the Gran Chaco is no sterile tract, like most parts of the Navajo country in the north, or the plains of Patagonia and the sierras of Arauco in the south.   Nor is it a humid, impervious forest, at seasons inundated, as with some portions of the Amazon valley and the deltas of the Orinoco.

Instead, what we do certainly know of the Chaco shows it the very country to invite colonization ; having every quality and feature to attract the settler in search of a new home.   Vast verdant savannas—natural clearings—rich in nutritious grasses, and groves of tropical trees, with the palm predominating ; a climate of unquestionable salubrity, and a soil capable of yielding every requisite for man's sustenance as the luxury of life.   In very truth, the Chaco may be likened to a vast park or grand landscape garden, still under the culture of the Creator !

But why not also submitted to the tillage of man?   The answer is easy : because the men who now hold it will not permit intrusion on their domain—to them hereditary—and they are hunters, not *agriculturists*. It is still in the pos-session of its red-skinned owners, the original lords of its soil, these warlike Indians, who have hitherto defied all attempts to enslave or subdue them, whether made by soldier, miner, or missionary. These independent savages, mounted upon fleet steeds, which they manage with the skill of Centaurs, scour the plains of the Chaco, swift as birds upon the wing. Disdaining fixed residence, they roam over its verdant pastures and through its perfumed groves, as bees from flower to flower, pitching their *toldos*, and making camp in whatever pleasant spot may tempt them. Savages though called, who would not envy them such a charming *insouciant* existence? Do not you, young reader?

I anticipate your answer, " Yes." Come with me, then ! Let us enter the " Gran Chaco," and for a time partake of it !

CHAPTER II.

PARAGUAY'S DESPOT.

NOTWITSTANDING what I have said of the Chaco remaining uncolonized and unexplored, I can tell of an exception. In the year 1836, one ascending the Pilcomayo to a point about a hundred miles from its mouth, would there see a house, which could have been built only by a white man, or one versed in the ways of civilization. Not that there was anything very imposing in its architecture; for it was but a wooden structure, the walls of bambo, and the roof a thatch of the palm called *cuberta*—so named from the use made of its fronds in covering sheds and houses. But the superior size of this dwelling, far exceeding that of the simple *toldos* of the Chaco Indians; its ample verandah pillared and shaded by a protecting roof of the same palm leaves; and, above all, several well-fenced enclosures around it, one of them containing a number of tame cattle, others under tillage—with maize, manioc, the plantain, and similar tropical products—all these insignia evinced the care and cultivating hand of some one else than an aboriginal.

Entering the house, still further evidence of the white man's presence would be observed. Furniture, apparently home-made, yet neat, pretty, and suitable; chairs and settees of the *caña brava*, or South American bamboo; bedsteads of the same, with beds of the elastic Spanish moss, and *ponchos* for coverlets; mats woven from fibres of another species of palm, with here and there a swung hammock. In addition, some books and pictures that appeared to have been painted on the spot; a bound volume of music, with a violin and guitar—all speaking of a domestic economy unknown to the American Indian.

In some of the rooms, as also in the outside verandah, could be noticed objects equally unlike the belongings of the aboriginal: stuffed skins of wild beasts and birds; insects impaled on strips of palm bark; moths, butterflies, and brilliant scarabæi; reptiles preserved in all their repulsive ugliness, with specimens of ornamental woods, plants, and minerals; a singular paraphernalia, evidently the product of the region around. Such a collection could only belong to a *naturalist*, and that naturalist could be no other than a white man. He was; his name Ludwig Halberger.

The name plainly speaks his nationality—a German. And such was he; a native of the then kingdom of Prussia, born in the city of Berlin.

Though not strange his being a naturalist—since the taste for and study of Nature are notably peculiar to the German people—it was strange to find Prussian or other European having his home in such an out-of-the-way place. There was no civilized settlement, no other white man's dwelling, nearer than the town of Assuncion; this quite a hundred miles off, to the eastward. And north, south, and west the same for more than five times the distance. All the territory around and between, a wilderness, unsettled, unexplored, traversed only by the original lords of the soil, the Chaco Indians, who, as said, have preserved a deadly hostility to the pale face, ever since the keels of the latter first cleft the waters of the Parana.

To explain, then, how Ludwig Halberger came to be domiciled there, so far from civilization, and so high up the Pilcomayo—river of mysterious note—it is necessary to give some details of his life antecedent to the time of his having established this solitary *estancia*. To do so a name of evil augury and ill repute must needs be introduced—that of Dr. Francia, Dictator of Paraguay, who for more than a quarter of a century ruled that fair land verily with a rod of iron. With this same demon-like tyrant, and the same almost heavenly country, is associated another name, and a reputation as unlike that of José Francia as Hyperion to the Satyr, and which justice to a godlike humanity forbids me to pass over in silence. I speak of Amadé, or, as he is better known, *Aimé* Bonpland—cognomen appropriate to this most estimable man—known to all the world as the friend and fellow-traveller of Humboldt; more still, his assistant and collaborateur in those scientific researches, as yet unequalled for truthfulness and extent—the originator and discoverer of much of that learned lore, which, with modesty unparalleled, he has allowed his more energetic and more ambitious *compagnon de voyage* to have credit for.

Though no name sounds more agreeably to my ears than that of Aimé Bonpland, I cannot here dwell upon it, nor write his biography, however congenial the theme. Some one who reads this may find the task both pleasant and profitable ; for though his bones slumber obscurely on the banks of the Parana, amidst the scenes so loved by him, his name will one day have a higher niche in Fame's temple than it has hitherto held—perhaps not much lower than that of Humboldt himself. I here introduce it, with some incidents of his life, as affecting the first character who figures in this my tale. But for Aimé Bonpland, Ludwig Halberger might never have sought a South American home. It was in following the example of the French philosopher, of whom he had admiringly read, that the Prussian naturalist made his way to the La Plata and up to Paraguay, where Bonpland had preceded him. But first to give the adventures of the latter in that picturesque land, of which a short account will suffice ; then afterwards to the incidents of my story.

Retiring from the busy world, of which he seems to have been somewhat weary, Bonpland took up his residence on the banks of the Rio Parana ; not in Paraguayan territory, but that of the Argentine Republic, on the opposite side of the river. There settled down, he did not give his hours to idleness; nor yet altogether to his favourite pursuit, the pleasant though somewhat profitless one of natural history. Instead, he devoted himself to cultivation, the chief object of his culture being the " yerba de Paraguay," which yields the well-known *maté*, or Paraguayan tea. In this industry he was eminently successful. His amiable manners and inoffensive character attracted the notice of his neighbours, the Guarani Indians—a peaceful tribe of proletarian habits —and soon a colony of these collected around him, entering his employ, and assisting him in the establishment of an extensive " yerbale," or tea plantation, which bid fair to become profitable.

The Frenchman was on the high-road to fortune, when a cloud appeared, coming from an unexpected quarter of the sky—the north. The report of his prosperity had reached the ears of Francia, Paraguay's then despot and dictator, who, with other strange theories of government, held the doctrine that the cultivation of " yerba " was a right exclusively Paraguayan—in other words, belonging solely to himself. True, the French colonist, his rival cultivator, was not within his jurisdiction, but in the state of Corrientes, and the territory of the Argentine Confederation. Not much, that, to Dr. Francia, accustomed to make light of international law, unless it were supported by national strength and backed by hostile bayonets. At the time Corrientes had neither of these to deter him, and in the dead hour of a certain night, four hundred of his myrmidons—the noted *quarteleros*—crossed the Parana, attacked the tea-plantation of Bonpland, and after making massacre of a half-score of his Guarani *peons*, carried himself a prisoner to the capital of Paraguay.

The Argentine Government, weak with its own intestine strife, submitted to the insult almost unprotestingly. Bonpland was but a Frenchman and foreigner ; and for nine long years was he held captive in Paraguay. Even the English *charge d'affaires*, and a Commission sent thither by the Institute of France, failed to get him free ! Had he been a lordling, or some little *viscomte*, his forced residence in Paraguay would have been of shorter duration. An army would have been despatched to "extradite" him. But Aimé Bonpland was only a student of Nature—one of those unpretending men who give the world all the knowledge it has, worth having—and so was he left to languish in captivity. True, his imprisonment was not a very harsh one, and rather partook of the character of *parole d'honneur*. Francia was aware of his wonderful knowledge, and availed himself of it, allowing his captive to live unmolested. But again the amiable character of the Frenchman had an influence on his life, this time adversely. Winning for him universal respect among the simple Paraguayans, it excited the envy of their vile ruler ; who once again, and at night, had his involuntary guest seized upon, carried beyond the confines of his territory, and landed upon Argentine soil—but stripped of everything save the clothes on his back !

Soon after, Bonpland settled near the town of Corrientes, where, safe from further persecution, he once more entered upon agricultural pursuits. And there, in the companionship of a South American lady—his wife—with a family of happy children, he ended a life that had lasted for fourscore years, innocent and unblemished, as it had been useful, heroic, and glorious.

CHAPTER III.

IN some respects similar to the experience of Aimé
Bonpland was that of Ludwig Halberger. Like the former,
an ardent lover of Nature, as also an accomplished naturalist, he too had selected South America as the scene of
his favourite pursuits. On the great river Parana—better,
though erroneously, known to Europeans as the La
Plata—he would find an almost untrodden field. For
although the Spanish naturalist, Azura, had there preceded
him, the researches of the latter were of the olden time, and
crude imperfect kind, before either zoology or botany had
developed themselves into a science.

Besides, the Prussian was moderately fond of the chase,
and to such a man the great *pampas* region, with its pumas
and jaguars, its ostriches, wild horses, and grand *guazuti*
stags, offered an irresistible attraction. There he could not
only indulge his natural taste, but luxuriate in them.

He, too, had resided nine years in Paraguay, and something more. But, unlike Bonpland, his residence there was
voluntary. Nor did he live alone. Lover of Nature though
he was, and addicted to the chase, another kind of love
found its way to his heart, making himself a captive. The
dark eyes of a Paraguayan girl penetrated his breast, seem-

ing brighter to him than the plumage of the gaudiest birds, or the wings of the most beautiful butterflies.

" *El Güero*," the blonde—as these swarthy complexioned people were wont to call the Teutonic stranger—found favour in the eyes of the young Paraguayense, who reciprocating his honest love, consented to become his wife; and became it. She was married at the age of fourteen, he being over twenty.

"So young for a bride!" many of my readers will exclaim. But that is rather a question of race and climate. In Spanish America, land of feminine precocity, there is many a wife and mother not yet entered on her teens!

For nigh ten years Halberger lived happily with his youthful *esposa;* all the happier that in due time a son and daughter—the former resembling himself, the latter a very image of her mother—enlivened their home with sweet infantine prattle. And as the years rolled by, a third youngster came to form part of the family circle—this neither son nor daughter, but an orphan child of the Señora's sister deceased. A boy he was, by name Cypriano.

The home of the hunter-naturalist was not in Assuncion, but some twenty miles out in the "*campo.*" He rarely visited the capital, except on matters of business. For a business he had; this of somewhat unusual character. It consisted chiefly in the produce of his gun and insect-net. Many a rare specimen of bird and quadruped, butterfly and beetle, captured and preserved by Ludwig Halberger, at this day adorns the public museums of Prussia and other European countries. But for the dispatch and shipment of these he would never have cared to show himself in the streets of Assuncion; for, like all true naturalists, he had no affection for city life. Assuncion, however, being the only shipping port in Paraguay, he had no choice but repair thither whenever his collections became large enough to call for exportation.

Beginning life in South America with moderate means, the Prussian naturalist had prospered : so much, as to have a handsome house, with a tract of land attached, and a fair retinue of servants; these last, all " Guanos," a tribe of Indians long since tamed and domesticated. He had been fortunate, also, in securing the services of a *gaucho*, named Gaspar, a faithful fellow, skilled in many callings, who acted as his *mayor-domo* and man of confidence.

In truth, was Ludwig Halberger in the enjoyment of a happy existence, and eminently prosperous. Like Aimé Bonpland, he was fairly on the road to fortune; when, just as with the latter, a cloud overshadowed his life, coming from the self-same quarter. His wife, lovely at fourteen, was still beautiful at twenty-four, so much as to attract the notice of Paraguay's Dictator. And with Dr. Francia to covet was to possess, where the thing coveted belonged to any of his own subjects. Aware of this, warned also ot Francia's partiality by frequent visits with which the latter now deigned to honour him, Ludwig Halberger saw there was no chance to escape domestic ruin, but by getting clear out of the country. It was not that he doubted the fidelity of his wife; on the contrary, he knew her to be true as she was beautiful. How could he doubt it, since it was from her own lips he first learnt of the impending danger?

Away from Paraguay, then—away anywhere—was his first and quickly-formed resolution, backed by the counsels of his loyal partner in life. But the design was easier than its execution; the last not only difficult, but to all appearance impossible. For it so chanced that one of the laws of that

:xclusive land—an edict of the Dictator himself—was to the point prohibitive ; forbidding any foreigner who married a native woman to take her out of the country, without having a written permission from the Executive Head of the State. Ludwig Halberger was a foreigner, his wife native born, and the Head of the State Executive, as in every other sense, was José Gaspar Francia !

The case was conclusive. For the Prussian to have sought permission to depart, taking his wife along with him, would have been more than folly—madness—hastening the very danger he dreaded.

Flight, then ? But whither, and in what direction ? To flee into the Paraguayan forests could not avail him, or only for a short respite. These, traversed by the *cascarilleros* and gatherers of yerba, all in the Dictator's employ and pay, would be no safer than the streets of Assuncion itself. A party of fugitives, such as the naturalist and his family, could not long escape observation ; and seen, they would as surely be captured and carried back. The more surely from the fact that the whole system of Paraguayan polity under Dr. Francia's regime was one of treachery and espionage, every individual in the land finding it to his profit to do dirty service for " El Supremo "—as they styled their despotic chief.

On the other side there was the river, but still more difficult would it be to make escape in that direction. All along its bank, to the point where it enters the Argentine territory, had Francia established his military stations, styled *guardias*, where sentinels kept watch at all hours, by night as in the day. For a boat to pass down, even the smallest skiff, without being observed by some of these Argus-eyed videttes, would have been absolutely impossible ; and if seen as surely brought to a stop, and taken back to Assuncion.

Revolving all these difficulties in his mind, Ludwig Halberger was filled with dismay, and for a long time kept in a state of doubt and chilling despair. At length, however, a thought came to relieve him—a plan of flight, which promised to have a successful issue. He would flee into the Chaco !

To the mind of any other man in Paraguay the idea would have appeared preposterous. If Francia resembled the frying-pan, the Chaco to a Paraguayan seemed the fire itself. A citizen of Assuncion would no more dare to set foot on the further side of that stream which swept the very walls of his town, than would a besieging soldier on the *glacis* of the fortress he besieged. The life of a white man caught straying in the territory of " El Gran Chaco " would not have been worth a withey. If not at once impaled on an Indian spear held in the hand of " Tova " or " Guaycuru," he would be carried into a captivity little preferable to death.

For all this, Ludwig Halberger had no fear of crossing over to the Chaco side, nor penetrating into its interior. He had often gone thither on botanizing and hunting expeditions. But for this apparent recklessness he had a reason, which must needs here be given. Between the Chaco savages and the Paraguayan people there had been intervals of peace—*tiempos de paz*—during which occurred amicable intercourse ; the Indians rowing over the river and entering the town to traffic off their skins, ostrich feathers, and other commodities. On one of these occasions the head chief of the Tovas tribe, by name Naraguana, having imbibed too freely of *guarapé,* and in some way got separated from his people, became the butt of some Paraguayan boys, who were behaving towards him just as the idle lads of London or the *gamins* of Paris would to one appearing intoxicated in the streets. The Prussian naturalist chanced to be passing at the time; and seeing the Indian, an aged man, thus insulted, took pity upon and rescued him from his tormentors.

Recovering from his debauch, and conscious of the service the stranger had done him, the Tovas chief swore eternal friendship to his generous protector, at the same time proffering him the " freedom of the Chaco."

The incident, however, caused a rupture between the Tovas tribe and the Paraguayan Government, terminating the *tiempo de paz,* which had not since been renewed. More unsafe than ever would it have been for a Paraguayan to set foot on the western side of the river. But Ludwig Halberger knew that the prohibition did not extend to him ; and relying on Naraguana's proffered friendship, he now determined upon retreating into the Chaco, and claiming the protection of the Tovas chief.

Luckily, his house was not a great way from the river's bank, and in the dead hour of a dark night, accompanied by wife and children—taking along also his Guano servants, with such of his household effects as could be conveniently carried, the faithful Gaspar guiding and managing all—he was rowed across the Paraguay and up the Pilcomayo. He had been told that at some thirty leagues from the mouth of the latter stream, was the *tolderia* of the Tovas Indians. And truly told ; since before sunset of the second day he succeeded in reaching it, there to be received amicably, as he had anticipated. Not only did Naraguana give him a warm welcome but assistance in the erection of

c

his dwelling; afterwards stocking his *estancia* with horses and cattle caught on the surrounding plains. These tamed and domesticated, with their progeny, are what anyone would have seen in his *corrals* in the year 1836, at the time the action of our tale commences.

CHAPTER IV.

THE house of the hunter naturalist was placed at some distance from the river's bank, its site chosen with an eye to the picturesque ; and no lovelier landscape ever lay before the windows of a dwelling. From its front ones—or, better still, the verandah outside them—the eye commands a view alone limited by the power of vision : verdant savannas, mottled with copses of acacia and groves of palm, with here and there single trees of the latter standing solitary, their smooth stems and gracefully-curving fronds cut clear as cameos against the azure sky. Nor is it a dead level plain, as *pampas* and prairies are erroneously supposed always to be. Instead, its surface is varied with undulations ; not abrupt as the ordinary hill and dale scenery, but gently swelling like the ocean's waves when these have become crestless after the subsidence of a storm.

Looking across this champaign from Halberger's house at almost any hour of the day, one would rarely fail to observe living creatures moving upon it. It may be a herd of the great *guazutt* deer, or the smaller *pampas* roe, or, perchance, a flock of *rheas*—the South-American ostrich—stalking along tranquilly or in flight, with their long necks extended far before, and their plumed tails streaming train-like behind them. Possibly they may have been affrighted by the tawny puma, or spotted jaguar, seen skulking through the long pampas grass like gigantic cats. A drove of wild horses, too, may go careering past, with manes and tails showing a wealth of hair which shears have never touched; now galloping up the acclivity of a ridge; anon disappearing over its crest to re-appear on one farther off and of greater elevation. Verily, a scene of Nature in its wildest and most interesting aspect !

Upon that same plain, Ludwig Halberger and his people are accustomed to see others than wild horses—some with men upon their backs, who sit them as firmly as riders in the ring; that is, when they do *sit* them, which is not always. Often may they be seen standing erect upon their steeds, these going in full gallop ! True, your ring-rider can do the same; but then his horse gallops in a circle, which makes it a mere feat of centrifugal and centripetal balancing. Let him try it in a straight line, and he would drop off like a ripe pear from the tree. No curving course needs the Chaco Indian, no saddle nor padded platform on the back of his horse, which he can ride standing almost as well as seated. No wonder, then, these savages—if savages they may be called—have obtained the fanciful designation of centaurs—the " Red Centaurs of the Chaco."

Those seen by Ludwig Halberger and his family are the " Tovas," already introduced. Their village, termed *tolderia*, is about ten miles off, up the river. Naraguana wished the white man to have fixed his residence nearer to him, but the naturalist knew that would not answer. Less than two leagues from an Indian encampment, and still more if a permanent dwelling-place, which this *tolderia* is, would make the pursuit of his calling something more than precarious. The wild birds and beasts—in short, all the animated creation—dislike the proximity of the Indian, and flee his presence afar.

It may seem strange that the naturalist still continues to form collections, so far from any place where he might hope to dispose of them. Down the Pilcomayo he dares not take them, as that would only bring him back to the Paraguay river, interdict to navigation, as ever jealously guarded, and, above all, tabooed to himself. But he has no thought, or intention, to attempt communicating with the civilized world in that way; while a design of doing so in quite another direction has occurred to him, and, in truth, been already all arranged. This, to carry his commodities overland to the Rio Vermejo, and down that stream till near its mouth; then again overland, and across the Parana to Corrientes. There he will find a shipping port in direct commerce with Buenos Ayres, and so beyond the jurisdiction of Paraguay's Dictator.

Naraguana has promised him not only an escort of his best braves, but a band of *cargadores* (carriers) for the transport of his freight; these last the slaves of his tribe. For the aristocratic Tovas Indians have their bondsmen, just as the Caffres, or Arab merchants of Africa.

Nearly three years have elapsed since the naturalist became established in his new quarters, and his collection has grown to be a large one. Safely landed in any European port, it would be worth many thousands of dollars; and thither he wishes to have it shipped as soon as possible. He has already warned Naraguana of his wish, and that the freight is ready; the chief, on his part, promising to make immediate preparations for its transport overland.

But a week has passed over, and no Naraguana, nor any

messenger from him, has made appearance at the *estancia.*
No Indian of the Tovas tribe has been seen about the
place, nor anywhere near it ; in short, no redskin has been
seen at all, save the *guanos,* Halberger's own male and
female domestics.

Strange all this ! Scarce ever has a whole week gone by
without his receiving a visit from the Tovas chief, or some
one of his tribe ; and rarely half this time without Naraguana's own son, by name Aguara, favouring the family
with a call, and making himself as agreeable as savage may
in the company of civilized people.

For all, there is one of that family to whom his visits are
anything but agreeable ; in truth, the very reverse. This
Cypriano, who has conceived the fancy, or rather feels conviction, that the eyes of the young Tovas chief rest too
often, and too covetously, on his pretty cousin, Francesca.
Perhaps, except himself, no one has noticed this, and he
alone is glad to count the completion of a week without
any Indian having presented himself at his uncle's
establishment.

Though there is something odd in their prolonged non-
appearance, still it is nothing to be alarmed about. On
other occasions there had been intervals of absence as long,
and even longer, when the men of the tribe were away from
their *tolderia,* on some foraging or hunting expedition. Nor
would Halberger have thought anything of it ; but for the
understanding between him and the Tovas chief, in regard
to the transport of his collections. Naraguana had never
before failed in any promise made to him. Why should he
in this ?

A sense of delicacy hinders the naturalist from riding over
to the **Tovas town, and** asking explanation why the chief

delays keeping his word. In all such matters, the American Indian, savage though styled, is sensitive as the most refined son of civilization ; and, knowing this, Ludwig Halberger waits for Naraguana to come to him.

But when a second week has passed, and a third, without the Tovas chief reporting himself, or sending either message or messenger, the Prussian becomes really apprehensive, not so much for himself, as the safety of his redskinned protector. Can it be that some hostile band has attacked the Tovas tribe, massacred all the men, and carried off the women? For in the Chaco are various communities of Indians, often at deadly feud with one another. Though such conjecture seems improbable, the thing is yet possible ; and to assure himself, Halberger at length resolves upon going over to the *tolderia* of the Tovas. Ordering his horse saddled, he mounts, and is about to ride off alone, when a sweet voice salutes him, saying :—

" Papa ! won't you take me with you ?"

It is his daughter who speaks, a girl not yet entered upon her teens.

" In welcome, Francesca. Come along !" is his answer to her query.

" Then stay till I get my pony. I sha'n't be a minute."

She runs back towards the corrals, calling to one of the servants to saddle her diminutive steed. Which, soon brought round to the front of the house, receives her upon its back.

But now another, also a soft, sweet voice, is heard in exhortation. It is that of Francesca's mother, entering protest against her husband either going alone, or with a companion so incapable of protecting him. She says :—

"Dear Ludwig, take Gaspar with you. There may be danger—who knows?"

"Let me go, *tio?*" puts in Cypriano, with impressive eagerness, his eyes turned towards his cousin as though he did not at all relish the thought of her visiting the Tovas village without his being along with her.

"And me, too?" also requests Ludwig, the son, who is two years older than his sister.

"No, neither of you," rejoins the father. "Ludwig, you would not leave your mother alone? Besides, remember I have set both you and Cypriano a lesson, which you must learn off to-day. There is nothing to fear, *querida!*" he adds, addressing himself to his wife. "We are not now in Paraguay, but a country where our old Friend Francia and his satellites dare not intrude on us. Besides, I cannot spare the good Gaspar from some work I have given him to do. Bah! 'Tis only a bit of a morning's trot there and back; and if I find there's nothing wrong, we'll be home again in little over a couple of hours. So *adios! Vamos*, Francesca!"

With a wave of his hand he moves off, Francesca giving her tiny roadster a gentle touch of the whip, and trotting by his side.

The other three, left standing in the verandah, with their eyes follow the departing equestrians, the countenance of each exhibiting an expression that betrays different emotions in their minds, these differing both as to the matter of thought and the degree of intensity. Ludwig simply looks a little annoyed at having to stay at home when he wanted to go abroad, but without any great feeling of disappointment; whereas Cypriano evidently suffers chagrin, so much that he is not likely to profit by the appointed lesson. With the Señora herself it is neither disappointment nor chagrin, but a positive and keen apprehension. A daughter of Paraguay, brought up to believe its ruler all powerful over the earth, she can hardly realize the idea of there being a spot where the hand of " El Supremo " cannot reach and punish those who have thwarted his wishes or caprices. Many the tale has she heard whispered in her ear, from the cradle upwards, telling of the weird power of this wicked despot, and the remorseless manner in which he has often wielded it. Even after their escape into the Chaco, where, under the protection of the Tovas chief, they might laugh his enmity to scorn, she has never felt the confidence of complete security. And now, that an uncertainty has arisen as to what has befallen Naraguana and his people, her fears became redoubled and intensified. Standing in the trellissed verandah, her eyes fixed upon the departing forms of her husband and daughter, she has a heaviness at the heart, a presentiment of some impending danger, which seems so near and dreadful as to cause shivering throughout her frame.

The two youths, observing this, essay to reassure her— one in filial duty, the other with affection almost as warm.

Alas ! in vain. As the crown of the tall hat worn by her husband, goes down behind the crest of a distant ridge, Francesca's having sooner disappeared, her heart sinks at the same time ; and, making a sign of the cross, she exclaims in desponding accents :—

" *Madre de Dios !* We may never see them more !"

CHAPTER V.

RIDING at a gentle amble, so that his daughter on her small palfrey may easily keep up with him, Halberger in due time arrives at the Indian village ; to his surprise seeing it is no more a village, or only a deserted one ! The toldos of bamboo and palm thatch are still standing, but un-tenanted—every one of them !

Dismounting, he steps inside them, one after the other, but finds each and all unoccupied—neither man, woman, nor child within ; nor without, either in the alleys between, or on the large open space around which the frail tenements are set, that has served as a loitering-place for the older members of the tribe, and a play-ground for the younger.

The grand council room, called *malocca*, he also enters with like result ; no one is inside it—not a soul to be seen anywhere, either in the streets of the village or on the plain stretching around !

He is alarmed as much as surprised ; indeed more, since he has been anticipating something amiss. But by degrees, as he continues to make an examination of the place, his apprehensions became calmed down, these having been for the fate of the Indians themselves. His first thought he had entertained while conjecturing the cause of their long absence from the *estancia*, was that some hostile tribe had attacked them, massacred the men, and carried captive the women and children. Such tragical occurrences are far from uncommon among the red aborigines of America, Southern or Northern. Soon, however, his fears on this score are set at rest. Moving around, he detects no traces of a struggle, neither dead bodies nor blood. If there had been a fight the corpses of the fallen would surely still be there, strewing the plain; and not a *toldo* would be standing or seen—instead, only their ashes.

As it is, he finds the houses all stripped of their furniture and domestic utensils; these evidently borne off not as by marauders, but taken away in a systematic manner, as when a regular move is made by these nomadic people. He sees fragments of cut *sipos* and bits of raw-hide thong—the overplus left after packing.

Though no longer alarmed for the safety of the Indians, he is, nevertheless, still surprised and perplexed. What could have taken them away from the *tolderia*, and whither can they have gone? Strange, too, Naraguana should have left the place in such unceremonious fashion, without giving him, Halberger, notice of his intention! Their absence on this occasion cannot be accounted for by any hunting or foraging expedition, nor can it be a foray of war. In any of these cases the women and children would have been left behind. Beyond doubt, it is an absolute abandonment of the place; perhaps with no intention of returning to it, or not for a very long time.

Revolving these thoughts through his mind, Halberger climbs back into his saddle, and sits further reflecting. His daughter, who has not dismounted, trots up to his side, she, too, in as much wonderment as himself; for, although but a very young creature, almost a child in age, she has passed through experiences that impart the sageness of years. She knows of all the relationships which exist between them and the Tovas tribe, and knows something of why her father fled from his old home; that is, she believes it to have been through fear of El Supremo, the "bogie" of every Paraguayan child, boy or girl. Aware of the friendship of the Tovas chief, and the protection he has extended to them, she now shares her father's surprise, as she had his apprehensions.

They exchange thoughts on the subject—the child equally perplexed with the parent; and after an interval passed in conjecturing, all to no purpose, Halberger is about to turn and ride home again, when it occurs to him he had better find out in what direction the Indians went away from their village.

There is no difficulty in discovering this; the trail of their ridden horses, still more that of their pack animals, is easily found and followed. It leads out from the village at the opposite end from that by which they themselves entered; and after following it for a mile or so along the river's bank, they see that it takes an abrupt turn across the *pampa.* Up to this point it has been quite conspicuous, and is also beyond; for although it is anything but recent, no rain has since fallen, and the hoof-prints of the horses can be here and there distinguished clean cut on the smooth sward, over which the mounted men had gone at a gallop. Besides, there is the broad belt of trodden grass where the pack animals toiled more slowly along; and upon this bits of broken utensils, with other useless articles, have been dropped and abandoned, plainly proclaiming the character of the cavalcade.

Here Halberger would halt, and turn back, but for a remembrance coming into his mind which hinders, at the same time urging him to continue on. In one of his hunting excursions he had been over this ground before, and remembers that some ten miles further on a tributary stream flows into the Pilcomayo. Curious to know whether the departing Tovas have turned up this tributary, or followed the course of the main river, he determines to proceed. For glancing skyward, he sees that the sun is just crossing the meridian, and knows he will have no lack of time before darkness can overtake him. The circumstances and events, so strange and startling, cause him to forget that promise made to his wife—soon to be back at the *estancia*.

Spurring his horse, and calling on Francesca to follow, he starts off again at a brisk gallop; which is kept up till they draw bridle on the bank of the influent stream.

This, though broad, is but shallow, with a selvidge of soft ooze on either side; and on that where they have arrived the mud shows the track of several hundred horses. Without crossing over, Halberger can see that the Indian trail leads on along the main river, and not up the branch stream.

Again he is on the balance, to go back—with the intention of returning next day, accompanied by Gaspar, and making further search for the missing Indians—when an object comes under his eye, causing him to give a start of surprise.

It is only the track of a horse; and strange that this should surprise him, among hundreds. But the one on which he has fixed his attention differs from all the rest in being the hoof-print of a *shod* horse, while the others are as Nature made them. Still even this difference would not make so much impression upon him were the tracks of the same *age.* Himself skilled as any Indian in the reading of *pampas* sign, at a glance he sees they are not. The hoof marks of the Tovas horses in their travelling train are all quite three weeks old ; while the animal having the iron on its heels, must have crossed over that stream within the week.

Its rider, whoever he was, could not have been in the company of the departing Tovas ; and to him now regarding the tracks, it is only a question as to whether he were a *white* man, or Indian. Everything is against his having been the former, travelling in a district tabooed to the pale faces, other than Halberger and his—everything, save the fact of his being on the back of a *shod* horse ; while this alone hinders the supposition of the animal being bestridden by an Indian.

For a long while the hunter-naturalist, with Francesca by his side, sits in his saddle contemplating the shod hoof-prints in a reverie of reflection. He at length thinks of crossing the tributary stream, to see if these continue on with the Indian trail, and has given his horse the spur, with a word to his daughter to do likewise, when voices reach his ear from the opposite side, warning him to pull in again. Along with loud words and ejaculations there is laughter ; as of boys at play, only not stationary in one place, but apparently moving onward, and drawing nearer to him.

On both sides of the branch stream, as also along the banks of the river, is a dense growth of tropical vegetation—mostly underwood, with here and there a tall *moriché* palm towering above the humbler shrubs. Through this they who travel so gleefully are making their way ; but cannot yet be seen from the spot where Halberger has halted. But just on the opposite bank, where the trail goes up from the ford, is a bit of treeless sward, several acres in extent, in all likelihood, kept clear of undergrowth by the wild horses and other animals on their way to the water to drink. It runs back like an embayment into the close-growing scrub, and as the trail can be distinguished debouching at its upper end, the naturalist has no doubt that these joyous gentry are approaching in that direction.

And so are they—a singular cavalcade, consisting of some thirty individuals on horseback ; for all are mounted. Two are riding side by side, some little way ahead of the others, who follow also in twos—the trail being sufficiently wide to admit of the double formation. For the Indians of *pampa* and prairie—unlike their brethren of the forest, do not always travel "single file." On horseback it would string them out too far for either convenience or safety. Indeed, these horse Indians not unfrequently march in column, and in line.

With the exception of the pair spoken of as being in the advance, all the others are costumed, and their horses caparisoned, nearly alike. Their dress is of the simplest and scantiest kind—a hip-cloth swathing their bodies from waist to mid-thigh, closely akin to the "breech-clout" of the Northern Indian, only of a different material. Instead of dressed buckskin, the loin covering of the Chaco savage is a strip of white cotton cloth, some of wool in bands of bright colour having a very pretty effect. But, unlike their red brethren of the North, they know nought of either leggings or moccasin. Their mild climate calls not for such covering ; and for foot protection against stone, thorn, or thistle, the Chaco Indian rarely ever sets sole to the ground—his horse's back being his home habitually.

Those now making way through the wood show limbs naked from thigh to toe, smooth as moulded bronze, and proportioned as if cut by the chisel of Praxiteles. Their bodies above also, nude; but here again differing from the red men of the prairies. No daub and disfigurement of chalk, charcoal, vermilion, or other garish pigment; but clear skins showing the lustrous hue of health, of bronze or brown amber tint, adorned only with some stringlets of shell beads, or the seeds of a plant peculiar to their country.

All are mounted on steeds of small size, but sinewy and perfect in shape, having long tails and flowing manes; for the barbarism of the clipping shears has not yet reached these barbarians of the Chaco.

Nor yet know they, or knowing, they use not saddle. A piece of ox-hide, or scrap of deer-skin serves them for its substitute; and for bridle a raw hide rope looped around the under jaw, without head-strap, bittless, and single reined, enabling them to check or guide their horses, as if these were controlled by the cruelest of curbs, or the jaw-breaking Mameluke bitt.

As they file forth two by two into the open ground, it is seen that there is some quality and fashion common to all; to wit, that they are all youths—not any of them over twenty—and that they wear their hair cropped in front, showing a square line across the forehead, but left untouched on the crown and back of the head. There it falls in full profuseness, reaching to the hips, and in the case of some mingling with the tails, of their horses.

Two, however, are notably different from the rest; they riding in the advance, with a horse's length or so of interval between them and their following. One of the two differs only in the style of his dress; being an Indian as the others, and, like them, quite a youth, to all appearance the youngest of the party. Yet also their chief, by reason of his richer and grander dress; his attire being of the most picturesque and costly kind worn by the Chaco savages. Covering his body, from the breast to half-way down his thighs, is a sort of loosely-fitting tunic of white cotton stuff. Sleeveless, it leaves his arm bare from nigh the shoulder to the wrist, around which glistens a bracelet with the sheen of solid gold. His limbs also are bare, save a sort of gartering below the knee, of shell and bead embroidery. On his head is a fillet band ornamented in like manner, with bright plumes, set vertically around it—the tail-feathers of the *guacamaya*, one of the most superb of South American parrots. But the most distinctive article of his apparel is his *manta*, a sort of cloak of the *poncho* kind, hanging loosely behind his back, but altogether different from the well-known garment of the gauchos, which is usually woven from wool. That on the shoulders of the young Indian is of no textile fabric, but the skin of a fawn, tanned and bleached to the softness and whiteness of a dress kid glove, the outward side being elaborately feather-worked in flowers and patterns, the feathers obtained from many a bird of gay plumage.

Of form perfectly symmetrical, the young Indian, save for his complexion, would seem a sort of Apollo, or Hyperion on horseback; while he who rides alongside him, withal that his skin is white, or once was, might well be likened to the Satyr. A man over thirty years of age, tall, and of tough, sinewy frame, with a countenance of the most sinister cast, dressed gaucho fashion, with the wide petticoat breeches lying loose about his limbs, a striped *poncho* over his shoulders, and a gaudy silken kerchief tied turban-like around his temples. But no gaucho he, nor individual of any honest calling; instead, a criminal of deepest dye, experienced in every sort of villany. For this man is Rufino Valdez, well known in Assuncion as one of Francia's familiars, and more than suspected of being one of his most dexterous *assassins.*

CHAPTER VI.

AN OLD ENEMY IN A NEW PLACE.

COULD the hunter-naturalist but know what has really occured in the Tovas tribe, and the nature of the party now approaching, he would not stay an instant longer on the banks of that branch stream ; instead, hasten back home with his child fast as their animals could carry them, and once at the estancia, make all haste to get away from it, taking every member of his family along with him. But he has no idea that anything has happened hostile to him or his, nor does he as yet see the troop of travellers, whose merry voices are making the woods ring around them : for, on the moment of his first hearing them, they were at a good distance, and are some considerable time before coming in sight. At first, he had no thought of retreating, nor making any effort to place himself and his child in concealment. And for two reasons : one, because ever since taking up his abode in the Chaco, under the protection of Naraguana, he has enjoyed perfect security, as also the consciousness of it. Therefore, why should he be alarmed now ? As a second reason for his not feeling so, an encounter with men, in the mood of those to whom he is listening, could hardly be deemed dangerous. It may be but the Tovas chief and his people, on return to the town they had abandoned; and, in all likelihood, it is they. *So,* for a time, thinks he.

But, again, it may not be; and if any other Indians—if a band of Anguité, or Guaycurus, both at enmity with the Tovas—then would they be also enemies to him, and his position one of great peril. And now once more reflecting on the sudden, as unexplained, disappearance of the latter from their old place of residence—to say the least, a matter of much mystery—bethinking himself, also, that he is quite twenty miles from his estancia, and for any chances of retreat, or shifts for safety, worse off than if he were alone, he at length, and very naturally, feels an apprehension stealing over him. Indeed, not stealing, nor coming upon him slowly, but fast gathering, and in full force. At all events, as he knows nothing of who or what the people approaching may be, it is an encounter that should, if possible, be avoided. Prudence so counsels, and it is but a question how this can best be done. Will they turn heads round, and go galloping back? Or ride in among the bushes, and there remain under cover till the Indians have passed? If these should prove to be Tovas, they could discover themselves and join them; if not, then take the chances of travelling behind them, and getting back home unobserved.

The former course he is most inclined to; but glancing up the bank, for he is still on the water's edge, he sees that the sloping path he had descended, and by which he must return, is exposed to view from the opposite side of the stream, to a distance of some two hundred yards. To reach the summit of the slope, and get under cover of the trees crowning it, would take some time. True, only a minute or two; but that may be more than he can spare, since the voices seem now very near, and those he would shun must show themselves almost immediately. And to be seen re-treating would serve no good purpose; instead, do him a damage, by challenging the hostility of the Indians, if they be not Tovas. Even so, were he alone, well-horsed as he believes himself to be—and in reality is—he would risk the attempt, and, like enough, reach his estancia in safety. But encumbered with Francesca on her diminutive steed, he knows they would have no chance in a chase across the *pampa*, with the red Centaurs pursuing. Therefore, not for an instant, or only one, entertains he thought of flight. In a second he sees it would not avail them, and decides on the other alternative—concealment. He has already made a hasty inspection of the ground near by, and sees, commencing at no great distance off, and running along the water's edge, a grove of *sumac* trees which, with their parasites and other plants twining around their stems and branches, form a complete labyrinth of leaves. The very shelter he is in search of; and heading his horse towards it, at the same time telling Francesca to follow, he rides in by the first opening that offers. Fortunately he has struck upon a *tapir* path, which makes it easier for them to pass through the underwood, and they are soon, with their horses, well screened from view. Perhaps, better would it have been for them had they continued on, without making any stop, though not certain this, for it might have been all one in the end. As it is, still in doubt, half under the belief that he may be retreating from an imaginary danger—running away from friends instead of foes—as soon as well within the thicket, Halberger reins up again, at a point where he commands a view of the ford as it enters on the opposite side of the stream. A little glade gives room for the two animals to stand side by side, and drawing Francesca's pony close up to his saddle-flap, he cautions her to keep it there steadily, as also to be silent herself. The girl needs not such admonition. No simple child she, accustomed only to the safe ways of cities and civilized life; but one knowing a great deal of that which is savage; and young though she is, having experienced trials, vicissitudes and dangers. That there is danger impending over them now, or the possibility of it, she is quite as conscious as her father, and equally observant of caution; therefore, she holds her pony well in hand, patting it on the neck to keep it quiet.

They have not long to stay before seeing what they half expected to see—a party of Indians. Just as they have got well fixed in place, with some leafy branches in front forming a screen over their faces, at the same time giving them an aperture to peep through, the dusky cavalcade shows its foremost files issuing out from the bushes on the opposite side of the stream. Though still distant—at least, a quarter of a mile—both father and daughter can perceive that they are Indians; mounted, as a matter of course, for they could not and did not, expect so see such afoot in the Chaco. But Francesca's eyes are sharper sighted than those of her father, and at the first glance she makes out more—not only that it is a party of Indians, but these of the Tovas tribe. The feathered *manta* of the young chief, with its bright gaudy sheen, has caught her eye, and she knows whose shoulders it should be covering.

" Yes, father," she says, in whisper, as soon as sighting it. " They are the Tovas! See yonder! one of the two leading—that's Aguara."

" Oh ! then, we've nothing to fear," rejoins her father, with a feeling of relief. "So, Francesca, we may as well ride back out and meet them.   I suppose it is, as I've been conjecturing ; the tribe is returning to its old quarters.   I wonder where they've been, and why so long away.   But we shall now learn all about it.   And we'll have their company with us, as far as their *tolderia ;* possibly all the way home, as, like enough, Naraguana will come on with us to the estancia.   In either case—ha ! what's that.   As I live, a white man riding alongside Aguara !   Who can *he* be ? "

Up to this, Halberger has neither touched his horse nor stirred a step ; no more she, both keeping to the spot they had chosen for observation.   And both now alike eagerly scan the face of the man, supposed to be white.

Again the eyes of the child, or her instincts, are keener and quicker than those of the parent ; or, at all events, she is the first to speak, announcing a recognition.

"Oh, papa !" she exclaims, still in whispers, "it's that horrid man who used to come to our house at Assuncion—him mamma so much disliked—the Señor Rufino."

"Hish !" mutters the father, interrupting both with speech and gesture ; then adds, "keep tight hold of the reins ; don't let the pony budge an inch ! "

Well may he thus caution, for what he now sees is that he has good reason to fear ; a man he knows to be his bitter enemy—one who, during the years of his residence in Paraguay, had repeatedly been the cause of trouble to him, and done many acts of injury and insult—the last and latest offered to his young wife.   For it was Rufino Valdez who had been employed by the Dictator previously to approach her on his behalf.

And now Ludwig Halberger beholds the base villain in company with the Tovas Indians—his own friends, as he had every reason to suppose them—riding side by side with the son of their chief! What can it mean?

Halberger's first thought is that Valdez may be their prisoner; for he, of course, knows of the hostility existing between them and the Paraguayans, and remembers that, in his last interview with Naraguana, the aged cacique was bitter as ever against the Paraguayan people. But no; there is not the slightest sign of the white man being guarded, bound, or escorted. Instead, he is riding unconstrained, side by side with the young Tovas chief, evidently in amicable relations—the two engaged in a conversation to all appearance of the most confidential kind!

Again Halberger asks, speaking within himself, what it can mean? and again reflecting endeavours to fathom the mystery: for so that strange juxtaposition appears to him. Can it be that the interrupted treaty of peace has been renewed, and friendship re-established between Naraguana and the Paraguayan Dictator? Even now, Valdez may be on a visit to the Tovas tribe on that very errand—a commissioner to arrange new terms of intercourse and amity? It certainly appears as if something of the kind had occurred. And what the Prussian now sees, taken in connection with the abandonment of the village alike matter of mystery—leads him to more than half suspect there has. For again comes up the question, why should the Tovas chief have gone off without giving him warning? So suddenly, and not a word! Surely does it seem as if there has been friendship betrayed, and Naraguana's protection withdrawn. If so, it will go hard with him, Halberger; for well knows he, that in such a treaty there would be little chance of his being made an object of special amnesty. Instead, one of its essential claims would sure be, the surendering up himself and his family. But would Nara-guana be so base? No; he cannot believe it, and this is why he is as much surprised as puzzled at seeing Valdez when he now sees him.

In any case things have a forbidding look, and the man's presence there bodes no good to him. More like the greatest evil; for it may be death itself. Even while sitting upon his horse, with these reflections running through his mind—which they do, not as related, but with the rapidity of thought itself—he feels a presentiment of that very thing. Nay, something more than a presentiment, something worse—almost the certainty that his life is near its end! For as the complete Indian cohort files forth from among the bushes, and he takes note of how it is composed—above all observing the very friendly relations between Valdez and the young chief—he knows it must affect himself to the full danger of his life. Vividly remembers he the enmity of Francia's *familiar*, too deep and dire to have been given up or forgotten. He remembers, too, of Valdez being noted as a skilled *rastrero*, or guide—his reputed profession. Against such a one the step he has taken to conceal himself is little likely to serve him. Are not the tracks of his horse, with those of the pony, imprinted in the soft mud by the water's edge where they had halted? These will not be passed over by the Indians, or Valdez, without being seen and con-sidered. Quite recent too! They must be observed, and as sure will they be followed up to where he and his child are in hiding. A pity he has not continued along the *tapir* path, still further and far away! Alas! too late now; the delay may be fatal.

In a very agony of apprehension thus reflecting, Ludwig

Halberger with shoulders stooped over his saddle-bow and head bent in among the branches, watches the Indian cavalcade approaching the stream's bank; the nearer it comes, the more certain he that himself and his child are in deadliest danger.

CHAPTER VII.

To solve the seeming enigma of Rufino Valdez travelling
in the company of the Tovas Indians, and on friendly terms
with their young chief—for he is so—it will be necessary to
turn back upon time, and give some further account of the
vaqueano himself, and his villanous master; as also to tell
why Naraguana and his people abandoned their old place
of abode, with other events and circumstances succeeding.
Of these the most serious has been the death of Naraguana
himself. For the aged cacique is no more; having died
only a few days after his latest visit paid to his pale-faced
protégé.

Nor were his last moments spent at the *tolderia*, now
abandoned. His death took place at another town of his
people some two hundred miles from this, and farther into
the interior of the Chaco ; a more ancient residence of the
Tovas tribe—in short, their "Sacred city" and burying-
place. For it is the custom of these Indians when any one
of them dies—no matter when, where, and how, whether by
the fate of war, accident in the chase, disease, or natural
decay—to have the body borne to the sacred town, and
there deposited in a cemetery containing the graves of their
athers. Not graves, as is usual, underground ; but scaffolds

standing high above it—such being the mode of Tovas interment.

Naraguana's journey to this hallowed spot—his last in life—had been made not on horseback, but in a *litera*, borne by his faithful braves.   Seized with a sudden illness, and the presentiment that his end was approaching, with a desire to die in the same place where he had been born, he gave commands for immediate removal thither—not only of himself, but everything and everybody belonging to his tribe. It was but the work of a day; and on the next the old settlement was left forsaken, just as the hunter-naturalist has found it.

Had the latter been upon the banks of that branch stream just three weeks before, he would there have witnessed one of those spectacles peculiar to the South American pampas ; as the prairies of the North.   That is the crossing of a river by an entire Indian tribe, on the move from one encampment, or place of residence, to another.   The men on horseback swimming or wading their horses ; the women and children ferried over in skin boats—those of the Chaco termed *pelotas*—with troops of dogs intermingled in the passage ; all amidst a *fracas* of shouts, the barking of dogs, neighing of horses, and shrill screaming of the youngsters, with now and then a peal of merry laughter, as some ludicrous mishap befalls one or other of the party.   No laugh, however, was heard at the latest crossing of that stream by the Tovas. The serious illness of their chief forbade all thought of merriment; so serious, that on the second day after reaching the sacred town he breathed his last ; his body being carried up and deposited upon that aërial tomb where reposed the bleaching bones of many other caciques—his predecessors.

His sudden seizure, with the abrupt departure following, accounts for Halberger having had no notice of all this—Naraguana having been delirious in his dying moments, and indeed for some time before. And his death has caused changes in the internal affairs of the Tovas tribe, attended with much excitement. For the form of government among these Chaco savages is more republican than monarchical; each new cacique having to receive his authority not from hereditary right, but by election. His son, Aguara, however, popular with the younger warriors of the tribe, carried the day, and has become Naraguana's successor.

Even had the hunter-naturalist been aware of these events, he might not have seen in them any danger to himself. For surely the death of Naraguana would not affect his relations with the Tovas tribe ; at least so far as to losing their friend-ship, or bringing about an estrangement. Not likely would such have arisen, but for certain other events of more sinister bearing, transpiring at the same period ; to recount which it is necessary for us to return still further upon time, and again go back to Paraguay and its Dictator.

Foiled in his wicked intent, and failing to discover whither his intended victims had fled, Francia employed for the finding of them one of his minions—this man of most ill repute, Rufino Valdez. It did not need the reward offered to secure the latter's zeal ; for, as stated, he too had his own old grudge against the German, brought about by a still older and more bitter hostility to Halberger's right hand man—Gaspar, the gaucho. With this double stimulus to action, Valdez entered upon the prosecution of his search, after that of the soldiers had failed. At first with confident expectation of a speedy success ; for it had not yet occurred to either him or his employer that the fugitives could have escaped clear out of the country ; a thing seemingly impossible with its frontiers so guarded.   It was only after Valdez had explored every nook and corner of Paraguayan territory in search of them, all to no purpose, that Francia was forced to the conclusion, they were no longer within his dominions. But, confiding in his own interpretation of international law, and the rights of extradition, he commissioned his emissary to visit the adjacent States, and there continue inquiry for the missing ones.   That law of his own making, already referred to, led him to think he could demand the Prussian's wife to be returned to Paraguay, whatever claim he might have upon the Prussian himself.

For over two years has Rufino Valdez been occupied in this bootless quest, without finding the slightest trace of the fugitives, or word as to their whereabouts.   He has travell.d down the river to Corrientes, and beyond to Buenos Ayres, and Monte Video at the La Plata's mouth.   Also up northward to the Brazilian frontier fort of Coimbra ; all the while without ever a thought of turning his steps towards the Chaco !

Not so strange, though, his so neglecting this noted ground ; since he had two sufficient reasons.   The first, his fear of the Chaco savages, instinctive to every Paraguayan ; the second, his want of faith, shared by Francia himself, tnat Halberger had fled thither.   Neither could for a moment think of a white man seeking asylum in the Gran Chaco ; for neither knew of the friendship existing between the hunter-naturalist and the Tovas chief.

It was only after a long period spent in fruitless inquiries, and while sojourning at Coimbra that the *vaqueano* first found traces of those searched for ; there learning from some Chaco Indians on a visit to the fort—that a white man with his wife, children, and servants, had settled near a *tolderia* of the Tovas, on the banks of the Pilcomayo river. Their description, as given by these Indians—who were not Tovas, but of a kindred tribe—so exactly answered to the hunter-naturalist and his family, that Valdez had no doubt of its being they. And hastily returning to Paraguay, he communicated what he had been told to the man for whom he was acting.

" El Supremo," overjoyed at the intelligence, promised to double the reward for securing the long-lost runaways. A delicate and difficult matter still; for there was yet the hostility of the Tovas to contend against. But just at this crisis, as if Satan had stepped in to assist his own sort, a rumour reaches Assuncion of Naraguana's death; and as the rancour had arisen from a personal affront offered to the chief himself, Francia saw it would be a fine opportunity for effecting reconciliation, as did also his emissary. Armed with this confidence, his old enmity to Halberger and gaucho, ripe and keen as ever, Valdez declared himself willing to risk his life by paying a visit to the Tovas town, and, if possible, induce these Indians to enter into a new treaty—one of its terms to be their surrendering up the white man, who had been so long the guest of their deceased cacique.

Fully commissioned and furnished with sufficient funds— gold coin which passes current among the savages of the Chaco, as with civilized people—the plenipotentiary had started off, and made his way up the Pilcomayo, till reaching the old town of the Tovas. Had Halberger's estancia stood on the river's bank, the result might have been different. But situated at some distance back, Valdez saw it not in passing, and arrived at the Indian village to find it

as did the hunter-naturalist himself, deserted. An experienced traveller and skilled tracker, however, he had no
difficulty in following the trail of the departed people, on to
their other town ; and it was the track of his horse on the
way thither, Halberger has observed on the edge of the
influent stream—as too well he now knows.

CHAPTER VIII.

WHAT the upshot of Valdez's errand as commissioner to the Tovas tribe may be told in a few words. That he has been successful, in some way, can be guessed from his being seen in close fellowship with him who is now their chief. For, otherwise, he would not be there with them or only as a prisoner. Instead, he is, as he appears, the accepted friend of Aguara, however false the friendship. And the tie which has knit them together is in keeping with the character of one, if not both. All this brought about without any great difficulty, or only such as was easily overcome by the Paraguayan plenipotentiary. Having reached the Tovas town—that where the tribe is now in permanent residence—only a day or two after Naraguana's death, he found the Indians in the midst of their lamentations ; and, through their hearts rendered gentle by grief, received friendly reception. This, and the changed *régime*, offered a fine opportunity for effecting his purpose, of which the astute commissioner soon availed himself. The result, a promise of renewal of the old peace treaty ; which he has succeeded in obtaining, partly by fair words, but as much by a profuse expenditure of the coin with which Francia had furnished him. This agreed to by the elders of the tribe ; since they had to be consulted.   But without a word said about their late chief's protégé—the hunter-naturalist—or aught done affecting him.   For the Paraguayan soon perceived, that the *sagamores* would be true to the trust Naraguana had left ; in his last coherent words enjoining them to continue protection to the stranger, and hold him, as his, unharmed.

So far the elders in council ; and the astute commisioner, recognizing the difficulty, not to say danger, of touching on this delicate subject, said nothing to them about it.

For all, he has not left the matter in abeyance, instead, has spoken of it to other ears, where he knew he would be listened to with more safety to himself—the ears of Aguara. For he had not been long in the Tovas town without making himself acquainted with the character of the new cacique, as also his inclinings—especially those relating to Francesca Halberger.   And that some private understanding has been established between him and the young Tovas chief is evident from the conversation they are now carrying on.

"You can keep the *muchachita* at your pleasure," says Valdez, having, to all appearance, settled certain preliminaries.   "All my master wants is, to vindicate the laws of our country, which this man Halberger has outraged.   As you know yourself, Señor Aguara, one of our statutes is that no foreigner who marries a Paraguayan woman may take her out of the country without permission of the President—our executive chief.   Now this man is not one of our people, but a stranger—*a gringo*—from far away over the big waters ; while the Señora, his wife, is Paraguayan, bred and born.   Besides, he stole her away in the night, like a thief, as he is."

Naraguana would not tamely have listened to such discourse.   Instead, the old chief, loyal to his friendship, would have indignantly repelled the allegations against his friend and protégé. As it is, they fall upon the ear of Naraguana's son without his offering either rebuke or protest.

Still, he seems in doubt as to what answer he should make, or what course he ought to pursue in the business between them.

"What would you have me do, Señor Rufino?" he asks in a patois of Spanish, which many Chaco Indians can speak; himself better than common, from his long and frequent intercourse with Halberger's family. "What want you?"

"I don't want you to do anything," rejoins the *vaqueano.* "If you're so squeamish about giving offence to him you call your father's friend, you needn't take any part in the matter, or at all compromise yourself. Only stand aside, and allow the law I've just spoken of to have fulfilment."

"But how?"

"Let our President send a party of his soldiers to arrest those runaways, and carry them back whence they came Now that you've proposed to renew the treaty with us, and are hereafter to be our allies—and, I hope, fast friends—it is only just and right you should surrender up those who are our enemies. If you do, I can say, as his trusted representative, that El Supremo will heap favours, and bestow rich presents on the Tovas tribe ; above all, on its young cacique—of whom I've heard him speak in terms of the highest praise."

Aguara, a vain young fellow, eagerly drinks in the fulsome flattery, his eyes sparkling with delight at the prospect of the gifts thus promised. For he is as covetous of wealth, as he is conceited about his personal appearance.

"But," he says, thinking of a reservation, "would you want us to surrender them all ?   Father, mother——"

"No, not all," rejoins the ruffian, interrupting.   "There is one," he continues, looking askant at the Indian, with the leer of a demon, "one, I take it, whom the young Tovas chief would wish to retain as an ornament to his court.   Pretty creature the *niña* was, when I last saw her ; and I have no doubt still is, unless your Chaco sun has made havoc with her charms.   She had a cousin about her own age, by name Cypriano, who was said to be very fond of her ; and rumour had it around Assuncion, that they were being brought up for one another."

Aguara's brow blackens, and his dark Indian eyes seem to emit sparks of fire.

"Cypriano shall never have her !" he exclaims in a tone of angry determination.

"How can you help it, amigo ?" interrogates his tempter. "That is, supposing the two are inclined for one another. As you know, her father is not only a pale-face, but *a gringo*, with prejudices of blood far beyond us Paraguayans, who are half-Indian ourselves.   Ah ! and proud of it too. Being such, he would never consent to give his daughter in marriage to a red man—make a *squaw* of her, as he would scornfully call it.   No, not even though it were the grandest cacique in the Chaco.   He would see her dead first."

"Indeed !" exclaims the Indian, with a disdainful toss of the head.

"Indeed, yes ;" asseverates Valdez.   "And whether they remain under your protection, or be taken back to Paraguay, 'twill be all the same as regards the señorita. There's but one way I know of to hinder her from becoming the wife of her cousin Cypriano, and that is——"

" What ? " impatiently asks Aguara.

" To separate them. Let father, mother, son, and nephew be taken back to where they belong; the *niña* to stay behind."

" But how can that be done ? "

" You mean without your showing your hand in it ? " asks Valdez, in a confidential whisper.

" I do. For know, Señor Rufino, that, though I'm now chief of our tribe, and those we have with us here will do as I bid them—obey me in anything—still the elders have control, and might make trouble if I did aught to injure the friend of my late father. I am not free, and dare not act as you propose."

" *Carramba !* you needn't act at all, as I've already told you. Only stand aside, and let others do the acting. 'Twill be easy enough. But give your consent to my bringing a pack of our Paraguayan wolves to this fold your father has so carefully shepherded, and I'll answer for sorting out the sheep we want to take, and leaving the lamb you wish left. Then you and yours can come opportunely up, too late for protecting the old ram and dam, but in time to rescue the bleating lambkin, and bear her away to a place of safety. Your own toldo, Señor Aguara ; where, take my word for't, no one will ever come to inquire after, much less reclaim her. You consent ? "

" Speak low ! " cautions the wily Indian, casting a glance over his shoulders as one willing to do a wicked deed, but without desiring it known. " Don't let them hear us. *You have my consent.*"

CHAPTER IX.

A RED-HANDED RUFFIAN.

JUST as the young cacique has yielded to the tempter, surrendering his last scruple of conscience, his horse dips hoof in the stream, that of the Paraguayan plunging into it at the same time. Knowing the ford well, and that it is shallow, with a firm bottom, they ride boldly on; their followers straggled out behind, these innocent of the foul conspiracy being hatched so near; still keeping up their rollicky mirth, and flinging about *jeux d'esprit* as the spray drops are tossed from the fetlocks of their wading horses.

It is a popular though erroneous belief, that the red men of America are of austere and taciturn habit. The older ones may be at times, but even these not always. Instead, as a rule they are given to jocularity and fun; the youth brimful of it as the street boys of any European city. At least one half of their diurnal hours is spent by them in play and pastimes; for from those of the north we have borrowed both Polo and La Crosse; while horse-racing is as much their sport as ours; and archery more.

Not strange, then, that the *jeunesse dorée* of the Tovas, escorting their youthful cacique, and seeing him occupied with the pale-face who has been on a visit to their town, take no heed of what passes between these two, but abandon themselves to merriment along the march. No more is it strange that Aguara, engrossed with the subject of conversation between him and the *vaqueano*, leaves them free to their frollicking.

Nothing occurs to change the behaviour either of the two who are in front, or those following, until the horses of the former have forded the stream, and stepped out on the bank beyond. Then the Paraguayan, as said, a skilled tracker and cunning as a fox, chancing to lower his eyes to the ground, observes upon it several hoof-marks of a horse. These at once fix his attention; for not only are they fresh—to all appearance made but the moment before—but the horse that made them must have been *shod*.

While in the act of verifying this observation, other hoof prints come under his eye, also shod, but much smaller, being the tracks of a pony. Recent too, evidently made at the same time as the horse's. He has no need to point them out to the young Indian, who, trained to such craft from infancy upward, has noted them soon as he, and with equally quick intuitiveness is endeavouring to interpret their significance.

Succeeding in this : for both the horse's track and that of the pony are known to, and almost instantly recognised by him. He has not lived two years in proximity to the estancia of Ludwig Halberger, all the while in friendly intercourse with the naturalist and his family, without taking note of everything; and can tell the particular track of every horse in its stables. Above all is he familiar with the diminutive hoof-marks of Francesca's pretty pony, which he has more than once trailed across the *campo*, in the hope of having a word with its rider. Perceiving them now, and so recently made, he gives out an ejaculation of pleased surprise; then looks around, as though expecting to see the pony itself, with its young mistress upon its back. There is no one in sight, however, save the *vaqueano* and his own followers; the latter behind, halted by command, some of them still in the water, so that they may not ride over the shod tracks, and obliterate them.

All this while Halberger and his child are within twenty paces of the spot, and seated in their saddles, as when they first drew up side by side. Screened by the trees, they see the Indians, themselves unobserved, while they can distinctly hear every word said. Only two of the party speak aloud, the young cacique and his pale-face companion; their speech, of course, relating to the newly-discovered "sign."

After dismounting, and for a few seconds examining 'it, Valdez leaps back into his saddle with a show of haste, as if he would at once start off upon the trail of horse and pony.

"There have been only the two here—that's plain," he says. "Father and daughter, you think? What a pity we didn't get up in time to bid 'good-day' to them! 'Twould have simplified matters much. You'd then have had your young chick to carry to the cage you intend for it, without the mother bird to make any bother or fluttering in your face; while I might have executed my commission sooner than expected."

"*Carramba!*" he continues after a short while spent in considering. "They can't have gone very far as yet. You say it's quite twenty miles to the place where the *gringo* has his headquarters. If so, and they've not been in a great hurry to get home—which like enough the girl would, since her dear Cypriano don't appear to be along—we may come up with them by putting on speed. Let us after them at once! What say you?"

The young Indian, passive in the hands of the older and more hardened sinner, makes neither objection nor protest. Instead, stung by the allusion to " dear Cypriano," he is anxious as the other to come up with the pony and its rider. So, without another word, he springs back upon his horse, declaring his readiness to ride on.

With eyes directed downward, they keep along the return tracks; having already observed that these come no farther than the ford, and turn back by the water's edge—

" Aha !" exclaims the *vaqueano*, pulling up again ere he has proceeded three lengths of his horse; " they've left the trail here, and turned off up stream! That wouldn't be their route home, would it ?"

" No," answers Aguara. " Their nearest way's along the river, down as far as our old *tolderia*. After that——"

" Sh !" interrupts the Paraguayan, leaning over, and speaking in a cautious whisper, " Did you not hear something ? Like the chinking of a bitt curb ? I shouldn't wonder if they're in among those bushes. Suppose you stay here and keep watch along the bank, while I go and beat up that bit of cover ?"

" Just as it please you," assents the young cacique, unresistingly.

" Give me two or three of your fellows along. Not that I have any fear to encounter the *gringo* alone—poor weak creature, still wearing his green spectacles, I suppose. Far from it. But still there's no harm in having help, should he attempt to give trouble. Besides, I'll want some one to look after the *muchachita !* "

" Take as many as you wish."

" Oh ! two will be sufficient ; that pair nearest us."

He points to the foremost file of the troop, two who **are** a little older than their friends, as also of more hardened and sinister aspect.   For, short as has been his stay among them, the subtle emissary has taken the measure of many members of the tribe ; and knows something of the two he thus designates.   His gold has made them his friends and allies; in short, gained them over to him as good for anything he may call upon them to do.

Aguara having signified assent, a gesture brings them up ; and, at a whispered word from the *vaqueano* himself, they fall in behind him.

Heading his horse for the *sumac* thicket he is soon at its edge, there seeing what rejoices him—the tracks of both horse and pony passing into it.   He has reached the spot where Halberger turned in along the *tapir* path.   Parting the leaves with a long spear—for he is so armed—he rides in also, the two Indians after.   And just as the tails of their horses disappear among the leaves, Aguara, who has kept his place, hears another horse neighing within the thicket at a point farther off.   Then there is a quick trampling of hooves, followed by a hurried rush, and the swishing of bent branches, as the *vaqueano* and his two aids dash on through the *sumacs*.

The young cacique and his followers continuing to listen, soon after hear shouts—the voices of men in angry exclamation—mingling with them the shriller treble of a girl's.   Then a shot, quick followed by a second, and a third ; after which only the girl's voice is heard, but now in lamentation.   Soon, however, it is hushed, and all over—everything silent as before.

The young Tovas chief sits upon his horse with heart audibly beating.   He has no doubt—cannot have—as to who were the pursued ones ; no more, that they have been overtaken. But with what result? Has the *vaqueano* killed both father and daughter? Or were the shots fired by Halberger, killing Valdez himself and the two who went with him? No; that cannot be; else why should the girl's lamenting cries be heard afterwards? But then again, why have they ceased so suddenly?

While thus anxiously conjecturing, he again hears the trampling of horses among the trees; this time evidently in return towards him. And soon after sees the horses themselves, with their riders—four of them. Three are the same as late left him, but looking differently. The Paraguayan has one arm hanging down by his side, to all appearance broken, with blood dripping from the tips of his fingers; while the steel blade of his spear, borne in the other, is alike reddened. And there is blood elsewhere—streaming down the breast of one of the young Indians who seems to have difficulty in keeping upon his horse's back. The fourth individual in the returning cavalcade is a young girl, with a cloth tied over her head, as if to hinder her from crying out; seated upon the back of a pony, this led by the Indian who is still unhurt.

At a glance, Aguara sees it is Francesca Halberger, though he needs not seeing her to know that. For he had already recognised her voice—well knew it, even in its wailing.

" Her father—what of him ? " he asks, addressing Valdez, soon as the latter is up to him, and speaking in undertone.

" No matter what," rejoins the ruffian, with a demoniac leer. " The father is my affair, and he has come very near making it an ugly one for me. Look at this !" he continues, indicating the left arm which hangs loose by his side. "And at that !" he adds, glancing up to the point of his spear.

"Blood on both, as you see. So, Señor Aguara, you may draw your deductions. Your affair is yonder," he nods towards the muffled figure on the pony's back; "and you can now choose between taking her home to her mother—her handsome cousin as well—or carrying her to *your* home, as the queen that is to be of the Tovas."

The young cacique is not slow in deciding which course to pursue. The allusion to the "handsome cousin" again excites his jealousy and his ire. Its influence is irresistible, as sinister; and when he and his followers take departure from that spot—which they do almost on the instant—it is to recross the stream, and head their horses homeward—Francesca Halberger carried captive along with them.

CHAPTER X.

GASPAR, THE GAUCHO.

OVER the broad undulating plain which extends between
Halberger's house and the deserted *tolderia* of the Tovas, a
horseman is seen proceeding in the direction of the latter.
He is a man about middle age, of hale, active appearance,
in no way past his prime. Of medium size, or rather above
it, his figure though robust is well proportioned, with strong
sinewy arms and limbs lithe as a panther's, while his countenance, notwithstanding the somewhat embrowned skin, has
a pleasant, honest expression, evincing good nature as a
habitually amiable temper, at the same time that his features
show firmness and decision. A keenly glancing eye, coal-
black, bespeaks for him both courage and intelligence;
while the way in which he sits his horse, tells that he is not
new to the saddle; instead, seeming part of it. His garb
is peculiar, though not to the country which claims him as
a native. Draping down from his shoulders and spreading
over the hips of his horse is a garment of woollen fabric,
woven in stripes of gaudy colours, alternating white, yellow,
and red, of no fit or fashion, but simply kept on by having
his head thrust through a slit in its centre. It is a *poncho*—
the universal wrap or cloak of every one who dwells upon
the banks of the La Plata or Parana. Under is another gar-

ment, of white cotton stuff, somewhat resembling Zouave breeches, and called *calzoneras*, these reaching a little below his knees ; while his feet and ankles are encased in boots of his own manufacture, seamless, since each was originally the skin of a horse's leg, the hoof serving as heel, with the shank shortened and gathered into a pucker for the toe. Tanned and bleached to the whiteness of a wedding glove, with some ornamental stitching and broidery, it furnishes a foot gear, alike comfortable and becoming. Spurs, with grand rowels, several inches in diameter, attached to the heels of these horse-hide boots, give them some resemblance to the greaves and ankle armour of mediæval times.

All this has he whose dress we are describing ; while surmounting nis head is a broad-brimmed hat with high-peaked crown and plume of *rheas* feathers—underneath all a kerchief of gaudy colour, which draping down over the nape of his neck protects it from the fervid rays of the Chaco sun. It is a costume imposing and picturesque ; while the caparison of his horse is in keeping with it. The saddle, called *recado*, is furnished with several coverings, one upon another, the topmost, *coronilla*, being of bright coloured cloth elaborately quilted ; while the bridle of plaited horse-hair is studded with silver joints, from which depend rings and tassels, the same ornamenting the breast-piece and neck straps attaching the martingale, in short, the complete equipment of a *gaucho*. And a gaucho he is—Gaspar, the hero of our tale.

It has been already said, that he is in the service of Ludwig Halberger. So is he, and has been ever since the hunter-naturalist settled in Paraguay ; in the capacity of steward, or as there called *mayor-domo ;* a term of very different signification from the *major-domo* or house-steward of European countries, with dress and duties differing as well. No black coat, or white cravat, wears he of Spanish America, no spotless stockings, or soft slipper shoes. Instead, a costume more resembling that of a Cavalier, or Freebooter; while the services he is called upon to perform require him to be not only a first-class horseman, but able to throw the lazo, catch a wild cow or colt, and tame the latter—in short, take a hand at anything. And at almost anything Gaspar can; for he is man-of-all-work to the hunter-naturalist, as well as his man of confidence.

Why he is riding away from the estancia at such an hour —for it is afternoon—may be guessed from what has gone before. For it is on that same day, when Halberger and his daughter started off to visit the Indian village ; and as these had not returned soon as promised, the anxiety of the wife, rendered keen by the presentiment which had oppressed her at their parting, became at length unbearable ; and to relieve it Gaspar has been despatched in quest of them.

No better man in all the pampas region, or South America itself, could have been sent on such an errand. His skill as a tracker is not excelled by any other gaucho in the Argentine States, from which he originally came ; while in general intelligence, combined with courage, no one there, or elsewhere, could well be his superior. As the Señora said her last words to him at parting, and listened to his in return, she felt reassured. Gaspar was not the man to make delay, or come back without the missing one. On this day, however, he deviates from his usual habit, at the same time from the route he ought to take—that leading direct to the Indian village, whither he knows his master and young mistress to have gone. For while riding along, going at a gentle canter, a cock "ostrich" starts up before his horse, and soon after the hen, the two trotting away over the plain to one side. It so chances that but the day before his master had given him instructions to catch a male ostrich for some purpose of natural history—the first he should come across. And here was one, a splendid bird, in full flowing plumage. This, with an observation made, that the ostriches seem less shy than is usual with these wary creatures, and are moving away but slowly, decides him to take after and have a try at capturing the cock. Unloosing his *bolas* from the saddle bow, where he habitually carries this weapon, and spurring his horse to a gallop, off after them he goes.

Magnificently mounted, for a gaucho would not be otherwise, he succeeds in his intent, after a run of a mile or so, getting close enough to the birds to operate upon them with his *bolas*. Winding these around his head and launching them, he has the satisfaction of seeing the cock ostrich go down upon the grass, its legs lapped together tight as if he had hard spliced them.

Riding on up to the great bird, now hoppled and without any chance to get away from him, he makes things more sure by drawing out his knife and cutting the creature's throat. Then releasing the *bolas*, he returns them to the place from which he had taken them—on the horn of his *recado*. This done, he stands over the dead *rhea*, thus reflecting :—

"I wonder what particular part of this beauty—it is a beauty, by the way, and I don't remember ever having met with a finer bird of the breed—but if I only knew which one or the identical parts the master wants, it would save me some trouble in the way of packing, and my horse no little of a load. Just possible the *dueño* only cares for the tail feathers, or the head and beak, or it may be but the legs. Well, as I can't tell which, there's but one way to make sure about it—that is, to take the entire carcase along with me. So, go it must."

Saying this, he lays hold of a leg, and drags the ostrich nearer to his horse, which all the time stands tranquilly by: for a gaucho's steed is trained to keep its place, without need of any one having care of it.

" *Carramba !* " he exclaims, raising the bird from the ground, "what a weight the thing is ! Heavy as a quarter of beef ! Now I think on't, it might have been better if I'd let the beast alone, and kept on without getting myself into all this bother. Nay, I'm sure it would have been wiser. What will the Señora say, when she knows of my thus dallying—trifling with the commands she gave me ? Bah ! she won't know anything about it—and needn't. She will, though, if I stand dallying here. I mustn't a minute longer. So up, Señor Avertruz, and lie there."

At which, he hoists the ostrich—by the gauchos called " *avertruz* "—to the croup of his *recado ;* where, after a rapid manipulation of cords, the bird is made fast, beyond all danger of dropping off.

This done, he springs upon his horse's back, and then looks out to see which direction he should now take. A thing not so easily determined ; for in the chase after it, the ostrich had made more than one double; and, although tolerably familiar with the topography of that plain, the gaucho is for the time no little confused as to his whereabouts. Nor strange he should be ; since the palm groves scattered over it are all so much alike, and there is no high hill, nor any great eminence, to guide him. Ridges there are, running this way and that; but all only gentle undulations, with no bold projection, or other landmark that he can remember.

He begins to think he is really strayed, lost; and, believing so, is angry with himself for having turned out of his path—as the path of his duty. Angry at the ostrich, too, that tempted him.

"*Avertruz, maldito!*" he exclaims, terms in the gaucho vernacular synonymous with "ostrich, be hanged!" adding, as he continues to gaze hopelessly around, "I wish I'd let the long-legged brute go its way. Like as not, it'll hinder me going mine, till too late. And if so, there'll be a pretty tale to tell! *Santissima!* whatever am I to do? I don't even know the way back to the house; though that wouldn't be any good if I did. I daren't go there without taking some news with me. Well; there's only one thing I can do; ride about, and quarter the pampa, till I see something that'll set me back upon my road."

In conformity with this intention, he once more puts his horse in motion, and strikes off over the plain; but he does not go altogether without a guide, the sun somewhat helping him. He knows that his way to the Indian village is westward, and as the bright luminary is now beginning to descend, it points out that direction, so taking his bearings by it, he rides on. Not far, however, before catching sight of another object, which enables him to steer his course with greater precision. This a tree, a grand vegetable giant of the species called *ombu*, known to every gaucho—beloved, almost held sacred by him, as affording shade to his sun-exposed and solitary dwelling. The one Gaspar now sees has no house under its wide-spreading branches; but he has himself been under them more than once while out on a hunt, and smoked his *cigarrito* in their shade. As his eye lights upon it, a satisfied expression comes over his features, for he knows that the tree is on the top of a little *loma*, or hill, about half-way between the estancia and the Indian town, and nearly in the direct route.

He needs nothing more to guide him now; but instead of riding towards the tree, he rather turns his back upon it, and starts off in a different direction. This because he had already passed the *ombu* before coming across the ostrich.

Soon again he is back upon the path from which he had strayed, and proceeds along it without further interruption, riding at a rapid pace to make up for the lost time.

Still, he is far from being satisfied with himself. Although he may have done that which will be gratifying to his master, there is a possibility of its displeasing his mistress. Most certainly will it do this, should he not find the missing ones, and have to go home without them. But he has no great fear of that; indeed, is not even uneasy. Why should he be? He knows his master's proclivities, and believes that he has come across some curious and rare specimens, which take time to collect or examine, and this it is which has been retarding his return. Thus reflecting, he continues on, every moment expecting to meet them. But as there is neither road nor any regular path between the two places, he needs to keep scanning the plain, lest on their return he may pass them unobserved.

But he sees nothing of them till reaching the *tolderia*, and there only the hoof marks of his master's horse, with those of his young mistress's pony, both conspicuous in the dust-covered ground by the doors of the *toldos*. But on neither does he dwell, for he, too, as were the others, is greatly surprised to find the place deserted—indeed alarmed, and for a time sits in his saddle as one half-dazed.

Only a short while, for he is not the man to give way to long irresolution, and recovering himself, he rides rapidly about, from *toldo* to *toldo*, all over the town, at the same time shouting and calling out his master's name.

For answer, he only has the echoes of his own voice, now and then varied with the howl of a wolf, which, prowling around like himself no doubt wonders, as he, at the place being abandoned.

After a hurried examination of the houses, and seeing there is no one within them, just as Halberger had done, he strikes off on the trail of the departed inhabitants; and with the sun still high enough to light up every track on it, he perceives those made by the *dueño's* horse, and the more diminutive hoof-prints alongside them.

On he goes following them up, and in a gallop, for they are so fresh and clear he has no need to ride slowly. On in the same gait for a stretch of ten miles, which brings him to the tributary stream at the crossing place. He rides down to the water's edge, there to be sorely puzzled at what he sees—some scores of other horse-tracks recently made, but turning hither and thither in crowded confusion.

It calls for all his skill as a *rastrero*, with some considerable time, to unwind the tangled skein. But he at length succeeds, so far as to discover that the whole horse troop, to whomsoever belonging, have recrossed the ford; and crossing it himself, he sees they have gone back up the Pilcomayo river. Among them is one showing a shod hoof; but he knows that has not been made by his master's horse, the bar being larger and broader, with the claw more deeply indented. Besides, he sees not the pony's tracks—though

A SIGHT MEETS HIS EYE, CAUSING THE BLOOD IN HIS VEINS
TO RUN COLD.

p. 69.

they are or were there—and have been trodden out by the ruck of the other animals trampling after.

The gaucho here turns back ; though he intends following the trail further, when he has made a more careful examination of the sign on the other side of the stream ; and re-crossing, he again sets to scrutinizing it. This soon leading him to the place where Halberger entered the *sumac* grove. Now the gaucho, entering it also, and following the *slot* along the *tapir* path, at a distance of some three hundred yards from the crossing, comes out into an open glade, lit up by the last rays of the setting sun, which fall slantingly through the trees standing around. There a sight meets his eye, causing the blood at one moment to run cold through his veins, in the next hot as boiling lava ; while from his lips issue exclamations of mingled astonishment and indignation. What he sees is a horse, saddled and with the bridle also on, standing with neck bent down, and head drooped till the nostrils almost touch the earth. But between them and the ground is a figure extended at full stretch ; the body of a man to all appearance dead ; which at a glance the gaucho knows to be that of his master !

CHAPTER XI.

ANOTHER sun is rising over the Chaco, and its rays, red
as the reflection from a fire, begin to glitter through the
stems of the palm-trees that grow in scattered topes upon the
plains bordering the Pilcomayo. But ere the bright orb
has mounted above their crowns, two horsemen are seen to
ride out of the *sumac* grove, in which Ludwig Halberger
vainly endeavoured to conceal himself from the assassin
Valdez and his savage confederates.

It is not where any of these entered the thicket that the
horsemen are coming out, but at a point some half-mile
further up the branch stream, and on its higher bank, where
it reaches the general level of the upper plain. Here the
sumac trees cover the whole slope from the water's edge to
the crest of the bordering ridge, on this ending abruptly.
Though they stand thinly, and there is room enough for two
horsemen to ride abreast, these are not doing so, but one
ahead, and leading the other's horse by a raw-hide rope attached to the bitt ring.

In this manner they have ascended the slope, and have
now the great plain before them; treeless, save here and
there a tope of palms or a scattering of willows around some

spot where there is water ; but the taller timber is behind them, and soon as they arrive at its edge, he riding ahead reins up his horse, the other stopping at the same time.

There is still a belt of bushes between them and the open ground, of stunted growth, but high enough to hinder their view. To see over them, the leading horseman stands up in his stirrups, and looks out upon the plain, his glances directed all around it. These, earnestly interrogative, tell of apprehension, as of an enemy he might expect to be there, in short, making a reconnaissance to see if the " coast be clear."

That he judges it so is evinced by his settling back into his saddle, and moving on across the belt of bushes; but again, on the skirt of this and before issuing out of it, he draws bridle, and once more makes a survey of the plain.

By this time, the sun having mounted higher in the heavens, shines full upon his face, showing it of dark complexion, darker from the apprehension now clouding it ; but of honest cast, and one which would otherwise be cheerful, since it is the face of Gaspar, the gaucho.

Who the other is cannot be easily told, even with the bright sun beaming upon him ; for his hat, broad-brimmed, is slouched over his forehead, concealing most part of his countenance. The head itself, oddly, almost comically, inclined to one side, droops down till the chin nigh touches his breast. Moreover, an ample cloak, which covers him from neck to ankles, renders his figure as unrecognizable as his face

With his horse following that of the gaucho, who leads him at long halter's reach, he, too, has halted in the outer selvidge of the scrub; still maintaining the same relative position to the other as when they rode out from the *sumacs*, and without speaking word or making gesture. In fact, he stirs not at all, except such motion as is due to the move ment of his horse; but beyond that he neither raises head nor hand, not even to guide the animal, leaving it to be lead unresistingly.

Were the gaucho of warlike habits, and accustomed to making predatory expeditions, he might be taken as return-ing from one with a captive, whom he is conducting to some safe place of imprisonment. For just like this his silent companion appears, either fast strapped to his own saddle, or who, conquered and completely subdued, has resigned all thoughts of resistance and hopes of escape. But Gaspar is essentially a man of peace, which makes it improbable that he, behind, is his prisoner.

Whatever the relationship between them, the gaucho for the present pays no attention to the other horseman, neither speaks to nor turns his eye toward him; for these are now all upon the plain, scanning it from side to side, and all round as far as he can command view of it. He is not him-self silent, however, though the words to which he gives utterance are spoken in a low tone, and by way of soliloquy, thus :—

"'Twill never do to go back by the river's bank. Who-ever the devils that have done this dastardly thing, they may be still prowling about, and to meet them would be for me to get served the same as they've served him, that's sure; so I'd best take another route, though it be a bit round the corner. Let me see. I think I know a way that should lead tolerably straight to the estancia without touching the river or going anywheres near it. I mustn't even travel within sight of it. If the Tovas have had any hand in this ugly business—and, by the Virgin, I believe they have, however hard it is to think so—some of them may still be near, and possibly a party gone back to their old *tolderia*. I'll have to give that a wide berth anyhow; so to get across this open stretch without being seen, if there be anyone on it to see me, will need manœuvring. As it is, there don't appear to be a soul, that's so far satisfactory."

Again he sweeps the grassy expanse with searching glance, his face brightening up as he observes a flock of ostriches on one side, on the other a herd of deer—the birds stalking leisurely along, the beasts tranquilly browsing. Were there Indians upon the plain, it would not be so. Instead, either one or the other would show excitement. The behaviour of the dumb creatures imparting to him a certain feeling of confidence, he says, continuing the soliloquy :—

"I think I may venture it. Nay, I must; and there's no help for't. We have to get home somehow—and soon. Ah! the Señora! poor lady! What will she be thinking by this time? And what when we get back? *Valga me Dios!* I don't know how I shall ever be able to break it to her, or in what way! It will sure drive her out of her senses, and not much wonder, either. To lose one of them were enough, but both, and—— Well, no use dwelling on it now; besides, there's no time to be lost. I must start off at once; and, maybe, as I'm riding on, I'll think of some plan to communicate the sad news to the Señora, without giving her too sudden a shock. *Pobrecita!* "

At the pitying exclamation he gives a last interrogative

glance over the plain ; then, with a word to his horse, and
a touch of the spur, he moves out into the open, and on ;
the other animal following, as before, its rider maintaining
the same distance and preserving the self-same attitude,
silent and gestureless as ever !

CHAPTER XII

SKULKING BACK.

WHILE the gaucho and his silent companion were still in halt by the edge of the *sumac* wood, another horseman could be seen approaching the place, but on the opposite side of the stream, riding direct down to the ford. Descried at any distance, his garb, with the caparison of his horse—the full gaucho panoply of bitted bridle, breast-plate, *recado*, and *caronilla*—would tell he is not an Indian. Nor is he; since this third traveller, so early on the road, is Rufino Valdez. As commissioner to the Tovas tribe, he has executed the commission with which he was entrusted, with something besides; and is now on return to make report to his master, El Supremo, leaving the latter to take such other steps as may deem desirable.

The *vaqueano* has passed the preceding night with the Indians at their camp, leaving it long before daybreak, though Aguara, for certain reasons, very much wished him to return with them to their town, and proposed it. A proposal, for reasons of *his* own, the cunning Paraguayan declined, giving excuses that but ill satisfied the young cacique, and which he rather reluctantly accepted. He could not, however, well refuse to let Valdez go his way. The man was not a prisoner moreover, his promise to be soon back, as the bearer of rich presents, was an argument irresistible ; and influenced by this, more than aught else, Aguara gave him permission to depart.

The young chief's reasons for wishing to detain him were of a kind altogether personal. Much as he likes the captive he is carrying with him, he would rather she had been made captive by other means, and in a less violent manner. And he is now returning to his tribe, not so triumphantly, but with some apprehension as to how he will be received by the elders. What will they say when the truth is told them, —all the details of the red tragedy just enacted? He would lay the blame, where most part of it properly belongs, on the shoulders of the Paraguayan, and, indeed, intends doing so. But he would rather have the latter with him to meet the storm, should there be such, by explaining in his own way, why he killed the other white man. For Valdez had already said something to them of an old hostility between himself and the hunter-naturalist, knowing that the Tovas, as well as other Chaco Indians, acknowledge the rights of the *vendetta.*

But just for the reason Aguara desires to have him along with him, is the *vaqueano* inclined to the opposite course ; in truth, determined upon it. Not for the world would he now return to the Tovas town. He has too much intelligence for that, or too great regard for his safety—his very life, which he believes, and with good cause, would be more than risked, were he again to show himself among a people whose hospitality he has so outraged. For he knows he ·ns done this, and that there will surely be that storm of w.. ·h the young cacique is apprehensive—a very tempest of indignation among the elders and friends of the deceased Naraguana, when they hear of the fate which has befallen the harmless stranger, so long living under their late chief's protection. Therefore, notwithstanding the many promises he has made, not the slightest thought of performing any of them, or even going back on that trail, has Rufino Valdez. Instead, as he rides down the ford of the stream he is thinking to himself, it will be the last time he will have to wade across it, gleeful at the thought of having so well succeeded in what brought him over it at all. Pondering on something besides, another deed of infamy yet to be done, but for which he will not have to come so far up the Pilcomayo.

In spite of his self-gratulation, and the gleams of a joy almost Satanic, which now and then light up his dark sinister countenance, he is not without some apprehensions; this is made manifest by his behaviour as he rides along. Although making what haste he can, he does not rush on in a reckless or careless manner. On the contrary, with due caution, at every turn of the path, stopping and making survey of each new reach before entering upon it. This he did, as the ford opened to his view, keeping under cover of the bushes, till assured there was no one there; then, striking out into the open ground, and riding rapidly for it. And while wading across the stream, his eyes are not upon the water, but sweeping the bank up and down with glances of keen scrutiny.

As he sees no one there, nor the sign of anyone having been—for it is not yet daylight, and too dark for him to note the tracks of Gaspar's horse—he says with a satisfied air,

"They're not likely to be coming after the missing pair at so early an hour. Besides, it's too soon. They'll hardly be setting them down as lost till late last night, and so couldn't have tracked them on here yet."

Riding up out of the water, he once more draws rein by its edge, and sits regarding the *sumac* grove with an expression in his eyes strangely repulsive.

" I've half a mind to go up in there," he mutters, "and see how things stand. I wasn't altogether satisfied with the way we left them, and there's just a possibility he may be still alive. The girl gave so much trouble in getting them parted, I couldn't be quite sure of having killed him outright. If not, he might manage to crawl away, or they coming after in search of him—*Carrai!* I'll make sure now. It can only delay me a matter of ten minutes, and," he adds glancing up at the blade of his spear, " if need be, another thrust of this."

Soon as forming his devilish resolve, the assassin gives his horse a prick of the spur, and passes on towards the *sumac* grove, entering at the same place as before, like a tiger skulking back to the quarry it has killed, and been chased away from.

Once inside the thicket, he proceeds along the *tapir* path, groping his way in the darkness. But he remembers it well, as well he may ; and without going astray arrives at a spot he has still better reason to recall ; that where, but a little more than twelve hours before, he supposes himself to have committed murder ! Delayed along the narrow tortuous track, some time has elapsed since his entering among the *sumacs*. Only a short while, but long enough to give him a clearer light, for the day has meanwhile dawned, and the place is less shadowed, for it is an open spot where the sanguinary struggle took place.

It is sufficiently clear for him, without dismounting, to distinguish objects on the ground, and note, which at a glance he does, that one he expected to see is not to be seen. No murdered man there; no body, living or dead !

CHAPTER XIII.

FOR some seconds, Rufino Valdez is in a state of semi-bewilderment, from his lips proceeding exclamations that tell of surprise, but more chagrin. Something of weird terror, too, in the expression upon his sallow, cadaverous face, as the grey dawn dimly lights it up.

"*Mil demonios !*" he mutters, gazing distractedly on the ground. "What does this mean? Is it possible the *gringo's* got away? Possible? Aye, certain. And his animal, too! Yes, I remember we left that, fools as we were, in our furious haste. It's all clear, and, as I half anticipated, he's been able to climb on the horse, and's off home! There by this time, like enough."

With this double adjuration, he resolves upon dismounting, to make better inspection of the place, and, if possible, assure himself whether his victim has really survived the murderous attack. But just as he has drawn one foot out of the stirrup and is balancing on the other, a sound reaches his ear, causing him to reseat himself in the saddle, and sit listening. Only a slight noise it was, but one in that place of peculiar significance, being the hoof-stroke of a horse.

"Good!" he ejaculates in a whisper, "it must be his."

Hearkening a little longer, he hears the sound again,

apparently further off, and as his practised ear tells him, the distance increasing.

" It must be his horse," he reiterates, still continuing to listen. "And who but he on the animal's back? Going off? Yes; slowly enough. No wonder at that. Ha! he's come to a halt. What's the best thing for me to do?"

He sits silently considering, but only for a few seconds; then glancing around the glade, in which yester eve he had shed innocent blood, at the same time losing some of his own, he sees another break among the bushes, where the *tapir* path goes out again. Faint as the light still is, it shows him some horse-tracks, apparently quite fresh, leading off that way.

He stays not for more, but again plying the spur, re-enters the thicket, not to go back to the ford, but on in the opposite direction. The *tapir* path takes him up an acclivity, from the stream's edge to the level of the higher plain, and against it he urges his horse to as much speed as the nature of the ground will permit. He has thrown away caution now, and presses forward without fear, expecting soon to see a man on horseback, but so badly crippled as to be easily overtaken, and as easily overcome.

What he does see, on reaching the summit of the slope, is something very different—two horses instead of one, with a man upon the back of each! And though one may be wounded and disabled, as he knows him to be, the other is not so, as he can well see. Instead, a man in full health, strength, and vigour, one Rufino Valdez fears as much as hates, though hating him with his whole heart. For it is Gaspar, the gaucho, once his rival in the affections of a Paraguayan girl, and successful in gaining them.

That the *vaqueano's* fear now predominates over his anti

pathy is evident from his behaviour. Instead of dashing on after to overtake the horsemen, who, with backs towards him, are slowly retiring, he shows only a desire to shun them. True, there would be two to one, and he has himself but a single arm available—his left, broken and bandaged, being now in a sling. But then only one of the two would be likely to stand against him, the other being too far gone for fight. Indeed, Halberger—for Valdez naturally supposes it to be he—sits drooped in his saddle, as though he had difficulty in keeping to it. Not that he has any idea of attacking them does the *vaqueano* take note of this, nor has he the slightest thought of attempting to overtake them. Even knew he that the wounded man were about to drop dead, he knows the other would be more than his match, with both his own arms sound and at their best, for they have been already locked in deadly strife with those of the gaucho, who could have taken his life, but generously forebore. Not for the world would Rufino Valdez again engage in single combat with Gaspar Mendez, and soon as setting eyes on the latter he draws bridle so abruptly that his horse starts back as if he had trodden upon a rattlesnake.

Quieting the animal with some whispered words, he places himself behind a thick bush, and there stays all of a tremble, the only thing stedfast about him being his gaze, fixed upon the forms of the departing travellers. So carefully does he screen himself, that from the front nothing is visible to indicate the presence of anyone there, save the point of a spear, with dry blood upon the blade, projecting above the bushes, and just touching the fronds of a palm-tree, its ensanguined hue in vivid contrast with the green of the leaves, as guilt and death in the midst of innocence and life !

Not till they have passed almost out of his sight, their heads gradually going down behind the culms of the tall pampas grass, does Rufino Valdez breathe freely. Then his nerves becoming braced by the anger which burns within—a fierce rage, from the old hatred of jealousy, interrupted by this new and bitter disappointment, the thwarting of a scheme, so far successful, but still only half accomplished—he gives utterance to a string of blasphemous anathemas, with threats, in correspondence.

" *Carajo !* " he cries, winding up with the mildest of his profane exclamations. " Ride on, señores, and get soon home ! While there, be happy as you best may. Ha, ha ! there won't be much merriment in that nest now, with the young chick out of it—pet bird of the flock ; nor long before the whole brood be called upon to forsake it. Soon as I can get to Assuncion and back with a dozen of our *quarteleros*, ah ! won't there be a wiping out of old scores then ? If that young fool, Naraguano's son, hadn't shown so chicken-hearted, I might have settled them now ; gone home with captives, too, instead of empty-handed. Well, it won't be so long to wait. Let me see. Three days will take me to Assuncion—less if this animal under me wasn't so near worn out ; three more to return with the troop. Say a week in all ; at the end of which, if there be a man named Gaspar Mendez in the land of the living, it won't be he whose head I see out yonder. That will be off his shoulders, or if on them only to help hold in its place the loop-end of my *lazo*. But I must make haste. For what if Halberger have recognized me ? I don't think he did or could ; 'twas too dark. If he have, what—aye, what? Of course they'll know that wasn't likely to be the last of it, and that there's something more to come. They'd be simpletons not to think so ; and thinking it, still greater fools if they don't take some steps to flee away from this new roost they've been perching upon. But whither can they? The young Tovas chief is compromised with them—dead declared as their enemy so long as he keeps that pretty creature captive in his toldo ; and there are others of the tribe will stand by me, I know. The glass beads and other glistening baubles will secure the young, while a few golden onzas skilfully distributed will do the same for the *sagamores.* No fear then, no failure yet ! With the Tovas on my side, there isn't a spot in th Chaco to shelter them. So, *caballeros !* you can keep on. In a week from this time, I hope to hold an interview with you, less distant and more satisfactory to myself."

After delivering this quaint rigmarole, he sits watching them till their heads finally sink below the sea of grass, the rheas feathers in Gaspar's high crowned hat being the last to disappear, as it were waving back defiance and to the death !

Soon as they are out of sight, and he no longer fears an encounter with his old enemy, Valdez turns to the consideration of some other things which have appeared strange to him. At first, why they are riding so slowly, for as long as seen they were proceeding in a walking-gait rarely witnessed upon the pampas, and never where the horseman is a gaucho ; for he gallops if it were but to the stream, within a stone's throw of his solitary cabin, to fetch a jar of water !

" Nothing in that," he mutters, " now I come to think of it. Only natural they should be going at snail's pace.

Carrai! the wonder is the *gringo* being able for even that, or go at all. I thought I'd given him his *quietus*, for surely I sent my spear right through his ribs! It must have struck button, or buckle, or something, and glinted off. Mad fool of me, when I had him down, not to make sure of my work! Well, it's no use blubbering about it now. Next time I'll take better care how the thing's done."

After a short pause, he resumes his strain of interrogative conjecture now on another matter, which has also struck him as being strange.

"Why are they going off that way, I wonder? It isn't their direct route homeward, surely? I don't know the exact spot where the *gringo* has established himself; but didn't Aguara say the nearest way to it is along the river's bank, down to their old *tolderia?* If so, certainly they're making a round about. Ha! I fancy I know the reason; natural, too, as the other. The Señor Ludwig must have known they were Tovas who attacked him, and under the belief that they've gone on to their former place of abode, dreads a second encounter with them. No wonder he should, having found them such treacherous allies—enemies instead of friends. Ha, ha, ha! won't that puzzle him? Of course, he hasn't yet heard of Naraguana's death—couldn't—they all said so. Well, it's a bit of good luck for me their going that round. My road lies direct down the river, and now I may proceed upon it without fear of being spied by them. That would never do just yet. They shall have sight of me soon enough—sooner than they'll like it. And this reminds me I mustn't waste any more time here; it's too precious. Now off, and home to El Supremo, who'll jump with very joy at the news I have for him."

Giving his horse a touch of the spur, he heads him along

the high bank, still keeping within the skirt of timber, and riding slowly through the tangle of obstructing bushes; but at length getting out upon the old trail, where it goes down to the ford, he turns along it, in the opposite direction, towards the deserted *tolderia*.　And now, with nothing further to obstruct him, he plies the spur vigorously, and keeps on at full gallop, not looking ahead, however, but with eyes all the while scanning the plain to his left, apprehensively, as fearing there to see a tall black hat, with a bunch of ostrich feathers floating above it.

CHAPTER XIV.

A NIGHT of dread suspense has been passed at the estancia of Ludwig Halberger. No one there has thought of sleep. Even the dark-skinned domestics—faithful Guano Indians—touched with sympathy for the señora, their mistress, do not retire to rest. Instead, retainers all, outside the house as within, sit up throughout the night, taking part with her in the anxious vigil.

As the hours drag wearily along, the keener become her apprehensions; that presentiment of the morning, which during all the day has never left her, now pressing upon her spirit with the weight of woe itself. She could scarce be sadder, or surer that some terrible mischance had happened to her husband and daughter, had she seen it with her own eyes. And were both to be brought back dead, 'twould be almost what she is anticipating.

In vain her son Ludwig, an affectionate lad, essays to cheer her. Do his best to assign or invent reasons for their prolonged absence, he cannot chase the dark shadow from her brow, nor lift the load off her heart. And Cypriano, who dearly loves his aunt, has no more success. Indeed, less, since almost as much does he need cheering himself. For although Francesca's fate is a thing of keen inquietude to the brother, it is yet of keener to the cousin. Love is the strongest of the affections.

But youth, ever hopeful, hinders them from despairing; and despite their solicitude, they find words of comfort for her who hears them without being comforted.

"Keep up heart, mother!" says Ludwig, feigning a cheerfulness he far from feels. "'Twill be all right yet, and we'll see them home to-morrow morning—if not before. You know that father has often stayed out all night."

"Never alone," she despondingly answers. "Never with Francesca. Only when Gaspar was along with him."

"Well, Gaspar's with him now, no doubt; and that'll make all safe. He's sure to have found them. Don't you think so, Cypriano?"

"Oh! yes," mechanically rejoins the cousin, in his heart far from thinking it so, but the reverse. "Wherever they've gone he'll get upon their tracks; and as Gaspar can follow tracks, be they ever so slight, he'll have no difficulty with those of uncle's horse."

"He may follow them," says the señora, heaving a sigh, "but whither will they lead him to. Alas, I fear——"

"Have no fear, *tia!*" interrupts the nephew, with alacrity, an idea occurring to him. "I think I know what's detaining them—at least, it's very likely."

"What?" she asks, a spark of hopefulness for an instant lighting up her saddened eyes; Ludwig, at the same time, putting the question.

"Well," replies Cypriano, proceeding to explain, "you know how uncle takes it, when he comes across a new object of natural history, or anything in the way of a curiosity. It makes him forget everything else, and everybody too. Suppose while riding over the campo he chanced upon something of that sort, and stayed to secure it? It may have been too big to be easily brought home."

"No, no!" murmurs the señora, the gleam of hope departing suddenly as it had sprung up. "It cannot be that."

"But it can, and may," persists the youth, "for there's something I haven't yet told you, *tia*—a thing which makes it more probable."

Again she looks to him inquiringly, as does Ludwig, both listening with all ears for the answer.

"The thing I'm speaking of is an ostrich."

"Why an ostrich? your uncle could have no curiosity about that.   He sees them every day."

"True, but it's not every day he can catch them.   And it was only yesterday I heard him tell Gaspar he wanted one, a cock bird, for some purpose or other, though what, he didn't say.   Now, it's likely, almost certain, that while on their way to the *tolderia*, or coming back, he has seen one, given chase to it, leaving Francesca somewhere to wait for him.   Well, *tia*, you know what an ostrich is to chase? Now lagging along as if you could easily throw the noose round its neck, then putting on a fresh spurt—'twould tempt any one to keep on after it.   Uncle may have got tantalized in that very way, and galloped leagues upon leagues without thinking of it.   To get back to Francesca, and then home, would take all the time that's passed yet.   So don't let us despair."

The words well meant, and not without some show of reason, fail, however, to bring conviction to the señora. Her heart is too sad, the presentiment too heavy on it, to be affected by any such sophistry.   In return, she says despairingly—

"No, *sobrino!* that's not it.   It your uncle had gone after
an ostrich, you forget that Gaspar has gone after him.   If
he had found them, they'd all have been back before this.
Ay de mi! I know they'll never be back—never more!"

"Nay, mamma! don't say that," breaks in Ludwig,
flinging his arms around her neck, and kissing the tears
from her cheek.   "What Cypriano says appears to me probable enough, and likely to be true.   But if it isn't, I think
I can tell what is."

Again the sorrowing mother looks inquiringly up; Cypriano, in turn, becoming listener.

"My idea," pursues Ludwig, "is that they went straight
on to the *tolderia*, and are there still—detained against
their will."

Cypriano starts, saying.

"What makes you think that, cousin?"

"Because of Naraguana.   You know how the old Indian's
given to drinking *guarapé*.   Every now and then he gets
upon a carousal, and keeps it up for days, sometimes weeks.
And he may be at that now, which would account for none
of them having been to see us lately.   If that's the reason,
the silly old fellow might just take it into his head to detain
father and Francesca.   Not from any ill will, but only some
crazy notion of his own.   Now, isn't that likely enough?"

"But Gaspar? they wouldn't detain him.   Nor would he
dare stay, after what I said to him at parting."

It is the señora who speaks, for Cypriano is now all
absorbed in thoughts which fearfully afflict him.

"Gaspar couldn't help himself, mamma, any more than
father or sister.   If the chief be as I've said—intoxicated—
all the other Indians will be the same, sure enough; and
Gaspar would have to stay with them, if they wished it.

Now, it's my opinion they have wished it, and are keeping all of them there for the night. No doubt, kindly entertaining them, in their own rough way, however much father and Francesca may dislike it, and Gaspar growl at it. But it'll be all right. So cheer up, *madre mia !* We'll see them home in the morning—by breakfast time, or before it."

Alas ! Ludwig's forecast proves a failure ; as his mother too surely expected it would. Morning comes, but with it no word of the missing ones. Nor is any sign seen of them by anxious eyes, that from earliest daybreak have been scanning the plain, which stretches away in front of the estancia. Nothing moves over it but the wild creatures, its denizens ; while above it, on widely extended wings, soars a flock of black vultures—ill omen in that moment of doubt and fear.

And so passes the hour of breakfast, with other hours, on till it is mid-day, but still no human being appears upon the plain. 'Tis only later, when the sun began to throw elongated shadows, that one is seen there, upon horseback, and going in a gallop ; but he is heading *from* the house, and not *toward* it. For the rider is Cypriano himself, who, no longer able to bear the torturing suspense, has torn himself away from aunt and cousin, to go in search of his uncle and another cousin—the last dearer than all.

CHAPTER XV

A TEDIOUS JOURNEY.

IT yet wants full two hours of sunset, as the gaucho and his companion come within sight of the estancia. Still, so distant, however, that the house appears not bigger than a dove-cot—a mere fleck of yellow, the colour of the *cana brava*, of which its walls are constructed—half hidden by the green foliage of the trees standing around it. The point from which it is viewed is on the summit of a low hill, at least a league off, and in a direct line between the house itself and the deserted Indian village. For although the returning travellers have not passed through the latter place, but, for reasons already given, intentionally avoided it, the route they had taken, now nearer home, has brought them back into that, between it and the estancia.

A slow journey they have made. It is all of eight hours since, at earliest sunrise, they rode out from among the *sumac* trees on the bank of the branch stream; and the distance gone over cannot be much more than twenty miles. Under ordinary circumstances the gaucho would have done it in two hours, or less.

As it is, he has had reasons for delaying, more than one. First, his desire to make the journey without being observed; and to guard against this, he has been zigzagging a good deal, to take advantage of such cover as was offered by the palm groves and scattered copses of *quebracho*.

A second cause retarding him has been the strange behaviour of his travelling companion, whose horse he has had to look after all along the way. Nothing has this rider done for himself, nor is yet doing ; neither guides the horse, nor lays hand upon the bridle-rein, which, caught over the saddle-bow, swings loosely about. He d' es not even urge the animal on by whip or spur. And as for word, he has not spoken one all day, neither to the gaucho, nor in soliloquy to himself! Silent he is, as when halted by the edge of the *sumac* wood, and in exactly the same attitude ; the only change observable being his hat, which is a little more slouched over his face, now quite concealing it.

But the two causes assigned are not the only ones why they have been so long in reaching the spot where they now are. There is a third influencing the gaucho. He has not wished to make better speed. Nor does he yet desire it, as is evident by his actions. For now arrived on the hill's top, within sight of home, instead of hastening on towards it he brings his horse to a dead halt, the other, as if mechanically, stopping too. It is not that the animals are tired, and need rest. The pause is for a different purpose ; of which some words spoken by the gaucho to himself, give indication. Still in the saddle, his face turned towards the distant dwelling, with eyes intently regarding it, he says :—

" Under that roof are three hearts beating anxiously now, I know. Soon to be sadder, though ; possibly, one of them to break outright. *Pobere señora !* what will she say when she hears—when she sees this ? *Santissima !* 'twill go well-nigh killing her, if it don't quite ! "

While speaking, he has glanced over his shoulder at the other horseman, who is half a length behind. But again facing to the house, and fixing his gaze upon it, he continues :—

"And Cypriano—poor lad! He'll have his little heart sorely tried, too. So fond of his cousin, and no wonder, such a sweet *chiquitita.* That will be a house of mourning, when I get home to it!"

Once more he pauses in his muttered speech, as if to consider something. Then, looking up at the sun, proceeds :

" It'll be full two hours yet before that sets. Withal I must wait for its setting. 'Twill never do to take him home in broad daylight. No ; she mustn't see him thus, and sha'n't —if I can help it. I'll stop here till it's dark, and, meanwhile, think about the best way of breaking it to her. *Carramba !* that will be a scene ! I could almost wish myself without eyes, rather than witness it. Ah! me ! It'll be enough painful to listen to their lamentations."

In conformity with the intention just declared, he turns his horse's head towards a grand *ombu*—growing not far off —the same which, the day before, guided him back to his lost way—and riding on to it pulls up beneath its spreading branches. The other horse, following, stops too. But the man upon his back stays there, while the gaucho acts differently ; dismounting, and attaching the bridles of both horses to a branch of the tree. Then he stretches himself along the earth, not to seek sleep or rest, but the better to give his thoughts to reflection, on that about which he has been speaking.

He has not been many minutes in his recumbent attitude before being aroused from it. With his ears so close to the ground, sounds are carried to him from afar, and one now reaching them causes him first to start into a sitting posture, and then stand upon his feet. It is but the trample of a horse, and looking in the direction whence it comes sees the animal itself, and its rider soon is seen, recognizing both.

"Cypriano!" he mechanically exclaims, adding, "*Pobrecito!* He's been impatient; anxious; too much to stay for my return, and now's coming after."

It is Cypriano, approaching from the direction of the house whence he has but lately started, and at great speed, urged on by the anxiety which oppresses him. But he is not heading for the *ombu*, instead, along the more direct path to the Indian town, which would take him past the tree at some three hundred yards' distance.

He does not pass it, nevertheless. Before he has got half way up the hill, Gaspar, taking the bridle of his own horse from the branch, leaps into the saddle, and gallops down to meet him. The gaucho has a reason for not hailing him at a distance, or calling him to come under the *ombu*, till he first held speech with him.

"Gaspar!" shouts the youth excitedly, soon as he catches sight of the other coming towards him. "What news? Oh? youv'e not found them! I see you haven't!"

"Calm yourself, young master!" rejoins the gaucho, now close up to him; "I have found them—that is, one of them."

"Only one—which?" half distractedly interrogates the youth.

"Your uncle—but, alas——"

"Dead—dead! I know it by the way you speak. But my cousin! Where is she? Still living? Say so, Gaspar! Oh, say but that!"

"Come señorito, be brave; as I know you are. It may not be so bad for the *niña*, your cousin. I've no doubt she's still alive, though I've not been successful in finding her. As for your uncle, you must prepare yourself to see something that'll pain you. Now, promise me you'll bear it bravely—say you will, and come along with me!"

At this Gaspar turns his horse, and heads him back for the *ombu*, the other silently following, stunned almost beyond the power of speech. But once under the tree, and seeing what he there sees, it returns to him. Then the gaucho is witness to an exhibition of grief and rage, both wild as ever agitated the breast of a boy.

CHAPTER XVI.

DEAD!

ONCE more the sun is going down over the pampa, but still nothing seen upon it to cheer the eyes of the Señora Halberger, neither those first missing, nor they who went after. One after another she has seen them depart, but in vain looks for their return.

And now, as she stands with eyes wandering over that grassy wilderness, she can almost imagine it a maelstrom or some voracious monster, that swallows up all who venture upon it. As the purple of twilight assumes the darker shade of night, it seems to her as though some unearthly and invisible hand were spreading a pall over the plain to cover her dear ones, somewhere lying dead upon it.

She is in the verandah with her son, and side by side they stand gazing outward, as long as there is light for them to see. Even after darkness has descended they continue to strain their eyes mechanically, but despairingly, she more hopeless and feeling more forlorn than ever. All gone but Ludwig! for even her nephew may not return. Where Gaspar, a strong man and experienced in the ways of the wilderness, has failed to find the lost ones, what chance will there be for Cypriano? More like some cruel enemy has made captives of them all, killing all, one after the other, and he, falling into the same snare, has been sacrificed as the rest !

Dark as is this hour of her apprehension, there is yet a darker one in store for her; but before it there is to be light, with joy—alas ! short-lived as that bright, garish gleam of sun which often precedes the wildest burst of a storm. Just as the last ray of hope has forsaken her, a house-dog, lying outstretched by the verandah starts to its feet with a growl, and bounding off into the darkness, sets up a sonorous baying.

Both mother and son step hastily forward to the baluster rail, and resting hands on it, again strain their eyes outward, now as never before, at the same time listening as for some signal sound, on the hearing of which hung their very lives.

Soon they both hear and see what gives them gladness unspeakable, their ears first imparting it by a sound sweeter to them than any music, for it is the tread of horses' hoofs upon the firm turf of the plain ; and almost in the same instant they see the **horses** themselves, each with a rider upon its back.

The exclamation that leaps from the mother's lips is the cry of a heart long held in torture suddenly released, and without staying to repeat it, she rushes out of the verandah and on across the patch of enclosed ground—not stopping till outside the palings which enclose it.

Ludwig following, comes again by her side, and the two stand with eyes fixed on the approaching forms, there now so near that they are able to make out their number.

But this gives them surprise, somewhat alarming them afresh. For there are but *three* where there should be four.

" It must be your father and Francesca, with Gaspar,"

says the señora, speaking in doubt. "Cypriano has missed them all, I suppose. But he'll come too——"

"No, mother," interrupts Ludwig, "Cypriano is there. I can see a white horse, that must be his."

"Gaspar then ; he it is that's behind."

She says this with a secret hope it may be so.

"It don't look like as if Gaspar was behind," returns Ludwig, hesitating in his speech, for his eyes, as his heart, tell him there is still something amiss. "Two of them," he continues, "are men, full grown, and the third is surely Cypriano."

They have no time for further discussion or conjecture— no occasion for it. The three shadowy figures are now very near, and just as the foremost pulls up in front of the palings, the moon bursting forth from behind a cloud flashes her full light upon his face, and they see it is Gaspar. The figures farther off are lit up at the same time, and the señora recognizes them as her husband and nephew. A quick searching glance carried behind to the croups of their horses shows her there is no one save those seated in the saddle.

"Where is Francesca?" she cries out in agonized ac- cents. "Where is my daughter?"

No one makes answer; not any of them speaks. Gaspar, who is nearest, but hangs his head, as does his master behind him.

"What means all this?" is her next question, as she dashes past the gaucho's horse, and on to her husband, as she goes crying out,

"Where is Francesca? What have you done with my child?"

He makes no reply, nor any gesture—not even a word'

to acknowledge her presence! Drawing closer she clutches him by the knee, continuing her distracted interrogatories.

"Husband! why are you thus silent? Ludwig, dear Ludwig, why don't you answer me? Ah! now I know. She is dead—dead!"

"Not *she*, but *he*," says a voice close to her ear—that of Gaspar, who has dismounted and stepped up to her.

"He! who?"

"Alas! señora, my master, your husband."

"O Heavens! can this be true?" as she speaks, stretching her arms up to the inanimate form, still in the saddle—for it is fast tied there—and throwing them around it; then with one hand lifting off the hat, which falls from her trembling fingers, she gazes on a ghastly face, and into eyes that return not her gaze. But for an instant, when, with a wild cry, she sinks back upon the earth, and lies silent, motionless, the moonbeams shimmering upon her cheeks, showing them white and bloodless, as if her last spark of life had departed!

CHAPTER XVII.

IT is the day succeeding that on which the hunter naturalist was carried home a corpse, sitting upright in his saddle. The sun has gone down over the Gran Chaco, and its vast grassy plains and green palm-groves are again under the purple of twilight. Herds of stately *quazutis* and troops of the *pampas* roebuck—beautiful creatures, spotted like fawns ot the fallow-deer—move leisurely towards their watering-places, having already browsed to satiety on pastures where they are but rarely disturbed by the hunter, for here no sound of horse nor baying of molossian ever breaks the stillness of the early morn, and the only enemies they have habitually to dread are the red puma and yellow jaguar, throughout Spanish America respectively, but erroneously, named lion (*leon*) and tiger (*tigre*), from a resemblance, though a very slight one, which these, the largest of the New World's *felidæ*, bear to their still grander congeners of the Old.

The scene we are about to depict is upon the Pilcomayo's bank, some twenty miles above the old *tolderia* of the Tovas Indians, and therefore thirty from the house of Ludwig Halberger—now his no more, but a house of mourning. The mourners, however, are not all in it, for by a camp-fire freshly kindled at the place we speak of, two of them are seen seated. One is the son of the murdered man, the other his nephew; while not far off is a third individual, who mourns almost as much as either. Need I say it is Gaspar, the gaucho?

Or is it necessary to give explanation of their being thus far from home so soon after that sad event, the cause of their sorrow? No. The circumstances speak for themselves; telling them to be there on an errand connected with that same crime; in short, in pursuit of the criminals.

' Who these may be they have as yet no definite knowledge. All is but blind conjectures, the only thing certain being that the double crime has been committed by Indians; for the trail which has conducted to the spot they are now on, first coming down the river's bank to the branch stream, then over its ford and back again, could have been made only by a mounted party of red men.

But of what tribe? That is the question which puzzles them. Not the only one, however. Something besides causes them surprise, equally perplexing them. Among the other hoof-marks, they have observed some that must have been made by a horse with shoes on; and as they know the Chaco Indians never ride such, the thing strikes them as very strange. It would not so much, were the shod-tracks only traceable twice along the trail; that is, coming down the river and returning up again, for they might suppose that one of the savages was in possession of a white man's horse, stolen from some of the settlements, a thing of no uncommon occurrence. But then they have here likewise observed a third set of these tracks, of older date, also going up, and a fourth, freshest of all, returning down again; the last on top of everything else, continuing on to the old *tolderia,* as they have noticed all the way since leaving it.

And in their examination of the many hoof-marks by the ford of the tributary stream, up to the *sumac* thicket—and along the *tapir* path to that blood-stained spot which they have just visited—the same tracks are conspicuous amid all the others, telling that he who rode the shod horse has had a hand in the murder, and likely a leading one.

It is the gaucho who has made most of these observations, but about the deductions to be drawn from them, he is, for the time, as much at fault as either of his younger companions.

They have just arrived at their present halting-place, their first camp since leaving the *estancia ;* from which they parted a little before mid-day : soon as the sad, funeral rites were over, and the body of the murdered man laid in its grave. This done at an early hour of the morning, for the hot climate of the Chaco calls for quick interment.

The sorrowing wife did nought to forbid their departure. She had her sorrows as a mother, too ; and, instead of trying to restrain, she but urged them to take immediate action in searching for her lost child.

That Francesca is still living they all believe, and so long as there seemed a hope—even the slightest—of recovering her, the bereaved mother was willing to be left alone. Her faithful Guanos would be with her.

It needed no persuasive argument to send the searchers off. In their own minds they have enough motive for haste ; and, though in each it might be different in kind, as in degree, with all it is sufficiently strong. Not one of them but is willing to risk his life in the pursuit they have entered upon ; and at least one would lay it down rather than fail in finding Francesca, and restoring her to her mother.

They have followed thus far on the track of the abductors,

but without any fixed or definite plan as to continuing. Indeed, there has been no time to think of one, or anything else; all hitherto acting under that impulse of anxiety for the girl's fate which they so keenly feel. But now that the first hurried step has been taken, and they can go no further till another sun lights up the trail, calmer reflection comes, admonishing them to greater caution in their movements. For they who have so ruthlessly killed one man would as readily take other lives—their own. What they have undertaken is no mere question of skill in taking up a trail, but an enterprise full of peril; and they have need to be cautious how they proceed upon it.

They are so acting now. Their camp fire is but a small one, just sufficient to boil a kettle of water for making the *maté*, and the spot where they have placed it is in a hollow, so that it may not be seen from afar. Besides, a clump of palms screens it on the western side, the direction in which the trail leads, and therefore the likeliest for them to apprehend danger.

Soon as coming to a stop, and before kindling the fire, Gaspar has gone all around, and made a thorough survey of the situation. Then, satisfied it is a safe one, he undertakes the picketing of their horses, directing the others to set light to the faggots; which they have done, and seated themselves beside.

CHAPTER XVIII.

WHILE waiting for the gaucho to rejoin them by the fire the two youths are not silent, but converse upon the event which saddens and still mystifies them. For up till this moment they have not seen anything, nor can they think of aught to account for the calamity which has befallen them—the double crime that has been committed. No more can they conceive who have been the perpetrators; though Cypriano all along has had his suspicions. And now for the first time he communicates them to his cousin, saying—

"It's been the work of Tovas Indians."

"Impossible, Cypriano!" exclaims Ludwig in surprise. "Why should they murder my poor father? What motive could they have had for it?"

"Motive enough; at least one of them had."

"One! who mean you?"

"Aguara."

"Aguara! But why he of all the others? And for what?"

"For what? Simply to get possession of your sister."

Ludwig starts, showing greater astonishment than ever.

"Cypriano!" he exclaims; "what do you mean?"

"Just what I've said, cousin. You're perhaps not aware

of what I've myself known for long; that the chief's son has been fixing his eyes on Francesca."

"The scoundrel!" cries Ludwig, with increasing indignation, for the first time apprised of the fact thus made known to him. Unobservant of such things generally, it had never occurred to him to reflect on what had long been patent to the jealous eyes of Cypriano. Besides, the thing seemed so absurd, even preposterous—a red-skinned savage presuming to look upon his sister in the light of a sweetheart, daring to love her—that the son of the Prussian naturalist, with all the prejudices of race, could not be otherwise than incredulous of it.

"Are you sure of that?" he questions, still doubting. "Sure of what you've said, Cypriano?"

"Quite sure," is the confident rejoinder; "more than once I've observed Aguara's free behaviour towards my cousin; and once would have thrashed the impudent redskin, but for uncle interfering. He was afraid it might get us into trouble with Naraguana."

"But did father himself know of it? I mean about Aguara and Francesca?"

"No. I rather think not. And I disliked telling him."

All this is new light to Ludwig, and turns his thoughts into the same channel of suspicion where those of Cypriano have been already running. Still, whatever he may think of Naraguana's son, he cannot bring himself to believe that Naraguana has been guilty. His father's friend, and hitherto their protector!

"It cannot be!" he exclaims; "surely it cannot be!"

"It may be for all that, and in my opinion is. Ah! cousin, there's no telling how an Indian will act. I never knew one who didn't turn treacherous when it served his purpose. Whether the old chief has been so or not, I'm quite sure his son has. Take my word for it, Ludwig, it's the Tovas Indians who've done this deed, and it will be with them we'll have to deal."

" But whither can they have gone? and why went they off so suddenly and secretly, without letting father or any of us know. All that certainly seems strange."

" Not so strange when we think of what's happened since. My idea is, it's been all a planned thing. Aguara got his father to agree to his carrying off Francesca; and the old chief, controlled by the young one, let him take his way. Fearing to face uncle he first went off, taking the whole tribe along; and they're now, no doubt, residing in some distant part of the Chaco, where they suppose we'll never go after them. But Francesca will be there too; and we must follow and find her—ay, if we have to lay down our lives when she's found. Shall we not, cousin ? "

" Yes; shall and will ! " is Ludwig's rejoinder in a tone of determination; their dialogue getting interrupted by Gaspar coming back to the camp fire, and saying—

"Now, *señoritos !* It's high time we had some supper."

On making this announcement the gaucho himself sets about preparing their evening repast. It requires no great effort of culinary skill; since the more substantial portion of it has been already cooked, and is now presented in the shape of a cold shoulder of mutton, with a cake of corn bread, extracted from a pair of *alparejas*, or saddle-bags. In the Chaco there are sheep—the Indians themselves breeding them—while since settling there the hunter-naturalist had not neglected either pastoral or agricultural pursuits. Hence the meal from which came that cake of maize bread.

With these two *pièces de résistance* nothing remains but to make a cup of "Paraguay tea," for which Gaspar has provided all the materials, viz., an iron kettle for boiling water, cups of cocoa-nut shell termed *matés*—for this is the name of the vessel, not the beverage—and certain tubes, the *bombillas*, to serve as spoons; the Paraguayan tea being imbibed, not in the ordinary way, but sucked up through these *bombillas*. All the above implements, with a little sugar for sweetening; and, lastly, the *yerba* itself, has the thoughtful gaucho brought along. No milk, however; the lacteal fluid not being deemed a necessary ingredient in the cup which cheers the Paraguayan people, without intoxicating them.

Gaspar—as all gauchos, skilled in the concoction of it—in a short time has the three *matés* brimful of the brew. Then the *bombillas* are inserted, and the process of sucking commences; suspended only at intervals while the more substantial mutton and maize-bread are being masticated.

Meanwhile, as a measure of security, the camp-fire has been extinguished, though they still keep their places around its embers. And while eating, converse; Cypriano imparting to Gaspar the suspicions he has already communicated to his cousin.

It is no new idea to the gaucho; instead, the very one his own thoughts have been dwelling upon. For he, too, had long observed the behaviour of the young Tovas chief towards the daughter of his *dueño*. And what has now occurred seems to coincide with that—all except the supposed treachery of Naraguana. A good judge of character, as most gauchos are, Gaspar cannot think of the aged cacique having turned traitor. Still, as Ludwig, he is at a loss what to think. For why should the Tovas chief have

made that abrupt departure from his late abiding place?
The reason assigned by Cypriano is not, to his view, satisfactory; though he cannot imagine any other. So, they
finish their suppers and retire to rest, without having
arrived at any certain conclusion, one way or the other.

With heads rested upon their saddles, and their ponchos
wrapped around them, they seek sleep, Ludwig first finding
it; next Cypriano, though he lies long awake—kept so by
torturing thoughts. But tired nature at length overpowers
him, and he too sinks into slumber.

The gaucho alone surrenders not to the drowsy god; but,
repelling his attacks, still lies reflecting. Thus run his reflections—as will be seen, touching near the truth:

"*Carramba!* I can think of but one man in all the
world who had an interest in the death of my dear master.
One there was who'd have given a good deal to see him dead
—that's El Supremo. No doubt he searched high and low
for us, after we gave him the slip. But then, two years
gone by since! One would think it enough to have made
him almost forget us. Forgive, no! that wouldn't be Señor
José Francia. He never forgives. Nor is it likely he has
forgotten, either, what the *dueño* did. Crossing him in his
vile purpose, was just the sort of thing to stick in his crop
for the remainder of his life; and I shouldn't wonder if it's
his hand has been here. Odd, those tracks of a shod horse;
four times back and forward! And the last of them, by
their look, must have been made as late as yesterday—
some time in the early morning, I should say. Beyond the
old *tolderia*, downward, they've gone. I wish I'd turned a
bit that way as we came up, so as to be sure of it. Well, I'll
find that out, when we get back from this pursuit; which I
very much fear will prove a wild goose chase."

For a time he lies without stirring, or moving a muscle, on his back, with eyes seemingly fixed upon the stars, like an ancient astrologer in the act of consulting them for the solution of some deep mystery hidden from mortal ken. Then, as if having just solved it, he gives a sudden start, exclaiming :

"*Sangre de Cristo!* that's the explanation of all, the whole affair ; murder, abduction, everything."

His words, though only muttered, awaken Cypriano, still only half asleep.

"What is it, Gaspar?" questions the youth.

"Oh, nothing, *señorito ;* only a mosquito that took a fancy to stick its bill into the bridge of my nose. But I've given Master *Zancudo* his quietus ; and he won't trouble me again."

Though the gaucho thinks he has at last got the clue to what has been mystifying them, like all skilled tacticians he intends for a time keeping it to himself. So, saying no more, he leaves his young companion to return to his slumbers : which the latter soon does. Himself now more widely awake than ever, he follows up the train of thought Cypriano had interrupted.

"It's clear that Francia has at length found out our whereabouts. I wonder he didn't do so long ago ; and have often warned the *dueño* of the danger we were in. Of course, Naraguana kept him constantly assured ; and with war to the knife between the Tovas and Paraguayans, no wonder my poor master was too careless and confident. But something has happened lately to affect their relations. The Indians moving so mysteriously away from their old place shows it. And these shod tracks tell, almost for sure, that some white man has been on a visit to them, wherever they are now. Just as sure about this white man being an emissary from El Supremo. And who would his emissary be? Who sent on such an errand so likely as *him?*"

The emphasis on the " him " points to some one not yet mentioned, but whom the gaucho has in his mind. Soon, however, he gives the name, saying :

" The scoundrel who bestrode that horse—and a thorough scoundrel too—is Rufino Valdez. Assassin, besides! It's he who has murdered my master. I'd lay my life on it."

After arriving at this conclusion, he adds :

" What a pity I didn't think of this before! If but yesterday morning! He must have passed along the trail going back, and alone? Ah! the chance I've let escape me! Such an opportunity for settling old scores with Señor Rufino! Well, he and I may meet yet; and if we do, one of us will have to stay on the spot where that encounter takes place, or be carried from it feet foremost. I think I know which would go that way, and which the other."

Thus predicating, the gaucho pulls his poncho around his shoulders, and composes himself for sleep ; though it is some time before he succeeds in procuring it.

But Morpheus coming to his aid, proves too many for the passions which agitate him ; and he at length sinks into a profound slumber, not broken till the curassows send up their shrill cries—as the crowing of Chanticleer—to tell that another day is dawning upon the Chaco.

CHAPTER XIX.

TRAVELLERS on such an errand as that which is carrying the gaucho and his youthful companions across the Chaco, do not lie abed late; and they are up and stirring as the first streak of blue-grey light shows itself above the horizon.

Again a tiny fire is kindled; the kettle hung over it; and the *matés*, with the *bombillas*, called into requisition.

The breakfast is just as was their supper—cold mutton, corn bread, and *yerba* tea.

By the time they have despatched it, which they do in all haste, it is clear enough to permit of their taking up the trail they have been following. So, saddling their horses, they return to, and proceed along it.

As hitherto, it continues up the bank of the Pilcomayo, and at intervals they observe the tracks of Francesca's pony, where they have not been trampled out by the other horses behind. And, as on the preceding day, they see the hoof-marks of the shod animal, both going and returning—the return track evidently the more recently made. They notice them, however, only up to a certain point—about twenty miles beyond the crossing place of that tributary stream, now so full of sad interest to them. Here, in a grove of *algarobias*, they come upon the spot where those they are in pursuit of must have made their night bivouac; this told by some fragments of food lying scattered around, and the grass burnt in two places—large circular discs where their camp-fires had been kindled. The fires are out, and the ashes cold now; for that must have been two nights before.

Dismounting, they too make halt by the *algarobia* grove —partly to breathe their horses, which have been all the morning kept at top speed, through their anxiety to overtake the Indians—but more for the sake of giving examination to the abandoned camp, in the hope that something left there may lead to further elucidation of the crime and its causes; possibly enable them to determine, beyond doubt, who have been its perpetrators.

At first nothing is found to give them the slightest clue; only the ashes and half-burned faggots of the fires, with some bits of *sipos*—which have been cut from creeping plants entwining the trees overhead—the corresponding pieces, in all likelihood, having been used as rope tackle for some purpose the gaucho cannot guess. These, and the fragments of food already referred to, with some bones of birds clean picked, and the shells of a half-score ostrich-eggs, are all the *débris* they can discover.

But none of these items give any indication as to who made bivouac there; beyond the fact, already understood and unquestioned, that they were Indians, with the further certainty of their having stayed on the spot over-night; this shown by the grass pressed down where their bodies had lain astretch; as also the circular patches browsed bare by their horses, around the picket pins which had held them.

Indians certainly; but of what tribe there is nothing on that spot to tell—neither sign nor token.

So concluding, Cypriano and Ludwig have climbed back into their saddles—the former terribly impatient to proceed —but Gaspar still stays afoot, holding his horse by the bridle at long reach, and leading the animal about from place to place, as if not yet satisfied with the search they have made. For there are spots where the grass is long, and the ground rough, overgrown also with weeds and bushes. Possibly among these he may yet discover something.

And something he does discover—a globe-shaped object lying half-hid among the weeds, about the size and colour of a cricket ball. This to you, young reader; for Gaspar knows nothing of your national game. But he knows everything about balls of another kind—the *bolas*—that weapon, without which a South American gaucho would feel as a crusader of the olden time lacking half his armour.

And it is a *bola* that lies before him; though one of a peculiar kind, as he sees after stooping and taking it up. A round stone covered with cow's skin; this stretched and sewed over it tight as that on a tennis ball.

But to the *bola* there is no cord attached, nor mark of where one has ever been. For there never has been such, as Gaspar at a glance perceives. Well knows the gaucho that the ball he holds in his hand has not been one of a pair strung together—as with the ordinary *bolas*—nor of three in like manner united, as is sometimes the case; but a *bola*, for still it is a *bola*, of a sort different from either, both in its make and the mode of using it, as also the effect it is designed to produce.

"What is it, Gaspar?" simultaneously interrogate the two,

as they see him so closely examining the thing he has picked up. At the same time they turn their horses' heads towards him.

" *Una bola perdida.*"

"Ah! a ball the Indians have left behind—lost, you mean."

"No, *señoritos;* I don't mean that, exactly. Of course, the redskins have left it behind, and so lost it. But that isn't the reason of my calling it a *bola perdida.*"

"Why, then, Gaspar?" asks Ludwig, with the hereditary instincts of the *savant*, like his father, curious about all such things. "Why do you call it a lost ball?"

"Because that's the name we gauchos give it, and the name by which it is known among those who make use of it —these Chaco Indians."

"And pray, what do they use it for? I never heard of the thing. What is its purpose?"

"One for which, I hope, neither it nor any of its sort will ever be employed upon us. The Virgin forbid! For it is no child's toy, I can assure you, *señoritos;* but a most murderous weapon. I've witnessed its effects more than once—seen it flung full thirty yards, and hit a spot not bigger than the breadth of my hand; the head of a horse, crushing in the animal's skull as if done by a club of *quebracha.* Heaven protect me, and you too, *muchachos*, from ever getting struck by a *bola perdida!*"

"But why a *lost* ball?" asks Ludwig, with curiosity still unsatisfied.

"Oh! that's plain enough," answers the gaucho. "As you see, when once launched there's no knowing where it may roll to; and often gets lost in the long grass or among bushes; unlike the ordinary *bolas*, which stick to the thing aimed at—that is, if thrown as they should be."

"What do you make of its being found here?" interrogates Cypriano, more interested about the ball in a sense different from the curiosity felt by his cousin.

"Much," answers Gaspar, looking grave, but without offering explantion; for he seems busied with some calculation, or conjecture.

"Indeed!" simultaneously exclaim the others, with interest rekindled, Cypriano regarding him with earnest glance.

"Yes, indeed, young masters," proceeds the gaucho. "The thing I now hold in my hand has once, and not very long ago, been in the hands of a Tovas Indian!"

"A Tovas!" exclaims Cypriano, excitedly. "What reason have you for thinking so?"

"The best of all reasons. Because, so far as is known to me, no other Chaco Indians but they use the *bola perdida*. That ball has been handled, mislaid, and left here behind by a Tovas traitor. You are right, *señorito*," he adds, speaking to Cypriano. "Whoever may have murdered my poor master, your uncle, Aguara is he who has carried off your cousin."

"Let us on!" cries Cypriano, without another word. "O, Ludwig!" he adds, "we mustn't lose a moment, nor make the least delay. Think of dear Francesca in the power of that savage beast. What may he not do with her?"

Ludwig needs no such urging to lead him on. His heart of brother is boiling with rage, as that of son almost broken by grief; and away ride they along the trail, with more haste and greater earnestness than ever.

CHAPTER XX.

IN their fresh "spurt," the trackers had not proceeded very far when compelled to slacken speed, and finally come to a dead stop. This from something seen before them upon the plain which threatens to bar their further progress —at least in the course they are pursuing.

The thing thus obstructing causes them neither surprise nor alarm, only annoyance; for it is one with which they all are familiar —a *biscachera*, or warren of *biscachas*.

It is scarce possible to travel twenty miles across the plains bordering the La Plata or Parana, without coming upon the burrows of this singular rodent; a prominent and ever-recurring feature in the scenery. There the *biscacha*, or *viscacha*—as it is indifferently spelt—plays pretty much the same part as the rabbit in our northern lands. It is, however, a much larger animal, and of a quite different species or genus—the *lagostomus trichodactylus*. In shape of head, body, and other respects, it more resembles a gigantic rat; and, like the latter, it has a long tapering tail, which strengthens the resemblance. But, unlike either rabbit or rat, its hind feet are furnished with but three toes; hence its specific name, *trichodactylus*. The same scarcity of toes is a characteristic of the *agoutis*, *capivaras*, and so called "Guinea pigs," all of which are cousins-german of the *biscacha*.

The latter makes its burrows very much in the same manner as the North American marmot (*Arctomys Ludoviciana*), better known by the name of "prairie dog;" only that the subterranean dwellings of the *viscacha* are larger, from the needs of a bigger-bodied animal. But, strange to say, in these of the pampa there exists the same queer companionship as in those of the prairie—a bird associating with the quadruped—a species of owl, the *Athene cunicularia*. This shares occupation with the *biscacha*, as does the other, an allied species, with the prairie dog. Whether the bird be a welcome recipient of the beast's hospitality, or an intruder upon it, is a question still undetermined; but the latter seems the more probable, since, in the stomachs of owls of the northern species, are frequently found prairie dog "pups;" a fact which seems to show anything but amicable relations between these creatures so oddly consorting.

There is yet another member of these communities, apparently quite as much out of place—a reptile; for snakes also make their home in the holes both of *biscacha* and prairie dog. And in both cases the reptile intruder is a rattlesnake, though the species is different. In these, no doubt, the owls find their staple of food.

Perhaps the most singular habit of the *biscacha* is its collecting every loose article which chances to be lying near, and dragging all up to its burrow; by the mouth of which it forms a heap, often as large as the half of a cart-load dumped carelessly down. No matter what the thing be— stick, stone, root of thistle, lump of indurated clay, bone, ball of dry dung—all seem equally suitable for these miscellaneous accumulations. Nothing can be dropped in the neighbourhood of a *biscacha* hole but is soon borne off, and added to its collection of *bric-a-brac.* Even a watch which had slipped from the fob of a traveller—as recorded by the naturalist, Darwin—was found forming part of one; the owner, acquainted with the habits of the animal, on missing the watch, having returned upon his route, and searched every *biscacha* mound along it, confident that in some one of them he would find the missing article—as he did.

The districts frequented by these three-toed creatures, and which seem most suitable to their habits, are those tracts of *campo* where the soil is a heavy loam or clay, and the vegetation luxuriant. Its congener, the *agouti*, affects the arid sterile plains of Patagonia, while the *biscacha* is most met with on the fertile pampas further north; more especially along the borders of those far-famed thickets of tall thistles—forests they might almost be called—upon the roots of which it is said to feed. They also make their burrows near the *cardonales*, tracts overgrown by the cardoon; also a species of large malvaceous plant, though quite different from the pampas thistles.

Another singular fact bearing upon the habits of the *biscacha* may here deserve mention. These animals are not found in the Banda Oriental, as the country lying east of the Uruguay river is called; and yet in this district exist conditions of soil, climate, and vegetation precisely similar to those on its western side. The Uruguay river seems to have formed a bar to their migration eastward; a circumstance all the more remarkable, since they have passed over the Parana, a much broader stream, and are common throughout the province of Entre Rios, as it name imports, lying between the two.

Nothing of all this occupies the thoughts of the three trackers, as they approach the particular *biscachera* which has presented itself to their view, athwart their path. Of such things they neither think, speak, nor care. Instead, they are but dissatisfied to see it there; knowing it will give them some trouble to get to the other side of it, besides greatly retarding their progress. If they ride right across it at all, they must needs go at a snail's pace, and with the utmost circumspection. A single false step made by any of their horses might be the dislocation of a joint, or the breaking of a leg. On the pampa such incidents are far from rare; for the burrows of the *biscachas* are carried like galleries underground, and therefore dangerous to any heavy quadruped so unfortunate as to sink through the surface turf. In short, to ride across a *biscachera* would be on a par with passing on horseback through a rabbit warren.

"*Caspita !*" is the vexed exclamation of the gaucho, as he reins up in front of the obstruction, with other angry words appended, on seeing that it extends right and left far as the verge of vision, while forward it appears to have a breadth of at least half a league.

"We can't gallop across that," he adds, "nor yet go at even a decent walk. We must crawl for it, *muchachos*, or ride all the way round. And there's no knowing how far round the thing might force us; leagues likely. It looks the biggest *biscachera* I ever set eyes on. *Carra-i-i !*"

The final ejaculation is drawled out with a prolonged and bitter emphasis, as he again glances right and left, but sees no end either way.

"Ill luck it is," he continues, after completing his reconnaissance. "Satan's own luck our coming upon this. A whole country covered with traps ! Well, it won't help us any making a mouth about it; and I think our best way will be to strike straight across."

" I think so too," says Cypriano, impatient to proceed.

" Let us on into it, then. But, *hijos mios ;* have a care how you go. Look well to the ground before you, and keep your horses as far from the holes as you can. Where there's two near together steer midways between, giving both the widest berth possible. Every one of them's a dangerous pitfall. *Caspita !* what am I prattling about ? Let me give you the lead, and you ride after, track for track."

So saying, he heads his horse in among the rubbish heaps, each with its hole yawning adjacent : the others, as admonished, close following, and keeping in his tracks.

They move onward at a creeping pace, every now and then forced to advance circuitously, but taking no heed of the creatures upon whose domain they have so unceremoniously intruded. In truth, they have no thought about these, nor eyes for them. Enough if they can avoid intrusion into their dwellings by a short cut downwards.

Nor do the *biscachas* seem at all alarmed at the sight of such formidable invaders. They are anything but shy creatures; instead, far more given to curiosity ; so much that they will sit squatted on their hams, in an upright attitude, watching the traveller as he passes within less than a score yards of them, the expression on their faces being that of grave contemplation. Only, if he draw too familiarly near, and they imagine him an enemy, there is a scamper off, their short fore-legs giving them a gait also heightening their resemblance to rats.

As a matter of course, such confidence makes them an easy prey to the *biscacha* catcher; for there are men who follow taking them as a profession. Their flesh is sweet and good to eat, while their skins are a marketable commodity; of late years forming an article of export to England, and other European countries.

Heeding neither the quadrupeds, nor the birds, their fellow-tenants of the burrow—the latter perched upon the summits of the mounds, and one after another flying off with a defiant screech as the horsemen drew near—these, after an hour spent in a slow but diligent advance, at length, and without accident, ride clear of the *biscachera,* and out upon the smooth open plain beyond it.

Soon as feeling themselves on firm ground, every spur of the party is plied; and they go off at a tearing pace, to make up for the lost time.

CHAPTER XXI.

A SHOULDER OUT OF JOINT.

WHEN Gaspar, on first sighting the *biscachera*, poured forth vials of wrath upon it, he little dreamt that another burrow of similar kind, and almost at the very same hour, was doing him a service by causing not only obstruction, but serious damage to the man he regards as his greatest enemy.

This second warren lay at least a hundred miles from the one they have succeeded in crossing, in a direction due east from the latter, and on the straight route for the city of Assuncion.

Let us throw aside circumlocution, and at once give account of the incident.

On this same day, and, as already said, almost the same hour, when the trackers are brought up by the *biscachera*, a single horseman is seen with head turned towards the Paraguay, and making as if to reach this river; from which he is distant some eighteen or twenty miles. He rides at a rapid rate ; and that he has been doing so for a long continuance of time, can be told by the lagging gait of his horse, and the sweat saturating the animal's coat from neck to croup. For all, he slackens not the pace ; instead, seems anxious to increase it, every now and then digging his spurs deep, and by strokes of a spear shaft he carries in his hands, urging his roadster onward. Anyone witness to his acting in this apparently frantic fashion, would suppose him either demented, or fleeing from pursuers who seek nothing less than his life. But as the plain over which he rides is smooth, level, and treeless for long leagues to his rear as also to right and left, and no pursuer nor aught of living thing visible upon it, the latter, at least, cannot be the case. And for the former, a glance at the man's face tells that neither is insanity the cause of his cruel behaviour to his horse. Rufino Valdez—for he is the hastening horseman—if bad, is by no means mad.

Superfluous to say, what the errand pressing him to such speed. In soliloquy he has himself declared it : hastening to communicate news which he knows will be welcome to the Paraguayan tyrant, and afterwards return to Halberger's *estancia* with a party of those hireling soldiers—quaintly termed *cuarteleros* from their living in barracks, or *cuartels*.

With this sinister purpose in view, and the expectation of a rich reward, the *vaqueano* has given his roadster but little rest since parting from the Tovas' camp; and the animal is now nigh broken down. Little recks its rider. Unlike a true gaucho, he cares not what mischance may befall his steed, so long as it serves his present necessity. If it but carry him to the Paraguay, it may drop down dead on the river's bank, for aught he will want, or think of it afterwards.

Thus free from solicitude about his dumb companion, he spurs and flogs the poor creature to the best speed it is able to make. Not much this; for every now and then it totters in its steps, and threatens going to grass, in a way different from what it might wish.

"About twenty miles," the *vaqueano* mutters to himself, with a glance, cast inquiringly ahead. "It can't be more than that to the river itself. Question is, whether I can make it anywheres near Assuncion. I'm not sure about this trail; evidently only a cattle run. It may lead me too much above or below. In any case," he adds, "I must bring out near one of the *guardias*, so thick along the bank, and the soldiers of the post will ferry me across. From there I'll have a good road to the town."

So consoling himself, he keeps on; no longer paying much attention to the doubtful cattle track, but rather taking guidance from the sun. This going down is directly behind his back, and so tells him the due course east, as well as west; for it is eastward he wishes to go. Now, near the horizon, it casts an elongated shadow of himself and his animal, far to the front; and after this he rides, as though following in the footsteps of some giant on horseback !

The sun soon after setting, the shadow changes, veering round to his rear. But it is now made by the moon, which is also low in the sky; only before his face, instead of behind his back. For it would be the season of harvest— were such known in the Chaco—and the moon is at her full, lighting up the *campo* with a clearness unknown to northern lands.

Were it otherwise, Rufino Valdez might have halted here, and been forced to stay in the Chaco for another night. But tempted by the bright moonlight, and the thought of his journey so near an end, he resolves differently; and once more pricking his tired, steed with spurs long since blood-clotted, he again forces it into a gallop.

But the pace is only for a short while sustained. Before going much further he feels his horse floundering between his legs; while a glance to the ground shows him he is riding through a *biscachera!*

Absorbed in thought—perhaps perfecting some wicked scheme—he had not noticed the burrow till now. Now he sees it—holes and heaps all around him—at the same time hearing the screeches of the owls, as the frightened birds fly up out of his path.

He is about to draw bridle, when the reins are suddenly jerked from his grasp—by his horse, which has gone headlong to the ground! At the same instant he hears a sound, like the cracking of a dead stick snapped crosswise. It is not that, but the shank of his horse, broken above the pastern joint! It is the last sound he hears then, or for some time after; he himself sustaining damage, though of a different kind—the dislocation of a shoulder-blade—that of the arm already injured—with a shock which deprives him of his senses.

Long lies he upon that moonlit plain, neither hearing the cries of the night birds nor seeing the great ratlike quadrupeds that, in their curiosity, come crowding close to, and go running around him!

And though consciousness at length returns, he remains in that same place till morning's light—and for the whole of another day and night—leaving the spot, and upon it his broken-legged horse, himself to limp slowly away, leaning upon his guilty spear, as one wounded on a battle-field, but one who has been fighting for a bad cause.

He reaches Assuncion—though not till the third day after—and there gets his broken bones set. But for Gaspar Mendez, there may have been luck in that shoulder-blade being put out of joint.

CHAPTER XXII

AFTER passing the *biscachera*, the trackers have not proceeded far, when Gaspar again reins up with eyes lowered to the ground. The others seeing this, also bring their horses to a stand ; then watch the gaucho, who is apparently engaged with a fresh inspection of the trail.

"Have you found anything else ?" asks Cypriano.

"No, *señorito*. Instead, I've lost something."

"What ?" inquire both, in a breath.

"I don't any longer see the tracks of that shod horse. I mean the big one we know nothing about. The pony's are here, but as for the other, they're missing."

All three now join in a search for them, riding slowly along the trail, and in different directions backward and forward. But after some minutes thus passed, their search proves fruitless ; no shod hoof-print, save that of the pony, to be seen.

"This accounts for it," mutters Gaspar, giving up the quest, and speaking as to himself.

"Accounts for what ?" demands Cypriano, who has overheard him.

"The return tracks we saw on the other side of the camp ground. I mean the freshest of them, that went over

the ford of the stream.   Whoever rode that horse, whether
red or white man, has parted from the Indians at their
camping place, no doubt after staying all night with them.
Ha ! there's something at the back of all this ; somebody
behind Aguara and his Indians—that very somebody I've
been guessing at.   He—to a dead certainty."

The last sentences are not spoken aloud ; for as yet he
has not confided his suspicions about Francia and Valdez
to his youthful comrades.

"No matter about this shod horse and his back-track,"
he continues, once more heading his own animal to the
trail.   " We've now only to do with those that have gone
forward, and forward let us haste."

While speaking he strikes his ponderous spurs against
his horse's ribs, setting him into a canter, the others start_
ing off at the same pace.

For nearly an hour they continue this rate of speed, the
conspicuous trail enabling them to travel rapidly and without interruption.   It still carries them up the Pilcomayo,
though not always along the river's immediate bank.   At
intervals it touches the water's edge, at others parting from
it ; the deflections due to " bluffs " which here and there
impinge upon the stream, leaving no room for path between
it and their bases.

When nearing one of these, of greater elevation than
common, Gaspar again draws his horse to a halt ; though
it cannot be the cliff which has caused him to do so.   His
eyes are not on it, but turned on a tree, which stands at
some distance from the path they are pursuing, out upon
the open plain.   It is one of large size, and light green
foliage, the leaves pinnate, bespeaking it of the order *legu-
minosæ*.   It is in fact one of the numerous species of

mimosas, or sensitive plants, common on the plains and mountains of South America, and nowhere in greater number, or variety, than in the region of the Gran Chaco.

Ludwig and Cypriano have, in the meantime, also drawn up; and turning towards the tree at which Gaspar is gazing, they see its long slender branches covered with clusters of bright yellow flowers, these evidently the object of his attention. There is something about them that calls for his closer scrutiny; since after a glance or two, he turns his horse's head towards the tree, and rides on to it.

Arrived under its branches, he raises his hand aloft, plucks off a spray of the flowers, and dismounting, proceeds to examine it with curious minuteness, as if a botanist endeavouring to determine its genus or species! But he has no thought of this; for he knows the tree well, knows it to possess certain strange properties, one of which has been his reason for riding up to it, and acting as he now does.

The other two have also drawn near; and dismounting, hold their horses in hand while they watch him with wondering eyes. One of them cries out—

"What now, Gaspar? Why are you gathering those flowers?" It is Cypriano who speaks, impatiently adding, "Remember, our time is precious."

"True, master," gravely responds the gaucho; "but however precious it is, we may soon have to employ it otherwise than in taking up a trail. If this tree tells truth, we'll have enough on our hands to take care of ourselves, without thinking of Indians."

"What mean you?" both interrogated together.

"Come hither, *señoritos*, and set your eyes on these flowers!"

Thus requested they comply, leading their horses nearer to the tree.

"Well?" exclaims Cypriano, "I see nothing in them; that is, nothing that strikes me as being strange."

"But I do," says Ludwig, whose father had given him some instruction in the science of botany. "I observe that the corollas are well nigh closed, which they should not be at this hour of the day, if the tree is in a healthy condition. It's the *üinay;* I know it well. We have passed several on the way as we started this morning, but I noticed none with the flowers thus shrivelled up."

"Stand still a while," counsels Gaspar, "and watch them."

They do as desired, and see what greatly surprises them. At least Cypriano is surprised; for the young Paraguayan, unlike his half-German cousin, unobservant of Nature generally, has never given a thought to any of its particular phenomena; and that now presented to his gaze is one ot the strangest. For while they stand watching the *üinay,* its flowers continue to close their corollas, the petals assuming a shrunk, withered appearance.

The gaucho's countenance seems to take its cue from them, growing graver as he stands contemplating the change.

"*Por Dios!*" he at length exclaims, "if that tree be speaking truth, and I never knew of the *üinay* telling lies, we'll have a storm upon us within twenty minutes' time; such a one as will sweep us out of our saddles, if we can't get under shelter. Ay, sure it's going to be either a *temporal* or *tormenta!* And this is not the where to meet it. Here we'd be smothered in a minute, if not blown up into the sky. Stay! I think I know of a place near by, where we may take refuge before it's down upon us. Quick, *muchachos!* Mount, and let us away from here. A moment lost, and it may be too late; *vamonos!*"

Leaping back into their saddles, all three again go off in a gallop; no longer upon the Indian trail, but in a somewhat different direction, the gaucho guiding and leading.

CHAPTER XXIII.

JUST about the same time that the party of trackers had turned to take departure from the barometer-tree, a cavalcade of a very different kind, and composed of a greater number of individuals, is moving over the plain, some forty or fifty miles distant. It is the party being tracked; Aguara and his band of young braves on return to the *tolderia* of their tribe; the one now become their permanent place of abode.

More than one change has taken place in the Indian cohort since it passed over the same ground going downward. In number it is still the same; but one of them does not sit erect upon his horse; instead, lies bent across the animal's back, like a sack of corn. There he is fast tied to keep him from falling off, for he could do nothing to prevent this—being dead! He it was who came forth from the *sumac* grove wounded by Halberger's bullet, and the wound has proved fatal; this accounting for the pieces of *sipos* seen at their camping-place.

Another change in the composition of the party is, that the white man, Valdez, is no longer with it. Just as Gaspar had conjectured, from seeing the return tracks of his horse, he had parted company with the Indians at their first encampment, on the night after the murder. Another and very different individual, has taken his place at the head of the troop. The daughter of the murdered man who now rides by the side of the young Tovas chief!

Though a captive, she is not bound. They have no fear of her attempting to escape ; nor does she even think of it. Though ever so well mounted, she knows such an attempt would be idle, and on her diminutive roadster, which she still rides, utterly hopeless. Therefore, since the moment of being made captive, no thought of escaping by flight had even entered her mind.

With her long yellow hair hanging dishevelled over her shoulders, her cheeks white as lilies, and an expression of utter woe in her eyes, she sits her saddle seemingly regardless of where she is going, or whether she fall off and get trampled under the hoofs of the horses coming behind. If alone, her pony might wander at will ; but alongside Aguara's horse it keeps pace with the latter, its meek, submissive look, seeming to tell of its being as much a prisoner as its mistress.

Beyond the bereavement she has suffered by her father's death—for she saw him struck down, and believes him to be dead—no ill-treatment has been offered her: not even insult. Instead, the young cacique has been making efforts to gain her good will! He pretends innocence of any intent to take her father's life, laying it all on the shoulders of Valdez. Giving reasons too, not without some significance, and an air of probability. For was not the *vaqueano* an old enemy of her father, while they were resident in Paraguay? The young Tovas chief has learnt this from Valdez himself, and does not fail to speak of it to his prisoner. Further, he pretends it was on account of this very crime the *vaqueano* has committed, that he parted company wiih them —in short, fled, fearing punishment had he accompanied them back to their town.

In this manner the wily Indian does all he can to mislead his captive, as they journey along together.

Captive, he does not call her; in this also feigning pretence.   He tells her that the reason for their not taking her direct to the *estancia* is, because of a party of Guaycurus, their enemies, being out on the war path, and it was to discover the whereabouts of these he and his followers were out scouting, when the sad mischance, as he flippantly terms it. arose.   That having learnt where the hostile Indians were, he had needs return at once and report to the warriors of his tribe ; thus the excuse for his not seeing her to her home.   They could not leave her alone in the wilderness, and therefore of necessity she was going with them to their town ; afterwards to be taken back to the *estancia*—to her mother.   With such false tales, cunningly conceived, does he endeavour to beguile the ears of his captive.

For all that they are not believed ; scarcely listened to. She, to whom they are told, has reasons for discrediting them.   Though but a child in years, Francesca Halberger s not childish in understanding.   The strange experiences and perils through which she, and all related to her, had passed, have given her the discernment of a more mature age ; and well comprehends she her present situation, with other misfortunes that have led to it.   She is not ignorant of the young chief's partiality for herself; more than once made manifest to her in signs unmistakable—by acts as well as words.   Besides, what he is not aware of, she had overheard part of the speech which passed between him and the *vaqueano*, as the latter was entering the *sumac* grove, to do that deed which has left her without a father. Instead, therefore, of Aguara's words deceiving her into a false confidence, they but strengthen the feeling of repulsion she has all along had for him. Whether listening or not, she makes no reply to what he says, nor even deigns to look at him. Sitting listless, dejected, with her eyes habitually bent upon the ground, she rides on as one who has utterly abandoned herself to despair. Too sad, too terribly afflicted with what is past, she appears to have no thoughts about the future, no hopes. Or, if at intervals one arises in her mind, it rests not on him now by her side, but her father. For as yet she knows not that Naraguana is dead.

If somewhat changed the *personnel* of the Indian troop, much more is it altered in the general aspect and behaviour of those who compose it—a very contrast to what was exhibited on their way downward. No longer mirthful, making the welkin ring with their jests and loud laughter ; instead, there is silence upon their lips, sadness in their hearts, and gloom—even fear—on their faces. For they are carrying home one of their number a corpse, and dread telling the tale of it. What will the elders say, when they hear what has occurred ? What do ?

The feeling among Aguara's followers may be learnt from a dialogue, carried on between two of them who ride in the rear of the troop. They have been speaking of their pale-face captive, and extolling her charms, one of them saying how much their young cacique is to be envied his good luck, in possession of such a charming creature.

" After all, it may bring him into trouble," suggests the more sage of the speakers, adding, " ay, and ourselves as well—every one of us."

" How that," inquires the other.

"Well; you know, if Naraguana had been living, he would never have allowed this."

"But Naraguana is not living, and who is to gainsay the will of Aguara? He's now our chief, and can do as he likes with this captive girl, or any other. Can't he?"

"No; that he can't. You forget the elders. Besides, you don't seem to remember the strong friendship that existed between our old cacique and him the *vaqueano* has killed. I've heard say that Naraguana, just before his death, in his last words, left a command we should all stand by the pale-faced stranger, her father, and protect him and his against every enemy, as long as they remained in the Chaco. Strange protection we've given him! Instead, help to the man who has been his murderer! And now returning home, with his daughter a captive! What will our people think of all this? Some of them, I know, were as much the white man's friend almost as Naraguana himself. Besides, they won't like the old cacique's dying injunction having been thus disregarded. I tell you, there'll be trouble when we get back."

"No fear. Our young chief is too popular and powerful. He'll not find any one to oppose his will; which, as I take it, is to make this little pale-face his wife, and our queen. Well, I can't help envying him; she's such a sweet thing. But won't the Tovas maidens go mad with jealousy! I know one—that's Nacena——"

The dialogue is interrupted by a shout heard from one who rides near the front of the troop. It is a cry as of alarm, and is so understood by all; at the same time all comprehending that the cause is something seen afar off.

In an instant every individual of the party springs up from his sitting posture, and stands erect upon the back of his horse, gazing out over the plain.   The corpse alone lies still ; the captive girl also keeping her seat, to all seeming heedless of what has startled them, and caring not what new misfortune may be in store for her.   Her cup of sorrow is already full, and she recks not if it run over.

CHAPTER XXIV.

CAUGHT IN A DUST STORM.

At the crisis described, the Indian party is no longer travelling upon the Pilcomayo's bank, nor near it. They have parted from it at a point where the river makes one of its grand curves, and are now crossing the neck of the peninsula embraced within its windings. This isthmus is in width at least twenty miles, and of a character altogether different from the land lying along the river's edge. In short, a sterile, treeless expanse, or " travesia "—for such there are in the Chaco—not barren because of infertility in the soil, but from the want of water to fertilize it. Withal, it is inundated at certain periods of the year by the river's overflow, but in the dry season parched by the rays of a tropical sun. Its surface is then covered with a white efflorescence, which resembles a heavy hoar frost ; this, called *salitré*, being a sort of impure saltpetre, left after the evaporation and subsidence of the floods.

They have entered this cheerless waste, and are about midway across it, when the cry of alarm is heard ; he who gave utterance to it being older than the others, and credited with greater knowledge of things. That which had caught his attention, eliciting the cry, is but a phenomenon of

Nature, though not one of an ordinary kind; still, not so rare in the region of the Chaco; since all of them have more than once witnessed it. But the thing itself is not yet apparent save to him who has shouted, and this only by the slightest sign giving portent of its approach. For it is, in truth, a storm.

Even after the alarmist has given out his warning note, and stands on his horse's hips, gazing off in a certain direction, the others, looking the same way, can perceive nothing to account for his strange behaviour. Neither upon the earth, nor in the heavens, does there appear anything that should not be there. The sun is coursing through a cloudless sky, and the plain, far as eye can reach, is without animate object upon it; neither bird nor beast having its home in the *salitré.* Nothing observable on that wide, cheerless waste, save the shadows of themselves and their horses, cast in dark *silhouette* across the hoary expanse, and greatly elongated ; for it is late in the afternoon, and the sun almost down to the horizon.

"What is it ?" asks Aguara, the first to speak, addressing himself to the Indian who gave out the cry. "You appear to apprehend danger ?"

"And danger there is, chief," returns the other. "Look yonder !" He points to the level line between earth and sky, in the direction towards which they are travelling. "Do you not see something ?"

"No, nothing."

"Not that brown-coloured stripe just showing along the sky's edge, low, as if it rested on the ground ?"

"Ah, yes ; I see that. Only a little mist over the river, I should say."

"Not that, chief. It's a cloud, and one of a sort to be

dreaded.　See! it's rising higher, and, if I'm not mistaken, will ere long cover the whole sky."

" But 'what do you make of it?　To me it looks like smoke."

" No; it isn't that either.　There's nothing out that way to make fire—neither grass nor trees; therefore, it can't be smoke."

" What, then?　You appear to know!"

" I do.　'Tis *dust.*"

" Dust!　A drove of wild horses?　Or may they be mounted?　Ah! you think it's a party of Guaycurus?"

" No, indeed.　But something we may dread as much—ay, more—than them.　If my eyes don't deceive me, that's a *tormenta.*"

" Ha!" exclaims the young cacique, at length compre-hending.　"A *tormenta*, you think it is?"

The others of the band mechanically mutter the same word, in like tones of apprehension.　For although slow to perceive the sign, even yet but slightly perceptible, all of them have had experience of the danger.

" I do, chief," answers he interrogated.　" Am now sure of it."

While they are still speaking it—the cloud—mounts higher against the blue background of sky, as also becomes more extended along the line of the horizon.　Its colour, too, has sensibly changed, now presenting a dun yellowish ap-pearance, like that mixture of smoke and mist known as a " London fog."　But it is somewhat brighter, as though it hung over, half-concealing and smothering, the flames of some grand conflagration.

And as they continue regarding it, red corruscations begin to shoot through its opaque mass, which they can ell to be flashes of lightning. Yet all this while, upon the spot where they have pulled up the sun is shining serenely, and the air still and tranquil as if gale or breeze had never disturbed it !

But it is a stillness abnormal, unnatural, accompanied by a scorching heat, with an atmosphere so close as to threaten suffocation.

This, however, lasts but a short while. For in less than ten minutes after the cloud was first descried, a wind reaches them blowing directly from it at first, in puffs and gusts, but cold as though laden with sleet, and so strong as to sweep several of them from the backs of their horses. Soon after all is darkness above and around them. Darkness as of night; for the dust has drifted over the sun, and its disc is no longer visible—having disappeared as in a total eclipse, but far more suddenly.

It is too late for them to retreat to any place of shelter, were one ever so near, which there is not. And well know they the danger of being caught in that exposed spot; so well that the scene now exhibited in their ranks is one of fright and confusion.

Terrified exclamations are sent up on all sides, but only one voice of warning, this from him who had first descried the cloud.

" From your horses !" he calls out, " take shelter behind them, and cover your faces with your *jergas !* If you don't you'll be blinded outright."

His counsel acts as a command ; though it is not needed, all of them, as himself, sensible of the approaching peril. In a trice they have dropped to the ground, and plucking the pieces of skins which serve them as saddles, from the backs of their horses, muffle up their faces as admonished.

Then each clutching the halter of his own, and holding it so as to prevent the animal changing position, they await the onslaught of the storm.

Meanwhile, Aguara has not been inactive. Instead of having seized the pony's bridle-rein, he has passed round to the rear of the troop, leading his captive along with him; for the wind strikes them in front. There in the lee of all, better sheltered, he dismounts, flings his arms around the unresisting girl, and sets her afoot upon the ground. He does all this gently, as though he were a friend or brother! For he has not lost hope he may yet win her heart.

"Star of my life," he says to her, speaking in the Tovas tongue, which she slightly understands. "As you see we're in some danger, but it will soon pass. Meanwhile, we must take steps to guard against it. So, please to lie down, and this will protect you."

While speaking, he takes the plumed cloak from his shoulders and spreads it over those of the captive, at the same time covering her head with it, as if it were a hood. Then he gently urges her to lie on the ground.

To all she submits mechanically, and without offering opposition; though she little cares about the dust storm— whether it blind or altogether destroy her.

Soon after it is on and over them in all its fury, causing their horses to cower and kick, many screaming in affright or from the pain they have to endure. For not only does the *tormenta* carry dust with it, but sand, sticks, and stones, some of the latter so large and sharp as often to inflict severe wounds. Something besides in that now assailing them; which sweeping across the *salitral* has lifted the sulphureous efflorescence, that beats into their eyes bitter and blinding as the smoke of tobacco. But for having muffled up their faces, more than one of the party would ,eave that spot sightless, if not smothered outright.

For nearly an hour the tempest continues, the wind roaring in their ears, and the dust and gravel clouting against their naked skins, now and then a sharp angled pebble lacerating them. At times the blast is so strong they have difficulty in keeping their places; still more in holding their horses to windward. And all the while there is lightning and thunder, the last loud and rolling continuously. At length the wind, still keenly cold, is accompanied by a sleety rain, which pours upon them in torrents, chill as if coming direct from the snowy slopes of the Cordilleras—as in all likelihood it does.

They know that this is a sign of the *tormenta* approaching its end, which soon after arrives; terminating almost as abruptly as it had begun. The dust disappears from the sky, that which has settled on the ground now covering its surface with a thick coating of mud—converted into this by the rain—while the sun again shines forth in all its glory, in a sky bright and serene as if cloud had never crossed it!

The *tormenta* is over, or has passed on to another part of the great Chaco plain.

And now the Tovas youths, their naked skins well washed by the shower, and glistening like bronze fresh from the furnace—some of them, however, bleeding from the scratches they have received—spring upon their feet, readjust the *jergas* on the backs of their horses, and once more remount.

Then their young chief, by the side of the captive girl, having returned to his place at their head, they forsake that spot of painful experience, and continue their journey so unexpectedly interrupted.

CHAPTER XXV.

IT is scarce necessary to say, that the storm that overtook the Indian party was the same of which the barometer-tree had given warning to Gaspar and his young companions. But although many a long league separated the
Indians from those following upon their trail, and it would
take the latter at least another day to reach the spot where
the former had met the *tormenta*, both were beset by it
within less than half-an-hour of the same time. The Indians first, of course, since it came from the quarter towards
which all were travelling, and therefore in the teeth of pursuers as pursued.

But the trackers were not called upon to sustain its
shock, as those they were tracking up. Instead of its
coming upon them in an exposed situation, before its first
puffs became felt they were safe out of harm's way, having
found shelter within the interior of a cavern. It was this
Gaspar alluded to when saying, he knew of a place that
would give them an asylum. For the gaucho had been
twice over this ground before—once on a hunting excursion
in the company of his late master; and once at an earlier
period of his life on an expedition of less pleasant remembrance, when, as a captive himself, he was carried up the

Pilcomayo by a party of Guaycuru Indians, from whom he was fortunate in making escape.

His knowledge of the cave's locality, however, was not obtained during his former and forced visit to the district they are now traversing; but in that made along with the hunter-naturalist; who, partly out of curiosity, but more for geological investigation, had entered and explored it.

" It's by the bank of a little *arroyo* that runs into the Pilcomayo, some three or four miles above the big river. And, as I take it, not much further from where we are now. But we must make a cross cut to reach it in the quickest time."

This Gaspar says as they part from the barometer-tree. Following out his intention he heads his horse towards the open plain, and forsakes the Indian trail, the others following his lead.

They now go in full gallop, fast as their horses can carry them; for they have no longer any doubts about the coming on of a *tormenta*. The forecast given them by the flowers of the *iïnay* is gradually being made good by what they see—a dun yellowish cloud rising against the horizon ahead. The gaucho well understands the sign, soon as he sees this recognizing it as the dreaded dust storm.

It approaches them just as it had done the Indians. First the atmosphere becoming close and hot as the interior of an oven; then suddenly changing to cold, with gusts of wind, and the sky darkening as though the sun were eclipsed.

But, unlike the others, they are not exposed to the full fury of the blast; neither are they in danger of being blinded by the sulphureous dust, nor pelted with sticks and stones. Before the storm has thus developed itself they reach the crest of the cliff overhanging the *arroyo;* and urging their horses down a sloping path remembered by Gaspar, they get upon the edge of the stream itself. Then, turning up it, and pressing on for another hundred yards, they arrive at the cavern's mouth, just as the first puff of the chilly wind sweeps down the deep rut-like valley through which the *arroyo* runs.

"In time!" exclaims the gaucho. "Thanks to the Virgin, we're in time! with not a second to spare," he adds, dismounting, and leading his horse into the arching entrance, the others doing the same.

Once inside, however, they do not give way to inaction; for Gaspar well knows they are not yet out of danger.

"Come, *muchachos,*" he cries to them, soon as they have disposed of their animals, "there's something more to be done before we can call ourselves safe. A *tormenta's* not a thing to be trifled with. There isn't corner or cranny in this cave the dust wouldn't reach to. It could find its way into a corked bottle, I believe. *Carramba!* there it comes!"

The last words are spoken as a whiff of icy wind, now blowing furiously down the ravine, turns into the cavern's mouth, bringing with it both dust and dry leaves.

For a moment the gaucho stands in the entrance gazing out; the others doing likewise. Little can they see; for the darkness is now almost opaque, save at intervals, when the ravine is lit up by jets of forked and sheet lightning. But much do they hear; the loud bellowing of wind, the roaring of thunder, and the almost continuous crashing of trees, whose branches break off as though they were but brittle glass. And the stream which courses past close to the cave's mouth, now a tiny rivulet, will soon be a raging, foaming torrent, as Gaspar well knows.

They stay not to see that, nor aught else. They have other work before them—the something of which the gaucho spoke, and to which he now hastily turns, crying out—

"Your ponchos, my lads! Get them, quick! We must close up the entrance with them, otherwise we'll stand a good chance of being smothered. *Vaya!*"

Neither needs urging to haste. Young as they are, they too have had experience of a *tormenta*. More than once they have witnessed it, remembering how in their house, near Assuncion, it drove the dust through the keyholes of the doors, finding its way into every crack and crevice, making ridges across the floor, just as snow in northern lands—of which, however, they know nothing, save from what they have read, or been told by one who will tell them of such things no more.

In a few seconds' time, three ponchos—for each possesses one—are snatched from the cantles of their saddles, and as speedily spread across the entrance of the cave— just covering it, with not an inch to spare. With like speed and dexterity, they join them together, in a rough but firm stitching done by the nimble fingers of the gaucho —his thread a strip of thong, and for needle the sharp terminal spine of the *pita* plant—one of which he finds growing near by. They attach them at top by their knife blades stuck into seams of the stratified rock, and at bottom by stones laid along the border; these heavy enough to keep them in place against the strongest gust of wind.

All this done, they breathe freely, now feeling secure;

and after a last look at the screen to assure himself of its being reliable, the gaucho turns to his companions, quietly remarking,

"Now, *muchachos*, I fancy we need have no more fear of Mr Tormenta."

CHAPTER XXVI.

AN UNWELCOME INTRUDER.

As they are now in the midst of amorphous darkness, it might be imagined nothing could be done but keep their places, or go groping idly about. Not so, however. Gaspar has no intention of letting the time pass in such an unprofitable manner; instead, he at once resumes speech, and along with it action.

"Now, young masters," he says, making a movement towards the place where they had left their horses, "since we are shut up here, I don't see why we shouldn't make ourselves as comfortable as we can under the circumstances; and the best way to begin will be with what's usually the winding up of a day's work—that's supper. Our bit of rough riding has given me the appetite of a wolf, and I feel as if I could eat one red-raw. Suppose we have another set-to at the shoulder of mutton? What say you, *señoritos?*"

They answer in the affirmative, both being as hungry as himself.

"We sha'n't have to eat in darkness either," he proceeds. "Luckily, I've brought with me a bit of candle—best wax at that. A costly affair it was when whole; being one of a pair I had to pay for when my poor mother died, to be used at her funeral, and for which the rascally *padres* charged me five *pesos* a-piece—because consecrated, as they called out. As they stood me so much, I thought I might as well save the stumps; which I did, and have got one of them here. Starting out, it occurred to me we might some time need it, as you see we do now; so I slipped it into my saddle-bags."

While speaking, he has moved on to his horse, and got beside him without much straying; for his former visit to the cavern has made him familiar with its topography, and he could go anywhere through it without a glimmer of light to guide him. Plunging his hand into his ample *alparejas*, and rummaging about for a short while, he gets hold of the bit of unburnt candle—souvenir of a melancholy ceremony, which, however, he had long ceased to mourn over, since his mother has been dead for many years.

He has drawn it out; removed the scrap of buckskin in which it was wrapped; and with flint and steel is proceeding to strike a light, when a sound reaches his ears that causes him to suspend operations, and stand intently listening for its repetition.

Simultaneously has it been heard by the other two, as also by the three horses; these last, on hearing it, showing their affright by a series of snorts, while they dance about over the floor of the cavern. For it is a sound which, heard in any part of tropical America, whether on sunlit plain or in shady forest, strikes terror to the heart of all who hear it, be it man, bird, or beast. No living creature in that land but dreads the cry of the jaguar.

" *El tigre!* " exclaims Gaspar in a subdued tone, his voice half-drowned by a second roar from the great feline, this time louder and more prolonged.

" Where is it ? " they ask one another hurriedly, and in whispers, fearing to speak out. For loud as is the creature's voice as it reverberates through the hollow cavity, what with the bellowing of the wind and the trampling of their horses' hoofs on the hard rock, it is impossible to tell whence it came, and whether the jaguar be outside the cavern or within. About this there is a difference of opinion among them, but only for an instant—all three agreeing, as for the third time the terrifying note is sounded. Then they believe it to have come from outside. But again they as quickly differ, at hearing a fourth repetition of it; this as certainly seeming to have been uttered inside the cavern. Once more changing their minds, when, for the fifth time, the beast gives out its grand roar; since along with it they hear another sound as of some heavy body hurling itself against the screen of spread ponchos, too solid to be mistaken for a puff of wind. Beyond doubt, it is the tiger seeking admittance to the cave !

Though but a few minutes have elapsed since its first fierce note fell upon their ears, they have not stood idly listening. Instead, all three have groped the way to their horses, got hold of their guns, and returned to take stand near the entrance. Gaspar, moreover, has lit the stump of candle, and stuck it upon a projecting point of rock; for he knows the *tigre*, like other cats, can see in the darkness, and would thus have the advantage of them.

Soon again it treats them to another bit of trumpeting, this time more angrily intoned, as if demanding shelter from the storm, and no doubt as much surprised as puzzled at the strange obstruction debarring entrance to the cave—in all likelihood its lair.

They have stationed themselves in a line facing the

screen, and with guns cocked stand ready to fire at the beast, should it persist in its intention to enter. But now, with the light shining upon the ponchos, they see what appears to be its body pressing against these from the outside, though quickly withdrawn, as if the creature recoiled from a thing that awes while perplexing it.

" Hadn't we better fire at it through the ponchos? Some one of us may hit it."

Cypriano makes the suggestion.

" No," dissents Gaspar, " we might all miss that way; and if we did, 'twould drive the *tigre* mad, and then——"

He is interrupted by another cry from the jaguar; this a fierce scream, showing the animal already maddened enough, or, at all events, madly impatient, and determined no longer to endure exclusion from the cave. For while still continuing that cry, it bounds up against the screen, plucking the knives from their places, tossing off the stones, and laying the entrance open. A gust of wind entering blows out the candle, and all is again darkness. But not silence; for there are noises close to where they stand, which they know must proceed from the jaguar, though different from its former utterances, and to them quite incomprehensible—a succession of growls, snorts, and coughs, as if the beast were being suffocated ; while at the same time a heavy body seems to be tumbling and struggling over the floor of the cavern !

" By St. Jago !" cries Gaspar, first to comprehend what it means, " the brute's caught in our ponchos ! He's bagged—smothered up ! Fire into him ! Aim where you hear the noise. *Tira !*"

At the word, their three guns go off together ; and then, to make sure, another shot additional from the double barreled piece of Cypriano; Ludwig's gun being the rifle that belonged to his father, found where the latter had fallen.

And sure work have their shots made of it. For as they stand in the darkness listening, they hear neither growl, nor snort, nor coughing; but, instead, only the wailing of wind and the rumbling of thunder.

" Dead as a door-nail !" pronounces Gaspar, feeling his way to where he had stuck the bit of bees'-wax, and once more setting it alight. Then returning towards the entrance, he sees that he has in everything rightly conjectured. For there, enveloped in the ponchos, with its claws stuck fast into the close-woven fabric of wool, lies the great spotted cat—not at full stretch, but doubled up into a shapeless lump, as it had worked itself in its efforts to get free! Though all their shots had hit it, some of the bullets passing through its body, a quivering throughout its frame tells that life is not yet extinct. But it is extinguished instantly after, by Gaspar laying hold of one of the knives, and giving *el tigre* the *coup de grace* by a cut across its throat; as he does so, saying—

" That's for your impudence—intruding yourself on three hungry travellers about sitting down to supper !"

CHAPTER XXVII

HAVING dragged the dead beast out of their ponchos, they are about to re-adjust these as before, when it strikes them there is no longer any need for closing the cave's mouth. The first blast of the *tormenta* having blown over, the dust borne upon it is now in less volume; while the wind, rushing direct down the ravine, carries everything along with it—only an occasional whiff seeking entrance into the cave.

"For the matter of our being blinded," remarks the gaucho in perceiving this, "we needn't trouble about shutting the door again. Though if I'm not greatly out in my reckoning, there's something else may need keeping out—a thing more dangerous than dust."

"What thing?" he is asked.

"Another *tigre*. I never knew one of these spotted beauties to be about alone. They always hunt in couples; and where there's a female, the male is sure to be with her. As you see, it's the lady we've closed accounts with, and for certain the gentleman isn't far off. Out in that storm, he'll be in the same way making for this snug shelter. So we may look for his worship to present himself at any moment."

Ludwig and Cypriano turn their eyes towards the entrance, as though they expected even then to behold the dreaded intruder.

" To keep him out," pursues Gaspar in a more serious vein, " 'twill be no use putting up the ponchos. We can't trust to the old Tom entangling himself, as did his *esposa*. That was all an accident. And yet we're not safe if we leave the entrance open. As we've got to stay here all night, and sleep here, we daren't close an eye so long as he's ranging about. Instead, we'd have to lie awake, and on the alert."

" Why can't we wall it up with those stones?" Cypriano thus interrogates, pointing to some scattered boulders lying about the cave—large blocks that have broken off from its roof, and fallen upon the floor.

" Not a bad idea," rejoins Gaspar, "and one quite practicable," he adds, with his eye taking in the dimensions of the cavern's mouth, but little larger than an ordinary stable door. " You're right, Señor Cypriano ; we can do that."

Without further speech, they set about the work; first rolling the larger masses of stalactite towards the entrance to form the foundation of the wall. But before having got half-a-dozen of them fixed in their places, a sound reaches their ears which causes them suddenly to desist; for all three recognize it as coming from the throat of a jaguar! Not a loud roar, or scream, such as they heard when that lying dead first made its presence known, but a sort of sniff or snort, as when it was struggling, half-choked by the ponchos. Soon, however, as they stand listening, the snorting changes into a long low growl, ending in a gruff bark ; as of a watch-dog awakened by some slight noise, for which he is not sure of its being worth his while to forsake his kennel, or spring upon his feet.

Not thus doubtful are they. Instead, the sounds now heard excite and terrify them as much as any that preceded; for they can tell that tiger No. 2 is, as themselves, *within the cave!*

"*Por Dios!*" exclaims Gaspar, in a low tone of voice, "it's the old Tom sure, and inside too! Ha! that accounts for our not being certain about the she. Both were yelling at the same time, answering one another. Where can the brute be?"

They turn their eyes toward the back of the cavern, but in the dim glimmer can see nothing like a tiger. They only hear noises of different kinds, made by their horses, then freshly affrighted, once more sniffing the air and moving uneasily about.

"Your guns!" cries Gaspar in hurried accents; "get them loaded again! If the *tigre* attack us, as it's almost sure to do, our knives will be of little use. *Viva, muschachos!*"

All together again lay hold of their guns; but where is the ammunition? Stowed in a pair of holsters on the pommel of Cypriano's saddle, as they well know—powder, balls, percussion-caps, everything. And where is the horse himself; for, left loose, he has moved off to another part of the cavern?

Cypriano taking the candle in hand, they go in search of him. Soon to see that the frightened animal has taken refuge in an angular embayment between two projecting buttresses of rock, where he stands cowering and trembling.

They are about to approach him, going cautiously and with timid steps, when, lo! on a ledge between, they perceive a long yellow body with black spots lying astretch at one end of it, a pair of eyes giving back the light of their candle, with a light almost as brilliant, and at intervals flashing like fire. It is the jaguar.

The sight brings them suddenly to a stand, even causing them to retreat a step or two. For the ledge on which the *tigre* crouches is directly between them and Cypriano's horse, and to approach the latter they must pass right under the former; since it is upon a sort of shelf, several feet above the level of the ground. They at once see there is no hope of reaching the needed ammunition without tempting the attack of the tiger; which, by their movements, is becoming at every moment more infuriated, and already seems about to spring upon them. Instinctively, almost mechanically, they move further away, having abandoned the idea of defending themselves with the guns, and fallen back on their only other weapons, the knives. Ludwig counsels retreating altogether out of the cave, and leaving their horses behind. Outside, the wind no longer rages, and the dust seems to have blown past. They but hear the pattering of rain, with peals of thunder, and the swish of the stream, now swollen. But nothing of these need they fear. To the course counselled Cypriano objects, as also Gaspar; fearing for their horses, almost sure to be sacrificed to the fury of the enraged jaguar. And where would they be then? Afoot in the midst of the Chaco, helpless as shipwrecked sailors on a raft in mid-ocean!

For a while they remain undecided; only a short while, when they are made aware of that which speedily brings them to a decision, and without any will of their own. In putting space between themselves and the dangerous beast, they have retreated quite up to the cavern's entrance. There, looking out, they see that egress is debarred them. The stream, swollen by the rain, still pouring down as in a deluge, has lipped up to the level of the cave's mouth, and rushes past in an impetuous torrent, crested, and carrying huge rocks, with the trunks and broken branches of trees upon its seething current. Neither man nor horse might dare ford it now. They are caught between a torrent and a tiger!

CHAPTER XXVII.

SAVED BY A SPITTING-DEVIL.

To be shut up in a room with a royal Bengal tiger, or what amounts to the same a cave of small dimensions, is a situation which no one will covet. Nor would it be much improved were the tyrant of the Asiatic jungles transformed into a jaguar—the despot of the American tropical forests. For, although the latter be smaller, and less powerful than the former, in an encounter with man it is equally fierce and dangerous. As regards size, the male jaguar often reaches the measurement of an Indian tigress; while its strength is beyond all proportion to its bulk. Humboldt has made mention of one that dragged the carcase of a horse it had killed across a deep, difficult ravine, and up to the top of a hill; while similar feats have been recorded by Von Tschudi, Darwin, and D'Orbigny.

Familiar with its character and capabilities, no wonder, then, that our gaucho and his companions should feel fear, as they take in the perils besetting them.

For there is no knowing how long the jaguar will keep its patience, or its place; and when it shifts they may "look out for squalls." They can still see it on the ledge; for although the light is feeble, with some dust floating about, through this its glaring eyeballs, as twin stars through

a thin stratum of cloud, gleam coal-like and clear.   They
can see its jaws, too, at intervals open to emit that cry of
menace, exposing its blood-red palate, and white serrature
of teeth—a sight horrifying to behold!   All the while its
sinewy tail oscillates from side to side, now and then
striking the rock, and breaking off bits of stalactites, that
fall in sparkling fragments on the floor.   At each repetition
of its growl the horses show fresh affright, and dance madly
about.   For the instinct of the dumb animals seems to
admonish them, they are caged with a dangerous companion—they and it alike unable to part company.   Their
masters know this, and knowing it, are all the more alarmed.
A fight is before them; and there appears no chance of
shunning it—a hand-to-hand fight, their short-bladed knives
against the sharp teeth and claws of a jaguar!

For a time they stand irresolute, even Gaspar himself
not knowing what to do.   Not for long, however.   It
would not be the gaucho to surrender to despair.   Instead,
a thought seems suddenly to have occurred to him—a way
of escape from their dilemma—as evinced by his behaviour,
to the others yet incomprehensible.

Parting from them, he glides off in the direction of his
horse; which happens to be nearest, like Cypriano's
cowering in a crevice of the rock.   Soon beside it, he is
again seen to plunge his hand into the *alparejas,* and grope
about, just as when searching for the stump of candle.

And now he draws forth something very similar—a
packet with a skin covering, tied with a bit of string.   Returning to them, and removing the wrapper, he exposes to
view a half-dozen little rolls, in shape somewhat like regalia
cigars, sharp-pointed at one end, and barbed as arrows.

At a glance, both boys see what they are.   They have

not been brought up in a country where bull-fighting, as in all Spanish America, is the principal pastime, without having become acquainted with most matters relating to it. And what Gaspar has brought before their eyes are some *torterillas,* or spitting-devils, used, along with the *banderillas* for rousing the fury of the bull while being goaded by the *picadores* round the arena, before the *matador* makes his final assault. Gaspar, who in early life has played *picador* himself in the bull-fights of San Rosario, knows how to manufacture all the implements pertaining to the *funcion de toros,* and has usually kept a stock of *torterillas* on hand, chiefly for the amusement of the Tovas youths, who were accustomed to visit the *estancia.*

Often, while dwelling at Assuncion, had he witnessed the wonder and delight with which the savages who came there regarded all sorts of fireworks; and it had occurred to him that, in the event of their encountering strange Indians, some "spitting-devils" might prove of service. So, at starting out on their present expedition, just as with the bit of wax candle, he had tossed a packet of them into his saddle-bags.

He does not give this explanation till afterwards. Now there is no time for talking; he must act, and instantly. But how he intends acting, or what he means to do with the *torterillas,* neither of his youthful comrades can tell or guess.

They are not kept long in ignorance. Snatching the candle from Cypriano, who has been carrying it—with this in one hand and a *torterilla* in the other—he moves off in the direction of the ledge, where luckily the jaguar still lies astretch. Possibly the reports of the guns have cowed it to keeping its place. Whether or no, it has kept it without change of attitude or position; though at intervals giving utterance to long low growls, with an occasional bark between.

Advancing cautiously, and in silence, the gaucho gets within six paces of it. This he deems near enough for his purpose; which, by this time, the others comprehend. It is to cast the *torterilla* at the tiger, and, if possible, get the barbed point to penetrate the creature's skin, and there stick.

He makes the attempt, and succeeds. First having put the primed end into the candle's flame, and set the fuse on fire, he launches the " Devil " with such sure aim, that it is seen to fix itself in the jaguar's back, just over the right shoulder.

The brute, feeling the sting, starts to its feet with an angry scream; this instantly changing to a cry of affright, as the caked powder catches fire, and fizzing up, envelopes it in a shower of sparks. Not a second longer stays it on the ledge, but bounding off makes for the cave's mouth, as if Satan himself had taken hold of its tail. So sudden and unexpected is its retreat, that Ludwig and Cypriano, to get out of the way, go tumbling over the stones; while Gaspar comes nigh doing the same; in the scramble dropping the candle, and of course extinguishing it. But the light goes out only with the jaguar itself; the brute bounding on with the sparks like the tail of a comet streaming behind, illumining the whole cavern, and causing the stalactites to glitter and sparkle, as if its roof were frosted with real diamonds!

In an instant after, all is darkness; simultaneously with the light going out, a sound reaching their ears, as of some solid body, falling heavily upon water—which they know to

THE CAKED POWDER CATCHES FIRE, AND FIZZING UP, ENVELOPES
THE BRUTE IN A SHOWER OF SPARKS.

p. 162.

be the tiger plunging into the stream. That puts out the "spitting-devil," and no doubt along with it, or soon after, the life of the animal it had so affrighted ; for even the king of American beasts could not escape being drowned in that foaming, seething flood.

Soon as satisfied that the enemy is *hors de combat*, and the coast clear, Gaspar gropes about for the candle, and finding, once more lights it. Then in his usual fashion, winding up with some quaint remark, he says :—

"No more caterwauling to-night, I fancy, unless the kittens be about too. If they be, it'll give us a bit of sport, drowning them. Now, *señoritos!* I think we may sit down to supper, without fear of being again baulked of our *maté* and mutton."

CHAPTER XXIX.

A ROCK-BOUND SLEEPING ROOM.

As the darkness, due to the storm, has now been succeeded by the more natural darkness of night, the trackers, for this day, cannot proceed further, were they ever so eager. Besides, there is another bar to their continuing; one still more directly obstructive, even forbidding their exit from the cave. This, the *arroyo*, which now in full flood fills the ravine up to the cliff's base, there leaving no path for either man or horse. That by which they approached is covered beyond fording depth, with a current so swift as to sweep the strongest animal from its feet, even were it an elephant. And to attempt reaching the opposite side by swimming, would only result in their getting carried down to be drowned to a certainty, or have the life crushed out of them on the rocks below.

Gaspar knowing all this, does not dream of making any such rash experiment. On the contrary, as he has signified, he designs them to remain all night in the cavern. Indeed, there is no alternative, as he observes, explaining how egress is forbidden, and assuring them that they are, in point of fact, as much prisoners as though the doors of a jail were shut and locked upon them.

Their imprisonment, however, need not last till the morning; so far as the flood is concerned. And this he also makes known to them, himself aware that the waters in the *arroyo*, will subside as rapidly as they had risen. It is one of those short rivulets, whose floods are over almost as soon as the rain which causes them. Looking out again near the hour of midnight, they see his prediction verified. The late swollen and fast-rushing stream has become reduced to nearly its normal dimensions, and runs past in gentle ripple, while the moon shining full upon it, shows not a flake of foam.

They could even now pass out of the cave, and on up the cliff where they came down, if they desired to do so. More, they might with such a clear moon, return to the river's bank and continue on along the trail they had forsaken. A trail so plain as it, could be followed in a light far more faint; at least, so think they. So believing, Cypriano, as ever impatient to get on, is greatly inclined to this course, and chafes at the irksomeness of delay. But Gaspar objects, giving his reasons.

"If we were to go on now," he says, "it wouldn't better us a bit. All we'd gain by it would be the league or so from this to the river. Once there, and attempting to travel up its bank, we'd find scores of little creeks that run into it, in full freshet, and have to swim our horses across them. That would only lose time, instead of gaining it. Now, by daybreak, they'll all be down again, when we can travel straight on without being delayed by so many stoppages. I tell you, Señor Cypriano, if we start now, it'll be only to find the old saying true, ' More haste, worse speed.' "

He to whom this speech is addressed perceives the application of the adage, and admitting it, yields the point.

"Besides," adds the gaucho, by way of clinching his argument, "we've got to spend part of the night somewhere, and have some sleep. If we keep on without that, it may end in our breaking dead down, which would be worse than being a little behind time. We all stand in need of rest now. Speaking for myself, I want it badly; and I'm sure so does Master Ludwig and you too, *señorito!* If we were to leave the cave, and seek for it anywhere outside, we'd find the ground soaking wet, and, like enough, every one of us get laid up with a spell of rheumatics. Here we'll be as snug as a *biscacha* in its hole; and, I take it, will sleep un-disturbed by the squalling of any more cats."

As Cypriano makes no further opposition, it is decided that they remain in the cave till morning.

The little incident as above, with the conversation which accompanies it, does not take place immediately after the tiger had been disposed of; for they have eaten supper since. By good luck, some sticks were found in the cave, half-burnt faggots, the remains of a fire no doubt left by a party of Indian hunters, who had also spent a night there. With these they were enabled to boil their kettle, and make a *maté* of their favourite *yerba* tea; while the "knuckle" of mutton and some cakes of corn bread still left, needed no cooking. It is after all this was over, and they had been some time conversing on the many strange incidents which occurred to them throughout the day, that they became aware of the flood having fallen, and escape from their rock-bound prison possible. Then succeeded the discussion recorded.

At its termination, as nothing more can be done, and all feeling fatigued, to go to rest is naturally the next move. Their horses have already been attended to by the removal of the riding gear, while some rough grass found growing against the cliff, near the cave's entrance outside, has been cut and carried in to them.

A slight grooming given to the animals, and it but remains to make their own beds. This done, by simply spreading their *jergas* and *caronillas* along the flinty stalagmites, each having his own *recado* for a pillow. Their ponchos, long since pulled apart, and the dust cuffed out of them, are to serve for what they really are—blankets; a purpose to which at night they are put by all gauchos and most Argentinos—as much as they are used during day time for cloak or greatcoat.

Each wrapping himself up in his own, all conversation ceases, and sleep is sought with closed eyes. This night it is found by them in a succession somewhat changed. As on that preceding, Ludwig is first asleep; but almost instantly after it is Gaspar, not Cypriano, who surrenders to the drowsy god; filling the hollow cavity with his snoring, loud as that often heard to proceed from the nostrils of a tapir. He well knows they are safe within that rock-bound chamber; besides that he is tired dead down with the day's exertion; hence his so soon becoming oblivious.

Cypriano is the last to yield. But he, too, at length gives way, and all is silent within the cavern, save the "crump-crump" of the horses munching their coarse provender, with now and then a hoof striking the hard rock. But louder than all is that raucous reverberation sent up by the slumbering gaucho.

CHAPTER XXX.

WHILE the pursuing party is peacefully reposing upon the stalagmites of the cavern, that pursued reaches its destination—the "Sacred town" of the Tovas.

The *tolderia*, so named, stands upon a level plain, near the shore of a large and beautiful lake, whose numerous low-lying islets, covered with a thick growth of the *moriche*, have the appearance of palm-groves growing direct out of the water itself.

A belt of the same stately trees borders the lake all around, broken here and there by projecting headlands; while away over the adjacent *campo*, on the higher and drier ground, are seen palms of other and different species, oth fan-leaved and pinnate, growing in copses or larger 'montes," with evergreen shrubs and trees of deciduous oliage interspersed.

At some three or four hundred yards from the lake's edge, a high hill rises abruptly above the plain—the only elevation within many miles. Thus isolated, it is visible from afar, and forms a conspicuous feature of the landscape; all the more remarkable on account of its singular shape, which is the frustrum of a cone. Though its sides are of steep pitch, they are thickly wooded to the summit; trees of large size standing upon its table-like top.   But something more than trees stand there; the scaffolds upon which are laid the bodies of the Tovas dead; hundreds of which may be seen in all stages of decay, or shrivelled and dessicated by the dry winds and sun of the Chaco till they resemble Egyptian mummies.   For it is the "Cemetery Hill," a spot hallowed in the hearts of these Indians, and so giving the title of "Sacred" to this particular place, as the town adjacent to it.   The latter is situated just under the hill, between its base and the shore of the lake.   No grand city, as might be supposed from such a high-sounding name, but simply a collection of palm and bamboo *toldos*, or huts, scattered about without any design or order; each owner having been left free to select the site of his frail tenement, since among the Tovas municipal regulations are of the simplest and most primitive character. True, some dwellings, grander and more pretentious than the common, are grouped around an open space; in the centre of which is one much larger than any of the others, its dimensions equalling a dozen of them.   This is not a dwelling, however, but the *Malocca*, or House of Parliament.   Perhaps, with greater propriety, it might be called "Congress Chamber," since, as already hinted at, the polity of the Tovas tribe is rather republican than monarchical.

Strange, as sad, that in this republic of red-skins, and so-called savages, should exist the same political contradiction as among some other republican communities, having the name of civilized.   For although themselves individually free, the Tovas Indians do not believe in the doctrine that all men should be so; or, at all events, they do not act up to it.   Instead, their practice is the very opposite, as shown by their keeping numbers of slaves.   Of these they have hundreds, most of them being Indians of other tribes, their enemies, whom they have made captive in battle. But to the Tovas master it signifies little what be the colour of his bondman's skin, whether white or red; and many of the former, women as well as men, may be seen doing drudgery in this same Sacred town—its hewers of wood and drawers of water. These are also captives, the spoil of predatory incursions across the Salado into the settlements of Santiago, Salto, and Tucuman.

Most of these slaves, employed in the care of cattle, live apart from their masters, in a sort of suburb, where the dwellings are of a less permanent character than the ordinary *toldos*, besides being differently constructed. They more resemble the tents, or wigwams, of the North-American Indians; being simply a number of poles set in a circle, and tied together at the tops; the hides of horses covering them, instead of the buffalo skins which serve a similar purpose on the northern prairies.

It may seem strange that captives with white skins, thus left unguarded, do not make their escape. But no; those so kept do not even seek or desire it. Long in captivity, they have become "Indianized," lost all aspirations for liberty, and grown contented with their lot; for the Tovas are not hard taskmasters.

On the night of that same day, when the *tormenta* overtook them, Aguara and his party approach the Sacred town, which is about twenty miles from the edge of the *salitral*, where the trail parts from the latter, going westward. The plain between is no more of saline or sterile character; but, as on the other side, showing a luxuriant vegetation, with the same picturesque disposal of palm-groves and other tropical trees.

The hour is late—nigh to midnight—as the captive train passes under the shadow of the Cemetery Hill, making round to where the *tolderia* stands ; for both lake and town are on the west side of the hill.

Well may the young cacique feel something of fear, his face showing it, as he glances up to that elevated spot where he so late laid the corpse of his father. Were that father living, he, the son, would not be passing there with the daughter of Ludwig Halberger as his captive. Even as it is, he can fancy the spirit of the deceased cacique hovering over the hill, and looking frowningly, reproachfully, down upon him !

As if to escape from such imaginary frowns, he gives the lash to his horse ; and setting the animal into a gallop, rides on alone—having first placed the captive under the charge of one of his followers.

On reaching the *tolderia*, however, he does not go direct to his own dwelling, which is the largest of those adjacent to the *malocca*. Nor yet enters he among the *toldos ;* but, instead, makes a wide circuit around them, taking care not to awake those sleeping within. The place for which he is making is a sort of half hut, half cave, close in to the base of the hill, with trees overshadowing, and a rocky background of cliff.

Arrived in front of this solitary dwelling, he dismounts, and, drawing aside the horse's skin which serves as a swing door, calls out :—

" Shebotha !"

Presently a woman appears in the opening—if woman she could be called. For it is a hag of most repulsive appearance ; her face half hidden by a tangle of long hair, black, despite old age indicated by a skin shrivelled and wrinkled as that of a chameleon. Add to this a pair of dark grey eyes, deep sunken in their sockets, for all gleaming brilliantly, and you have the countenance of Shebotha—sorceress of the Tovas tribe—one of cast as sinister as ever presented itself in a doorway.

She speaks not a word in answer to the friendly salutation of the cacique; but stands silent in bent, obeisant attitude, with her skinny arms crossed over her breast, as if waiting to hear what he would further say. His words are by way of command:

"Shebotha! I've brought back with me a captive—a young girl of the pale-faces. You must take charge of her, and keep her here in your hut. She's not yet come up, but will presently. So get things ready to receive her."

Shebotha but bends lower, with an inclination of the head, to imply that his instructions will be attended to. Then he adds—

"No one must see, or converse with her; at least, not for a time. And you mustn't admit any one inside' your *toldo*, except the witless white creature, your slave. About him it don't signify. But keep out all others, as I know you can. You understand me, Shebotha?"

She makes answer in the affirmative, but, as before, only by a nod.

"Enough!" is the young chief's satisfied rejoinder, as he vaults back upon his horse, and rides off to meet the captive train, which he knows must be now near.

That night, as for other nights and days succeeding, Francesca Halberger has this horrid hag for a hostess, or rather the keeper of her prison; since the unhappy girl is in reality kept and guarded as a prisoner.

CHAPTER XXXI.

Long before daylight penetrates the interior of the cavern, or shows its first streak on the sky outside, the trackers are up and active.

A hasty breakfast is prepared ; but, as the mutton bone is now quite bare, they have to fall back on another kind of fleshmeat, which the provident Gaspar has brought along. This is *charqui,* or as it is called by English-speaking people "jerked beef;" in all likelihood a sailor's pseudonym, due to some slight resemblance, between the English word "jerked," and the Guarani-Indian one *charqui,* as pro nounced by South American people.

Charqui is simply beef cut into long, thin strips, then hung over a rope or rail, and exposed to a hot sun—in the absence of this, to a fire—till the juices are thoroughly dried out of it. Thus prepared, it will keep for weeks, indeed months.

The reason for so preserving it, is the scarcity of salt, which in the districts where *charqui* prevails, is difficult to be got at, and, in consequence, dear. Most of the beef imported from the La Plata, under the name of "jerked beef," is not *charqui,* but simply meat cured with salt.

Beef is preserved by a similar process throughout most

parts of Spanish America, as in Mexico, and California, and for the same reason; but in these countries it is termed *tasajo*, and sometimes *cecina*.

Charqui is by no means a dainty viand; not nice either to the nose or palate. Those portions of it which have not had sufficient sun in the drying process, become tainted, and the odour is anything but agreeable. For all, it serves a purpose in those countries where salt is a scarce commodity; and cooked—as all Spanish Americans cook it—with a plentiful seasoning of onions, garlic, and chilé, the "gamey" flavour ceases to be perceptible. Above all, it is a boon to the traveller who has a long journey to make through the uninhabited wilderness, with no inns nor post-houses at which he may replenish his spent stock of provisions. Being dry, firm, and light, it can be conveniently carried in haversack, or saddle-bags.

By Gaspar's foresight, there is a packet of it in Ludwig's *alparejas*, where all the other provisions are stowed; and a piece cut from one of the strips, about the length of a Bologna sausage, makes breakfast for all three. Of the Paraguay tea they have a good store, the *yerba* being a commodity which packs in small space.

Their morning meal is dismissed with slight ceremony; and soon as eaten, they recaparison their horses; then leading them out of the cavern, mount, and are off.

As the *arroyo* has long since shrunk to its ordinary level, and the path along the base of the bluff is dry as when trodden by them in their rush for shelter from the storm, they have no difficulty in getting out. So on they ride up the steep acclivity to the cliff's crest; which last is on a level with the pampa itself.

But on reaching it, a sight meets their eyes—it is now

daylight—causing a surprise to Ludwig and Cypriano; but to Gaspar something more—something akin to dismay. For the sage gaucho mentally sees further than either of his less experienced companions; and that now observed by him gives token of a new trouble in store for them. The plain is no longer a green grassy savanna, as when they galloped across it on the afternoon preceding, but a smooth expanse, dark brown in colour, its surface glittering under the red rays of the rising sun, whose disc is as yet but half visible above the horizon !

" *Santos Dios !* " exclaims the gaucho, as he sits in his saddle, contemplating the transformation, to him no mystery. " I thought it would be so."

" How very strange ! " remarks Ludwig.

'Not at all strange, *señorito;* but just as it should be, and as we might have expected."

" But what has caused it ? "

" Oh, cousin," answered Cypriano, who now comprehends all. "Can't you see? I do."

" See what ? "

" Why, that the dust has settled down over the plain ; and the rain coming after, has converted it into mud."

" Quite right, Señor Cypriano," interposes Gaspar ; " but that isn't the worst of it."

Both turn their eyes upon him, wondering what worse he can allude to. Cypriano interrogates :—

" Is it some new danger, Gaspar ? "

" Not exactly a danger, but almost as bad ; a likelihood of our being again delayed."

" But how ? "

" We'll no longer have track or trace to guide us, if this abominable sludge extend to the river ; as I daresay it does.

There we'll find the trail blind as an owl at noontide. As you see, the thing's nearly an inch thick all over the ground. 'Twould smother up the wheel-ruts of a loaded *carreta.*"

His words, clearly understood by both his young companions, cause them renewed uneasiness. For they can reason, that if the trail be obliterated, their chances of being able to follow the route taken by the abductors will be reduced to simple guessing; and what hope would there be searching that way over the limitless wilderness of the Chaco?

"Well?" says Gaspar, after they had remained for some moments gazing over the cheerless expanse which extends to the very verge of their vision, " it won't serve any good purpose, our loitering here. We may as well push on to the river, and there learn the worst—if worst it's to be. *Vamonos !*"

With this, the Spanish synonym for " Come along !" the gaucho gives his horse a dig in the ribs, with spur rowels of six inches diameter, and starts off at a swinging pace, the others after.

And now side by side go all three, splashing and spattering through the mortar-like mud, which, flung up in flakes by their horses' hoofs, is scattered afar in every direction.

Half an hour of quick cantering brings them back upon the Pilcomayo's bank; not where they had parted from it, but higher up, near the mouth of the *arroyo.* For Gaspar did not deem it necessary to return to that prophetic tree, whose forecast has proved so unfailing. To have gone back thither would have been a roundabout of several miles, since they had made a cross-cut to reach the cavern ; and as on the way they had seen nothing of the Indian trail, it must needs have continued up the river.

But now, having reached this, they cannot tell ; for here, as on all the plain over which they have passed, is spread the same coating of half-dried dirt, fast becoming drier and firmer as the ascending tropical sun, with strengthened intensity, pours his hot beams upon it. It has smothered up the Indian's trail as completely as if snow several inches deep lay upon it. No track there, no sign to show, that either horses or men ever passed up the Pilcomayo's bank.

" *Caspita !* " exclaims the gaucho, in spiteful tone. " It is as I anticipated ; blind as an old mule with a *tapojo* over its eyes. May the fiends take that *tormenta !* "

CHAPTER XXXII.

FOR a time the trackers remain at halt, but without forsaking their saddles, pondering upon what course they should pursue, or rather, what direction they ought to take.

Only a short while are they undecided. It seems good as certain that the Indians have kept to the river, for some distance further on, at all events. Therefore, it will be time enough to enter upon a more prolonged deliberation, when they come to a point where this certainty ceases. Thus reflecting, they start off afresh, with their horses' heads as before.

Going at good speed as ever, in a few minutes they arrive at the confluence of the *arroyo* with the greater river; the former here running between banks less "bluffy" than above, where it passes the cavern. Still they are of sufficient elevation to make a sharp descent towards the channel of the stream, and a corresponding ascent on its opposite side. But instead of an impediment, the trackers find this an advantage; giving them evidence that the Indians have gone across the *arroyo*. For their horses' tracks are distinctly traceable on the steep faces of both banks; the dust either not having settled there, or been washed off by the rain which fell after.

Without difficulty they themselves ride across; for the rapid-running stream has returned to its ordinary dimensions, and is now quite shallow, with a firm gravelly bed. Once on its western side, however, and up to the level of the *campo* beyond, they are again at fault; in fact, have reached the point spoken of where all certainty is at an end. Far as they can see before them, the surface is smeared with mud, just as behind, and no sign of a trail visible anywhere. Like enough the Indians have still continued on along the river, but that is by no means sure. They may have turned up the *arroyo*, or struck off across the pampa, on some route known to them, and perhaps leading more direct to whatever may be their destination.

It is all conjecture now; and upon this they must rely. But the weight of probablility is in favour of the pursued party having kept to the river, and Gaspar is of this opinion. After riding some distance up the western bank of the *arroyo*, and seeing no trail or track there, he again returns to where they had crossed, saying :—

" I think we may safely stick to the river. I'm acquainted with its course for at least thirty leagues further up. At about half that distance from here it makes a big elbow, and just there, I remember, an old Indian path strikes off from it, to cross a *traveria*. Ha ! that's good as sure to be the route these redskins have taken. For now, I think of it, the path was a big, broad road, and must have been much travelled by Indians of some kind or other. So, *muchachos ;* we can't do better than keep on to where it parts from the water's edge. Possibly on the *traveria*, which chances to be a *salitral* as well, we may find the ground clear of this detestable stuff, and once more hit off the *rastro* of these murderous robbers."

His young companions, altogether guided by his counsels, of course offer no objection ; and off they again go up the bank of the broad deep river.

Nor less swiftly do they speed, but fast as ever. For they are not impeded by the necessity of constantly keeping their eyes upon the earth, to see if there be hoofmarks on it. There are none; or if any, they are not distinguishable through the thick stratum of slime spread over all the surface. But although going at a gallop, they do not get over much ground ; being every now and then compelled to pull up—meeting obstructions they had not reckoned upon. These in the shape of numerous little streamlets, flowing into the river, most of them still in freshet from the late rain. One after another they ford them, none being so deep as to call for swimming. But they at length come upon one of greater depth and breadth than any yet passed, and with banks of such a character as to bring them to a dead stop, with the necessity of considering whether it can be crossed at all. For it is a watercourse of the special kind called *riachos*, resembling the *bayous* of Louisiana, whose sluggish currents run in either direction, according to the season of the year, whether it be flood-time or during the intervals of drought.

At a glance, Gaspar perceives that the one now barring their onward progress is too deep to be waded ; and if it be possible to pass over it, this must be by swimming. Little would they regard that, nor any more would their animals ; since the pampas horse can swim like an otter, or *capivara*. But, unfortunately, this particular *riacho* is of a kind which forbids even their swimming it ; as almost at the same glance, the gaucho observes, with a grunt expressing his discontent. On the stream's further shore, the bank, instead of being on a level with the water surface, or gently shelving away from it, rises abruptly to a height of nigh six feet, with no break, far as can be seen, either upward or downward. Any attempt to swim a horse to the other side, would result in his being penned up, as within the lockgates of a canal!

It is plainly impossible for them to cross over there; and, without waiting to reflect further, the gaucho so pronounces it; saying to the others, who have remained silently watching him :—

"Well, we've got over a good many streams in our morning's ride, but this one beats us. We can't set foot on the other side—not here, at all events."

"Why?" demands Cypriano.

"Because, as you can see, *señorito*, that water's too deep for wading."

"But what of that? We can swim it, can't we?"

"True, we could; all that and more, so far as the swimming goes. But once in there, how are we to get out again? Look at yonder bank. Straight up as a wall, and so smooth a cat couldn't climb it, much less our horses; and no more ourselves. If 'twere a matter of wading we might; but, as I can see, all along yonder edge it's just as deep as in mid-stream; and failing to get out, we'd have to keep on plunging about, possibly in the end to go under. *Carramba!* we mustn't attempt to make a crossing here."

"Where then?" demands Cypriano, in torture at this fresh delay, which may last he knows not how long.

"Well," rejoins the gaucho, reflectingly, "I think I know of a place where we may manage it. There's a ford which can't be very far from this; but whether it's above or below, for the life of me I can't tell, everything's so changed by

that detestable *tormenta*, and the ugly coat of plaster it has
laid over the plain! Let me see," he adds, alternately
turning his eyes up stream and down, " I fancy it must be
above ; and now I recollect there was a tall tree, a *quebracha*,
not far from the ford. Ha !" he exclaims, suddenly catching sight of it, " there's the bit of timber itself ! I can tell
it by that broken branch on the left side. You see that,
don't you, *hijos mios ?* "

They do see the top of a solitary tree with one branch
broken off, rising above the plain at about two miles'
distance ; and they can tell it to be the well-known species
called *quebracha*—an abbreviation of *quebrahacha*, or " axe-
breaker," so named from the hardness of its wood.

" Whether it be by wading or swimming," Gaspar remarks
in continuance, "we'll get over the *riacho* up yonder, not
far from that tree. So, let's on to it, *señoritos !* "

Without another word, they all wheel their horses about,
and move off in the direction of the *quebracha*.

CHAPTER XXXIII.

As they make towards the tree, which has erst served others than themselves as a guide to the crossing-place, the nature of the ground hinders their going at great speed. Being soft and somewhat boggy, they are compelled to creep slowly and cautiously over it.

But at length they get upon a sort of ridge slightly elevated above the general level, though still unsafe for fast travelling. Along this, however, they can ride abreast, and without fear of breaking through.

As they proceed onward, Gaspar gives them some further information about the ford they are making for.

" We can easily wade it," he says, " if this awkward and ill-timed dust-storm hasn't changed it, as everything else. When poor dear master and I went across—that would be about six months ago—the water wasn't quite up to our stirrups ; but, like as not, last night's downpour has raised it too, and we'll have a swim for it. Well, that won't matter much. There, at all events, we can get the horses out ; as the bank slopes off gently. So there'll be no fear of our being stuck or sent floundering in the stream. A regular Indian road, crosses the *riacho* there, and has worn a rut running down to the channel on both sides."

His hearers are pleased at this intelligence ; Cypriano signifying so by the laconic rejoinder—

"*Esta bueno.*"

Then follows an interval of silence ; after which Gaspar, as if some new thought had occurred to him, suddenly exclaims—

"*Santos Dios !* I'd forgotten that."

"Forgotten what ? " both inquire, with a surprised, but not apprehensive look ; for the gaucho's words were not in this tone.

"Something," he answers, "which we ought to find at this very crossing place. A bit of good luck it's being here."

" And what do you expect from it ? " questions Cypriano.

" I expect to learn whether we're still on the right track, or have strayed away from it. We've been going by guess-work long enough ; but, if I don't greatly mistake we'll there see something to tell us whether our guesses have been good or bad. If the redskins have come up the river at all, it's pretty sure they also have crossed the *riacho* at this very ford, and we should there see some traces of them. Sure to find them on the sloping banks, as we did by the *arroyo.* That will count a score in our favour."

By the time he has ceased speaking, they have reached the *quebracha ;* and, soon as under its shadow, Gaspar again reins up, telling the others to do the same. It is not that he has any business with the beacon tree, as with that which served them for a barometer ; but simply, because they are once more within sight of the stream—out of view since they left its bank below. The ford is also before their eyes, visible over the tops of some low bordering bushes.

But what has now brought the gaucho to a stop is neither the stream, nor its crossing place ; but a flock of large birds wading about in the water, at the point where he knows the ford to be. Long-legged creatures they are, standing as on stilts, and full five feet high, snow-white in colour, all but their huge beaks, which are jet black, with a band of naked skin around their necks, and a sort of pouch like a pelican's, this being of a bright scarlet. For they are *garzones soldados*, or "soldier-cranes," so called from their red throats bearing a fancied resemblance to the facings on the collar of a soldier's coat, in the uniform of the Argentine States.

"*Bueno !*" is the pleased exclamation which proceeds from the gaucho's lips, as he sits contemplating the cranes. "We sha'n't have any swimming to do here ; the rain don't seem to have deepened the ford so much as a single inch. You see those long-legged gentry ; it barely wets their feet. So much the better, since it ensures us against getting our own wetted, with our baggage to the boot. Stay !" he adds, speaking as if from some sudden resolve, "let's watch the birds a bit. I've a reason."

Thus cautioned, the others hold their horses at rest, all with their eyes fixed upon the soldier-cranes ; which still unconscious of intruders in such close proximity, continue the occupation in which they were engaged when first seen —that of fishing.

Every now and then one darts its long bayonet-like beak into the water, invariably drawing it out with a fish between the mandibles ; this, after a short convulsive struggle, and a flutter or two of its tail fins, disappearing down the crane's capacious throat.

"Having their breakfast," observes the gaucho, "or, I should rather call it dinner," he adds, with a glance upward to the sky. "And the height of that sun reminds me of its being high time for us to do something in the same line, if I hadn't been already reminded of it by a hollow I feel here." He places his spread palm over the pit of his stomach, and then continues, "So we may as well dine now; though, sad to say, we haven't a morsel to make a meal upon but that juiceless *charqui*. *Santissima!* what am I thinking about? I verily believe my brains have got bemuddled, like everything else. Nothing but *charqui*, indeed! Ha! we'll dine more daintily, if I know what's what. Here, *señoritos!* back your horses behind those bushes. Quick, gently."

While speaking, he turns his own out of the path, and rides crouchingly to the rear of the bushes indicated, thus putting a screen between himself and the soldier-cranes.

Following his example, the others do likewise, but without the slightest idea of what he is going to be after next.

Cypriano inquiring, receives the very unsatisfactory answer—

" You'll see."

And they do see ; first himself dismounting and tying his bridle to a branch ; then detaching his lazo from its ring in the saddle-tree, and carefully adjusting its coils over his left arm. This done, he separates from them, as he walks away, speaking back in a whisper :—

" Keep your ground, young masters, till I return to you, and if you can help it, don't let the horses make any noise, or budge an inch. For yourselves, *silencio !*"

As they promise all this, he parts from them, and is soon out of sight; their last glance showing him to be making for the ford, going with bent body and crouched gait, as cat or cougar stealing upon its prey.

For some ten minutes or so, they neither see nor hear

more o him; and can only conjecture that the design he has so suddenly conceived, has something to do with the *garzones.* So believing, curiosity prompts them to have another peep at these piscatory birds; which by standing up in their stirrups—for they are still seated in the saddle—they can. Looking over the tops of the bushes, they see that the cranes continue fishing undisturbed, and seemingly unaware of an enemy being near, or that danger threatens them.

But not much longer are they left to enjoy this feeling of security. While the two youths are still regarding them, first one, then another, is observed to elevate its head to the full height of its long slender neck; while here and there throughout the flock are heard cries of warning or alarm; the frightened ones letting fall the fish already in their beaks, while those not quite so much scared, suddenly swallow them. But in another instant, all, as if by one impulse, give out a simultaneous scream; then, rising together, spread their broad, sail-like wings, and go flapping away.

No, not all. One stays in the *riacho;* no longer to look after fish, but with both wings outspread over the surface of the stream, beating the water into froth—as it does so, all the while drawing nearer and nearer to the nether bank! But its movements are convulsive and involuntary, as can be told by something seen around its neck resembling a rope. And a rope it is; the youths knowing it to be the *lazo* they late saw coiled over Gaspar's arm, knowing also that he is at the other end of it. He is hauling it in, hand over hand, till the captured bird, passing under the high bank, disappears from their view.

Soon, however, to reappear; but now carried under the gaucho's arm.

He cries out as he approaches them :—

" *Viva! muchachitos !* Give me congratulation, as I intend giving you a good dinner. If we can call *charqui* flesh, as I suppose we must, then we shall have fish, flesh, and fowl, all the three courses. So we'll dine sumptuously, after all."

Saying which, he draws out his knife, and cuts open the crane's crop, exposing to view several goodly-sized fish, fresh as if just cleared from a draw-net ! They are of various sorts ; the riverine waters of South America being noted for their wonderful multiplicity of both genera and species. The Amazon and its tributaries, are supposed to contain at least three thousand distinct species ; a fact upon which the American naturalist, Agassiz—somewhat of an empiric, by the way—has founded a portion of his spurious fame, on the pretence of being its discoverer. It was pointed out by a real naturalist, Alfred Wallace, ten years before Agassiz ever set eyes on the Amazon ; and its record will be found in the appendix to Wallace's most interesting work relating to this, the grandest of rivers.

In the La Plata, and its confluent streams, are also many genera and species ; a question that gives Gaspar not the slightest concern, while contemplating those he has just made the *garzon* disgorge. Instead, he but thinks of putting them to the broil. So, in ten minutes after they are frizzling over a fire ; in twenty more, to be stowed away in other stomachs than that of the soldier-crane.

CHAPTER XXXIV.

ATTACKED BY GYMNOTI.

GASPAR'S promise to give them a dinner of the three orthodox courses—fish, flesh, and fowl—was only meant in a jocular sense. For the flesh, their stock of *charqui* is not drawn upon; and as to fowl, the soldier-crane would be a still more unpalatable morsel. So it results in their dining simply upon fish; this not only without sauce, but swallowed at second-hand!

While they are occupied in the eating it, the gaucho, seeming more cheerful than usual, says :—

"I've a bit of good news for you, *hijos mios.*"

"Indeed! what?" is their eager inquiry.

"That we are still upon the right road. The redskins have gone past here, as I supposed they would."

"You've discovered fresh traces of them, then?"

"I have; ever so many scratches of their horses' feet, where they slipped in stepping down to the stream. Quite plain they are; I could distinguish them some way off, and with half an eye, as I was hauling in the *soldado*. Good news, I call it; since we won't have to take the back track anyhow. What's before us remains to be seen. Possibly, on the other side we may light on something else, to tell the direction they've taken. So, we'd better lose no time, but cross over."

Hurriedly finishing their primitive repast, they spring back upon their *recados*, and ride down to the ford.

Once in the water, they find it not quite so shallow, as they had supposed from seeing the *garzones* wading about with but the slightest portion of their shanks below the surface.   For at the bottom is a substratum of mud ; a soft slimy ooze, firm enough to support the light birds, but through which the heavier quadrupeds, further weighted with themselves and their baggage, sink to their bellies.

Gaspar is surprised at finding the ford in this condition. It was not so when he passed over it before, and he can only account for the change by the dust from the *tormenta* having been blown in large quantities into the stream, then carried down by the current, and settling over the shallow crossing place.

Whatever the cause, they find it awkward work to wade through the sticky slime.   Still, they might have accomplished the crossing without accident, and doubtless would have done so, but for an impediment of another kind—one not only altogether unexpected, but far more to be dreaded than any danger of their going head and ears over into the ooze.   For just as they have reached mid-stream, and are splashing and floundering on, Gaspar, who is riding ahead, and shouting back directions to the others, all at once finds his attention fully occupied in looking to himself, or rather to his horse.   For the animal has come to a stop, suddenly and without any restraint of the rein, and stands uttering strange snorts, while quivering throughout every fibre of its frame !

Glancing over his shoulder, the gaucho sees that the other horses have also halted, and are behaving in a precisely similar manner, their riders giving utterance to excited exclamations. Ludwig looks a picture of astonishment; while, strange to say, on Cypriano's countenance the expression is more one of alarm! And the same on the face of the gaucho himself; for he, as the young Paraguayan comprehends the situation, and well knows what has brought their horses so abruptly to a halt.

"What is it, Gaspar?" questions Ludwig, now also alarmed at seeing the others so.

"Eels!" ejaculates the gaucho.

"Eels! Surely you're jesting?" queries the incredulous youth.

"No, indeed," is the hurried rejoinder. "I only wish it were a jest. It's not, but a dire, dangerous earnest. *Santissima!*" he cries out, in addition, as a shock like that of a galvanic battery causes him to shake in his saddle, "that's a *lightning eel*, for sure! They're all round us, in scores, hundreds, thousands! Spur your horses! Force them forward, anyway! On out of the water! A moment wasted, and we're lost!"

While speaking, he digs the spurs into his own animal, with his voice also urging it onward; they doing the same.

But spur and shout as they may, the terrified quadrupeds can scarce be got to stir from the spot where first attacked by the electric eels. For it is by these they are assailed, though Gaspar has given them a slightly different name.

And just as he has said, the slippery creatures seem to be all around them, coiling about the horses' legs, brushing against their bellies, at intervals using the powerful, though invisible, weapon with which Nature has provided them; while the scared quadrupeds, instead of dashing onward to get clear of the danger, only pitch and plunge about, at intervals standing at rest, as if benumbed, or shaking as though struck by palsy—all three of them, breathing hard and loud, the smoke issuing from their nostrils, with froth which falls in flakes, whitening the water below.

Their riders are not much less alarmed: they too sensibly feeling themselves affected by the magnetic influence. For the subtle current passing through the bodies of their horses, in like manner, and almost simultaneously enters their own. All now aware that they are in real danger, are using their utmost efforts to get out of it by spurring, shouting to their animals, and beating them with whatever they can lay their hands on.

It is a desperate strife, a contest between them and the quadrupeds, as they strive to force the latter forward, and from out of the perilous place. Fortunately, it does not last long, or the end would be fatal. After a short time, two of the three succeeded in reaching the bank: these Gaspar and Cypriano; the gaucho, as he feels himself on firm ground, crying out :—

"Thank the Lord for our deliverance!"

But scarce has the thanksgiving passed his lips, when, turning face towards the stream, he sees what brings the pallor back into his cheeks, and a trembling throughout his frame, as if he were still under the battery of the electric eels. Ludwig, lagging behind, from being less able to manage his mount, is yet several yards from the shore, and what is worse, not drawing any nearer to it. Instead, his horse seems stuck fast in the mud, and is making no effort to advance; but totters on his limbs as though about to lose them! And the youth appears to have lost all control not only of the animal but himself; all energy to act, sitting lollingly in his saddle, as if torpid, or half-asleep!

At a glance Gaspar perceives his danger, knowing it of no

common kind. Both horse and rider are as powerless to leave that spot, as if held upon it in the loop ot a *lazo*, with its other end clutched in the hands of a giant.

But a *lazo* may also release them; and at this thought occurring to him opportunely, the gaucho plucks his own from the horn of his *recado*, and with a wind or two around his head, casts its running noose over that of the imperilled youth. It drops down over his shoulders, settling around both his arms, and tightening upon them, as Gaspar, with a half wheel of his horse, starts off up the sloping acclivity. In another instant, Ludwig is jerked clean out of his saddle, and falls with a splash upon the water. Not to sink below its surface, however; but be drawn lightly along it, till he is hoisted high, though not dry, upon the bank.

But the gaucho's work is still unfinished; the horse has yet to be rescued from his dangerous situation; a task, even more difficult than releasing his rider. For all, it is not beyond the skill of Gaspar, nor the strength of his own animal. Hastily unloosing his long, plaited rope from the body of the boy, and readjusting the loop, he again flings it forth; this time aiming to take in, not the head of Ludwig's horse, but the pommel and cantle of his high-back saddle. And just as aimed, so the noose is seen to fall, embracing both. For Gaspar knows how to cast a lasso, and his horse how to act when it is cast; the well-trained animal, soon as he sees the uplifted arm go down again, sheering round without any guidance of rein, and galloping off in the opposite direction.

In the present case, his strength proves sufficient for the demand made upon it, though this is great; and the debilitated animal in the water, which can do nought to help itself, is dragged to the dry land nearly as much dead as alive.

But all are saved, horses as well as riders.   The unseen, but dangerous, monsters are deprived of the prey they had come so near making capture of; and Gaspar again, even more fervently than before, cries out in gratitude,—

"Thank the Lord for our deliverance!"

CHAPTER XXXV.

AN attack by electric eels, however ludicrous the thing may seem, is not so looked upon by those whose ill luck it has been to experience it. That these slippery creatures possess a most dangerous power, and know how to exert it, there is ample evidence in the accounts given of them by many a truthful traveller.

More than enough of it have had our heroes; for while escaping with their lives, they have not got off altogether scatheless — neither themselves, nor their horses. For, though now beyond reach of their mysterious assailants, the latter stand cowering and quivering, evidently disabled for that day, at least. To continue the journey upon them, while they are in this condition, is plainly impossible. But their riders do not think of it; they, too, feeling enfeebled —Ludwig actually ill. For the electricity still affects them all, and it may be some time before their veins will be freed from its influence.

Nolens volens, for a time they must stay where they are, however they may chafe at this fresh halt—as before, a forced one. But the gaucho, with spirits ever buoyant, puts the best face upon it, saying,

"After all, we won't lose so much time. By this, our

horses would have been pretty well done up, anyhow, after such a hard day's work, floundering through so much mud and crossing so many streams. Even without this little bit of a bother, we'd have had to stop soon somewhere to rest them. And what better place than here? Besides, as you see, the sun's wearing well down, and it's only a question of three or four hours at most. We can make that up by an earlier start, and a big day's journey, to-morrow; when it's to be hoped we'll meet with no such obstructions as have beset us to-day."

Gaspar is not using arguments; for no one wishes to dispute with him. Only speaking words of comfort; more especially addressing them to Cypriano, who is, as ever, the impatient one. But he, as the gaucho himself, sees the impossibility of proceeding further, till they and their animals have had a spell of rest.

For the purpose of obtaining this, they go in search of a suitable camping-place; which they soon find within a grove of *algarobias*, at some three or four hundred yards' distance from the ford. The trees cover the sides of a little mound, or hillock; none growing upon its summit, which is a grassy glade. And as the dust has either not settled on it, or been washed off by the rain, the herbage is clean and green, so too the foliage of the trees overshadowing it.

" The very place for a comfortable camp," says Gaspar, after inspecting it—the others agreeing with him to the echo.

Having returned to the ford for their horses, and led them up to the chosen ground, they are proceeding to strip the animals of their respective caparisons, when, lo! the *alparejas*, and other things, which were attached to the croup of Ludwig's saddle, and should still be on it, are not there ! All are gone—shaken off, no doubt, while the animal was plunging about in the stream—and with as little uncertainty now lying amidst the mud at its bottom.

As in these very saddle-bags was carried their commissariat—*yerba*, *charqui*, maize bread, onions, and everything, and as over the cantle-peak hung their kettle, skillet, *matés*, and *bombillas*, the loss is a lamentable one ; in short, leaving them without a morsel to eat, or a vessel to cook with, had they comestibles ever so abundant !

At first they talk of going back to the ford, and making search for the lost chattels. But it ends only in talk ; they have had enough of that crossing place, so dangerously beset by those *demonios*, as Gaspar in his anger dubs the electric eels. For though his courage is as that of a lion, he does not desire to make further acquaintance with the mysterious monsters. Besides, there is no knowing in what particular spot the things were dropped; this also deterring them from any attempt to enter upon a search. The stream at its crossing place is quite a hundred yards in width, and by this time the articles of metal, as the heavily-weighted saddle-bags, will have settled down below the surface, perhaps trampled into its slimy bed by the horse himself in his convulsive struggles. To seek them now would be like looking for a needle in a stack of straw. So the idea is abandoned ; and for this night they must resign themselves to going supperless.

Fortunately, none of the three feels a-hungered; their dinner being as yet undigested. Besides, Gaspar is not without hope that something may turn up to reprovision them, ere the sun goes down. Just possible, the soldier-cranes may come back to the ford, and their fishing, so that another, with full crop, may fall within the loop of his *lazo*.

Having kindled a fire—not for cooking purposes, but to dry their ponchos, and other apparel saturated in the crossing of the stream—they first spread everything out ; hanging them on improvised clothes-horses, constructed of *caña brava*—a brake of which skirts the adjacent stream. Then, overcome with fatigue, and still suffering from the effects of the animal electricity, they stretch themselves alongside the fire, trusting to time for their recovery.

Nor trust they in vain. For, sooner than expected, the volatile fluid—or whatever it may be—passes out of their veins, and their nervous strength returns ; even Ludwig saying he is himself again, though he is not quite so yet.

And their animals also undergo a like rapid recovery, from browsing on the leaves and bean-pods of the *algarobias ;* a provender relished by all pampas horses, as horned cattle, and nourishing to both.   More than this, the fruit of this valuable tree when ripe, is fit food for man himself, and so used in several of the Argentine States.

This fact suggesting itself to Gaspar—as he lies watching the horses plucking off the long siliques, and greedily devouring them—he says :—

" We can make a meal on the *algarobia* beans, if nothing better's to be had.   And for me, it wouldn't be the first time by scores.   In some parts where I've travelled, they grind them like maize, and bake a very fair sort of bread out of their meal."

" Why, Gaspar ! " exclaims Ludwig, recalling some facts of which he had heard his father speak, " you talk as if you had travelled in the Holy Land, and in New Testament times !   These very trees, or others of a similar genus, are the ones whose fruit was eaten by St. John the Baptist You remember that passage, where it is said : ' his meat was locusts and wild honey.' Some think the locusts he ate were the inserts of that name; and it may be so, since they are also eaten by Arabs, and certain other tribes of Asiatic and African people. But, for my part, I believe the beans of the 'locust tree' are meant; which, like this, is a species of acacia that the Arabs call *carob;* evidently the root from which we take our word *algarobia.*"

Gaspar listens, both patiently and pleased, to this learned dissertation. For he is rejoiced to perceive, that the thoughts of his young companion are beginning to find some abstraction and forgetfulness, of that upon which they have been so long sadly dwelling. Cypriano, too, appears to take an interest in the subject of discourse; and to encourage it the gaucho rejoins, in gleeful tones :

"Well, Señor Ludwig; I don't know much about those far-away countries you speak of, for I've not had any great deal of schooling. But I do know, that *algarobia* beans are not such bad eating; that is if properly prepared for it. In the States of Santiago and Tucuman, which are the places I spoke of having travelled through, the people almost live on them; rich and poor, man as well as beast. And we may be glad to make breakfast on them, if not supper; though I still trust something more dainty may drop upon us. I'm not so hopeful as to expect manna, like that which rained down upon Moses; but there's many an eatable thing to be had in this Chaco wilderness, too—for those who know how to look for it. *Ay Dios !*" he adds, after a pause, with his eyes turned towards the ford, "those long-legged gentry don't seem to care about coming back there. No doubt, the screams of that fellow I throttled have frightened them off for good. So I suppose we must give the birds up, for this night anyhow. Just possible, in the morning they'll be as hungry as ourselves, and pay their fishing-ground a very early visit."

Saying this, the gaucho relapses into silence, the others also ceasing to converse. They all feel a certain lethargy, which calls for repose ; and for a while all three lie without speaking a word, their heads resting on their *recados*—the only sound heard being the " crump-crump " of their horses' teeth grinding the *algarobia* pods into pulp.

CHAPTER XXXVI.

A CHAT ABOUT ELECTRIC EELS.

THE silence of the camp is not of long continuance; Gaspar being the first to break it. For the gaucho, having a stronger stomach, and consequently a quicker digestion than the others, feels some incipient sensations of hunger.

" I only wish," he says, " we could get hold of one of the brutes that battered us so in the stream. If we could, it would furnish us with a supper fit for a king."

" What !" exclaims Ludwig, raising his head in surprise, " one of the electric eels? Is it that you're speaking of, Gaspar ? "

" Aye, *señorito ;* just that."

" Surely you wouldn't eat *it,* would you ? "

" Wouldn't I ? If I had one here now, you'd soon see."

" But are they really good to eat ? "

" Good to eat ! I should think they are ; and if you could but taste them yourself, *señorito*, you'd say so. A lightning eel's about the daintiest morsel I ever stuck teeth into ; though they do have their dwelling place in mud, and as some say, feed upon it. Before cooking them, however, something needs being done. You must cut away a portion of their flesh ; the spongy part, which it's said gives them power to make their lightning play. In that lies the dangerous stuff, whatever sort of thing it is."

"But what are they like, Gaspar? I've never seen one."

It is Ludwig who still interrogates; but to his last question Cypriano, not Gaspar, gives the answer, saying:

"Oh, cousin! Do you mean to say you've never seen an electric eel?"

"Indeed do I. I've heard father speak of them often, and I know them by their scientific name, *gymnotus.* I believe there are plenty of them in the rivers of Paraguay; but, as it chances, I never came across one, either dead or alive."

"I have," says Cypriano, "come across more than one, and many times. But once I well remember; for an awkward circumstance it was to myself."

"How so, *sobrino ?* "

"Ah! that's a tale I never told you, Ludwig; but I'll tell it now, if you wish."

"Oh! I do wish it."

"Well, near the little village where, as you know, I was born, and went to school before coming to live with uncle at Assuncion, there was a pond full of these fish. We boys used to amuse ourselves with them; sending in dogs and pigs, whenever we had the chance, to see the scare they would get, and how they scampered out soon as they found what queer company they'd got into. Cruel sport it was, I admit. But one day we did what was even worse than frightening either dogs or pigs; we drove an old cow in, with a long rope round her horns, the two ends of which we fastened to trees on the opposite sides of the pond, so that she had only a little bit of slack to dance about upon. And dance about she did, as the eels electrified her on every side ; till at last she dropped down exhausted, and, I suppose, dead ; since she went right under the water, and didn't come up again. I shall never forget her pitiful, aye, reproachful look, as she stood up to the neck, with her head craned out, as if making an appeal to us to save her, while we only laughed the louder. Poor thing ! I can now better understand the torture she must have endured."

"But is that the awkward circumstance you've spoken of?"

"Oh, no. *It* was altogether another affair ; and for me, as all the others, a more serious one. I hadn't come to the end of the adventure—the unpleasant part of it—which was the chastisement we all got, by way of reward for our wickedness."

"Chastisement ! Who gave it to you ?"

"Our worthy schoolmaster. It so chanced the old cow was his ; the only one he had at the time giving milk. And he gave us such a thrashing ! Ah ! I may well say, I've a lively recollection of it ; so lively, I might truly think the punishment then received was enough, without the additional retribution the eels have this day inflicted on me."

Cypriano's narration ended, his cousin, after a pause, again appeals to Gaspar to give him a description of the creatures forming the topic of their conversation. To which the gaucho responds, saying :—

"Well, Señor Ludwig, if you want to know what a lightning eel is like, take one of the common kind—which of course you've seen—a full-sized one ; make that about ten times as thick as it is, without adding much to its length, and you'll have the thing, near as I can think it. So much for the reptile's bulk ; though there are some both bigger round, and longer from head to tail. As for its colour, over the back it's a sort of olive green—just like *yerba* leaves when they've been let stand a day or two after plucking. On the throat, and under the belly, it's paler, with here and there some blotches of red. I may tell you, however, that the lightning eels change colour same as some of the lizards; partly according to tneir age, but as much from the sort of water they're found in—whether it be a clear running stream, or a muddy stagnant pond, such as the one Señor Cypriano has spoken of. Besides, there are several kinds of them, as we gauchos know; though, I believe, the *naturalutas* are not aware of the fact. The most dangerous sort, and no doubt the same that's just attacked us, have broad heads, and wide gaping mouths full of sharp teeth, with flat tails and a pair of fins close to the nape of the neck. *Carramba!* they're ugly devils to look at, and still uglier to have dealings with ; that is, when one's in the water alongside them—as we ourselves know. Still they don't always behave so bad, as these did to-day. When I crossed this stream before, with the *dueño*, neither he nor I felt the slightest shock to tell of eels being in it. I suppose it's the *tormenta* that's set them a stirring. Like enough, there's some connection between their lightning and that of the sky. If so, that's what has quickened the brutes, and made them so mad. Well," he adds, as if drawing his account to a conclusion, " mad as they are, I'd like to have one frizzling over this fire."

" But who eats them, Gaspar ? " interrogates Ludwig, still incredulous on the question of their being a fit article of diet. " I've never heard of their being eaten, nor brought to market like other fish."

" Hundreds, thousands of people eat them, *hijo mio.* They're in great request in some places ; aye, all over the country. Both whites and Indians relish them ; but more especially the redskins. Some tribes prefer them to any other food, be it fish, flesh, or fowl ; and make a regular business of catching them."

"Ah ! how are they caught ? "

" There are various ways ; but the usual one is by spearing them. Sometimes the slippery fellows glide out of their mud beds and come to the surface of the water, as it were to amuse themselves by having a look round. Then the fisherman gets a chance at them, without any search-ing, or trouble. He is armed with a long pole of *caña brava*, one end having an iron point barbed like a spear. This, he launches at them, just as I've heard say whalers do their harpoons. For, if he kept the shaft in his hands, he'd catch it from their lightning, and get strokes that would stagger him. Still, he doesn't let go altogether ; as there's a cord attached to the spear, and with that he can haul in the fish, if he has struck it. But he must have a care to keep his cord out of the water ; if it gets wetted he'll have a fit of the trembles upon him, sure. For it's a fact—and a curious one you'll say, *señoritos*—that a dry cord won't conduct the eel's lightning, while a wet one will."

" It *is* a fact," says Ludwig, endorsing the statement. " I've heard father speak of it."

" Very singular," observes Cypriano.

" And I can tell you of another fact," pursues the gaucho, " that you'll say is still more singular. Would you believe, that from one of these fish a man may strike sparks, just as by a flint and steel—aye, and kindle a fire with them ? I know it's an old story, about fish having what's called phosphorus in them ; but it isn't everybody who knows that real fire can be got out of the lightning eels."

"But can that be done, Gaspar?" asks Ludwig.

"Certainly it can. I've seen it done. And he who did it was your own dear father, Señor Ludwig. It was one day when we were out on a ramble, and caught one of the eels in a pool, where it had got penned up by the water having dried around it. The *dueño* took out a piece of wire, and with one end tickled the eel ; the other end being stuck into some gunpowder, which was wrapped loosely in a piece of paper. The powder flashed and set the paper ablaze, as also some leaves and dry sticks we'd laid around it. Soon we had a fire ; and on that same fire we broiled the eel itself, and ate it. *Por dios!* I only wish we had one broiling over this fire. I'd want no better thing for supper."

So ended the chat about electric eels, the subject seeming exhausted. Then the conversation changing to other and less interesting topics, was soon after brought to a close. For the darkness was now down, and as their ponchos, and other softer goods had become thoroughly dry, there was no reason why they should not go to rest for the night. But since the soldier-cranes had declined coming back—by this time no doubt roosted in some far-off " cranery "—and no other source of food supply offering, they must needs go to bed supperless, as they did. Their appetites were not yet sufficiently sharp, to have an inordinate craving for meat.

CHAPTER XXXVII.

NOTHING FOR BREAKFAST.

UNDER the shadow of the *algarobias* the trackers sleep undisturbed. Ludwig, however, has troubled dreams, in which gymnoti play a conspicuous part. He imagines himself still floundering amidst these monsters, assailed from all sides by their galvanic batteries, and that they have dragged him down into the mud, where he is fast getting asphyxiated. When in his last gasp, as it were, he is relieved, by awaking from his uneasy slumbers; which he does suddenly, and with a terrified cry.

Finding it has been all a dream, and glad to think it so, he says nothing; and the others not having heard his half-stifled cry, soon again falls asleep. This time his slumber is lighter, as also more profound; and, on the whole, he has a tolerable night's rest; in the morning feeling fairly refreshed, as likewise do Cypriano and Gaspar.

All three are astir a good half-hour before there is any sign of day; and their camp fire is rekindled. This not for culinary purposes—since they have nothing to be cooked— but rather because the air is chilly cold, as it often is in the tropics, and they need to warm themselves before setting about aught else.

When warmed, however, they begin to think of breakfast,

as also to talk about it. What is it to be, or of what con-
sist, are the questions which interest them without being
easily answered. There are the *algarobia* beans; but their
skillet has been lost along with the kettle, and there is left
them no utensil in which these legumes might be boiled.
True, they can roast them in the ashes; but Gaspar still
clings to the hope that something more toothful may turn up.
As the early dawn is the best time to find wild animals
abroad, both birds and quadrupeds—the best also for approaching them—the gaucho feels pretty confident either
one or other will stray within reach of their guns, bolas,
or lazos.

In the end it proves that his confidence has not been misplaced. Just as the first red rays of the Aurora are reflected
from the tops of the trees around their camp, more faintly
lighting up the lower level of the pampa beyond, Gaspar,
peering through a break between the branches of the *algarobias*, sees a brace of large birds moving about over the
plain. Not soldier-cranes, though creatures with necks and
legs quite as long; for they are *rheas*.

"*Gracios a Dios !*" is the gaucho's gratified exclamation
at sight of them; continuing in low tone and speaking over
his shoulder, "A couple of *avestruz !*"

The others, gliding up to him, and looking through the
leaves, also behold the birds, seeing them from head to foot.
For they are out upon the open ground, striding to and fro,
now and then pausing to pick up some morsel of food, or it
may be but a pebble to aid in the digestion of what they
have already eaten. While thus engaged, they are gradually
drawing nearer to the bank of the *riacho*, as also the edge
of the *algarobia* grove in which the trackers are encamped.
Their proximity to the latter most interests those in the

camp, and all three instantly lay hold of their guns, which lucikily have been reloaded, two of them with ball. Gaspar, foremost of the trio, has got his barrel through the branches, and, seeing that the *rheas* are now within bullet-range, is about to blaze away at the one nearest, which chances to be the cock bird, when the latter, suddenly elevating its head, and uttering a loud hiss succeeded by a snort, as from a badly-blown trumpet, turns tail and makes off over the plain ; its mate turning simultaneously, and legging it alongside . All this to the surprise of the gaucho ; who knows that he has not exposed his person and sees that neither have the others, nor yet made any noise to account for the behaviour of the birds.

"What can have frightened them?" is the question he would ask, when casting his eyes upward he perceives what has done it—their smoke of their camp-fire ! The blue stream ascending over the tops of the trees, as if out of a chimney, had just then, for the first time, been caught sight of by the ostriches, sending them off in quick scare. Nor strange it should, being a spectacle to which the wild denizens of the Chaco are not accustomed, or only familiar with as denoting an enemy near—their greatest enemy, man.

"*Maldita sea !*" exclaims the gaucho, as the birds show their backs to him, an exclamation morally the reverse of that he uttered on seeing them with heads turned the opposite way. "That confounded fire ! what a pity we kindled it ! the thing's done us out of our breakfast. Stay ! no."

The negative ejaculation comes from his perceiving that the ostriches, instead of rushing onwards in long rapid strides, as they had started, are gradually shortening step and slackening the pace. And while he continues looking after them, they again come to a stop, and stand gazing back at the dark blue pillar of smoke rising spirally against the lighter blue background of sky. But now they appear to regard it less with alarm than curiosity; and even this after a time wearing off, they once more lower their beaks, and return to browsing, just as a couple of common geese, or rather a goose and gander. For all, they do not yet seem quite tranquillized, every now and then their heads going up with a suddenness, which tells that their former feeling of security is not restored; instead, replaced by uneasy suspicions that things are not as they ought to be.

"Our guns will be of no use now," says Gaspar, laying his own aside. "I know the nature of *avestruz* well enough to say for certain, that, after the scare they've had they'll stay shy for several hours, and 'twill be impossible to approach them; that is, near enough for the longest-range gun we've got. And to run them down with our horses would be to lose a day's journey at least. We can't afford that, for the sake of a bit of breakfast. No, 'twould never do. We'll have to go without, or else, after all, break our fast upon these beans."

Saying which, he glances up to the *algarobias*, from which the long siliques droop down in profusion, more plentiful than tempting to him.

"*Caspita!*" he resumes, after a pause, once more bending his eyes covetously upon the birds, and as if an idea had suddenly occurred to him, "I think I know of a way by which we may circumvent these two tall stalkers."

"How?" eagerly asks Cypriano.

"By going at them—*garzoneando.*"

"*Garzoneando!*" exclaims Ludwig in echo. "Good Gaspar, whatever do you mean by that?"

"You'll see, young master, soon as I've made things

ready for it. And your cousin here, he's the fittest for the part to be played. I'd undertake it myself, but I'm a bit too bulky to counterfeit a creature of such slender proportions as the *garzon soldado;* while Señor Cypriano's figure will just suit to a nicety.

Neither of the two youths has the slightest idea of what the gaucho designs doing ; but, accustomed to his quaint, queer ways, and knowing that whatever he intends is pretty sure to be something of service to them—as likely to have a successful issue—they await his action with patience and in silence.

CHAPTER XXXVIII.

GASPAR allows no time to be lost, but instantly commences taking measures for the *garzoneando*—whatever that may be. As yet neither of his young companions has been told what it is, though they soon begin to have a guess.

While they stand watching, they see him once more plunge his hand into those capacious saddle-bags, where for a time it rummages about. When drawn out again, it is seen to grasp a folded bundle of soft goods, which, on being shaken open, shows to be a shirt. No common cotton thing, however, but an affair of the finest linen, snow white, with an embroidered bosom and ruffles; in short, his gala shirt, such as are worn by gauchos when they appear at *fiestas* and *fandangoes*.

"A pity to use my best *camisa* for such a purpose," he observes, while in the act of unfolding it. "Still it won't likely get much damage; and a wash, with a bit of starch, will set it all right again."

Then turning to Cypriano, he adds, "Now, señorito; be good enough to strip off everything, and draw this over your shoulders."

Without a word of protest, or objection, the young Paraguayan does as requested, and is soon inside the holiday shirt; his own having been laid aside, as also his *jaqueta*, *calzoneras*, and every other article of dress worn by him.

Meanwhile, Gaspar has been engaged getting ready several other things for the change of costume intended; one of these being a silk handkerchief of a bright scarlet colour, also taken out of the inexhaustible *alparejas*. This he ties about Cyprian's neck, not as an ordinary cravat, but loosely folded, so as to expose a breadth of several inches all round.

The gaucho's next move is to snatch from off the fire one of the faggots still only half consumed; from which with his knife he scrapes the red coal, leaving the surface black, at the same time paring the stick to a sharp point. With some wet gunpowder he further blackens it; then placing the thick end against Cypriano's forehead, he binds it fast with a piece of raw hide thong, the last carried around and firmly knotted at the back of the neck.

A few more touches and the toilet is complete; transforming Cypriano into what, at a distance, might be supposed a soldier-crane! At all events, the ostriches will so suppose him, as Gaspar knows; for he is but copying a scheme often practised by South American Indians for the capture of these shy birds.

"*Muy bien!*" he exclaims, as he stands contemplating his finished task. "By my word, *muchacho mio*, you look the character to perfection. And if you act it cleverly, as I know you can and will, we'll make breakfast on something better than beans. Now, señorito; you're in costume to go *garzoneando.*"

Long ere this, Cypriano has come to comprehend what is required of him, and is quite eager to have a try at the ruse so cunningly contrived. Declaring himself ready to start out, it but remains to be decided what weapon he ought to take with him. For they have the three kinds—gun, *bolas*, and *lazo;* and in the use of the two last he is almost as skilled as the gaucho himself.

"The gun might be the readiest and surest," remarks Gaspar; "and it will be as well to have one with you, in case of your not getting a good chance to cast either of the others. But just now the less noise that's made the better. Who knows, but that some of these traitorous redskins may be still straggling about? Hearing shots they'd be sure to come up to us; which we don't want, though ever so much wishing to come up with them. Therefore, I say, use either the balls or the rope."

"All the same to me," observes the young Paraguayan. "Which do you think the better?"

"The *bolas*, decidedly. I've known the *lazo* slip over an ostrich's head, after the noose had been round its neck. But once the cord of the *bolas* gets a turn round the creature's shanks, it'll go to grass without making another stride. Take this set of mine. As you see, they're best *boliadores*, and you can throw them with surer aim."

The weapon which the gaucho hands to him differs from the ordinary *bolas*, in having a longer stretch of cord between the balls; but Cypriano is himself as well acquainted with this kind as with the other, and can cast them as skilfully.

Taking hold of the weapon, along with his double-barrelled gun, and concealing both as he best can under the gaucho's shirt, he starts off upon the stalk; for he now knows what he has to do, without any further instruction from Gaspar. It is simply a question of getting near enough to one of the birds to make capture of it with the *boliadores;*

or, failing this, bring it down with a bullet—one barrel of his gun being loaded with ball.

As he goes off, Gaspar and Ludwig looking after him can see that his chances of success are good. For by this the *rheas* have pretty well recovered from their scare, and are again tranquilly striding about. Moreover, they have moved somewhat nearer to the bank of the *riacho*, where a bordering of leafy evergreens offers to the stalker cover of the best kind. Taking advantage of it, he, in the guise of a *garzon*, steps briskly on, and steals in among the bushes. There he is for a time unseen, either by those watching him from the summit of the knoll, or the creatures being stalked. The latter have already noticed the counterfeit, but without showing any signs of fear; no doubt supposing it to be what it pretends—a bird as themselves, with neck and legs as long as their own. But no enemy; for often have they passed over that same plain, and fed in a friendly way alongside soldier-cranes—scores of them. Even when this solitary specimen again appears by the skirting of the scrub within less than twenty paces of them, they do not seem at all alarmed, though possibly a little surprised at its being there all alone.

Nor do they make any attempt to stir from the spot, till a movement on the part of the *garzon*, with some gestures that seem odd to them, excite their suspicions afresh; then raising their heads, and craning out their long necks, they regard it with wondering glances. Only for an instant; when seeming at last to apprehend danger, the birds utter a hiss, as if about to beat a retreat.

For one of them it is too late, the cock, which chances to be nearest the bushes, and who before he can lift a leg feels both embraced by something which lashes them tightly together ; while at the same time something else hits him a hard heavy blow, bowling him over upon the grass, where he lies stunned and senseless.

"*Bueno! Bravo!*" simultaneously shout Gaspar and Ludwig, the two together rushing down from the hillock, and on for the prostrate *rhea ;* while the counterfeit crane comes forth from the bushes to meet them, as he draws near, saying :—

"I could have shot the hen, but for what you said, Gaspar, about making a noise."

"No matter for the hen," rejoins the gaucho. "We don't want her just now. This beauty will not only give us enough meat for breakfast, but provide dinners and suppers for at least a couple of days to come."

So saying, he draws his knife across the *rhea's* throat, to make sure before releasing its legs from the thong. After which the *boliadores* are detached ; and the huge carcase, almost as heavy as that of a fatted calf, is carried in triumph to the camp.

CHAPTER XXXIX.

Soon after the trio of trackers have re-entered the *algarobia* grove, a frizzling, sputtering noise is heard therein; while an appetising odour spreads all around, borne afar on the balmy breeze of the morning. Both the sound and the smell proceed from some choice tit-bits which Gaspar has taken from the body of the great bird—chiefly slices from the thigh bone and breast.

By the time Cypriano has doffed the masquerading dress, and resumed his proper travelling costume, the cooking is done, and breakfast declared ready.

While eating it, by way of accompaniment they naturally converse about the bird. Not the particular one which exclusively forms their repast, but of ostriches in general, and more especially those of South America commonly called *rheas;* though to the gauchos better known by the name *avestruz.*

Both the boys are pretty well acquainted with these birds and their habits; Cypriano having several times taken part in their chase; while Ludwig best knows them in a scientific sense. Still there are many of their ways, and strange ones, of which neither one nor the other has ever heard, but that Gaspar has been witness to with his own eyes. It is the gaucho, therefore, who imparts most of the information, the others being little more than listeners.

" Though the thing isn't generally known," he says, " there are several distinct kinds of *avestruz* in different parts of the country. Of myself I've seen three. First, a very small sort, not much bigger than a turkey cock. It's darker coloured than the kind we're eating, with shorter legs and feathered further down. It don't lay so many eggs either; but, strange to say, they are almost as big as those of the other sort, only differently shaped, and with a tinge of blue on the shell. It I saw when I once went on an expedition with the Buenos Ayres army down south to the plains of Patagonia. There the climate is much colder than up here, and the *avestruz petise,* as the bird's called, seems to like that best; since it's never seen on the warm pampas farther north. On the other hand, the sort we have here, which is the biggest of all, never strays down to these very cold districts, but goes all over the *Chaco* country, where it's hottest. The third kind I've seen is in bulk about midways between the two; but it's a very rare bird, and I believe not known to the learned *naturalistas.* Isn't that so, Señor Ludwig ? "

" Indeed, yes. I never heard of a third species, though father has told me of the *avestruz petise ;* which, as you say, is only found far south, ranging from the Rio Negro to the Straits of Magellan."

" Well," continues Gaspar, resuming his account, " I'm sure of there being there sorts; though I don't know much about the other two, only this we've met here. Of them I ought to know a good deal, having hunted them as often as there are days in the year. One thing there's been no end of disputation about; and that is whether several hens lay

their eggs in the same nest. Now, I can say for certain
they do. I've seen several go to the same nest, one after
the other, and on the same day too. What should take
them there if not to lay their eggs? True, they drop them
about everywhere, in a very loose, careless way; as can be
told by their being seen scattered all over the *campo*, and
far from any nest. What this is for I cannot myself tell;
though I've heard some gauchos say that these stray eggs—
huachos we call them—are laid here and there for the young
birds to feed upon. But that can't be so, since the *huachos*
are never found pecked or broken, but always whole, whether
they be fresh or addled. I think it's more likely that the
hens drop these stray eggs because they have no nest in
which to put them; that where they have laid their others
being already full. Besides, there is the cock sitting upon
it; who won't let any of them come near, once he has taken
to hatching?"

"Is it true, then, that the cock does the hatching?" interrogates Ludwig.

"Quite true—all of it; and he's got a good many eggs to
cover. I've counted over fifty in one nest. That of itself
shows no single hen could have laid them; for, as it would
take her a long time, the first ones would be rotten before
the last came. As for the cock when sitting, he's as cross
as an old duck doing the same, but ten times more dangerous to go near. I've known of a gaucho getting a kick
from one he'd started from off the nest, almost as hard as
if it had been given by a mule. And to hear them hiss
then! Ah! that was nothing we've just heard from this
fellow."

"Is it true they can swim, Gaspar?" again questions
Ludwig.

"Like swans. No, I'm wrong there, for nothing can be more unlike. So far as the swimming goes, the *avestruz* can do it, but in quite a different way from swans. They swim with their bodies under water, and only their shoulders, with the head and neck, above. It's a funny sight to see a flock of them crossing one of the big rivers ; and scores of times I've been eye-witness to that bit of comicality. *Carramba !* a curious bird, the *avestruz* is altogether, and a useful one, as we've now good reason to know. So, *señoritos,* let us be thankful to Providence that there's such a plenty of them on these *pampas,* and above all, for guiding the steps of this fine specimen, as to place it so directly and opportunely in our way."

The discourse about ostriches is brought to a close with the breakfast upon that which had led to it ; both, along with the incident of the bird's capture, having occupied little more time than is here taken in telling of them. So little, indeed, that the sun's disc is not yet all above the horizon, when, having completed the repast, the trackers start up from their seats around the fire, and proceed to caparisoning their animals.

Nor do they spend many moments at this. Ever mindful of what has brought them thither—no mere excursion for pleasure's sake, but an expedition forced upon them through sad, painful necessity—they waste not a second that can be saved. Quickly, therefore, their horses are got under saddle, and bridled, with every article of their *impedimenta* fixed and fastened in its respective place, besides, some-thing on the croup of Ludwig's *recado,* which was not hitherto there. Where the lost traps had been carried, are now seen the two thigh-bones of the cock ostrich, with most of the flesh still adhering, each as large as a leg of mutton.

There is a heart, liver, and gizzard also stowed away in a wrap of a *vihao*, or wild plantain leaves, which, tied in a secure packet, dangles alongside ; the whole, as Gaspar declared, enough to keep them provisioned for at least a couple of days.

But although everything seems in readiness, they are not yet prepared to take a final departure from the place. A matter remains to be determined, and one of the utmost importance—being no less than the direction in which they should go. They have thought of it the night before, but not till darkness had come down upon them. Still unrecovered from the excitement consequent on the attack of the *gymnoti*, and afterwards occupied in drying their wet garments, with other cares of the occasion, even Gaspar had failed during daylight to examine the nether side of the ford at its outcoming, where he supposed he might hit upon the trail they were in search of. It was not because he had forgotten it, but that, knowing they would stay there all night, he also knew the tracks, if any, would keep till the morning.

Morning having arrived, from earliest daybreak and before, as is known, they have been otherwise occupied ; and only now, at the moment of moving off, do they find time to look for that which must decide their future course and the route they are to take.

With a parting glance at the place of bivouac, and each leading his own horse, they move out of the *algarobia* grove, and on down to the edge of the *riacho*, stopping at the spot where they came across.

But not a moment spend they there, in the search for hoof marks other than those of their own horses. They see others soon as arrived at the stream's edge ; scores of them, and made by the same animals they have been all along tracking. Not much in this it might appear; since unfortunately, these hoof-marks can be distinguished no farther than to the summit of the sloping bank. Beyond they are covered up, as elsewhere, by the mud. But Gaspar's keen eye is not to be thus baffled; and a joyful ejaculation escaping his lips tells he has discovered something which gives him gladness. On Cypriano asking what it is, he makes answer—

" Just what we're wanting to find out; the route the redskins have taken after parting from this place. Thanks to the Virgin, I know the way they went now, as well as if I'd been along with them."

" How do you know that?" questions Cypriano, who with Ludwig has been examining the Indian trail down by the water's edge—apart from the gaucho, who had followed it up to the summit of the slope.

" Come hither!" he calls out. " Look there!" he adds as they get beside him, " You see that these tracks have the toes all turned down stream; which tells me the horses did the same, and, I should say, also their riders. Yes! Soon as out of the water they turned down; proof good as positive that they've gone along the *riacho* this side, and back again to the big river. So it's no use our delaying longer here; there's nothing farther to be learnt, or gained by it."

So says Gaspar; but Cypriano, and also Ludwig, think otherwise. Both have a wish—indeed, an earnest desire—once more to look upon the tracks of the pony on which they know Francesca to have been mounted. And communicating this to the gaucho, he holds their horses while they return to search for them.

To their satisfaction they again beheld the diminutive hoof-marks; two or three of which have escaped being trampled out by the horses that came behind. And after regarding them for a time with sad glances, Ludwig turns away sighing, while his cousin gives utterance to what more resembles a curse, accompanied by words breathing vengeance against the abductors.

Rejoining the gaucho, all three mount into their saddles; and, without further dallying, ride off down the *riacho*, to make back for the main river.

But, again upon the latter's bank, they find the trail blind as before, with nothing to guide them, save the stream itself. To the gaucho, however, this seems sufficient, and turning his horses's head upward, he cries out—

" Now, *muchachos mios !* we must on to the *salitral !* "

And on for this they ride; to reach the point where it commences, just as the sun's lower limb touches, seeming to rest on the level line of the horizon.

And now, having arrived on the edge of the *salitral*, they make halt, still keeping to their saddles, with eyes bent over the waste which stretches far beyond and before them. Greater than ever is the gloom in their looks as they behold the sterile tract, which should have shown snow-white, all black and forbidding. For the *salitral*, as all the rest of the campo, is covered with a stratum of mud, and the *travesia* across it has been altogether obliterated.

Gaspar only knows the place where it begins; this by the bank of the river which there also commences its curve, turning abruptly off to the south. He thinks the route across the *salitral* is due westward, but he is not sure. And there is no sign of road now, not a trace to indicate the direction. Looking west, with the sun's disc right before their faces, they see nothing but the brown bald expanse, treeless as cheerless, with neither break nor bush, stick nor stone, to relieve the monotony of its surface, or serve as a land-mark for the traveller.   And the same thing both to the right and left, far as their eyes can reach ; for here the river, after turning off, has no longer a skirting of trees ; its banks beyond being a low-lying saline marsh—in short, a part of the *salitral.*   To ride out upon that wilderness waste, to all appearance endless, with any chance or hope of finding the way across it, would be like embarking in an open boat, and steering straight for the open ocean.

Not on that night, anyhow, do they intend making the attempt, as the darkness will soon be down upon them.   So dismounting from their horses, they set about establishing a camp.

But when established they take little delight in its occupation.   Now more than ever are they doubtful and dejected; thinking of that terrible *travesia,* of which all traces are lost, and none may be found beyond.   To Cypriano no night since their starting out seemed so long as this.

Little dream they, while seated around their camp fire, or lying sleepless alongside it, that the tract of country they so much dread entering upon, will, in a few hours' time, prove their best friend.   Instead of sending them further astray it will put them once more on the lost trail, with no longer a likelihood of their again losing it.

Unaware of this good fortune before them, they seek rest with feelings of the utmost despondency, and find sleep only in short snatches.

CHAPTER XL.

ON THE SALITRAL.

NEXT morning the trackers are up at an early hour—the earlier because of their increased anxiety—and after breakfasting on broiled ostrich leg, make ready to recommence their journey.

Nolens volens, they must embark upon that brown, limitless expanse, which looks unattractive in the light of the rising sun as it did under that of the setting.

In their saddles, and gazing over it before setting out, Gaspar says—

"*Hijos mios ;* we can't do better than head due westward. That will bring us out of the *salitral*, somewhere. Luckily there's a sun in the sky to hold us to a straight course. If we hadn't that for a guide, we might go ziz-zagging all about, and be obliged to spend a night amidst the saltpetre ; perhaps three or four of them. To do so would be to risk our lives ; possibly lose them. The thirst of itself would kill us, for there's never drinkable water in a *salitral.* However, with the sun behind our backs, and we'll take care to keep it so, there won't be much danger of our getting bewildered. We must make haste, though. Once it mounts above our heads, I defy Old Nick himself to tell east from west. So let's put on the best speed we can take out of the legs of our animals."

With this admonition, and a word to his horse, the gaucho goes off at a gallop; the others starting simultaneously at the same pace, and all three riding side by side. For on the smooth, open surface of the *salitral* there is no need for travelling single file. Over it a thousand horsemen —or ten thousand for that matter—might march abreast, with wide spaces between.

Proceeding onward, they leave behind them three distinct traces of a somewhat rare and original kind—the reverse of what would be made by travellers passing over ground thinly covered with snow, where the trail would be darker than the surrounding surface. Theirs, on the contrary, is lighter coloured—in point of fact, quite white, from the saltpetre tossed to the top by the hooves of their galloping horses.

The gaucho every now and then casts a glance over his shoulder, to assure himself of the sun's disc being true behind their backs; and in this manner they press on, still keeping up the pace at which they had started.

They have made something more than ten miles from the point where they entered upon the *salitral;* and Gaspar begins to look inquiringly ahead, in the hope of sighting a tree, ridge, rock, or other land-mark to tell where the *travesia* terminates. His attention thus occupied, he for awhile forgets what has hitherto been engaging it—the position of the sun.

And when next he turns to observe the great luminary, it is only to see that it is no longer there—at least no longer visible. A mass of dark cloud has drifted across its disc, completely obscuring it. In fact, it was the sudden darkening of the sky, and, as a consequence, the shadow coming over the plain before his face, which prompted him to turn round—recalling the necessity of caution as to their course.

" *Santos Dios !* " he cries out, his own brow becoming shadowed as the sky ; " our luck has left us, and——"

"And what?" asks Cypriano, seeing that the gaucho hesitates, as if reluctant to say why fortune has so suddenly forsaken them. "There's a cloud come over the sun ; has that anything to do with it?"

"Everything, señorito. If that cloud don't pass off again, we're as good as lost. And," he adds, with eyes still turned to the east, his glance showing him to feel the gravest apprehension, "I am pretty sure it won't pass off— for the rest of this day at all events. *Mira!* It's moving along the horizon—still rising up and spreading out!"

The others also perceive this, they too, having halted, and faced to eastward.

" *Santissima !* " continues the gaucho in the same serious tone, " *we're lost as it is now !* "

" But how lost? " inquires Ludwig, who, with his more limited experience of pampas life, is puzzled to understand what the gaucho means. "In what way?"

"Just because there's *no way*. That's the very thing we've lost, señorito. Look around! Now, can you tell east from west, or north from south? No, not a single point of the compass. If we only knew one, that would be enough. But we don't, and, therefore, as I've said, we're lost—dead, downright lost ; and, for anything beyond this, we'll have to go a groping. At a crawl, too, like three blind cats."

"Nothing of the sort !" breaks in Cypriano, who, a little apart from the other two, has been for the last few seconds to all appearance holding communion with himself. "Nothing of the sort," he repeats riding towards them with a cheerful expression. "We'll neither need to go groping, Gaspar, nor yet at a crawl. Possibly, we may have to slacken the pace a bit ; but that's all."

Both Ludwig and the gaucho, but especially the latter, sit regarding him with puzzled looks. For what can he mean ? Certainly something which promises to release them from their dilemma, as can be told by his smiling countenance and confident bearing. In fine, he is asked to explain himself, and answering, says :—

"Look back along our trail. Don't you see that it runs straight ? "

"We do," replies Gaspar, speaking for both. "In a dead right line, thank the sun for that ; and I only wish we could have had it to direct us a little longer, instead of leaving us in the lurch as it has done. But go on, señorito ! I oughtn't to have interrupted you."

"Well," proceeds the young Paraguayan, "there's no reason why we shouldn't still travel in that same right line —since we can."

"Ha !" ejaculates the gaucho, who has now caught the other's meaning, "I see the whole thing. Bravo, Señor Cypriano ! You've beaten me in the craft of the pampas. But I'm not jealous—no. Only proud to think my own pupil has shown himself worthy of his teacher. *Gracias a Dios !* "

During all this dialogue, Ludwig is silent, seated in his saddle, a very picture of astonishment, alike wondering at what his cousin can mean, and the burst of joyous enthusiasm it has elicited from the gaucho's lips. His wonder is brought to an end, however, by Cypriano turning round to him, and giving the explanation in detail.

"Don't you see, *sobrino mio,* that one of us can stay by the end of the trail we've already made, or two for that matter, while the third rides forward. The others can call after to keep him in a straight line and to the course. The three of us following one another, and the last giving the directions from our trail behind, we can't possibly go astray. Thanks to that white stuff, our back-tracks can be seen without difficulty, and to a sufficient distance for our purpose."

Long before Cypriano has reached the end of his explanatory discourse, Ludwig, of quick wit too, catches his meaning, and with an enthusiasm equalling that of the gaucho, cries out :—

"*Viva, sobrino mio !* You're a genius !"

Not a moment more is lost or spent upon that spot; Ludwig being the one chosen to lead off, the gaucho following, with a long space between them, while the rear is brought up by Cypriano himself; who for this go, and not Gaspar, acts as guide and director.

CHAPTER XLI.

An odd spectacle the trio of trackers would afford to anyone seeing them on the *salitral* now, without knowing what they are at; one riding directly in the wake and on the track of the other, with over a hundred yards between each pair. And, as all are going at full gallop, it might be supposed that the foremost is fleeing from the other two— one of the pursuers having a blown horse and fallen hopelessly behind !

Nor do they proceed in silence. Instead, the hindmost is heard to utter loud shouts which the one midway repeats, as if in echo; while he ahead alone says nothing. Even this would strengthen the supposition of its being a chase; the pursued party speechless from the intensity of his fears, and the effort he is making to escape his pursuers.

One near enough, however, to note the expression upon the faces of all three, and hear the words spoken, would know that the three galloping horsemen, though oddly apart, are in friendly communication with one another. Since in their shouts, though loud, is nothing to tell of hostility or anger. Nor yet any great variety of speech— only the two words, "right" and "left;" these uttered at short but irregular intervals, first by the hindmost, then taken up by the one riding midway, and passed on to him who leads; the last, as he hears them, shaping his course in accordance.

In this quaint fashion they have proceeded several leagues, when the leader, Ludwig, is seen to swerve suddenly to the left, without any direction having reached him from behind; this, too, at an angle of full fifty degrees.

" Right !" calls Cypriano from the rear, the tone of his voice telling of surprise, while the same is visible on his face.

Gaspar repeats the word in like accent of astonishment. Cypriano once more vociferating, " Right ! to the right !"

But, although Ludwig must have heard them both, to neither gives he ear, nor pays the slightest attention to the directions called out to him. Instead, he still holds on in the new course, which he seems to have chosen for himself.

Has his horse shied, and escaped from his control ? That is the first thought of the other two, who by this time have both reined up, and sit looking after him. Then a more painful apprehension forces itself upon them ; he may have gone astray in another sense, than from the track he should have taken. Is he still under the influence of the animal electricity, which might account for his seemingly eccentric behaviour ? For eccentric it certainly appears, if not something worse—as indeed they half-suspect it to be.

While they continue watching him, they see, as well as hear, what goes far towards confirming their suspicions. For after galloping some two or three hundred yards, and without once looking back, he suddenly pulls up, raises the hat from his head, and holding it aloft, waves it round and round, all the while uttering cries as of one in a frenzy !

" *Pobrecito !*" mutters Gaspar to himself, " the excitement has been too much for him. So long on the strain—no wonder. *Ay de mi ?* Another of that poor family doomed —and to worse than death !"

At the same time Cypriano is reflecting in a somewhat similar fashion, though he makes no remark. The strange exhibition saddens him beyond the power of speech. His cousin has gone crazed !

They had headed their horses, and were about to ride rapidly after, when they saw him stop; and now moving gently forward with their eyes on him, they see him replace the cap upon his head, and bend downward, with gaze given to the ground. Some new fancy dictated by a disordered brain, think they. What will he do next? What will they see ?

And what *do* they see on drawing nearer to him ? That which makes both of them feel foolish enough; at the same time that it rejoices them to think they have been the victims of a self-deception. For before they are quite up to the spot where he has halted, they perceive a large space of whitish colour, where the surface mud has been tossed and mixed up with the substratum of saltpetre—all done by the hoofs of horses, as even at a distance they can tell.

"Come along here, you laggards !" cries Ludwig in a tone of triumph; "I've something to show you. Feast your eyes upon this ! "

While speaking he nods to the ground by his horse's head, indicating the disturbed tract; then, adding as he raises his hand, and points outward—

" And on that ! "

The " that " he refers to is a white list leading away westward as far as they can see—evidently the trail taken by those they are in pursuit of.

Long ere this, both Gaspar and Cypriano have full comprehension of what perplexed while alarming them. But neither says a word of the suspicions they had entertained concerning him. Each in his own mind has resolved never to speak of them, the gaucho, as he comes up again, crying out—

"Bravo!" then adding with an air of gracious humility, "So, Señor Ludwig, you, too, have beaten me! Beaten us all! You've set us on the right trail now; one which, if I mistake not, will conduct us to the end of our journey, without need of sunshine, or any other contrivance."

"And that end," interposes Cypriano, "will be in a town or camp of Tovas Indians, at the tent of the scoundrel Aguara;" then, adding excitedly, "Oh! that I were there now!"

"Have patience, *hijo mio;*" counsels Gaspar; "you'll be there in good time, and that very soon. For, from something I remember, I don't think we've much more journey to make. But before proceeding further, let us take a look at this curious thing here, and see what we can make of it. Besides, our animals need breathing a bit."

So saying, he dismounts, as do the others; and leaving their horses to stand at rest, all three commence examination of the tract which shows stirred and trampled.

They see hoof-marks of horses—scores of them—all over the ground for the space of several perches, and pointed in every direction; among them also the foot-prints of men, with here and there smooth spots as if where human bodies had reclined. That both men and horses had been there is evident, and that they had gone off by the trace running westward, equally so. But how they came thither is a question not so easily answered; since the same halting-place shows no track of either horse or man leading towards it!

Odd all this might appear, indeed inexplicable, to one unacquainted with the nature of a dust-storm, or unaware of the incidents which have preceded. But to Gaspar, the gaucho, everything is as clear as daylight; and, after a short inspection of the "sign," he thus truthfully interprets it :—

"The redskins had just got thus far, when the *tormenta* came on. It caught them here, and that's why we see these smooth patches; they lay down to let it blow by. Well; there's one good turn it's done us: we now know the exact time they passed this spot; or, at all events, when they were on it. That must have been just after we entered the cave, and were engaged with the *tigre*—I mean it Number 1. No doubt by the time we tackled the old Tom, they were off again. As, you see, *muchachos*, some little rain has sprinkled that trail since they passed over it, which shows they went away in the tail of that terrific shower. So," he adds, turning round, and stepping back towards his horse, "there's nothing more to be done but ride off after them; which we may now do as rapidly as our animals can carry us."

At this they all remount, and setting their horses' heads to the Indian trail, proceed upon it at a brisk pace; no longer travelling tandem, but broadly abreast.

CHAPTER XLII

PICKING UP PEARLS.

FROM their new point of departure, the trackers have no difficulty about the direction; this traced out for them, as plain as if a row of finger-posts, twenty yards apart, were set across the *salitral*. For at least a league ahead they can distinguish the white list, where the saline efflorescence has been turned up, and scattered about by the hoofs of the Indian horses.

They can tell by the trail that over this portion of their route the party they are in pursuit of has not ridden in any compact or regular order, but straggled over a wide space; so that, here and there, the tracks of single horses show separate and apart. In the neighbourhood of an enemy the Indians of the Chaco usually march under some sort of formation; and Gaspar, knowing this, draws the deduction that those who have latest passed over the *salitral* must have been confident that no enemy was near—either in front or following them. Possibly, also, their experience of the *tormenta*, which must have been something terrible on that exposed plain, had rendered them careless as to their mode of marching.

Whatever the cause, they now, taking up their trail, do not pause to speculate upon it, nor make any delay. On the contrary, as hounds that have several times lost the scent, hitherto faint, but once more recovered, and now fresher and stronger than ever, they press on with ardour not only renewed, but heightened.

All at once, however, a shout from Cypriano interrupts the rapidity of their progress—in short, bringing them to a halt—he himself suddenly reigning up as he gives utterance to it. Gaspar and Ludwig turn simultaneously towards him for an explanation. While their glances hitherto have been straying far forward, he has been giving his habitually to the ground more immediately under his horse's head, and to both sides of the broad trail; his object being to ascertain if among the many tracks of the Indians' horses, those of Francesca's pony are still to be seen.

And sure enough he sees the diminutive hoofmarks plainly imprinted—not at one particular place, but every here and there as they go galloping along. It is not this, however, which elicited his cry, and caused him to come so abruptly to a stop. Instead, something which equally interests, while more surely proclaiming the late presence of the girl, in that place, with the certainty of her being carried along a captive. He has caught sight of an object which lies glistening among the white powder of the *salitré*— whitish itself, but of a more lustrous sheen. Pearls—a string of them, as it proves upon closer inspection! At a glance he recognizes an ornament well known to him, as worn by his girlish cousin; Ludwig also, soon as he sees it, crying out :—

" It's sister's necklet ! "

Gaspar, too, remembers it; for pearls are precious things in the eyes of a gaucho, whose hat often carries a band of such, termed the *toquilla*.

Cypriano, flinging himself from his saddle, picks the necklace up, and holds it out for examination. It is in no way injured, the string still unbroken, and has no doubt dropped to the ground by the clasp coming undone. But there are no traces of a struggle having taken place, nor sign that any halt had been made on that spot. Instead, the pony's tracks, there distinctly visible, tell of the animal having passed straight on without stop or stay. In all likelihood, the catch had got loosened at the last halting-place in that conflict with the storm, but had held on till here.

Thus concluding, and Cypriano remounting, they continue onward along the trail, the finding of the pearls having a pleasant effect upon their spirits. For it seems a good omen, as if promising that they may yet find the one who had worn them, as also be able to deliver her from captivity.

Exhilarated by the hope, they canter briskly on; and for several leagues meet nothing more to interrupt them; since that which next fixes their attention, instead of staying, but lures them onward—the tops of tall trees, whose rounded crowns and radiating fronds tell that they are palms.

It still lacks an hour of sunset, when these begin to show over the brown waste, and from this the trackers know they are nearing the end of the *travesia*. Cheered by the sight, they spur their horses to increased speed, and are soon on the edge of the *salitral;* beyond, seeing a plain where the herbage is green, as though no dust-storm had flown over it. Nor had there, for the *tormenta*, like cyclones and hurricanes, is often local, its blast having a well-defined border.

Riding out upon this tract—more pleasant for a traveller —they make a momentary halt, but still remaining in their saddles, as they gaze inquiringly over it.

And here Cypriano, recalling a remark which Gaspar had made at their last camping place, asks an explanation of it. The gaucho had expressed a belief, that from something he remembered, they would not have much further to go before arriving at their journey's end.

"Why did you say that?" now questions the young Paraguayan.

"Because I've heard the old *cacique*, Naraguana, speak of a place where they buried their dead. Strange my not thinking of that sooner; but my brains have been so muddled with what's happened, and the hurry we've been in all along, I've forgotten a good many things. He said they had a town there too, where they sometimes went to live, but oftener to die. I warrant me that's the very place they're in now; and, from what I understood him to say, it can't be very far t'other side this *salitral*. He spoke of a hill rising above the town, which could be seen a long way off: a curious hill, shaped something like a wash-basin turned bottom upwards. Now, if we could only sight that hill."

At this he ceases speaking, and elevates his eyes, with an interrogative glance which takes in all the plain ahead, up to the horizon's verge. Only for a few seconds is he silent, when his voice is again heard, this time in grave, but gleeful, exclamation :—

"*Por todos Santos!* there's the hill itself!"

The others looking out behold a dome-shaped eminence, with a flat, table-like top recognizable from the quaint description Gaspar has just given of it, though little more than its summit is visible above the plain—for they are still several miles distant from it.

"We must go no nearer to it now," observes the gaucho,

adding, in a tone of apprehension, " we may be too near already. *Caspita!* Just look at that! "

The last observation refers to the sun, which, suddenly shooting out from the clouds hitherto obscuring it, again shows itself in the sky. Not now, however, as in the early morning hours, behind their backs, but right in front of them, and low down, threatening soon to set.

" *Vayate!* " he continues to ejaculate in a tone of mock scorn, apostrophizing the great luminary, " no thanks to you now, showing yourself when you're not needed. Instead, I'd thank you more if you'd kept your face hid a bit longer. Better for us if you had."

" Why better?" asks Cypriano, who, as well as Ludwig, has been listening with some surprise to the singular monologue. " What harm can the sun do us now more than ever?"

" Because now, more than ever, he's shining inopportunely, both as to time and place."

" In what way?"

" In a way to show us to eyes we don't want to see us just yet. Look at that hill yonder. Supposing now, just by chance, any of the Indians should be idling upon it, or they have a vidette up there. Bah! what am I babbling about? He couldn't see us if they had; not here, unless through a telescope, and I don't think the Tovas are so far civilized as to have that implement among their chattels. For all, we're not safe on this exposed spot, and the sooner we're off it the better. Some of them may be out scouting in this direction. Come, let us get under cover, and keep so till night's darkness gives us a still safer screen against prying eyes. Thanks to the Virgin! yonder's the very place for our purpose."

He points to a clump of trees, around the stems of which

appears a dense underwood; and, soon as signalling this, he rides toward and into it, the others after him.

Once inside the copse, and for the time feeling secure against observation, they hold a hasty counsel as to which step they ought next to take. From the sight of that oddly-shaped hill, and what Gaspar remembers Naraguana to have said, they have no doubt of its being the same referred to by the old chief, and that the sacred town of the Tovas is somewhere beside it. So much they feel sure of, their doubts being about the best way for them to approach the place and enter the town, as also the most proper time. And with these doubts are, of course, mingled many fears; though with these, strange to say, Ludwig, the youngest and least experienced of the three, is the least troubled. Under the belief, as they all are, that Naraguana is still living, his confidence in the friendship of the aged *cacique* has throughout remained unshaken. When the latter shall be told of all that has transpired; how his pale-faced friend and protegé met his death by the assassin's hand—how the daughter of that friend has been carried off—surely he will not refuse restitution, even though it be his own people who have perpetrated the double crime?

Reasoning thus, Ludwig counsels their riding straight on to the Indian town, and trusting to the good heart of Naraguana—throwing themselves upon his generosity, Cypriano is equally eager to reach the place, where he supposes his dear cousin Francesca to be pining as a prisoner; but holds a very different opinion about the prudence of the step, and less believes in the goodness of Naraguana. To him all Indians seem treacherous—Tovas Indians more than any —for before his mental vision he has ever the image of Aguara, and can think of none other.

As for the gaucho, though formerly one of Naraguana's truest friends, from what has happened, his faith in the integrity of the old Tovas chief is greatly shaken. Besides, the caution, habitual to men of his calling and kind, admonishes him against acting rashly now, and he but restates his opinion: that they will do best to remain under cover of the trees, at least till night's darkness comes down. Of course this is conclusive, and it is determined that they stay.

Dismounting, they make fast their horses to some branches, and sit down beside them—*en bivouac.* But in this camp they kindle no fire, nor make any noise, conversing only in whispers. One passing the copse could hear no sound inside it, save the chattering of a flock of macaws, who have their roosting-place amid the tops of its tallest trees.

CHAPTER XLIII.

THAT same sun which became so suddenly obscured over the *salitral*, to shine again in the later hours of the afternoon, is once more about to withdraw its light from the Chaco—this time for setting. Already appears its disc almost down upon the horizon; and the strangely-shaped hill, which towers above the Tovas town, casts a dark shadow over the plain eastward, to the distance of many miles. The palms skirting the lake reflect their graceful forms far over the water, whose surface, undisturbed by the slightest breath of air, shows smooth and shining as a mirror; broken, however, here and there, where water-fowl disport themselves upon it. Among these may be observed the great musk duck, mis-named "Muscovy," and the black-necked swan; both in-digenous to the Chaco; while in the shallower places along shore, and by the edges of the islets, appear various species of long-legged waders, standing still, or stalking about as if on stilts; the most conspicuous of all being the scarlet flamingo, side by side with the yet taller *garzon*, already known to us as "soldier-crane."

A scene of tranquil yet picturesque beauty—perhaps no fairer on earth—is the landscape lying around the Sacred Town of the Tovas.

And on this same day and hour, a stranger entering within the precincts of the place itself might not observe anything to contrast with the tranquillity of the scene outside. Among the *toldos* he would see children at play, and, here and there, seated by their doors young girls engaged in various occupations; some at basket work, others weaving mats from the fibres of split palm leaves, still others knitting *redes*, or hammocks. Women of more mature age are busied with culinary cares, preparing the evening repast over fires kindled in the open air; while several are straining out the honey of the wild bee, called *tosimi*, which a party of bee-hunters, just returned to the *tolderia*, has brought home.

A few of the men may also be observed moving about, or standing in groups on the open ground adjoining the *malocca;* but at this hour most of them are on horse-back out upon the adjacent plain, there galloping to and fro, gathering their flocks and herds, and driving them towards the *corrals;* these flocks and herds composed of horned cattle, sheep, and goats—the Tovas Indians being somewhat of a pastoral people. No savages they, in the usual sense of the term, nor yet is hunting their chief occupation. This they follow now and then, diversifying the chase by a warlike raid into the territory of some hostile tribe, or as often some settlement of the pale faces. For all civilization of a certain kind has made progress among them; having its origin in an early immigration from Peru, when the " Children of the Sun " were conquered by Pizarro and his *conquistadores*. At that time many Peruvians, flee-ing from the barbarous cruelty of their Spanish invaders, sought asylum in the Chaco, there finding it; and from these the Tovas and other tribes have long ago learnt many of the arts of civilized life; can spin their own thread, and sew skilfully as any sempstress of the pale faces ; weave their own cloth, dress and dye it in fast colours of becoming patterns ; in short, can do many kinds of mechanical work, which no white artizan need feel ashamed to acknowledge as his own. Above all, are they famed for the "feather-work," or plume embroidery—an art peculiarly Indian—which, on their first becoming acquainted with it, astonished the rough soldiers of Cortez and Pizarro, as much as it delighted them.

To this day is it practised among several of the South American tribes, notably those of the Gran Chaco, while the Tovas particularly excel in it.

But perhaps the highest evidence of these Indians having some civilization, is their form of government, which is in reality Republican. For their *cacique*, or chief, although sometimes allowed to rule by hereditary succession, is more often chosen by the sub-chiefs and warriors ; in short, elected just as the President of a Republic.

This gives the key to Aguara's doubts and fears on returning to the Sacred Town with Francesca Halberger as his captive. Nor are the latter yet allayed, despite three days having elapsed since his return. Though he has done all in his power to conceal from his people the true facts in relation to her father's death, still certain details of the tragedy have leaked out ; and it has become known to most, that the hunter-naturalist is not only dead, but died by the hand of an assassin. This last, however, they suppose to have been the other white man late on a visit to them— Valdez the *vaqueano*. For the same tale which Aguara had told to his captive on the way, he has repeated, with some variations, to the elders of the tribe assembled in council within the *malocca*. So far not much of a fiction ; only that part accounting for the death of the young brave who fell to Halberger's bullet—a stray shot, while the latter was defending himself against Valdez.

And the daughter of the murdered man has been brought back with them, not as a prisoner, but because it was inconvenient to take her direct to her own home. She can and will be sent thither at the first opportunity which offers. So promises the deceitful son of Naraguana to those of the tribe who would call him to account.

Meanwhile, the girl has been entrusted to the charge and safe keeping of Shebotha, a sort of "mystery woman," or sorceress, of much power in the community; though, as all know, under the influence of Aguara himself. But he has not dared to take the youthful captive to his own *toldo*, or even hint at so doing; instead, he still keeps his wicked purpose to himself, trusting to time and Shebotha for its accomplishment.

According to his own way of thinking, he can well afford to wait. He has no thought that anyone will ever come after the captive girl; much less one with power to release her. It is not probable, and from a knowledge possessed only by himself, scarcely possible. Her father is dead, her mother doomed to worse than death, as also her brother and that other relative—his own rival. For before parting with him, Rufino Valdez had said what amounted to so much; and possibly by this time the Señora Halberger, with what remained of her family, would be on the way back to Paraguay; not returning voluntarily, but taken back by the *vaqueano*. With this belief—a false one, as we know—the young Tovas chief feels secure of his victim, and therefore refrains from any act of open violence, as likely to call down upon him the censure of his people. Though popular with the younger members of the tribe, he

is not so much in favour with the elders as to fly in the face
of public opinion; for were these aware of what has really
taken place, it would go ill with him.   But as yet they are
not; silence having been enjoined on the youths who accompanied him in that ill-starred expedition, which they,
for their own sakes, have hitherto been careful to keep.

For all, certain facts have come to light in disjointed,
fragmentary form, with deductions drawn from them, which
go hard against the character of the young *cacique;* and as
the hours pass others are added, until discontent begins to
show itself among the older and more prominent men of
the tribe, chiefly those who were the friends of his father.
For these were also friends of her father, now alike father-
less, though made so by a more cruel fate. Low murmurings
are here and there heard, which speak of an intent to prosecute inquiry on the subject of Halberger's assassination—
even to the carrying it into Paraguay. Now that they have
re-entered into amity with Paraguay's Dictator, they may
go thither, though the purpose be a strange one; to arraign
the commissioner who acted in restoring the treaty!

With much whispering and murmurs around, it is not
strange that the young *cacique,* while dreaming of future
pleasures, should also have fears for that future. His own
passion, wild as wicked, has brought him into danger, and a
storm seems brewing that, sooner or later, may deprive him
of his chieftainship.

CHAPTER XLIV.

AN INDIAN BELLE.

IF the Tovas chief be in danger of receiving punishment from his people for carrying into captivity the daughter of his father's friend, there is also danger to the captive herself from another and very different source. Just as the passion of love has been the cause of her being brought to the Sacred Town of the Tovas, that of jealousy is like to be the means of her there finding an early grave.

The jealous one is an Indian girl, named Nacena, the daughter of a sub-chief, who, like Naraguana himself, was an aged man held in high regard; and, as the deceased *cacique*, now also sleeping his last sleep in one of their scaffold tombs.

Despite her bronzed skin, Nacena is a beautiful creature; for the brown is not so deep as to hinder the crimson blush showing its tint upon her cheeks; and many a South American maiden, boasting the blue blood of Andalusia, has a complexion less fair than she. As on this same evening she sits by the shore of the lake, on the trunk of a fallen palm tree, her fine form clad in the picturesque Indian garb, with her lovely face mirrored in the tranquil water, a picture is presented on which no eye could look, nor thought dwell, without a feeling of delight; and, regarding her thus, no one would believe her to be other than what she is—the belle of the Tovas tribe.

Her beauty had not failed to make impression upon the heart of Aguara, long before his having become *cacique.* He has loved her too, in days gone by, ere he looked upon the golden-haired pale-face. Both children then, and little more yet; for the Indian girl is only a year or two older than the other. But in this southern clime, the precocity already spoken of is not confined to those whose skins are called white, but equally shared by the red.

Nacena has been beloved by the son of Naraguana, and knew, or at least believed it. But she better knows, that she has been deceived by him, and is now slighted, about to be cast aside for another. That other will, ere long, be chieftainess of the Tovas tribe, while she——

She has reflected thus far, when the bitter thought overpowering causes her to start to her feet, a cry escaping her lips as if it came from a heart cleft in twain.

Nothing of this, however, shows in her face. The expression upon it is rather that of anger, as a *jaguarete* of her native plains, whose rage has been aroused by the arrow of the Indian hunter suddenly piercing its side. Hitherto silent, she is now heard to speak; but, though alone, the words to which she gives utterance are not in soliloquy; instead, as if spoken to some one who is near, though unseen. It is an apostrophe meant for no mortal ears, but addressed to the Divinity of the lake!

"Spirit of the Waters!" she cries, with arms outstretched and head aloft, "hear my prayer! Tell me if it be true! Will he make her his wife?"

She is silent for a second or two, as though expecting a reply, and listening for it. It comes, but not from the deity addressed. Out of her own heart she has the answer.

"He will; yes, surely will! Else, why has he brought her hither? A false tale he has told in the council of the elders; false as himself! Where are his words, his vows, made to me with lips that gave kisses? Perjured—broken —gone as his love, given to another! And I am soon to see her his queen, salute her as mine, and attend upon her as one of her waiting maids! Never! No, Spirit of the Waters! Rather than do that, I shall go to you; be one of your attendants, not hers. Rather than that, thou shalt take me to thy bosom!"

High-sounding speeches from an Indian girl, scarce fifteen years of age? But love's eloquence is not confined to age, race, or rank, no more than that of jealousy. Both passions may burn in the breast of the savage maiden, as in the heart of the high-born lady—perhaps tearing it more. Not strange they should find like expression on the lips.

"Why not now?" continues Nacena in a tone that tells of despair, while the cloud upon her brow is seen to grow darker. "Ah! why not? No need waiting longer; I know all. A leap from yonder rock, and all would be over, my suspense, as my sufferings."

For a moment she stands with eyes fixed upon a rocky promontory, which juts out into the lake near by. Its head overhangs the water, three fathoms deep, as she knows. Many the time has she sprung from that projecting point to swim, naiad-like, underneath it. But the plunge she now meditates is not for swimming, but to sink!

"No!" she exclaims, after a pause, as she withdraws her gaze from the rock, the expression upon her face changing back to that of the *jaguarete!* "No, Spirit of the Waters!

not yet. Nacena fears not to die, but that is not the death for the daughter of a Tovas chief. If wronged, she must resent it, and will. Revenge first, and the deceiver shall first die. After that, O Spirit, thou canst take me; Nacena will no longer care to live."

As she says this, the sad look returns to her countenance, replacing that of anger; and for a time she stands with head drooped down to her bosom, and arms hanging listlessly by her side—a very picture of despair.

At length, she is about to leave the spot, when a footstep warns her of one making approach; and, turning, she sees who it is. A youth, but to manhood grown, and wearing the insignia of a sub-chief. Though many years older than herself, he is her brother.

"Sister!" he says, coming up to her, and closely scanning her face, "you have thoughts that trouble you. I would know what they are."

"Oh, nothing," she rejoins, with an effort to appear calm. "I've only been looking over the lake, at the birds out yonder. How they enjoy themselves this fine evening!"

"But you're not enjoying yourself, Nacena; nor haven't been for some time past. I've noticed that; and more, I know the reason."

She starts at his words; not to turn pale, but with the blood mantling into her brown cheeks. Still she is silent.

"You need neither deny, nor declare it," he continues. "'Tis all known to me, save one thing. That alone I wish to ask you about. I must have an answer, and a truthful one. As your brother I demand it, Nacena."

She fixes her eyes upon him, in a look half-frightened, then timidly asks:

"What thing, Kaolin?"

"Has he deceived you?"

"Deceived!" she echoes, the blush upon her cheeks mounting up to her brow, and becoming deeper red. "Brother! Had any one but you asked that question, I would —— Deceived! No; your sister would die before that could have been. As you seem to know all, I will no longer conceal the truth from you. You speak of Aguara. I loved him; ah! love him still. And he told me my love was returned; spoke it solemnly; vowed it. Now I know his words were false, and he was but beguiling me."

"Then he has trifled with you," exclaims the brother, his indignation now beyond bounds. "You, *my* sister, the daughter of a Tovas chief, of birth and blood equal to his own! But he shall repent it, and soon. The time has not come; it will ere long. Enough now, Nacena. Not a word to anyone of what has passed between us. Be patient and wait. For your wrongs, I promise, you shall have revenge."

And with this threat, he turns away; leaving her on the lake's edge, as he found her.

Soon as he is out of sight, and his footfall beyond hearing, she reseats herself on the trunk of the palm; and, supporting her head upon her hands, gives way to weeping—a very cataract of tears.

It seems to relieve her from the tumult of emotions late harassing her heart, and after a time she looks up with an expression in her eyes different from all that have preceded. It is of hope; as can be told by the words which fall in low murmuring from her lips:

"After all I may be mistaken. Can I? If so, and he is still true, then I am wronging him, and Kaolin may commit a crime that will bring both punishment and repentance. Oh, that I knew the truth! But surely, Shebotha knows, and can tell it me. She will, for the reward I shall offer her. This night she has promised to meet me on the hill, and then, then——"

She breaks off abruptly, and with countenance again clouding over. For the words "I shall learn the worst" are on her lips, and the thought in her mind.

It is hope's last spark, love-lighted from embers nearly extinguished, still flickering, faint, and vainly struggling to burn on.

CHAPTER XLV.

AN ELEVATED GRAVEYARD.

JUST as the last glimmer of twilight is taking departure from the plain, the three who had sought concealment under the roosting-place of macaws, slip quietly out of the copse, and ride away from it, leaving the noisy birds, now silent, behind them.

There is yet light enough to enable them to take bearings by the hill, which, as they have rightly conjectured, rises over the Tovas town ; and, heading direct towards it, after a couple of hours spent in riding at a brisk pace, they arrive at the rocky steep forming a periphery to its base. As there is now a clear moonlight, caution dictates their again getting under cover ; which they do by drawing their horses close in to the adjacent cliff, whose shadow sufficiently conceals them. But it is not intended to stay long there. At their last halting-place they had considered everything, and decided upon the steps to be taken ; so far as they can, from what is known to them. If the circumstances change, or turn out different from what they are expecting, they must be guided in their action accordingly.

Still in the belief of Naraguana being alive, Ludwig is again of the opinion that they should push on to the town without further delay. The place cannot now be far off ; for at the hill's base they have struck a broad and much-travelled trail denoting the proximity of a settlement. Cypriano is undecided, but Gaspar, as before, goes strongly against proceeding directly onward.

"You speak of delay, Señor Ludwig," he says; "but in this case, the old adage, 'More haste less speed,' might be true, as it often is. Besides, what would we gain by entering their town now? It isn't likely we should accomplish anything to-night. You forget the hour it is—nigh unto midnight. And as the custom of most Chaco Indians is early to bed and early to rise, we'd no doubt find every redskin of them asleep, with only their dogs to receive us. *Carrai!* A nice reception that would be! Like as not some scores of half-famished curs to fall upon us—perhaps drag us out of our saddles. Whereas, in the morning all would be different, with the people up to protect us from such an assault. But whether we enter at night, or by day, I still stick to the belief, that it will be better to do so by stealth; at least, one of us should first slip in that way, and learn how the land lies. In any case, we ought to have a squint at this Sacred Town, before trusting ourselves within its walls—if walls it have. From the look of things here, I fancy it lies on the other side of this hill. By climbing the hill now, and staying on its top till daybreak, we'll get a good view of the town, which will, no doubt, be right under us. We can see all through the streets, and what's going on in them. That will give us a hint of how to act afterwards, and if things look favourable, we might then ride boldly in; which, after all, may be the best way of introducing ourselves—only it should be done in the daylight."

Cypriano sees that the gaucho's reasoning is correct; and Ludwig also acknowledging it to be so, it is finally decided that they ascend the hill, and remain upon its summit for the rest of that night.

But now comes a question not hitherto asked, or thought of. How is the ascent to be made, and where is there a path practicable for making it? Not only is it steep, but its sides are thickly overgrown with trees, and between their trunks a dense tangle of underwood.

"It must be on its summit, they have their burying-ground," observes Gaspar, gazing upward. "Yes; Naraguana spoke of its being on the top of a hill, and there's no other hill near. If that be the case, and they carry their dead up, there'll sure be some sort of a road for their funeral processions. That would likely be on the other side, straight up from the town. But I warrant there's a trail starts from this side too, and runs right over the hill. Let's ride along a bit, and see if there be."

The gaucho's conjecture is correct, as they soon discover. Before they have ridden three score lengths of their horses, keeping close along the base of the hill, they perceive an opening in the timber which skirts it, marked by certain insignia denoting the entrance to a much-frequented path. For though narrow, it shows well trampled and trodden. Diverging abruptly from the broad road running on round the hill, it strikes in under a tall cotton tree, a *ceiba*, this conspicuous from being bent over, as if half-blown down. The path enters between its trunk and a gigantic *pita* plant (*agave*), whose stiff spinous leaves almost bar up the entrance as with an iron gate.

"That's the way we've got to go," says Gaspar, pointing to it, at the same time setting his horse's head in the direction of the *ceiba*; then adding, as he nods towards the *pita* plant; "have a care of your heads, *hijos mios!*

Look out for this queer customer on the left, or you may get your soft cheeks scratched a bit."

On delivering the admonition he ducks his own head, and passing under the thorny leaves of the *agave*, commences the ascent of the hill.

Cypriano and Ludwig do likewise ; and all three are soon climbing the steep, one behind the other, now in silence, the only sounds heard being the hoof-strokes of the horses, with their hard breathing as they strain up the acclivity.

A quarter of an hour's tough climbing carries them up the wooded slope, and out upon the open summit, where they have a spectacle before their eyes peculiar, as it is original. As already said, the hill is table-topped, and being also dome-shaped the level surface is circular, having a diameter of some three or four hundred yards. Nothing strange in this, however, since hills of the kind, termed *mesas*, are common throughout most parts of Spanish America, and not rare in the Gran Chaco. All three are familiar with such eminences. But what they are not familiar with—and indeed none of them have ever seen before—are some scores of queer-looking structures standing all over the summit, with alley-like spaces between ! Scaffolds they appear, each having two stages, one above the other, such as might be used in the erection of a two-storey house !

And scaffolds they are, though not employed in any building purposes ; instead, for that of burial. They are the tombs on which are deposited the bodies of the Tovas dead ; or those of them that during life were dignitaries in the tribe.

On this elevated cemetery the moon is shining brightly, though obliquely, throwing the shadows of the scaffolds aslant, so that each has its counterpart on the smooth turf by its side, dark as itself, but magnified in the moonlight. Gaspar and his companions can see that these singular mausoleums are altogether constructed of timber, the supporting posts being trunks of the *Cocoyol* palm, the lower staging of strong canes, the *caña brava*, laid side by side, while the upper one, or roof, is a thatch of the leaves of another species of palm—the *cuberta*.

After contemplating them for an instant, Gaspar says :

" This is the burying-ground Naraguana spoke to me about, beyond a doubt.   And not such a bad sort of place either to take one's final rest in, after life's worries are over. I shouldn't much object to being laid out in that style myself.   Only I'd need friends to live after me, and keep the structure in repair ; otherwise the frail thing might some day come tumbling down, and my poor bones along with it."

At the conclusion of this quaint speech, he gives the rein to his horse, and moves on among the tombs, making for the opposite side of the cemetery, the others following in silence.   For from the brow of the hill on its westward side, they expect to look down upon the Indian town.

" It must be on t'other side," observes the gaucho, as they proceed.   " I remember the old chief saying the *toldería* was west of the hill."

When half-way across he again reins up, halting his horse alongside one of the scaffolds, conspicuous among the rest by its larger size, as also a certain freshness about the timbers of which it is constructed ; some chips scattered around the supports, where these have been chopped and barked, telling of recent erection.   It is not this, however, has prompted Gaspar to make stop beside it ; but simply that he there sees a place suitable for the stalling of their horses.

There is no need to take the animals on to the other side, but better leave them there, and themselves go forward afoot.

Thus reflecting, all three dismount, and attach their horses to the corner posts of the scaffold, each choosing one for his own. Then, with cautious steps, they continue to the outer edge of the circle, and pushing through some trees that skirt it, look to the plain below. Sure enough, there is the thing they expected to see—an Indian town or *tolderia*. A large lake lies beyond, on whose tranquil surface the moon makes a mirror, as if it were glass. But their eyes rest only upon the town, their ears bent to catch any sound that may come up from it.

It is not long till sounds do ascend, the barking of dogs, with now and then the lowing of cattle, and neighing of horses; but no human voice, nothing to tell that the place is inhabited by man. For there is no smoke from the houses, no lights anywhere, everybody seeming to be asleep.

Nothing strange in all this; nor do they looking down from the hill think it so. Instead, things are just as they should be and as Gaspar anticipated they would. For it is now the midnight hour, and since red men must have rest as well as white ones, the Tovas have all retired to their beds or hammocks.

So concluding, and satisfied with what they see—reflecting further that nothing more can be done till morning—the gaucho and his companions go back to their horses, with the intention of taking off the saddles, and otherwise disposing of them for the night.

It was at first proposed to keep them tied to the scaffold posts, but on a second inspection of the place, Gaspar sees

It is not the best one either for their animals or themselves to pass the night in. Should they go to rest under the scaffold, while asleep, their horses turning restive might pull down the posts, and bring rattling about their ears the bones of some dead *cacique!* Besides, the ground underneath is not nice to repose upon ; being without herbage and trampled all over, some parts seeming freshly turned up. The gaucho would prefer a patch of soft grass to lay his limbs along, and this very thing he has noticed while they were out on the brow of the eminence overlooking the town. Here a grand fig-tree had attracted his attention, under its branches seeming the most proper place for them to encamp. Its far-spreading and umbrageous boughs drooping back to the ground and there taking root—as the Indian *banyan* of which it is the New World representative —enclosed a large space underneath. It would not only give them a shelter from the dews of the night, but concealment from the eyes of anyone who might chance to be passing that way.

With these manifest advantages in favour of the ground under the fig-tree as a camping place, and the disadvantages of that beneath the scaffold, the latter is without further ado forsaken, and the former taken possession of.

As no camp fire can be safely kindled, nor food cooked, they must go to sleep supperless.

Fortunately none of them is a-hungered, all having made a hearty meal while within the *macaw's* grove. There they had polished off the grand " drumsticks " of the ostrich, by good luck already roasted. So caring not for supper, after having disposed of their horses by tying them to branches of the fig-tree, they stretch themselves along the ground, and seek repose, which on this night they all need, as much as on any other since starting upon their long-protracted expedition.

Still, they do not intend to be all asleep at the same time. In such a place, with the danger of being found in it, that would never do. One of the three must remain awake and on watch; so it is arranged that they take the duty of sentinel in turns. As the present hour appears to be the one calling for keenest vigilance, Gaspar volunteers for the first turn of guard; and the other two wrapping their ponchos around them, and resting their heads upon their *recados*, with a mutual *Buenas noches!* become silent, if not asleep.

CHAPTER XLVI.

WHETHER his young companions be sleeping or awake,
the gaucho does not stay by their side ; but, almost as
soon as seeing them disposed along the earth, slips out
from under the fig-tree, and facing towards the central part
of the cemetery, walks off in that direction.   His object is
to revisit the scaffold lately left by them, and make a more
detailed examination of it.   Not that he cares aught about
the structure itself.   It is not the first time for him to have
seen similar burying places of the Chaco Indians, and he
knows as much about them as he cares to know.   Nor is
his object, in returning to this particular one, of a very
definite character ; but rather because a vague idea or
instinct has come into his mind which prompts him to the
act—a sort of presentiment that he may there see something to throw light on much of what has been all along
mystifying him.   To go thither will in no way interfere with
his duties as a sentinel, since he can perform these equally
well or better by moving about.   Besides, it will help to
beguile the time, as also make him familiar with the ground
they have got upon—a familiarity that may hereafter prove
of service to them.   As already stated, he had observed

that the scaffold is of recent erection, telling that the man or woman laid upon it cannot have been very long dead. He had, moreover, noticed, while attaching his bridle to one of the uprights, that a series of notches was cut in the post, evidently to facilitate ascent. ' In all likelihood, the surviving relatives of the deceased are in the habit of coming thither at periodical intervals, to adorn the tomb with flowers or other tokens of affectionate memory; perhaps bring votive offerings to the spirit which presides over that consecrated spot. But whatever the purpose of the notches, the gaucho knows they will enable him to climb up with ease, and see what rests upon the platform.

Approaching the catafalque with silent tread, he stands for a time gazing at it without making any movement to mount up. Not from curiosity does he so regard it; but something akin to awe has stolen over his spirit, and he almost fears further to intrude on the sacredness of the place. Besides, the act requires caution. What if some of the Indians given to nocturnal straying should chance to come that way, and see him up those stairs, desecrating the abode of the dead? Even were there no other reason for his fearing to be found in that place, the act itself would make him liable to punishment—possibly no less than death! For among the Tovas, as many other tribes of South American Indians—infidels though they are called— the tombs of their dead are held as sacred as those of the Spanish Christians who so designate them.

Notwithstanding all this, Gaspar the gaucho is not to be baulked in his design. He has not come to the bottom of that curious catafalque, to go away again without seeing what is above. And though he stands hesitating, it is only for a short while, finally making up his mind to ascend.

Ascend he does; laying hold of one of the notched corner posts, and climbing the primitive ladder, as it were, set ready and awaiting him.

As the moon is by this far down in the sky, its beams are not obstructed by the roof thatch, but fall obliquely upon the floor of the platform beneath. There, lying at full length, the gaucho perceives a form, easily recognizable as that of a human being, though swathed in various kinds of cloths, which cover it from head to foot. The body of a man, moreover, as can be told by its size and shape; while beside, and arranged around it, are certain insignia proclaiming it to be that of some distinguished chieftain of the Tovas. There are spears, shields, *macanas*, lazoes, bolas—among them the *bola perdida*, some of these weapons placed upon the platform alongside the corpse, others suspended from the beams and poles supporting the thatch of the roof. There is horse-gear as well—the multifarious trappings which appertain to the caparison of a gaucho's steed—recado, carona, caronilla, jerga, with Mameluke bitts and spurs of immensely large rowels; for all these are possessed by the higher order of pampas Indians, and notably their chiefs—property they have picked up in some plundering expedition, where gauchos themselves have been their victims.

Just such a thought passes through the mind of gaucho Gaspar, as his eyes rest on the grand array displayed on the *cacique's* tomb. For that it is the tomb of a *cacique*, and one of grand note, he has not a doubt, seeing such a selection of trophies. In addition to the war weapons and implements of the chase, there are articles of dress and adornment; bracelets of gold, bead necklets and belts, with coronets of bright-coloured plumes; while most conspicuous of all is a large feather-embroidered *manta,* covering the corpse from head to foot, even concealing the face.

Still there is nothing in all this to astonish Gaspar Mendez, or in any way give him a surprise. He has seen the like before, and often among the Auracanian Indians, who are kindred with the tribes of the Chaco. He but makes the reflection, how silly it is in these savages thus to expose such fine commodities to the weather, and let them go to loss and decay—all to satisfy a heathen instinct ot superstition! And thus reflecting, he would in all probability have lowered himself back to the ground, but for that presentiment still upon him. It influences him to remain a moment longer balancing himself upon the notched upright, and gazing over the platform. Just then the moon getting clear of some cirrhous clouds, and shining brighter than ever, lights up an object hitherto unnoticed by him, but one he recognizes as an old acquaintance. He starts on beholding a felt hat of the Tyrolese pattern, which he well remembers to have seen worn by his master, the hunter-naturalist, and by him given to the aged *cacique* of the Tovas as a token of friendship. And now he feels the presentiment which has been upon him all explained and fulfilled. Springing up on the platform, and uncovering the face of the corpse, he beholds—Naraguana!

p. 274.

CHAPTER XLVII.

" Naraguana dead ! " exclaims the gaucho, as standing upon the scaffold he gazes upon the form at his feet. " *Santissima !* this is strange ! "

" But is it certainly the old *cacique?* " he adds, again stooping down and raising the selvedge of feather cloth, which had fallen back over the face. Once more exposed to view, the features deeply-furrowed with age—for Naraguana was a very old man—and now further shrivelled by the dry winds of the Chaco, with the skin drawn tight over high-cheek bones, and hollow, sightless sockets, where once shone a pair of eyes coal-black and keen—all this under the pale moon-light, presents a spectacle at once weird-like and ghastly, as if of a death's head itself !

Still it is the face of Naraguana, as at a glance the gaucho perceives, muttering,

" Yes ; ĥ's the old chief, sure enough. Dead, and dried up like a mummy ! Died of old age, no doubt. Well," he continues, in graver tone, " by whatever way he may have come to his end, no greater misfortune could have befallen us. *Carrai !* it's Satan's own luck ! "

Having thus delivered himself, he stands for a while on the platform, but no longer looking at the corpse, nor any

of the relics around it. Instead, his eyes are turned towards
the tree, under whose shadow his youthful comrades are
reclining, and as he supposes asleep. On that side is the
moon, and as her light falls over his face, there can be
seen upon it an expression of great anxiety and pain—
greater than any that has marked it since that moment,
when in the *sumac* grove he bent over the dead body of his
murdered master.

But the troubled look now overspreading his features
springs not from grief, nor has anger aught to do with it.
Instead, it is all apprehension. For now, as though a
curtain had been suddenly lifted before his eyes, he sees
beyond it, there perceiving for himself and his companions
danger such as they had not yet been called upon to encounter. All along the route their thoughts were turned to
Naraguana, and on him rested their hopes. Naraguana
can do nothing for them now.

"No!" reflects the gaucho, despairingly; "we can
expect no help from him. And who else is there to give
it? Who, besides, would have the power to serve us, even
if the will be not wanting? No one, I fear. *Mil Diablos !*
it's a black look-out, now—the very blackest!"

Again facing round to the corpse, and fixing his eyes
upon the still uncovered face, he seems to examine it as
though it were a trail upon the pampas, in order to discover
what tale it may tell. And just for a like purpose does he
now scrutinize the features of the dead *cacique*, as appears
by his soliloquy succeeding.

"Yes; I understand it all now—everything. He's been
dead some time—at least two or three weeks. That
explains their leaving the other town in such haste, and
coming on here. Dead, or deadly sick, before he left it,

the old chief would have himself to think of, and so sent no word to us at the *estancia*. No blame to him for not doing so. And now that the young one's in power, with a fool's head and a wolf's heart, what may we expect from him? Ah, what? In a matter like this, neither grace nor mercy. I know he loves the *muchachita*, with such love as a savage may—passionately, madly. All the worse for her, poor thing! And all the poorer chance for us to get her away from him. *Por Dios!* it does look dark."

After a pause, he continues:

"His making her a captive and bringing her on here, I can quite understand; that's all natural enough, since his father being dead, there's no longer any one to hinder him doing as he likes. It's only odd his chancing to meet master out that day, so far from home. One would suppose he'd been watching the *estancia*, and saw them as they went away from it. But then, there were no strange tracks about the place, nor anywhere near it. And I could discover none by the old *tolderia* that seemed at all fresh, excepting those of the shod horse. But whoever rode him didn't seem to have come anywhere near the house; certainly not on this side. For all that, he might have approached it from the other, and then ridden round, to meet the Indians afterwards at the crossing of the stream. Well, I shall give the whole ground a better examination once we get back."

"Get back!" he exclaims, repeating his words after a pause, and in changed tone. "Shall we ever get back? That's the question now, and a very doubtful one it is. But," he adds, turning to descend from the scaffold, "it won't help us any on the road my remaining up here. If the old *cacique's* body still had the breath in it, may be it might. But as it hasn't the sooner I bid good-by to it the better. *Adios*, Naraguana ! *Pasa V. buena noche !*"

Were death itself staring him in the face, instead of seeing it as he does in the face of another man, Gaspar the gaucho, could not forego a jest, so much delights he to indulge in his ludicrous humour.

After unburdening himself as above, he once more closes his arms around the notched post, and lowers himself from the platform.

But again upon the ground, and standing with face toward the fig-tree, the gravity of its expression is resumed, and he seems to hesitate about returning to the place of bivouac, where his youthful companions are now no doubt enjoying the sweets of a profound slumber.

" A pity to disturb them !" he mutters to himself; "and with such a tale as I have now to tell. But it must be told, and at once. Now that everything's changed, new plans must be thought of, and new steps taken. If we're to enter the Indian town at all, it will have to be in a different way from what we intended. *Caspita !* how the luck's turned against us !"

And with this desponding reflection, he moves off from the scaffold ; and, making his way among the mausoleums, once more approaches the spot where the South American banyan casts its sombre shadow over them.

CHAPTER XLVIII.

GASPAR has been mistaken in supposing the other two asleep. One of them is—Ludwig, who sleeps soundly, and to all appearance peacefully. Not that he is indifferent to the seriousness of the situation, or less anxious about the upshot, than Cypriano. He but slumbers, because he is naturally of a more somnolent habit than his cousin, as also, being the weaker of the two, from the effects of a journey so long sustained, and travelling at such a pace. Moreover, he is not even yet quite recovered from the damage done him by the gymnoti; their electricity still acting on his nervous system, and producing a certain lassitude.

There is yet another reason why Ludwig has let himself go to sleep—one of a moral nature. As is known, he still adheres to his belief in the fidelity of Naraguana, and, so believing, is least of them all apprehensive about the result. At this moment he may be dreaming of the old *cacique*, though little dreams he that his dead body is so near!

Altogether different is it with Cypriano. This night there is no sleep for him, nor does he think of taking any. Though he lay down alongside his cousin, wrapping himself in his poncho, he did not long remain recumbent. Instead, soon starting to his feet again, he has been pacing to and fro under the fig-tree, wondering where Gaspar has gone. For, as known, the gaucho had slipped off without making noise, or saying word.

Missing him, the young Paraguayan would call out his name. But he fears to raise his voice, lest it reach other ears than those for which it was intended. Reflecting, moreover, that Gaspar is pretty sure to have some good reason for absenting himself, and that his absence will not likely be for long, he awaits his return in silence. Therefore, when the gaucho in coming back draws nigh to the fig-tree, he sees a form within the periphery of its shadow, that of Cypriano, standing ready to receive him.

The latter first speaks, asking :

" Where have you been, Gaspar? "

" Oh ! only taking a turn among the tombs."

" And you've seen something among them to make you uneasy ? "

" Why do you say that, Señorito? "

" Because I can see it in your countenance."

The gaucho, as he approaches, has the moon full upon his face, and by her light the other has observed the troubled look.

" What is it ? " the youth goes on to ask, in a tone of eager anxiety, all the more from seeing that the other hesitates to give the explanation. " You've discovered something—a new danger threatens us ? Come, Gaspar, you may as well tell me of it at once."

" I intend telling you, *hijo mio.* I was only waiting till we were all three together. For now, I think, we'll have to rouse Master Ludwig. You've conjectured aright, as I'm sorry to say. I *have* seen something that's not as we would wish it. Still, it may not be so bad as I've been making it."

Notwithstanding this hopeful proviso, Cypriano is himself now really alarmed; and, impatient to learn what the new danger is, he stoops down over his cousin, takes hold of his arm, and shakes him out of his slumbers.

Ludwig, starting to his feet, confusedly inquires why he has been disturbed. Then Gaspar, coming close to them, so that he need not speak in a loud voice, gives an account of what he has discovered, with his own views relating to it.

As he himself did, both the boys at once comprehend the changed situation, with a like keen sense of the heightened danger to result from it. Naraguana's death has extinguished all hope of help from him. It may be both the cause and forecast of their own !

Their prospects are now gloomy indeed; but they do not idly dwell on them, or give way to utter despondency. That would be unavailing; besides, there is no time for it. Something must be done to meet the altered circumstances. But what ? A question to which none of them makes an immediate answer, since none can.

For awhile all three stand silent, considering. Only a short while, when Gaspar is again stirred to activity, by reflecting that even now they are not safe. One of their horses, frightened by an owl that has flapped its wings close to its face, has snorted, striking the hard ground with his hoof, and making a noise that reverberates throughout the cemetery, echoing among the scaffolds. What if he should set to neighing, in answer to that which now and then comes up from the town below ? The thing is too probable, and the result manifest. A single neigh might betray them;

for what would horses be doing up there upon the sacred hill ?
So would any Indian ask who should chance to hear it.

"We must muffle our animals," says Gaspar. "And
what's more, take them back to the other side, where we
came up. There we can better conceal them among the
bushes. Besides, if it should come to our being under the
necessity of a speedy retreat, we'll be nearer to the back
track, and have a fairer chance of getting off. Señoritos !
get your jergas, and wrap them round your horses' heads."

He sets the example by so disposing of his own ; and,
accustomed to quick action in matters of the kind, all three
soon have their animals "tapado." Then, leading them
across to where the path ascends on the opposite side, they
place them under cover of some thick bushes growing neai
by, Gaspar saying :

" 'They'll be safe enough here, I take it ; at all events till
the morning. Then we may move them elsewhere, and if
we're to have a run for it, remember, *hijos mios*, 'twill be a
race for our lives. There's no Naraguana now to stand
between us and that young wolf, who I fear has got the dear
little lamb in his clutches, so fast we'll have great——"

The effect of his words are such, upon those listening to
them, that he suddenly interrupts himself in what he was
about to say, and in changed tone continues : "*Carramba !*
we'll rescue her yet, Naraguana, or no Naraguana. It can
be done without him, and I think I know the way."

In saying so, Gaspar is practising a slight deception, his
object being to cheer his young companions, over whom his
last speech seemed to cast the gloom of despair. For he
has as yet thought of no way, nor conceived any definit
plan of action. When asked by Cypriano to explain himself, he is silent ; and appealed to, he answers by evasion

The truth is, that up to the instant of his finding Naraguana's body upon the scaffold, he too had been trusting all
to what the latter would do for them ; and no more than
Ludwig could he believe the good old chief to have turned
traitor to the pale-faced friend so long under his protection,
much less connived at his assassination. Now, the gaucho
knows he has had no hand either in the murder of his master,
or the abduction of that master's daughter. These events
must have occurred subsequent to his death, and, while
they were in the act of occurrence, Naraguana was sleeping
his last sleep under his plumed *manta* upon that elevated
platform. His son and successor—for Gaspar doubts not
that Aguara has succeeded him in the chieftainship—is
answerable for the deed of double crime, whoever may have
been his aiders and abettors.

Of course, this makes the case all the more difficult to
deal with, since the new *cacique*, by this time established in
full plenitude of power, will have it all his own way, and
can carry things with a high hand, as he most surely will.
To make appeal to him for the restitution of the captive
would be manifestly idle, like asking a tiger to surrender the
prey it holds between its teeth or in its claws. The gaucho
has no thought of so appealing, any more than either of the
others. And no more than they has he formed a plan of
future action. Only now, after their disposal of the horses,
is his brain busy in the conception of some scheme suited
to the changed circumstances ; and hence, on Cypriano
asking him to tell the way he knew of, he but replies
evasively, saying :

"Be patient, Señorito ! Wait till we've got things a little
snug, then I'll take pleasure in telling you. But we mustn't
remain here. On the other side of this queer cemetery,

where the road runs down to the *tolderia*—as I've no doubt
there is such—that will be the place for us to spend the
night in.   There we can see and hear what passes on the
plain, and should any one stray up we'll be warned of it,
either by our eyes or ears, in good time to get out of their
way.   So let us cross over.   And we must step silently," he
adds, pointing to the *cacique's* scaffold tomb, " lest we disturb
the sleep of old Naraguana, up yonder."

With this facetious remark, made partly in the indulgence
of his usual humour, but as much to raise the spirits of his
young companions, he strides off among the odd structures,
making direct for the other side of the cemetery, Ludwig
and Cypriano following in single file.

CHAPTER XLIX.

As they might truly anticipate, the gaucho's conjecture
proves to be correct. A road runs up to the summit of the
hill on its western side ; not direct, but somewhat zigzagged,
in consequence of the slope on that face being steeper, and
the ground more rocky and uneven. Withal, it is much
wider than that by which they ascended, the latter being
only a path leading out to the uninhabited pampa ; while
the former is the main thoroughfare between town and
cemetery. It debouches on the level summit through a
slight hollow, or defile, possibly due to the wear and tear of
travel, continued through the long ages. Many a funeral
procession, and from the most remote time, may have wound
its way up that steep slope, passing between two cliffs, which,
like the posterns of some grand gateway, mark the entrance
to this elevated burial-place.

They do not go direct to the point where the town road
enters the cemetery ground, but first back to the fig-tree to
get their guns, ponchos, and some other articles left under
it in their haste to put the horses in a better place of
security. Having recovered the weapons and chattels, they
proceed in search of the road. It is easily found, as all
the paths between the separate scaffolds run into it. The

point where it comes up out of the defile is but a short distance from the fig-tree; and on reaching this point they take their stand under the cliff; the one on the right hand side: for the moon being behind this, its shadow is projected more than half across the causeway of the road, so giving them a safe spot to stand in.

But they do not remain long upon their feet. Gaspar, observing a low bench of rock at the cliff's base behind them, repeats a Spanish synonym of the old saw, "It's as cheap sitting as standing;" and with this drops down upon the ledge, the others doing likewise.

The spot thus chosen is in every way answerable for the object they have in view. They are right over the Indian town, and can see into its streets, so far as is permitted by the moon's declining light. It commands, moreover, a view of the road, for a good reach below, to the first angle of the zigzag, and no one could ascend beyond that point without being seen by them so long as there is light; while there is no danger of being themselves seen. One passing up, even when opposite the place where they are seated, would not perceive them; since, in addition to the shadowing cliff, there is a thick scrub between them and the travelled track, effectually screening them.

The advantages of the position are apparent to all; and, soon as settled in it, Cypriano once more calls upon Gaspar to make known the plan he has hinted at.

Thus again challenged, the gaucho, who has meanwhile been doing his best to trace out some course of action, responds, speaking in a slow, meditative way. For as yet he has but a vague idea of what ought to be done.

"Well," he says, "there's but one plan I can think of as

at all likely to be successful. It may be, if dexterously managed ; and I dare say we can so manage it."

He pauses, seeming to deliberate within himself; which the two youths perceiving, refrain to ask further questions, leaving him to continue at his own time.

Which at length he does, with the odd observation :—

"One of us must become an Indian."

"Become an Indian !" exclaims Ludwig. "What mean you by that, Gaspar?"

"I mean counterfeit a redskin ; get disguised as one, and so steal into their town."

"Ah ! now, I understand. But that will be a dangerous thing to do, Gaspar. If caught ——"

"Of course it will be dangerous," interrupts the gaucho. "If caught, whoever of us it be, would no doubt get his skull crushed in by a *macana,* or maybe his body burnt over a slow fire. But as you see everything's dangerous for us now, one may as well risk that danger as any other. As to counterfeiting an Indian, I propose taking the part myself; and I should be able to play it pretty well, having, as you both know, had some experience in that line. It was by a trick of the same sort I got off from the Guaycurus when I was their prisoner up the Pilcomayo ; and if I hadn't done it neatly, you shouldn't now see me here."

"How did you manage it?" queries Ludwig mechanically, or rather, to know how he intended doing it now.

"Well, I borrowed the costume of an ugly savage, who was set to keep guard over me, having first taken a loan of his hardwood club. The club I returned to him, in a way he wouldn't have wished had he been awake. But he was silly enough to go to sleep, and was sleeping when I took it —ah ! and slept on after I returned it—ever after. His dress I kept, and wore for more than a week—in short, till I got back to Paraguay, for I was over a week on the road. It fitted me well; so well, that with some colouring stuff I found in the fellow's pouch, I was able to paint Indian, pass among the tents of the Guaycurus, and through a crowd of the savages themselves, without one of them suspecting the trick.   In that way I slipped out of their camp and off. So, by something of the same I may be able to get the dear little *niña* out of this town of the Tovas."

"Oh! do it, Gaspar!" exclaims Cypriano; "do that, and all I have will be yours."

"Yes! all we both have," adds Ludwig; "all there is at the *estancia*.   But rescue sister, and I'm sure my mother will make you welcome to everything."

"*Ta-ta!*" returns the gaucho, in a tone of reproach at being thus bargained with; gentle, however, as he knows it is from their anxiety about Francesca.   "Why, *hijos mios*, what are you speaking of? Promises to me,—a bribe for but doing my duty! 'Twill be a far day before Gaspar Mendez will need that for service done to either friend or relative of his dear dead master—aye, to the laying down of my life. *Carramba!* are we not all embarked in the same boat, to swim or sink together? But we sha'n't sink yet; not one of us. No; we shall swim out of this sea of troubles, and triumphantly. Cease despairing, then; for after all there mayn't be so much danger. Though Naraguana be dead, there's one above him, above all, up there in Heaven, who will not forsake us in this our extremity. Let us kneel and pray to Him."

And they do kneel; Ludwig, as called upon by Gaspar repeating the Lord's prayer, with a solemnity befitting the occasion.

CHAPTER L.

RISING from their knees, and resuming their seats upon the ledge, they return to the subject of discourse, interrupted by their devotional interlude; Gaspar declaring it his fixed intention to disguise himself as an Indian, and so seek entrance into the town. No matter what the danger, he is ready to risk it.

The others consenting, the next question that comes before them is, how the disguise is to be got up. About this there seems a difficulty to Ludwig, and also to Cypriano; though recalling the transformation of the latter into a soldier-crane, so quickly done by the deft hands of the gaucho, they doubt not that he will also find the ways and means for transforming himself into a redskin.

"If we only had a Tovas Indian here," he says, "as I had that sleepy Guaycuru, I'd not be long in changing clothes with him. Well, as we can't borrow a dress, I must see what can be done to make one. Good luck, there's no great quantity of cloth in a Tovas suit, and the stitching isn't much. All that's needed is a bit of breech-clout, which I can make out of the tail of my shirt; then the poncho over my shoulders, that will cover everything."

"But the colour of your skin, Gaspar! Wouldn't that betray you?"

Ludwig thus interrogates, not thinking how easily the dexterous gaucho can alter his complexion, nor recalling what he has said about his having done so to disguise himself as a Guaycuru.

"It might," returns Gaspar; "and no doubt would, if I left it as it is; which I don't intend doing. True, my face is not so fair as to need much darkening, beyond what the sun has done for it. I've seen some Tovas Indians with cheeks nigh as white as my own, and so have you, señoritos. As for my arms, legs, and body, they'll require a little browning, but as it so happens I've got the stuff to give it them. After the service rendered me by a coat of that colour, you may trust this gaucho never to go on any expedition over the pampas without a cake of brown paint stowed away in some corner of his *alparejas.* For the poncho, it won't be out of place. As you know, there are many of the common kind among the Tovas Indians, worn and woven by them; with some of better sort, snatched, no doubt, from the shoulders of some poor gaucho, found straying too far from the settlements."

"But, Gaspar," says Ludwig, still doubting the possibility of the scheme; "surely such a disguise as you speak of will never do? In the daylight they'd see through it."

"Ah! in the daylight, yes, they might. But I don't intend giving them that chance. If I enter their town at all, and I see no other way for it, that entry must be made in the darkness. I propose making it to-morrow evening, after the sun's gone down, and when it's got to be late twilight. Then they'll all be off guard, engaged in driving their animals into the *corrales,* and less likely to notice any one strolling about the streets."

"But supposing you get safe into the place, and can go

about without attracting attention, what will you do?" questions Ludwig.

"What can you?" is the form in which Cypriano puts it.

"Well, señoritos, that will depend on circumstances, and a good deal on the sort of luck in store for us. Still you mustn't suppose I'm trusting all to chance. Gaspar Mendez isn't the man to thrust his hand into a hornet's nest, without a likelihood—nay, a certainty, of drawing some honey out of it."

"Then you have such certainty now?" interrogates Cypriano, a gleam of hope irradiating his countenance. For the figurative words lead him to believe that the gaucho has not yet revealed the whole of his scheme.

"Of course I have," is Gaspar's rejoinder. "If I hadn't we might as well give everything up, and take the back track home again. We won't do that, while there's a chance left for taking the *muchachita* along with us."

"Never!" exclaims Cypriano, with determined emphasis. "If I have to go into their town myself, and die in it, I'll do that rather than return without my cousin."

"Be calm, *hijo mio!*" counsels Gaspar in a soothing tone, intended to curb the excitement of the fiery youth; "I don't think there will be any need for you either to enter the town, or lay down your life in it. Certainly neither, unless my plan get spoiled by the ill-luck that's been so long hanging about us. It isn't much of a plan after all; only to find one of the Indians, to whom I did a service when they were living at their old place. I cured the man of a complaint, which, but for the medicine I administered, would have carried him off to the happy hunting grounds—where just then he didn't wish to go. That medicine wasn't mine either. I had it from the *dueño.* But the sick man gave me credit for it all the same, and swore if I ever stood in need of his services, I could count upon receiving them, sure. From what I saw of him afterwards, and we came to know one another pretty well, I think I can. If ever there was a redskin to be trusted it's he. Besides, he's one of some authority in the tribe—a sort of sub-chief."

"I know another," breaks in Ludwig, as if suddenly recollecting ; "one who'd help us too—if we could only have a word with him. That's Nacena's brother, Kaolin."

Cypriano casts at his cousin a glance of peculiar meaning —something like surprise. Not because the latter has made mention of an Indian girl and her brother, both known to himself; but his giving the girl's name first, as though she were uppermost in his thoughts. And she is ; though that is a secret the young naturalist has hitherto kept close locked within his own breast.

Without noticing the glance of scrutiny bent upon him, he proceeds to explain himself.

"You may remember, Kaolin and I were the best of friends. He often went fishing with me, or rather I went with him. And I'm sure he'd stand by me now, in spite of Aguara."

"So much the better," rejoins Gaspar. " If my man fail me, we can fall back upon yours. What I propose doing, then, is this. We must keep quiet, and of course concealed, all day to-morrow till after sunset. We can employ ourselves in the preparation of my masquerading costume. When it comes on twilight, or a little later, I can slip down among those *toldos,* and go sauntering about, like any other redskin, till I find my old patient. He being a big fellow, there shouldn't be much difficulty in doing that. When found I'll make appeal to him, to help us in getting the *niña* out of——" he has it on his tongue to say "Aguara's clutches," but thinking of the effect of such a phrase falling upon Cypriano's ears, he concludes with the words, "whatever place they're keeping her in."

Gaspar's scheme thus at length declared, seeming feasible enough—and indeed the only one which any of them can think of as at all practicable—the other two signify assent to it; and its execution, or the attempt, is finally determined upon.

Going on to discuss the steps next best to be taken, they are interrupted by the sound of footsteps—some one ascending from below! The footfall is a light one, but distinct enough for them to tell, that whoever makes it is continuing on towards them, though yet unseen. As already said, the causeway is in part overshadowed by the cliff, and within this shadow keeps the person approaching. For all, on the footsteps drawing near, there is light enough for them to make out a figure; the better from its being clad in a drapery of white, loose and flowing, as though the wearer were a woman.

And so is she, or, to speak more correctly, a girl; her sex and age revealed to them, as at a certain point she steps to the off side of the path, and the moonlight falling upon her, exposes to their view a face beautiful as youthful.

Gaspar and Cypriano both recognize the face, but say nothing. Different Ludwig, who at the first glance got of it, unable to restrain himself, mechanically mutters the name—

"Nacena !"

CHAPTER LI.

FORTUNATELY Ludwig's exclamation has been uttered in
a subdued tone of voice; but lest in his agitation he may
speak louder, the gaucho grasps him by the arm, and
cautions silence, enjoining the same on Cypriano.

For several seconds not another word passes between
them, all three remaining motionless, and silent as sphinxes.

Meanwhile the Indian girl having come opposite the
place where they are seated, passes onward with cautious
step and eyes that interrogate the ground in front, as if she
anticipated seeing some one; like a young hind that has
stolen timidly out of the covert, on hearing the call-bleat
of the stag.

Soon she is far enough beyond to give them an opportunity of exchanging speech without her overhearing it; and
of this the gaucho avails himself, whispering—

"She's keeping an appointment with her lover, I suppose."

He little thinks of the painful effect his words have
produced upon Ludwig, as he adds—

"We'll do best to let her go on to their place of meeting,
which is no doubt somewhere near. She must return this
way, and then we can have *our* interview with her. But

where's the *amanté?* A laggard, to let the girl be on the ground before him! That wasn't my way, when—— See! she's coming to a stop."

And to a stop she comes, just where the sloping path passes out at the upper end of the defile, entering among the scaffolds. There standing erect, she glances inquiringly around, her gaze ranging along the open spaces between the structures and the shadows underneath them.

For a minute or two she remains in this attitude, without changing it, or making the slightest noise—evidently looking for a form or listening for a footstep. But neither seeing the one, nor hearing the other, she at length calls out a name; at first timidly, but after an interval in bolder tone,

"Shebotha!"

"Not her lover after all!" mutters Gaspar, who remembers the name thus pronounced, while Ludwig is relieved at hearing it, he also knowing something of the sorceress.

"Only that old hag!" the gaucho goes on; "I wonder now what the young sprout can be wanting with her, up here and at this hour of the night! Some mischief between them, I haven't a doubt."

His conjectures are suddenly brought to a close by a new noise now reaching their ears; a sort of scraping or shuffling, diversified by grunts and coughs—all coming up from below. Turning their eyes that way, they see ascending what appears to be a human figure, but stooped forward so as more to resemble a creature crawling on all fours. At the same instant the Indian girl has caught sight of it; and standing poised on the platform's edge, she silently awaits its approach, knowing the bent form to be Shebotha's.

Scrambling on up the steep, at intervals stopping to take breath, while she intermittently gives out hoarse grunts, the hag passes by them, at length reaching the spot where the girl stands awaiting her. Stopping by the side of the latter, both are now seen face to face in the full moonlight; and never did moon shine upon faces or figures more contrasting. On the one side age indicated by a spare body, thin skinny arms, features furrowed with wrinkles, of most repulsive aspect, and eyes sparkling with a sinister light; on the other, youth, with all its witching charms, **a figure** lithe and graceful as any palm growing on the plain below, features of classic type, and a face exquisitely beautiful, despite its tint of bronze, the eyes bright with the glow of a burning passion. For it is this last that has brought the girl thither.

Only a second or two do they remain silent, till the sorceress recovers breath; for it is she who breaks the silence, saying :—

" Nacena wants to speak with Shebotha? On what subject ? "

" Need I tell you, Shebotha; you know ! "

" I know that the sister of Kaolin is in love with our young *cacique.* That is no secret to others, any more than to me."

" Oh ! do not say that ! I thought no one knew of it but——"

" But everybody," interrupts the unfeeling hag. " And what if they do ? Nacena is beautiful, the belle of our tribe, and need fear no rival ; not even her with the eyes of blue, and the tresses of gold, who sleeps under Shebotha's roof. Nacena is jealous of the pale-face captive ; she has no cause."

" O, good Shebotha ! " cries the young girl, in passionate tone, her heart heaving with rekindled hope, " can you assure me of that ? If so, you shall have all I can give you; my armlets, neck ornaments, *mantas, hamacas,* everything. Fear not my rewarding you well ! "

" Nacena is generous," rejoins the sorceress, her eyes sparkling with pleasure at such a wholesale proffer of chattels. " She shall have that assurance; for Shebotha can give it without fail. See this ! "

While speaking, she has drawn out, from under the skin robe that covers her bony breast, what appears to be a small horn, converted into a phial with bottom and stopper.

" In this," she says, holding it up to the light, " is a fluid, one drop of which, given to Aguara will turn his heart whichever way Shebotha wishes it turned ; make him love whomsoever she wants him to love ; and that will be as Nacena wants it."

" Oh ! it is good of you, Mam Shebotha so good ! How shall I ever enough thank or reward you ? "

" No matter about thanks," responds the hag with a knowing leer; " Shebotha likes better the reward. And what you've promised will content her. But promises, as Nacena herself knows, are sometimes badly kept, and should have something to secure them, by way of earnest. What can you give me now ? "

The girl glances down to her breast, upon which lie several pendants, sustained by a massive chain of gold passing around her neck. Then she holds out her arms to show bracelets upon the wrists, beset with pearls and precious stones, that no doubt once clasped other wrists than hers—those of pale-faced *doncellas* dwelling in Santiago or Salta. Unclasping the armlets, one after another, she delivers them to Shebotha.

But the avaricious beldame is not yet satisfied. With her eyes upon the chain necklet and its glittering attachments, she nods towards it, as much as to say, "That too." And it, also, is detached; and handed over to her. Then her greedy eyes go to the fillet around the girl's temples, and an embroidered belt which encircles her waist. But these, though pretty ornaments, are not of great intrinsic value; and as Shebotha has in view a further levy of black mail at a future time, she can then take them too.

For the present she appears content, all the more as she gloats over the treasure, which for a while she feasts her eyes upon without speaking. Then slipping the various articles, one after another, into the bosom of her dress, she resumes speech, saying—

"Shebotha has other spells besides that spoken of; one powerful above all, which puts to sleep—ah! a sleep from which the sleeper never awakes. If the other should fail to act, and Aguara——"

"But you said it could not fail," breaks in the girl, her countenance again clouding over. "Is there a doubt, Mam Shebotha?"

"There's always uncertainty in these things," rejoins the sorceress; "and in the *love-spell* more than any other. As you know, love is the strongest passion, and therefore the most difficult to control."

All this, by way of making safe her bargain, for well knows she her spell will not bring back Aguara's love, lost to Nacena; and as the bulk of the reward promised will depend upon this, she has yet another proposal to make that may ensure its payment. She acts as one who would hedge a bet, and drawing closer to the victim of her delusion, she says—

"If Nacena should ever want the pale face put to sleep by that other spell, Shebotha will administer it."

As the fiendish suggestion is spoken in a whisper, the three listeners do not hear what it is. They can only guess by the behaviour of the young girl that some offer has been made which she indignantly rejects. This can be told by her rejoinder, and the air in which she delivers it.

"No!" she exclaims, starting back with an expression of horror upon her countenance. "Never, never! If Aguara be untrue to me, it is no fault of the pale-face. I know that; and have no vengeance for her. But for him—ah! if he have deceived me, it is not she, but he should suffer punishment. And punished he shall be—by my brother."

"Oh! your brother!" returns the sorceress with a sneer, evidently in anger at having her offer so rejected. "If Kaolin can right your wrongs, let him." And she adds, making to move off, "I suppose you haven't any more need for me, or my services."

"If she haven't I have," cries Gaspar, springing out from the place of concealment and seizing hold of the hag, while at the same instant Cypriano flings his arms around the Indian girl.

"Come, Mam Shebotha!" continues the gaucho, "it's my turn to have a talk with you."

She makes an effort to escape, and would cry out; but cannot, with his sinewy fingers around her throat.

"Stop your struggling!" he commands, giving her a shake till her old bones crackle at every joint. "A cry, a word from you above a whisper, and I'll close your windpipe so that you'll never grunt through it again. Come, *muchachos!* Let's to the other side! One of you bring on the girl. *Vamos!*"

Raising the hag in his arms he bears her off, with no more care for her comfort than if she were a trapped wolf. Nacena is borne more tenderly in Ludwig's arms, into which she has been transferred, by a sort of tacit understanding between him and his cousin—the latter walking alongside. No threat hears the girl, nor needs it to enforce silence. For she is no more apprehensive of injury, now knowing him who carries her as her brother's old playfellow. Above all, does she feel reassured, on hearing whispered in her ear—

" Have no fear, Nacena ! Am not I the bosom friend of your brother? *I will not deceive you.*"

Does she note the earnestness of his words, and the significant emphasis given to those last pronounced? Whether or not, she refrains making rejoinder : but suffers herself to be borne on through the scaffold tombs without resistance, and silent as the forms reposing upon them.

CHAPTER LII.

A FRIEND UNEXPECTED.

STRAIGHT across the cemetery goes Gaspar, with Shebotha in his arms, nor stops he till back on the spot where
the path leads down to the outer plain. Arriving there, he
deposits his living burden upon the earth ; not gently, but
dumping her down with a rude violence, as though it were a
bunch of faggots. Still he does not let her out of his arms
altogether ; but with a threat, once more warning her to be
silent, retains fast hold of her, till Cypriano has brought
him a *lazo* from the saddle of one of the horses near by.
Looping this round the body of the sorceress, and taking a
few turns of it about her arms and ankles, he spreads his
poncho over her head, then knots the rope around her neck,
and so muffles her beyond the chance of either hearing or
making herself heard. All this done, he again raises her
from the ground, and carrying her some distance back
among the scaffolds, he binds her to a corner post of one
with the end of the *lazo* yet unused. His purpose in thus
disposing of her is not clear to his companions, both of
whom he has left in charge of the Indian girl ; who, on her
part, makes no attempt to escape. Instead, released from
Ludwig's arms, she stands silently by his side, neither
trembling nor showing sign of fear. Why should she, with

those words of friendly assurance which have been once
more whispered in her ear?

And now Gaspar getting back to where they stand, and
speaking in the Tovas tongue sufficiently well to be understood by her, says to Nacena—

" *Muchacha mia !* you see who we are, and know all three
of us. We know you, Nacena—even to your tenderest
secret ; which has been revealed to us in the dialogue just
held between yourself and Mam Shebotha. Every word of
that we've heard, with the lies she's been telling you. And
let me tell you, that of all the wicked impostor's promises,
there's but one she could have kept—that to rid you of her
you deem a rival. And she could only have done that by
doing murder ; which was what she meant by her sleeping
draught."

The young girl shudders listening to what she knows is
but the truth.

" 'Twas good of you to reject the foul proposal," goes on
the gaucho, " and indignantly, as we know you did. We
saw and heard it all. And now, I have a proposal to offer,
which you won't reject ; I'm sure you won't, Nacena."

She makes no rejoinder, but stands waiting to receive it.

" It is," he continues, " that you can still rid yourself of
that rival, not by doing wrong, but right and justice. With
your help we shall take her away to a place where Aguara
will never more set eyes upon her. But as I've said, we
stand in need of your assistance, and you must give it."

" You will, you will !" interposes Cypriano, in tones of
earnest appeal.

" Yes, dear Nacena," follows Ludwig, in tenderer tones ;
" I'm sure you will. Remember, she is my sister, and that
you yourself have a brother ! "

Had they but known it, there was no need for all this petitioning. Even while Gaspar was speaking, and long before he had finished, the Indian girl, with the quick, subtle instinct of her race, divined what they were aiming at —the very end she herself desires, and might have proposed to them. The same instinct, however, prompts her to feign ignorance of it, as evinced by her interrogative rejoinder :—

" How can Nacena assist you ? In what way ? "

" By helping us to get the pale-face out of her prison." It is Gaspar who speaks. " She is imprisoned, is she not ? "

"She is."

"And where is she kept ? " further questions the gaucho.

Cypriano trembles as he listens for the answer. He fears, half expecting it to be, " In the *toldo* of the *cacique.*"

It is a relief to him, when Nacena, pointing towards the dark object bound to the scaffold post, says : " She has charge of the pale-face captive."

'' *Bueno !* " ejaculates Gaspar with delight in his eyes, as in those of Cypriano. " Nothing could be better than that. And now that we have Shebotha here, no one will be guarding the prisoner—will there ? "

" Alas, yes ! " responds the Indian girl, her words with their tone telling that she has entered into the spirit of their enterprise.

" Who ? " interrogates Gaspar. " What is he—if it be a man ? "

" Yes, a man. A white man, like yourselves ; one who has been long with our tribe—a captive taken many years ago from some of the countries south. He is Shebotha's own slave, and watches over the pale-face when she is out of the *toldo*."

Again the gaucho ejaculates, "*Bueno !*" adding, in *sotto voce*, to his two companions, "It seems better still ; a bit of rare good luck ; that is, if this white man, whoever he be, isn't grown Indianized, as I've known some to be." Then to the girl. "Shebotha's slave, you say? In that case, he should be wanting to regain his liberty, and we may give him the chance. If need be, we can take him along, too. You understand, Nacena?"

"I do."

"Then you agree to assist us?"

"Say yes !" urges Cypriano.

"*My* sister, Nacena !" adds Ludwig.

In response to their united appeals, she points to the sorceress, saying—

"Her vengeance is to be dreaded. If I do as you wish me, Shebotha——"

"Won't hurt a hair of your head," says Gaspar, interrupting. "Nor can't. She'll not be near enough to do you any injury. That worthy woman is on the eve of a long journey, to be made in our company, if you agree to assist us in getting the pale-face away. You do agree to it, *amiga mia ?*"

The girl fully comprehending, and relieved at the thought of the dreaded sorceress being taken out of the way, at length not only signifies assent to their scheme, but embraces it with alacrity. Its success will be to her advantage as theirs, ridding her of that rival feared, and it may be, restoring to her the affections of him on whom she has fixed her own.

And now that confidence is established between her and

her captors, she gives them a full account of how things stand in the *toldería*, and the place where the captive is confined. Having heard which, Gaspar counsels her how to act, as a last word, saying—

" Tell this white man, who has charge of the *niña*, he need no longer be a prisoner himself, nor Shebotha's slave. Say to him, that men of his own race and colour are near, ready to rescue and take him back to his people, wherever they may be. Surely that will be enough to gain him to our side, and get his help also."

Nacena hesitates for a time ; then answering, says,—

" No, not enough, I fear."

" But why ? "

" The white man is not in his senses. He has lost them long ago. The little left him is given to Shebotha. He fears her, as all our people do; but he more than any. She has surely left him with commands to keep a close watch. He does not disobey her ; and it may be impossible for me to speak with the pale-face, much more get her away from him."

"*Caspita !*" exclaims Gaspar, his countenance again turning grave. " There will be a difficulty there, I see it ; if the man's crazed, as you say he is, Nacena. You think he won't let you speak with the prisoner, unless you have permission from Shebotha ? "

" He will not—I am sure he will not."

" In that case all may be idle, and our scheme go for nought. *Por Dios !* what's to be done ? "

Pressing his head between his hands, the gaucho stands considering, while the other three in silence await the result. His deliberation is not for long ; a bright idea has flashed across his brain, and with his countenance also recovering brightness, he exclaims—

"*Gracios a Dios!* I know how it can be managed; I think I know."

Ludwig and Cypriano have it on their tongues to inquire what he means. But before either can say a word, he is off and away in a rush toward the scaffold-post to which Shebotha is tied.

Reaching it, he is seen with arms outstretched and in rapid play, as though he were setting her free. Far from that, however, is his intention. He but undoes the knot around her neck, and raising the poncho, clutches at something which encircles her throat. He had noticed this something while throttling her when first caught; it had rattled between his fingers as the beads of a rosary, and he knew it to be such, with a slight difference—the beads being human teeth! A remembrance, moreover, admonishes him that this ghastly necklace was worn by the sorceress, not for adornment, but to inspire dread. It is, in fact, one of her weapons of weird mystery and power, and an idea has occurred to him that it may now be used as an instrument against herself.

Having detached it from her neck, and replaced the poncho upon her head, he returns to where he had left the others, and holding out the string of teeth, says to Nacena—

"Take this. Present it to the crazy pale-face; tell him Shebotha sent it as a token authorizing you to act for her; and, if he be not altogether out of his wits, I warrant it'll get you admission to the presence of the pale-face. For anything beyond, you will best know how to act of yourself."

The girl grasps the hideous symbol, a gleam of intelligence

lighting up her swarth but beautiful face. For she, too, anticipates the effect it will have on Shebotha's slave, from actual knowledge—not by guessing, as with Gaspar.

Knowing herself now at liberty and free to depart, without saying another word, she turns her back upon them ; and gliding away with the agile, stealthy step peculiar to her race, soon passes beyond their sight.

They stand looking after her, till her dark figure disappears amid the shadows of the scaffolds. But they have no doubt of her fidelity—no fear that she will fail to do what she can for the fulfilment of her promise. The keeping it is secured by her own interested motives : for the passion impelling her to act on their behalf, though purely selfish, can be trusted as truth itself."

CHAPTER LIII.

A DELUDED JAILER.

MIDNIGHT's hour is past, the moon has gone down, and in the Indian town there is darkness and silence. Every one is asleep, or seems to be ; since no light shines either in *toldo* or tent, neither can a human figure be seen in the streets, or anywhere around.

At some distance from the houses, however, among thickly-standing trees, and close into the base of the hill, is the quaint dwelling-place of Shebotha—half cave, half hut—and inside this flickers a faint light, from a dip candle of crude beeswax, with a wick of the fibre of the *pita* plant. By its red flame, mingled with much smoke. a collection of curious objects is dimly discernible ; not articles of furniture, for these are few, but things appertaining to the craft in which Shebotha is supposed to have skill—demonology. There are the bones and skins of monkeys, with those of snakes, lizards, and other reptiles ; teeth of the alligator and jaguar ; the proboscis-like snouts of the *tapir* and *tamanoir*, or great ant-bear, with a variety of other like oddities, furnished by the indigenous creatures of the Chaco in every department of the zoological world—birds, quadrupeds, insects, reptiles, and fishes.

This motley conglomeration is for the most part arranged

against the inner wall of the hut, and opposite the entrance, so as to be observable by any one looking in at the door, or even passing by it. For its purpose is to impress the superstitious victims of Shebotha's craft with a belief in her witching wa s. And to give this a more terrifying and supernatural character, a human skull, representing a death's head, with a pair of tibia for crossbones underneath, is fixed centrally and prominently against the wall.

The same light that so faintly illuminates this paraphernalia of repulsive objects, also shines upon one that is pleasing—this the figure of a young girl, with a face wonderfully fair. For she is Francesca Halberger.

At the hour spoken of she is the sole occupant of the hut ; its owner, Shebotha, being abroad. For it is the self-same hour and instant when the sorceress has the rosary of teeth snatched so rudely from her neck. She is seated on the edge of a *catré*, or cane bedstead, of the pallet kind, her head buried in her hands, through the white fingers of which her long golden tresses fall in rich profusion, scattered over and mingling with the fur of the great pampas wolf which serves as a sort of mattrass for the bed.

The candle has burnt down into the socket of its rude stick, but at intervals flares up, with a crackling, sputtering noise ; as it it does so, showing upon her features that same sad look as when she was being carried hither, a captive ; only that her face is now paler, and the expression upon it telling of a despair deeper and more settled. She has slept but little from the day of her entrance under Shebotha's roof, and no great deal since she last lay on her own bed at home. What sleep she now gets is only in short snatches ; when tired nature can no longer continue the struggle with thoughts all the while torturing her. No wonder at sweet slumber being thus long denied her, with such memories to keep her awake! In fancy, ever before her seems the face of her father with that look of agony she last saw upon it, as he lay upon the ground, weltering in his gore. And in fancy also, she beholds the ruffian, Valdez, standing above the prostrate form, waving over it his blood-stained spear, a very demon exultant!

But her painful thoughts are not all of the past. She has doubts and fears also for the future, dark as she reflects on her own situation, and what will be done to her; but still darker when she thinks of those left behind and far away. What will become of her dear mother and brother? What of him—dear, ah! perhaps dearer than either—her handsome cousin? For Cypriano's affection for her is fully reciprocated.

Not strange then the sadness overspreading her features, nor the weight of woe in her heart; as she dwells on the fate that may be his and theirs. For she knows they are all in danger—great and certain danger; has known it ever since seeing Valdez, the *vaqueano*, consorting with the Tovas Indians, and on friendly terms with their chief. Oft had she asked herself the question whither he went afterwards! Did he return to Paraguay, or go direct to the *estancia*, there to complete his diabolical work—begun by murder, to end in the same with other crimes? In any case he would not likely leave them unharmed, as the captive girl too truly apprehends.

With such terrible thoughts to agitate her breast, no wonder she should be awake while everyone around seems slumbering. But on this night, and at this hour, something besides hinders her from seeking repose; that being the absence of Shebotha, which, for certain reasons, makes her more than ordinarily apprehensive. In truth, she is greatly alarmed by it. Never before has the sorceress been out of her *toldo* to stay for any continued time; above all, never during the hours of night. Why should she be absent now, and so long?

While asking herself these questions, the captive has not the slightest intention to take advantage of Shebotha's absence, and make trial to escape. Well knows she that would be idle, and she could not get away if she tried. For though the owner of the hut is off watch, there is one on it —a man sitting, or squatted, just outside the door. No red man, but one with a white skin; himself a prisoner, and who possibly once, as she, felt distressed by his captivity. It may have been this very feeling which has made him what he now is—a witless idiot, resigned to his fate. In any case, he seems to be contented as Shebotha's slave; and, perhaps ignorant of there being any better, serves her with a fidelity worthy of a better mistress. No watch-dog at that *toldo's* door were more to be trusted than he.

She inside has no intention, nor ever had, of tempting him to be untrue to his trust. Even could he be induced to let her pass out, what purpose would it serve? She could not make her way home; and he is not the sort of man to see her safe through more than two hundred miles of wilderness. The idea is too hopeless to be entertained, and she does not for an instant entertain it.

The thoughts that now occupy her mind are not of how she may escape from her captivity, but dwelling upon a theme altogether different. She is thinking who will be the next one to darken the door of the hut; fearing it may be neither Shebotha herself, nor yet her slave, but the man who is master of both—Aguara!

True, the young *cacique* has not as yet offered her either outrage or insult; instead still approaches her with courtesy, and a pretence of friendship. For all, something—it may be instinct—admonishes her that he is acting under a mask, which he may at any moment cast aside, revealing the monster, as she believes him to be. And with sufficient reason, recalling that tragedy which deprived her of a father; and sure, despite all his protestations, that Aguara played a willing part in it.

While thus apprehensively reflecting, she hears footsteps, as of some one approaching the place. The sound causes her to start to her feet, and stand listening, with a heightened expression of fear upon her face. For, although the footfall is distant, and only distinguishable as such by the rustle it makes among the dead leaves, she can tell it is not that of Shebotha, with whose halting gait and shuffling step her ear has grown familiar. Whose, then? Who would be coming to the hut at that time of night—now morning—save She-botha herself? None but she, and those of her belonging, dare do so either by night or by day? For the *toldo* of the sorceress is a sort of sanctuary, tabooed to the people of the tribe, and no one may enter or approach its sacred pre-cincts, without having her permission, or being bidden by her. Yes; one may, and can—Aguara.

Still darker shows the fear upon the face of the captive girl, as she thinks of this special privilege accorded to the *cacique*, of which she has been made aware. It must be he who is drawing near, and with him a danger she has long vaguely apprehended.

For some seconds she remains intently listening, her young heart pulsing audibly within her breast. It beats easier as the footfall draws nigher, and she can tell it is not

that of a man. The tread is too light and elastic. It cannot be Aguara who approaches.

She is still surer of its not being he, as the footsteps,
having come close up to the hut, cease to be heard, and in
their place a different sound enters through the open door
—a feminine voice speaking in soft, dulcet tones.

The speech is not addressed to the captive herself, but to
him who watches outside. After an interchange of ordinary
salutation, and an inquiry by the watcher as to what is
wanted—this evidently in tone of surprise—the soft voice
responds,

" I want to speak with the little pale-face."

"You cannot. Shebotha forbids it. No one may enter
here without her permission."

" But I have more than her permission—her commands.
She has sent me with a message to the pale-face. At this
moment Mam Shebotha has a matter elsewhere, and could
not come nersell.'

"You may be speaking the truth, but how am I to
know?" questions the man, as he regards the intruder with
an incredulous stare. " I don't go so far as to say you are
telling a lie. All I say is, that the thing isn't at all likely.
Mam Shebotha's not the sort to trust her affairs to such a
chiquitita as you."

"You know me, don't you?"

"Oh, yes; you are Kaolin's sister—her they call the belle
of the tribe; your name's Nacena."

" It is so ; and surely you'll believe me? The sister of
Kaolin would not speak false. You cannot suppose I am
deceiving you ?"

" Ah !" he rejoins, with his words heaving a sigh , 'it is
often those who are most beautiful who most deceive."

Possibly the memory of some such deception, an experience of times long past, has been awakened within him. It embitters his speech as he continues,—

"I can't—I won't believe you—though you are Kaolin's sister, and ever so fair to look upon."

"But you will, when you look upon this."

She draws out the string of teeth snatched from the neck of the sorceress, and holds it up to his eyes, adding,—

"That I bring from Shebotha herself. She gave it me to show you as a sign that I have her permission to speak with the pale-face—nay, her command, as I've said. Now!"

At sight of the hideous symbol, which he instantly recognizes, his incredulity is at an end. For he knows how jealously the sorceress guards this token, and that no one could have obtained it from her without some special purpose, or to do a service to herself. What it may be he questions not, nor longer forbids entrance to the hut, but nods towards the door, as much as to say,—

"You can go in."

CHAPTER LIV.

AN UNLOOKED-FOR DELIVERER.

THOUGH the dialogue between Nacena and Shebotha's slave was in the Tovas tongue, she who has overheard them inside the hut has sufficient acquaintance with it to make out that the Indian girl is seeking an interview with herself. But for what purpose, she has not the most distant idea, and cannot conceive why it should specially he sought at that strange hour, when everybody else is abed. She knows Nacena by name, as by sight; having on many occasions seen her at the old *tolderia*. But the two have never had acquaintance, nor held conversation; the sister of Kaolin always seeming shy with her, and never visiting the *estancia*, as did the other girls of the tribe. More than this, she remembers that whenever of late she by chance met the savage maiden, she had observed a scowl upon the latter's face, which she could not help fancying was meant for herself. Nor had her fancy been astray; since in reality for her was that black look. Though for what reason Francesca could not tell, having never that she could think of done aught that should give offence to Kaolin's sister. Besides, was not Kaolin himself the bosom friend of her brother Ludwig? Still, recalling that scowl so often seen upon Nacena's

x

countenance—with a suspicion, purely intuitive, of what may have caused it—not strange she should deem the visit of the Indian girl boding no good to her, but instead something of ill.

As the latter steps inside the *toldo*, however, and the light falls upon her face, the captive can there see no sign of malice, nor token of hostility. Instead, it is lit up by a smile which seems rather to speak of friendship and protection. And, in truth, such are among the sentiments now moving the Indian girl to action. At the prospect of being for ever rid of a rival she sees so helpless, the feeling of jealousy has passed away out of her heart, as its frown from her face, and she approaches the captive with the air of one who has both the wish and the power to give liberty. She is the first to speak, asking abruptly—

"Do you wish to be free?"

"Why do you ask that?" is the interrogative rejoinder, in a tone distrustful. For that smile may be but to deceive.

"Because Nacena has it in her power to give you freedom if you desire it."

"Desire it!" exclaims the captive. "Nacena is but mocking me," she adds, involuntarily falling into the figurative mode of speech peculiar to the American Indian. "Indeed, I do desire it. But how could Nacena set me at liberty?"

"By taking the pale-face to her people."

"They are far away—hundreds of miles. Would Nacena herself take me to them?"

"No. That is not needed. The pale-face is mistaken. Her friends are not far away, but near. They wait for her to come out to them."

The captive gives a start of surprise, the light of hope and joy, long absent from her eyes, rekindling in them, as another light breaks upon her.

"Of whom does Nacena speak?"

"Of your brother the fair-haired youth, your cousin the dark Paraguayan, and the gaucho who has guided them hither. All three are close to the *tolderia*, on the other side of the hill—as I've said, expecting you. Nacena has spoken with them, and promised she will conduct you to where they are. White sister!" she adds, in a tone of unmistakeable sincerity, at the same time drawing closer to the captive, and tenderly taking her by the hand, " do not show distrust, but let Nacena keep her word. She will restore you to your friends, your brother; ah! to one who waits for you with anxiety keener than all!"

At the last words the captive bends upon her would-be deliverer a wildered, wondering look. Is it possible Nacena has knowledge of her tenderest secret? It must be so; but how can she have learnt it? Surely Cypriano—whom she says she has seen outside and spoken with—surely, he could not have revealed it; would not! Francesca forgets that the Indian girl was for years a near neighbour to her father's *estancia ;* and though never visiting there, with the keen intuition of her race was like enough to have learnt, that the relationship between her cousin and herself had something in it beyond mere cousinly affection.

While she is still cogitating as to how Nacena could have come to this knowledge, and wondering the while, the latter breaks in upon her wonderment, and once more urges her to flight, again speaking of him who is near and dear, so anxiously expecting her.

It needs not such pressing appeal. For the captive girl,

her surprise once past, is but too willing to embrace the opportunity so unexpectedly offered, and by one so unlikely to offer it. Therefore, without further hesitation, she signifies acceptance, saying,

"I will trust you, Nacena. You have called me your white sister, and I believe you sincere. You would not speak so if you meant me harm. Take me where you will; I am ready to go with you."

Saying which, she holds out her hand, as if offering to be led.

The Indian girl taking it, turns her face for the door, and is about to step towards it, when she remembers the watcher without; and obstruction she had for the time forgotten. Will he bar their exit? A cloud comes over her brow, as she asks herself the question; for, mentally answering it, she thinks he most probably will.

The other observing her hesitation, and quite comprehending it, makes no inquiry about the cause. That is already declared in the dialogue lately overheard by her; and as he outside is likely to be listening, the two now take counsel together, speaking in whispers.

Nacena, from a better knowledge of the situation, is of course the chief adviser, and it ends in her determining to show a bold front, and pass out as if already armed with Shebotha's permission. If interrupted, they can then make a rush for it. In short, after a hurried consultation, they can think of no other way, much less a better one. For by the shuffling of footsteps, and a wheezing noise—Shebotha's slave being afflicted with asthma—they can tell that he is close by the entrance.

Soon as resolved how to act, the Indian girl, still holding the captive by the hand, leads her on to the door; and, passing over the threshold side by side, they present them-selves to the sentry, Nacena saying:

"In going in I forgot to tell you my errand from Mam Shebotha. She bad me bring the pale-face to where she is herself. You see, I am taking her."

"You cannot take her out of the *toldo*," rejoins the man in a tone of dogged denial. "You must not; Shebotha would kill me if I permitted it."

"But I have Shebotha's command to do so."

"How am I to know that?"

"You forget what I have said, and what I've given you."

She points to the strange rosary, which he had taken from her, and still retains—possibly as a voucher against any mis-take that may arise.

"No, I don't," he rejoins, holding the string up before her eyes, and shaking it till the teeth rattle. "There it is; but withal, I can't allow her, the pale-face, to go with you. It might be as much as my life is worth."

"But what is your life worth without liberty?"

It is not Nacena who puts this question, but the pale-face herself; speaking to him in her native tongue, as his. He gives a sudden start on hearing it, and regards the young girl with a stare of astonishment, rubbing his eyes as though just awakened from a long-continued sleep.

"Ah—eh!" he exclaims, excitedly. "What's that? Liberty, did you say? Liberty? Mine's gone long ago. I'm but a poor slave—Shebotha's slave. I can never be free again; no, *never!*"

"You may be free now—this very moment—if you wish it."

"If I wish it! Ha, ha, ha! That's a good joke! If I

wish it ! Only show me the way, and let Mam Shebotha go to ——"

" Never mind Mam Shebotha.   Listen to me, who am of the same race and people as yourself.   There are some of them now near, who have come to take me home to my friends.   You must have friends too, whom you left long ago.   Why should you not go back to them ? "

" *Carramba !* " he cries out, as if the sound of his native tongue had brought back to remembrance one of its most common exclamations, and along with it a desire to return to the place where he last heard it spoken.   " Why should I not ?   If you say you'll take me, I will."

" Ah !   I'll not only take you, but be glad of your company. *Nos vamos !*"

It is still Francesca who speaks, and at the last words, pronounced in a tone of half encouragement, half command, she stretches out her hand, and taking hold of that of her late jailer, leads him off, as a rough pampas colt just tamed and gentled.

Nacena, astonished at the spirit shown by the little pale-face, and delighted with a success which may prove advantageous to herself, says not a word ; but steps off forward in front of the other two—making mute pantomimic signs to guide them in the direction they are to go.

CHAPTER LV.

Soon as Nacena had started on return to the town, the gaucho and his companions commence making preparations to descend from the hill. Not by the road leading down to the *tolderia*, but the path by which they came up. For before her parting with them the Indian girl and Gaspar had held further speech; she imparting to him additional information of how things stood in the tribe; he, in turn, giving her more detailed instructions how to act, in the event of her being able to obtain an interview with the pale-face captive, and to get her off from the place where confined. In the programme arranged between them, the final part to be played by Nacena would be her conducting her charge round to the other side of the hill, where the rescuers would be in waiting to receive her. Delivered to them, the action of the Indian girl would be at end, so far as that affair was concerned, while theirs had yet to be considered.

The place where they were to await her was, of course, mutually understood—by the entrance to the uphill path, under the great *ceiba* tree. Nacena knew it well, having oft traversed that path, reclined in the shadow of the tree, and played under it from the earliest days of childhood. For it was a pretty spot, much frequented by the younger members of the community when out for promenade on the plain, or nutting among the palm-groves that studded it. A sort of rendezvous, or stopping place, from the two routes to the town here diverging; the shorter, though by far the more difficult, being that over the Cemetery Hill. Of the round-about one, Gaspar, of course, had no knowledge. But he knew the *ceiba*, and the way back to it, all that they needed. The girl had trodden both, hundreds of times, and was ac-quainted with their every reach and turning. She would come anyhow, and no fear of her not finding the way; their only fear was of her coming unaccompanied.

Least of all has Ludwig this apprehension; instead, full confidence that the Indian girl will bring Francesca back with her. Strange this; but stranger still, that, while over-joyed with the thought of his sister being delivered from captivity, his joy should have a tinge of sadness in it, like a mingling of shadow and sun. This due to his suspicion of the motives actuating her who has promised to be his sister's deliverer. Nacena is not their friend for mere friendship's sake; nor his, because of the former fellowship between him and her own brother. Instead, jealousy is her incentive, and what she is doing, though it be to their benefit, is but done for the thwarting of Aguara.

Though Ludwig has expressed his opinion that they will soon see Francesca, he is silent about these suspicions. There is no time to speak of them if he would. For in a few seconds after Nacena's separating from them, Gaspar gives the signal for action, and all three become engaged in getting ready their horses for a return to the plain.

" *Por Dios !* " mutters the gaucho, while slipping on his bridle. " I don't much fancy remaining longer in this melancholy place. Though high and airy, it mayn't be wholesome. If, after all, that brown beauty should change her mind, and play us false, we'd be in a bad predicament up here—a regular trap, with no chance of retreating from it. So the sooner we're back to the bottom of the hill, the safer 'twill be. There we'll at least have some help from the speed of our horses, if in the end we have to run for it. Let us get below at once !"

Having by this finished adjusting his bridle, he hands the rein to Cypriano, adding—

" You hold this, señorito, while I go after Shebotha. Botheration take that old hag ! She'll be a bother to us, to say nothing of the extra weight for our poor horses. After all, she's not very heavy—only a bag of bones."

" But, Gaspar ; are you in earnest about our taking her along with us ? " asks Cypriano.

" How are we to help it, *hijo mio !* If we leave her here, she'd be back in the town before we could get started ; that is, if we have the good luck to get started at all. I needn't point out what would be the upshot of that. Pursuit, as a matter of course, pell mell, and immediate. True, we might leave her tied to the post, and muffled as she is. But then she'd be missed by to-morrow morning, if not sooner, and they'd be sure to look for her up here. No likelier place for such as she, among these scaffolds ; except tied to a scaffold of another sort, and in a somewhat different style."

The gaucho pauses, partly to enjoy his own jest, at which he is grinning, and partly to consider whether Shebotha can be disposed of in any other way.

Cypriano suggests another, asking—

" Why couldn't we take her in among these trees, and tie

her to one of them ?   There's underwood thick enough to conceal her from the eyes of anyone passing by, and with the muffle over her head, as now, she couldn't cry out that they'd hear her."

"'Twould never do," rejoins Gaspar, after an instant of reflection. " Hide her as we might, they'd find her all the same. These redskins, half-naked though they are, can glide about among bushes, even thorny ones, like slippery snakes. So many of them, they'd beat every bit of thicket within leagues, in less than no time. Besides, you forget their dogs. Scores they have—aye, hundreds, some ol them keen-scented as beagles. *Carrai !* they'd smell the nasty witch half-a-mile off, and so discover her whereabouts to their masters."

" True," returns Cypriano, seeing the plan he has proposed would not do. " In that way they would find her, no doubt."

" And if they didn't," interposed Ludwig, speaking from a sentiment of humanity, " it would be dreadful."

" Dreadful ! what do you mean ?" asks Cypriano, looking puzzled. " For them *not* to find her is just what we want."

" Ah, cousin ! how would it be for *her ?* Tied to a tree, with no hope—no chance of getting loosed from it—she'd die of hunger or thirst—miserably perish. Wicked as Shebotha is, we'd be worse than she if we left her to such a fate as that, to say nothing of our bringing it upon her. Aye, and for doing so we'd deserve the same ourselves, or something as bad."

" Well, Señor Ludwig," rejoins the gaucho, with an air of submission rather than conviction, " you may be right in what you say, and I'm not the man to deny it. But there

need be no difference of opinion on that point. Leaving
Shebotha tied to a tree wouldn't do on any account, for the
reasons I've stated. It might—most likely would, and, as
you say, it ought—end in ourselves getting tied to trees or
stakes, with a bundle of faggots between our legs set to the
tune of a slow fire. But," he adds, after a second or two
spent considering, " there's only one other way I can think
of to deal with the witch, if we're not to take her with us."

" What's the other?" asks Cypriano, seeing that the
gaucho hesitates to declare it.

" Why, knock her on the head, or draw the blade of a
cuchilla across her throat, and so stop her grunting at once
and for ever. The old wretch deserves no better fate and
hanging's too good for her. But they'd find her dead body
all the same; though not with a tongue in it to tell who
stopped her wind, or, what's of more consequence, how
and which way we went off. Besides, I dare say, the Señor
Ludwig wouldn't agree to our getting disembarrassed of her
in that fashion."

" Oh! no, no!" ejaculates the humane youth, horrified
at the thought of such cruelty, " anything but that,
Gaspar."

" Well, there isn't anything but what I propose doing—
that is, taking her along. I'm willing to accommodate her
on the croup of my *recado*, and will show her all the gal-
lantry she deserves. If you're jealous, Señor Ludwig, you
may have her behind you; and as your horse is the lightest
laden, that might be best. When we're crossing back over
that *riacho* where you left your saddle-bags, if you're tired of
riding double, you can drop her down among the lightning-
eels, and let them play their batteries upon her old bones
till every joint of them cracks asunder."

Were it not for the gravity of the situation, Gaspar's young companions would be greatly amused at his quaint rhodomontade. But as both are too anxious about the future, and in no humour for a jest, Ludwig only answers with a faint smile; while Cypriano, alone thinking of Francesca, has somewhat impatiently listened to it. Having hold of the bridle-rein which the gaucho has handed to him, on the latter ceasing to speak, he says in urgent tone —

"Bring her along, then, good Gaspar; and be quick about it! As you've said, we should get down to the plain as soon as possible."

The admonition is not needed, for Gaspar does not waste time over his jokes, nor allow them to interfere with his action. And while delivering the last sally, he has been looking to his horse gear, to see that his *recade* is in a proper condition to receive her who is to be his double.

Satisfied it will do, he strides off to where Shebotha is tied; and in a few seconds returns bearing the sorceress in his arms, as though she were but a bundle of rags.

Hoisting her up to his horse's withers, and with a stern threat and a shake, telling her to stay there, he springs upon the saddle behind her. It would not be their relative positions, then riding double, were they starting out on a long journey. But it will do for the half-mile or so, to the bottom of the hill, and for that short distance it seems idle either to bind her to his own body or to the saddle. So thinks Gaspar; but in this the gaucho, with all his prudent sagacity, is for once incautious to a fault. As they are groping their way down the steep slope, zigzagging among the tree trunks that stand thickly on both sides of the path, a troop of ring-tailed monkeys asleep in their tops, having their slumbers disturbed by the clink-clink of the hoofs against stones, set up a lugubrious howling. All the three horses are affrighted by the unearthly noise, but Gaspar's more than any ; so much, that rearing erect upon its hind legs, with the ground so uneven, the animal loses balance, and stumbles over on its side.

As the gaucho gathers himself, stunned and somewhat dazed by the fall, 'tis to learn that for that night his riding double is at an end. with Shebotha sharing the saddle ; for the sorceress is no longer to be seen !

CHAPTER LVI.

THERE is no mystery about Shebotha's disappearance nor aught out of the way save in the adroitness with which the aged crone contrived to effect her escape. Soon as touching the ground, and feeling herself free from the arms hitherto holding her on horseback, she has darted into the underwood, and off; not even rising erect to her feet, but on all fours, and silently as a snake. For although the hill-side is so thickly overgrown with thorny scrub that a pointer would with difficulty quarter it, the supple old savage worms her way through, without making any more noise than would a badger just got out of the barrel, and away from the dogs that have been baiting it.

In her retreat, she does not proceed for any great distance in a direct line, nor long continue crawling through the tangle of bushes. She is acquainted with every inch of that wooded slope, and all the paths traversing it, even to the tiniest trace of bird or quadruped; and soon coming into one of these, she at length stands upright. But not to stay there for any time, only long enough to give a glance to the right and left, in order that she may assure herself as to which of the two she had best take. Deciding in an instant, she is off again in crouched attitude, but with the agility of youth itself. Up the hill she goes, back towards the Cemetery. And one who saw her ascending before seeing her now, would with difficulty believe it to be the same person. Then, however, she was taking it leisurely, with no particular call for haste nor the taxing of her strength; now there is a motive for her making speed, with every exertion in her power. Indeed, more than one; for she is urged by two of the strongest passions that can agitate the human breast—cupidity and vengeance. While depriving her of her ghastly necklace, Gaspar had taken the occasion to possess himself of the more elegant and valuable ornaments stripped from the person of Nacena; not with any thought to appropriate them to himself, but the intention of restoring them to their rightful owner, when the latter should re-appear to claim them. Coming back, and bringing with her the captive, the Indian girl would well deserve restitution of her trinkets.

Thwarted in her infernal schemes, stung to fury by their failure, Shebotha goes panting up the hill; but, despite her hard breathing, without stopping to take breath. Nor rests she on reaching the summit, but glides on across the Cemetery, finding her way through the wooden structures as one who knows every scaffold there, and whose bones are mouldering upon it.

It is not from fear of being followed that she is now so hastening her steps. She knows that they from whom she has escaped will not return thither. For although hindered from hearing their conversation with Nacena, and so becoming acquainted with their plans, if not fully comprehending, she at least surmises them. For, having recognized the gaucho and his companions—all three of them—what purpose could they have there other than to release the pale-face girl she has in her charge? And fiom the fact ot their having themselves released Nacena—let her go without further detention than would be required to come to an understanding—she concludes that this has been come to, and the Indian girl consented to aid them in their intended rescue. But it will not be successful if she, Shebotha, can prevent it; and desperately bent on doing so, she rushes on through the scaffolds, and down the road to the *tolderia*, as if some danger threatened her from behind.

Arriving by the door of her own hut, she utters an exclamation of surprise at not there seeing her slave. Still another, after having called out his name, and received no answer. Her astonishment is complete and her rage at full height, when, having stepped up to the threshold of the *toldo*, she sees there is no one inside. The beeswax dip, burnt low and flickering in the socket, faintly lights up the hideous objects of her craft and calling; but shows no form of human being !

It is only a mechanical act her entering within the hut, and proceeding on to its inner apartment; for she is quite as sure it, too, will be found empty—as she finds it.

Almost instantly returning to the door, she stands gazing out into the darkness. Were there a light in front, her eyes would be seen to glare in their sunken sockets with the brightness of fire-balls; while in her breast is burning the fury of a concentrated vengeance. Once again she calls out the name of her slave, but as before getting no answer; and now sure that he, too, has either betrayed her, or been himself betrayed, she glides silently out of the *toldo*, and off towards that in which sleeps Aguara.

Soon she reaches its door, which she finds wide open; for it is within the tropics, and the night is a warm one.

Craning her head inside, and listening for a second or two, she can tell by his breathing that the *cacique* is asleep. A slumber abruptly broken by her calling out—

"Son of Naraguana, awake !"

"Shebotha !" he exclaims, recognizing her shrill treble. "What is it ?" he adds, raising his head over the edge of his *hamaca*.

"Arise, Aguara ! and make all haste. Know that there are enemies near, and treason in your tribe. You've been betrayed, and so has Shebotha !"

"Betrayed ! How ?" he asks in wonderment, but without leaving the hammock. "Who are these enemies you speak of? Who the traitors ?"

"You'll learn that in time, chief. It may be enough for you now to know, that your pale-face captive has escaped."

"Escaped !" he cries out, bounding down upon the floor, and coming forward to the entrance. "The pale-face escaped, you say? Are you speaking truth, Mam Shebotha ?"

"Come to my *toldo*, and see for yourself."

"No, that's not needed, if you say she's gone. Tell me how, when, and whither. Be quick !"

In hurried phrase she recounts the incidents which have occurred to her and Nacena on the Cemetery Hill, adding her conjectures as to what may have transpired since, and may still be in the act of occurrence. Among these last are her suspicions, well founded as we know, that Kaolin's sister has aided the pale-face to escape ; and that her own slave, who should have hindered, has not only connived at it, but taken himself away as well. In short, the cage is empty, and the bird with its keeper both flown !

What direction the fugitives have taken, is a question to

which the sorceress can give answer without the need of any doubtful surmise or conjecture. She knows it as well as if she herself had appointed the place of rendezvous, given by Gaspar to the Indian girl. For while riding double with the gaucho, she had heard him speak of it to his companions ; heard, despite the poncho spread over her ears, the word *ceiba*, with others, which told of their intention to stay by that tree.

The *cacique* knows the noted spot, as well as Nacena herself, he too having oft played beneath its shade, or climbed up its grand trunk and disported himself among its branches, when more of a boy than he is now.

But he reflects not on these past times, so full of innocence and happiness. Instead, wild with rage, and wretched as he is angry, he stays not to reflect at all ; but hastily, and little better than half-dressed, he rushes forth from his *toldo*, calling loudly for his horse.

Meanwhile, the sorceress has aroused others of the tribe ; several of whom, in obedience to their chief's command, start off for the *corrals* to procure the horses necessary for a pursuit of the fugitives.

Aguara's is on the ground first ; and, without waiting for companion or attendant of any kind, he vaults upon the animal's back, and goes off at a gallop along the path, which, after turning around close to the hill, at about a mile's distance, farther on passes the *ceiba* tree.

CHAPTER LVII.

IMPOSSIBLE to describe the feelings of Gaspar, when having recovered his feet after the tumble out of his *recado*, he finds that Shebotha has got away from him. It is some consolation to know that neither himself nor his horse has received serious injury. Still not sufficient to satisfy him, nor allay the wild exasperation burning within his breast, which seeks to vent itself in a string of maledictions poured plenteously from his lips.

As the hag, however, has surely succeeded in getting off, and it would be idle to attempt pursuing through the thick scrub, his anathemas hurled after her are all in vain ; and, at thought of this, he soon ceases to pronounce them. For the reflection quick follows, that he and his companions have now something else to think about—their own safety. doubly endangered by Shebotha's escape.

" *Mil demonios !* " is his last exclaim of the kind, after getting his horse upright again and himself back into the saddle, " who'd have believed the old beldame had so much suppleness in her joints ? But it's no joking matter. Only to think of it ! Everything looking so bright, and now Satan's luck once more back upon us—bad, if not worse, than ever ! Well, we mustn't dilly-dally here. If there's still a chance left us, we'll have to look for it down below, by that big cotton tree."

Saying which, he again gives the rein to his horse, and continues the descent of the hill, the others head and tail close after.

On reaching the said cotton tree, however, Gaspar changes his mind about that spot being the best for their temporary abiding place. Since its being arranged as a rendezvous with Nacena, the circumstances have sadly altered, and, on reflection, he deems it better, as do the others, to keep on along the road towards the *tolderia*—at least for some little distance. There can be no harm in that, nor danger of their going astray. The path is a plain one, much trampled by horses and cattle, and, notwithstanding the darkness of the night, easily discernible. If fortune so far favour them, that the captive will be coming that way, under the guidance of the Indian girl, the sooner these be met the more chance for all eventually getting safe off, rescuers as rescued.

So concluding, they make scarce a moment's halt by the *ceiba;* but, passing under its umbrageous branches, head their horses along the trail leading to the town.

At this moment were it daylight, or even a clear moonlight, one placed upon the brow of the hill fronting southeastward, and looking down to the level plain by its base, would behold two separate parties moving upon it, but in opposite directions, so that, if they continue to advance, they must meet. One party is mounted, the other afoot; the former being Gaspar and his two companions, while the latter is also composed of three individuals—Nacena, Francesca, and Shebotha's slave. The two girls, going in a half-run, are side by side, and ahead of the man; who, less free of foot, has fallen behind them to a distance of some twenty or thirty paces. Nacena, who knows the way, guides the escaping captive, and has hold of her by the hand. They are now not more than half-a-mile from the mounted party, coming the opposite way, and in a few minutes should meet it, if nothing prevent. Already within hailing distance, they might hear one another's voices; but neither being aware of this mutual proximity, all advance in silence—the trio on horseback proceeding at a slow pace for caution's sake, lest the tread of their animals should betray them.

But if their own be not heard afar, there are other hoofs making a noise to disturb the stillness of the night. Just as the Indian girl has whispered to her pale-face *protégée* some words of cheer, saying that her friends are now no great way off, she is startled by the hoof-stroke of a horse, which her practised ear tells her to be ridden; while the rapid repetition of the sound denotes the animal going in a gallop.

Suddenly she stops, and listens. Clearer rings the "tramp - tramp," as nearer the horseman approaches. Coming up behind, from the direction of the town, who can it be but one in pursuit of them? And if a pursuer, what other than Aguara?

Still Nacena is in doubt, and deems it strange. As they stole away from Shebotha's hut, and through the straggling suburb of the *tolderia*, all was darkness and silence, everybody seeming asleep. Who or what could have awakened the *cacique*, and apprized him of the flight of his captive?

In asking herself these questions, Kaolin's sister is under the belief, that the sorceress is herself still a prisoner, in the keeping of that stalwart and redoubtable gaucho. Hence her surprise at their being pursued, with the uncertainty that they are so, and the further doubt of the pursuer being Aguara.

He it is, notwithstanding; and as yet pursuing alone. For although soon can be heard the hoof-strokes of other horses than his also following, these are faint and far off. He himself hears them ; knows it is a party of his young braves pressing on after, but will not wait for them to come up. For he hopes to overtake the fugitives, ere they can reach the place of rendezvous Shebotha has spoken of, and recover his captive before she can fling herself into the arms of protecting friends.

In this hope, alas! he is not disappointed. Dashing on through the darkness along a road with every foot of which both he and his horse are familiar, he first comes up with the half-witted creature lagging behind, soon as beside him putting the question—

" Where is the pale-face, your prisoner ? "

The man, frightened at seeing it is the *cacique*, in his confusion hesitates to make reply. But Aguara does not wait for it. He hears voices ahead—soft and sweet, though raised in tones of alarm—and knows she must be there. Giving his horse's head a wrench, so as to shave close past the delinquent jailer, he raises his *macana*, and dealing a downward blow, strikes the latter to the earth : then hastens on after the others.

Nacena now knows for certain that they are pursued, as also who is the pursuer. She has heard the question asked by Aguara, recognizing his voice ; heard also the dull thud of his club as it descended on the skull of the unfortunate man ; and now again hears the trampling of hoofs renewed and drawing nearer. She has still hold of Francesca's hand, and for a moment debates within herself what is best to be done, and whether she should not release it, and turning show front to the pursuer.

Too late for that, or aught else likely to be of service either to herself or *protegée*. Before any resolve reaches her the *cacique* is by their side ; and flinging himself from his horse, grasps both by the wrists, wrenching asunder their joined hands. Then turning upon the Indian girl with a cry of rage—a curse in the Tovas tongue—he strikes her with his shut fist, inflicting a blow which sends her reeling to the earth. Before she can regain her feet he is once more upon his horse, and heading back for the *tolderia*—his recovered captive in his arms !

CHAPTER LVIII.

In a rush Aguara goes, fast as his animal can be urged by heel and voice. For, while so roughly separating the two girls, these had shouted in alarm, and his ear had caught other cries raised at a distance, and as if responsive. Now he hears them again; men's voices, and mingling with them the trampling of hoofs—clearly several horses coming on in a gallop. She, he has in his arms, hears them too, but listens not in silence or unresisting. Instead, she struggles and shrieks, calling " Help, help ! " with the names " Ludwig, Cypriano, Gaspar ! "

She is heard by all three; for it is they who responded to the cries of herself and Nacena, knowing who gave utterance to them. Near they are now, and riding as in a race; they, too, pressing their horses to utmost speed. But the darkness is against them, as their ignorance of the ground, with which the man pursued is familiar. By this, at every step, they are obstructed ; and but for the screams of Francesca, still continued, might as well abandon the chase for any chance they have of overtaking him.

And overtake him they never would, nor could, were fortune not in their favour. An accident it may appear ; at the same time seeming a divine retribution for wrong—a very Nemesis in the path of the wicked Aguara. On returning past the spot where he had struck down Shebotha's slave, he sees the unfortunate man stretched along the ground, and, to all appearance, still insensible. Nought cares he for that, but his horse does; and, at sight of the prostrate form, the animal, with a snort of affright, shies to one side, and strikes off in a new direction. Going at so swift a pace, and in such a dim light, in a few bounds it enters among some bushes, where it is brought up standing. Before its rider can extricate it, a strong hand has hold of it by the head, with a thumb inserted into its nostrils, while the fingers of another are clutching at his own throat. The hand on the horse's muzzle is that of Gaspar the gaucho, the fingers that grope to get a gripe on the rider's neck being those of Cypriano.

It is a crisis in the life of the young Tovas *cacique*, threatening either death or captivity. But subtle as all Indians are, and base as any common fellow of his tribe, instead of showing a bold front, he eludes both, by letting go the captive girl, himself slipping to the ground, and, snake like, gliding off among the bushes.

On the other side of his horse, which he has also abandoned, Francesca falls into the arms of her brother, who embraces her with wild delight. Though not wilder, nor half so thrilling, as that which enraptures the ear of Cypriano—to whose arms she is on the instant after transferred.

But it is not a time for embraces, however affectionate, nor words to be wasted in congratulation. So Gasper tells them, while urging instant departure from that perilous spot.

"Our lucky star's gone up again," he says, with a significant nod to Aguara's horse, which he has still hold of. "There is now four of us; and as I take it this brisk little *musteño* is fairly our property, there'll be no need for any of us riding double—to say nothing of one having a witch behind his back. Without such incumbrance, it'll be so much the better for the saving of time; which at this present moment presses, with not the hundredth part of a second to spare. So *hijos mios*, and you, *hija mia querida*, let us mount and be off!"

While the gaucho is yet thus jocularly delivering himself, Cypriano has lifted his cousin, Francesca, to the back of the *cacique's* abandoned steed; on which he well knows she can keep her seat, were it the wildest that ever careered across *campo.* Then he remounts his own, the other two taking to their saddles at the same time.

A word about the route, and all four start together; not to go back along the trail towards the *ceiba* tree, but striking straight out for the open plain, in a direction which Gaspar conjectures to be the right one.

They would willingly diverge from it to ascertain whether the poor creature clubbed by Aguara be dead or still living; and, if the latter, take him along. But Gaspar urges the danger of delay; above all, being burdened with a man not only witless, but now in all likelihood disabled by a wound which would make the transporting him an absolute impossibility.

Ludwig and his sister are more desirous to turn aside, and learn how it is with Nacena. But again the gaucho, not greatly given to sentiment, objects. Luckily, as if to relieve them from all anxiety, just then they hear a voice, which all recognize as that of the Tovas belle, calling out in tolerably pure Castilian :—

"*Va con Dios !*"

Standing up in his stirrups, with a shout and counter salute, the gaucho returns the valediction ; then, spurring forward and placing himself at the head of the retreating party, they ride on, with no thought of again halting so long as their horses can keep their feet.

CHAPTER LIX.

THE solitary *estancia* which for two years had been the happy home of Ludwig Halberger and his family, but late the abode of deepest sorrow, is once more revisited by a gleam of joy. For the rescuing party has returned to it, bringing Francesca back safe and still unharmed. In the tumult of gratified emotions at recovering her lost child, —or rather children, for she had begun to think them all for ever gone from her—the widow almost forgets that she is widowed.

Only for a brief moment, however. The other great bereavement has been too recent to remain long out of her thoughts, and soon returns to them in its full afflicting bitterness.

But she has no time to dwell upon it now. The tale of actual experience which the rescuers have brought back, with Gaspar's surmises added, has given her a full and clear comprehension of everything; not only explaining the tragic event already past, but foreshadowing other and further dangers yet to come, and which may, at any moment, descend upon herself and the dear ones still left to her.

She has no longer any doubts as to the hand that has

dealt her such a terrible blow; neither of the man who actually committed the murder, nor of him who instigated it. For Francesca's recognition of Valdez has confirmed all the gaucho's conjectures.

And the Dictator of Paraguay is not the man to leave unfinished either his cruel deeds or designs. Surely will he further prosecute them, either by hastening himself to the *estancia*, or sending thither his myrmidons. Yes, at any hour, any minute, a party of these may appear approaching it from the east, while in like short time the pursuing Tovas, headed by their enraged *cacique*, may show themselves coming from the west.

No wonder that the moments of mutual congratulation between the Señora Halberger and those just returned to her are brief, and but little joyful. The fugitives have reached home, but not to find it a refuge. For them it is no more a place of safety; instead, the most perilous in which they could now or ever after sojourn. But where are they to go—whither further flee? In all the Chaco there is not a spot that can shelter them from such pursuers as they are expecting!

It is now near noon of the fourth day since they left the Sacred Town of the Tovas, and in the interval they had been riding hard and fast, day and night, scarce allowing themselves either sleep or rest. But, fast as they have travelled, they know that Aguara, with his braves, will not be far behind; and although less than an hour has elapsed since their arrival at the *estancia*, Gaspar has already made preparations for their departure from it. Assisted by the faithful Guano Indians, who of course are to accompany them in their flight, he has caught up and caparisoned fresh horses, with the mules belonging to the establishment.

Still the question remains unanswered—Whither are they to go? Throughout all the vicissitudes of his eventful life, never had the gaucho one so perplexing him, or fraught with such fears.

In the hope of finding an answer, and the better to reflect upon it, he has drawn a little apart from the house, with the hurry and bustle going on around it. A slight eminence, not far off in front, gives a commanding view of the *campo;* and, taking stand upon its top, he first casts a sweeping glance around the horizon, then fixes it only in one direction —that southwards, towards the old *tolderia.* For, although expecting enemies both from east and west, he knows that, coming from either side, they will most likely approach by the Pilcomayo's bank; the former by the trail leading up the river, the latter by the same going down. It is not the first time for him to be standing on that elevated spot. Every ten minutes since their return to the *estancia,* he has been upon it, gazing out in the same way, and for the self-same purpose. Still, as yet, he observes nothing to add to his apprehensions, already keen enough. No living thing —much less human being—stirs over the wide expanse of green grassy plain. For it is near the meridian hour, and the tropical sun, pouring its fervid rays vertically down, has forced both birds and quadrupeds inside the cooler shadow of their coverts. Only two of the former are seen—a brace of *urubus,* or "king vultures," soaring in circles aloft— beautiful birds, but less emblematic of life than death. A bad omen he might deem their presence ; and worse, if he but saw what they see. For, from their more elevated position, they command a view of the plain to a much greater distance, and see mounted men upon it; not a single party, but three distinct groups of them, leagues distant from each other, though all bound for the *estancia*. They are approaching it by separate routes, and from different quarters of the compass; one party coming up the Pilcomayo's bank, and making straight for the old *tolderia ;* a second moving towards the same place on the down-river trail; while the third, away from the river, and out upon the open plain, is heading more direct for the *estancia* itself. The first cohort, which is the smallest, is composed of some forty or fifty horsemen, riding " by twos;" their regular formation on the march, but more the uniformity in their dress, arms, and accoutrements, telling them to be soldiers. For such they really are—the *cuarteleros* of Paraguay, with Rufino Valdez riding at their head ; not as their commanding officer, but in the exercise of his more proper and special calling of *vaqueano*, or guide. Ghastly and pallid, with his arm supported in a sling, he is on the way back to Halberger's *estancia*, to complete the ruffian's task assigned to him by the Dictator of Paraguay, and make more desolate the home he had already enough ruined. But for his mischance in the *biscachera*, the rescuers would have found it empty on their return, and instead of a lost daughter, it would have been the mother missing.

The second band of horsemen, coming from the opposite quarter and down the river, is no other than the pursuing party of Tovas, with Aguara at their head. They are mostly young men, the *cacique's* particular friends and partizans, nearly a hundred in number, all armed with *bolas* and long spears. Hastily summoned together, they had started in pursuit soon as they could catch up their horses ; but with all their speed the rescuing party had so far kept ahead, as to have arrived at the *estancia* some time before them. But they are pressing on for it now, fast as their horses can carry them, urged forward by their leader, who, in his rage, is not only determined to retake the escaped captive, but kill cousin, brother, all who aided in her escape

The third party, also approaching from the west, but by a route leading direct to the house, with the river far southward on their right, is, as the second, composed entirely of Tovas Indians. But, instead of them being the youths or the tribe, they are, for the most part, men of mature age. though a young man is at their head, and acting as their commander. There is a girl riding by his side, a beautiful girl, at a glance recognizable as Nacena—he himself being her brother, Kaolin.

They and their party are also pursuing. Though not to retake, the pale-face captive ; instead, to protect her—the object of their pursuit being Aguara himself. For soon as the latter had started off on his reckless chase—braving public opinion, and defying the opposition of the elders—a revolution had arisen in the tribe ; while a council meeting, hastily called in the *malocca*, had, with almost unanimous vote, deposed him from the chieftainship, and chosen Kaolin *cacique* in his stead. Needless to say, that to all this Nacena was a consenting party. And something more—since she gave the cue to her brother, who was chief instigator in the revolt. That blow which laid her along the earth, with the cause for which it was given, had severed the last link of love that bound her to Aguara, and for him her heart is now full of hate and burning with vengeance. While pressing on in pursuit of his escaped captive, little dreams the deposed *cacique* of the Tovas, either that he has been deposed of his chieftainship or that others are pursuing him.

But his pursuers are not now behind him ; instead, in

front, or, at all events, nearer to the *estancia* than he.　For Kaolin's followers, availing themselves of a route known to one of their number—a shorter cut across the *pampas*—have passed the party led by Aguara, and will be the first to arrive at the objective point aimed at by both.

And they are first sighted by Gaspar, though the gaucho has not been looking in their direction, little expectant of pursuers to come from that quarter.　The *urubus* have guided him, or rather their shadows gliding over the grassy sward ; these, as the birds making them, having suddenly passed away towards the west.　Following them with his eyes, he sees what causes him to exclaim—

" *Santos Dios !* we are lost.　Too late—too late ; 'tis all over with us now !"

His cry, sent up in accent of deepest despair, brings Ludwig and Cypriano to his side ; and the three stand watching the dark cohort advancing towards them.　None of them speaks or thinks of retreat.　That would be idle, and any attempt at escape must surely result in failure ; while to resist would but hasten the disaster impending over them.　Convinced of this, they no longer contemplate either flight or resistance, but stand in sullen silence to await the approach of the pursuers, for such they suppose them to be.　Deeming them avengers also, as well they may, recalling their last encounter with the young Tovas chief.

Never did mistaken men more rejoice at their mistake than do they, when, on the band of Indian braves galloping up to the ground, they behold at its head, and evidently in command of it, not the *cacique* Aguara, but the sub-chief, Kaolin, and beside him his sister Nacena !　She who aided

z

them in effecting the escape of the captive, and, as a last word, bade them " God speed," would not be with pursuers who are hostile.

Nor is she, as they soon learn ; instead, along with friends who come but to give comfort and protection !

CHAPTER LX.

SPEEDY RETRIBUTION.

SHORT time stays Kaolin and his party by the *estancia*,
for the newly-elected chief of the Tovas is a man of
ready resolves and quick action, and soon as his story is
told, with that of the others heard in return, he again
mounts, and makes ready for the march—this time to be
directed towards the old *tolderia*. He knows that his rival
cacique must come that way, as also the other enemy of whom
Gaspar has given him information, and who may be expected
as soon, if not sooner, than Aguara himself.

The gaucho goes along with him, as so would Cypriano
and Ludwig, but that Gaspar forbids it ; urging them to
remain at the *estancia* as company, and, if need be, protection, for the *señora* and *niña*. Thus influenced, they both
stay.

Straight off over the *pampa* rides Kaolin, at the head of
his hundred stalwart warriors, his sister still by his side. She
also had been counselled to remain behind, an advice she
disdainfully rejected. The revenge burning in her breast
will not let her rest, till she has seen her false lover, her
insulter, laid low.

Her brother, too, and all his band of braves, are alike
eager for the conflict to come. It was not so before their

arrival at the *estancia*. Then they only thought of dealing with their deposed *cacique* and his youthful followers, foolish as himself; nor dreamt they aught of danger. But now, with the prospect of meeting another and very different enemy, more dangerous and more hated, their savage nature is roused within them to an ire uncontrollable. By chance, Kaolin himself has a special dislike for the *vaqueano* Valdez; while as to the others, despite the restored treaty forced upon them by Aguara, their friendship has not been restored with it ; and they urge their horses forward, burning for an encounter with the *cuarteleros* of Paraguay.

Though the gaucho rides at the head of the quick marching party, and alongside their leader, it is not to guide them. They know the ground as well, and better than he; for oft and many a time have they quartered that same *campo*, in pursuit of *gama*, *guazuti*, and ostrich.

Kaolin directs his march in a straight course for the old *tolderia*, though not now designing to go so far. His objective point for the present is a high bluff which hems in the valley of the Pilcomayo, and from which a view may be obtained of the river for long leagues upward and downward, as of the deserted village, at no great distance off upon its bank. Through a ravine that cuts this bluff transversely, the latter can alone be reached from the elevated plain over which they are advancing.

Arrived at the upper end of the gorge, they do not go down it. Instead, commanding his warriors to make halt, Kaolin himself dismounts; and signing to the gaucho to keep him company, the two step crouchingly forward and upward to the outer edge of the cliff.

Soon as reaching it they get sight of what they had more than half expected to see : two bands of men mounted and upon the march, one with the horses' heads directed down the stream, the other up it. The first, as can be seen at a glance, is the pursuing party of Tovas youths led by Aguara; while the sun shining upon gilt buttons, with the glittering of lance blades and barrels of guns, tells the other to be a troop of soldiers, beyond doubt the looked for *cuarteleros !* Both are at about a like distance from the abandoned town, heading straight for it; and while Kaolin and the gauc' o continue watching them they ride in among the *toldos* from opposite sides, meeting face to face on the open space by the *malocca.*

At sight of one another the two sets come to a sudden halt; and, for a second or two, seem engaged in a mutual and suspicious reconnaissance. But their distrust is of short continuance; for there is a rogue at the head of each, and these, as if instinctively recognizing one another, are seen to advance and shake hands, while their followers mutually mingle and fraternize.

Amicable relations being thus established between them, the men on both sides are observed to dismount, as if they intended to make stay in the *tolderia.* A movement, which puzzles Kaolin and the gaucho, who were about going back to the gorge with the design of taking steps for defending it. Instead, they remain upon the cliff's crest to watch the enemy below.

And they continue watching there till the sun goes down, and the purple of twilight spreads itself over the plain bordering the Pilcomayo; this succeeded by a mist rising from the river, and shrouding the deserted village in its murky embrace. But before night's darkness is altogether on they see a mounted troop, filing by twos, out from among the *toldos,* with lances carried aloft, and pennons

floating over their heads—surely the *cuarteleros*.   There is
just light enough left to show two men in the lead, dressed
differently from these following.   One of these resplendent
in a feather-embroidered *manta*, Kaolin recognizes as his
rival Aguara; while the gaucho identifies the other as his
oldest, deadliest, and most dangerous enemy, Valdez, the
vaqueano.

They remain not a moment longer on the cliff; for, eager
as Gaspar Mendez may be to rid himself of that enemy, he
is not more so than the Indian to send to his long account
the man who insulted his sister.   Now more than ever determined upon avenging her wrongs, he rushes back to his
braves, and hurriedly puts them in ambush near the head
of the gorge, at a point where the defile is narrowest; himself taking stand on a ledge, which commands the pass, in
such manner, that with his long spear he can reach across
it from side to side.

At length has the opportunity arrived for the angry
brother to take the retribution he has resolved upon—
Naccna herself being a witness to it.   For she is near by,
standing on a higher bench behind, in posed attitude, with
her features hard set and lips compressed, as one about to
be spectator to a sad and painful scene.   But if she feel
sadness, it is not for the death now threatening Aguara.
That blow had changed her fond love to bitterest resent-
ment; and instead of doing aught, or saying word, to stay
her brother's hand, she but by her presence and silence
incites him to the deed of vengeance.

It is soon and quickly done.   Scarce has the ambuscade
been set, when the trampling of horses heard down the
defile tells of a cavalcade coming up, and presently the
foremost files appear rounding an angle of rock.   Dim as is

the light, the horseman leading can be told to be the young Tovas *cacique*, while the one immediately in his rear is recognizable as Rufino Valdez. At sight of the latter the gaucho, who is close to Kaolin, feeling all his old hatred revived, and recalling, too, the murder of h's beloved master, with difficulty restrains himself from springing down and commencing the conflict. He is prevented by a sign from Kaolin; who, on the instant, after leaning forward lounges out with his spear. A wild cry tells that it has pierced the body of Aguara; then drawn instantly back and given a second thrust, it passes through that of the *vaqueano*—both dropping from their horses dead, as if by a bullet through the brain!

The soldiers coming on behind are brought to a sudden stop; scarce comprehending why, till they hear the wild Tovas war-cry raised above their heads, at the same time being saluted with a shower of *bolas peridas* rained down from the rocks, these terrible missiles crushing in every skull with which they came into contact.

The scared *cuarteleros* stay for no more; but, with a cry of treason, turn their horses' heads, and hurry back down the ravine. Nor stop they at the *tolderia*; but still under the belief of having been betrayed, continue their retreat down the river, and on toward Paraguay, leaving over a dozen of them dead in that dark defile.

As for the followers of Aguara, they make no show of fight. Now that their leader is no more, there is no cause of quarrel between them and the warriors of the tribe, and not a hand is raised to avenge their young *cacique*. For on learning the full character of his designs, and his complicity with the cruel *vaqueano*, all acknowledge that both men have but met the death they deserved.

CHAPTER LXI.

AFTER a day's rest at their old *tolderia*, the two parties of Tovas, now united in amity, set out on return to their Sacred Town. And along with them goes the Señora Halberger, with all the members of her family—including the Guano Indian domestics, and, needless to say, not leaving Gaspar Mendez behind. And, alike idle to declare, that they go not as captives; but guests, to be honoured and better cared for than ever before. Better protected, too; for, as ever do they need protection; now more than ever likely to be under the ban of the Paraguayan despot. That solitary *estancia* would no longer be a safe place of residence for them, and they well know it.

Perfect safety they find at the Sacred Town, and hospitality too, great as when Naraguana himself dispensed it. For is not Kaolin now *cacique*—he who saved them from death and destruction?

Kindly he extends his protection, and generously bestows his hospitality. But they do not for long need the former, nor are they called upon to abuse the latter by a too protracted stay. Shortly after their arrival at the Sacred Town, they get news which, though of death, gives them joy, as it only could and should; since it is the death of that man who has been the cause of all their miseries. José Francia, feared far and wide throughout Paraguay, and even beyond its borders, has at length paid the debt due by all men, whether bad or good. But although dead, strange to say, in the land he so long ruled with hard ruthless hand, still dreaded almost as much as when living; his cowed and craven subjects speaking of him with trembling lips and bated breath, no more as " El Supremo," but " El Defunto ! "

The Señora Halberger believes she may now return to her native country, without fear of further persecution from him. But Gaspar thinks otherwise; deeming it still unsafe, and pointing out the danger of their being called to account for what they were not guilty of—the slaughter of the *cuarteleros* in the defile. In fine, he urges her to make her future home in the Argentine States; a pleasanter land to live in, besides being a land of liberty, and, above all, the orthodox country of his own class and kind, the *gauchos.*

Observing the justness of his arguments, she consents to follow his advice ; and to the Argentine States they all go, journeying across many great rivers and through hundreds of miles of wilderness. But they are not permitted to travel either unprotected or alone ; for Kaolin accompanies them, with a band of his best braves—Nacena also forming one of the escort.

The Tovas *cacique* sees them over the Salado river, and within safe distance of the outlying settlements of San Rosario, there leaving them. But when he parts company, to return to the Sacred Town, his sister returns not with him. Though as a brother he be dear to her, she has found one dearer, with whom she prefers to stay. And does stay,

Kaolin himself consenting; since the dearer one is his own friend and former playmate. The gentle Ludwig has at length succeeded in winning the heart of the savage maiden —still whole, despite the tearing of a misplaced passion, long since passed away.

Our tale could be prolonged, and the characters who have figured in it followed further; but not through scenes of the same exciting character as those already detailed. Instead, the record of their after life, though not devoid of stirring incident, is more signalized by scenes of peace and prosperity. The reader will be satisfied with a peep at it, obtained some ten years later than the date of their settling down in the Argentine States. A traveller at this time passing from San Rosario to the German Colonies recently established on the Salado river, near the old but abandoned missionary settlement of Santa Fe, could not fail to observe a grand *estancia ;* a handsome dwelling-house with outbuildings, *corrals* for the enclosure of cattle, and all the appurtenances of a first-class *ganaderia*, or grazing establishment. Should he ask to whom it belongs, he would have for answer, " The Señora Halberger ; " and if curiosity led him to inquire further, he might be told that this lady, who is *una viuda,* is but the nominal head of the concern, which is rather owned conjointly by her son and nephew, living along with her. Both married though ; the latter, Señor Cypriano, to her daughter and his own cousin ; while the former, Señor Ludwig, has for his wife an Indian woman ; with possibly the remark added, that this Indian woman is as beautiful and accomplished as though she were a white.

Were the traveller to deviate a little from his route, and approach near enough to the house, he might see the members of this double though united family, surrounded by several pretty children of both sexes, strolling about in happy harmony, and with that freedom from care which speaks of wealth, at the same time telling of its having been honestly acquired.

Whether or not such a tableau be presented to the traveller's eye, one man who should figure in it would sure be seen moving about the place. For he is the *mayor-domo* of the estate, and if not actual master, the manager of all. As in that old *estancia* near the northern bank of the Pilcomayo, so in this new and grander one on the southern side of the Salado, everything is entrusted, as safely it may be, to

GASPAR, THE GAUCHO.

Reprinted from Stereotype Plates by JAS. TRUSCOTT & SON. LTD., London, E.C.

www.ingramcontent.com/pod-product-compliance
Lightning Source LLC
Chambersburg PA
CBHW021727110726
47902CB00005B/1380